DOCTOR PASCAL

DOCTOR PASCAL

EMILE ZOLA

Translated from the French by
VLADIMIR KEAN

Introduction by
HUGH SHELLEY

LONDON
ELEK BOOKS

I dedicate this book
which is the recapitulation and
conclusion of all my labours

to

the memory of
MY MOTHER
and to
MY DEAR WIFE

INTRODUCTION

by

HUGH SHELLEY

"REALLY and truly," Zola said to Edmond de Goncourt, "the book which appeals to me, which beckons to me, is the last of all .." *Doctor Pascal* was of such importance to its author, and is so fascinating to read to-day, not only because it tells the final story in the bloody saga of the Rougon-Macquart family (in countless characters and incidents a right culmination of what has gone before) but also because it is the most personal of the series. Zola told an English journalist that the novel was to be an apology for its forerunners.

"People, especially abroad," he said, "have accused me of being a pornographer. This I shall refute through Pascal. It has been said that all my characters are people of bad lives. Pascal will explain that this is not so. Zola has been charged with a lack of tender-heartedness. Pascal will show that this is not so."

But *Doctor Pascal* is a "personal" novel in two closer senses. First, Zola puts into Pascal's mouth so many views that express his own philosophy—and it is worthy of note that Zola later stayed at the Grosvenor Hotel in London under the name of "M. Pascal". Secondly, Dr Pascal's niece, Clotilde, with whom he falls in love, is an idealized portrait of Zola's mistress Jeanne Rozerot, like Clotilde, nearly a quarter of a century his junior. Although the printed dedication to the book reads: "To the memory of my Mother, and to my Dear Wife, I dedicate this novel which summarizes and concludes my whole work," Zola sent a copy to Jeanne inscribed: "To my darling Jeanne—to my Clotilde, who has given me the royal banquet of her youth .."

Doctor Pascal was written and published in 1893. In it Zola epitomises the struggle between religion and science, that so disturbed his contemporaries, in the story of this elderly doctor who has devoted his life to the study of heredity. His material is in voluminous files on each member through five generations of his own family, the Rougon-Macquart. His mother, the eighty-year-old Madame Rougon, is determined that the family honour shall not be tarnished by their publication and she works on the religious susceptibilities of Pascal's niece, Clotilde, who lives with him as his secretary, and of his old servant, finally convincing them that her son's soul is endangered by his work. Pascal surprises Clotilde in the act of stealing his files and, in the first of the book's great emotional scenes, wins her over to the cause of science. The peaks of the novel are this and the last mighty and macabre scene in which Clotilde, becomes Pascal's mistress and the future mother of his child, sleeps by his deathbed whilst below, Madame Rougon and the servant make a bonfire of his papers. The story of Pascal and Clotilde's love, weathering the storms of family and financial disasters, presents Zola with the opportunity to affirm his revived faith in life. It is an uneven work and bears signs of Zola's anxiety to complete with it the series that had taken twenty years of labour, but its very defects—the clumsy switching from lyricism to pedestrian realism; the chunks of undigested medical theory—add to a remarkably clear picture of Zola as he was when he wrote it. Furthermore, they throw into vivid relief the many superb descriptive passages and dramatic incidents that bring to life, in Zola's unequalled fashion, the good and the evil, the weakness and the strength, of those Rougons and Macquarts whose violent personalities are such that one almost expects to find them chronicled in the histories of nineteenth-century France.

CHAPTER ONE

OUTSIDE, it was a torrid July afternoon. Inside, thanks to the shutters over the three windows, it was a haven of tranquillity. Narrow shafts of sunshine filtered through the cracks in the old woodwork, bathing everything in a soft, diffuse glow of tremulous light. Compared with the raw heat of the sun, which was burning the facade outside, the room was relatively cool.

Doctor Pascal was standing in front of the cupboard, facing the windows. He was looking for a page of notes. The immense carved-oak cupboard was wide open. It was a period piece of the previous century and was ornamented with heavy, finely-wrought iron-work. The shelves were crammed with an extraordinarily untidy accumulation of papers, files and manuscripts. For more than thirty years the doctor had thrown into it everything he had written, from short notes to the complete texts of his great works on heredity. It was no easy matter to find what he was looking for. He went on searching patiently and smiled when he finally succeeded. He stood by the cupboard, engrossed in the notes. His figure was outlined in a ray of golden sunshine which fell from the middle window. Although he was nearly sixty, with snow-white hair and beard, he appeared robust and vigorous. His face was unlined, his complexion fresh, his eyes clear and his features finely chiselled. In his tight-fitting brown velvet jacket he seemed more like a young man with powdered hair.

"Please copy these notes for me, Clotilde," he said. "Ramond would never be able to decipher my execrable writing."

He put the paper down on the high desk at which the young woman was standing, in the embrasure of the window on the right.

"Very good, uncle!" she replied.

She was so preoccupied with her crayon drawing, which she was slashing with bold strokes, that she did not even turn around. Her eyes were fixed on a spray of long-stemmed hollyhocks of a peculiar purple colour, striped with yellow, that stood in a vase in front of her. The profile of her small round head, with its fair hair cropped short, was exquisite. Her expression serious, her forehead straight, the skin faintly wrinkled by a frown of concentration. The eye was sky-blue in colour, the nose delicate and the chin firm. There was

7

something adorably childish about the curve of the back of her neck, with its milk white skin, disappearing under the profusion of curls. She wore a long black overall, which made her look tall and slender. Her neck was also slender and delicately modelled. Her body had the long supple lines of those divine figures of the Renaissance. In spite of her twenty-five years, the bloom of childhood still clung to her and she looked barely eighteen.

"And," added the doctor, "you might try and tidy up the cupboard. It will soon be impossible for me to find anything."

"Very well, uncle!" she repeated, without raising her head. "Presently!"

Pascal sat down at his desk at the other end of the room, in front of the window on the left. It was a plain table of some dark, almost black wood, covered with pamphlets and papers of all kinds. There was silence in the room, an islet of twilit peace in the overwhelming heat of outdoors. It was a vast room, ten yards long and six yards wide, scantily furnished; apart from the cupboard there were two bookcases filled to overflowing with books and a few antique chairs and armchairs scattered at random about the room. There were no ornaments, except for some pastels depicting flowers of strange and unearthly hues. These were nailed on the walls, which were covered in faded wallpaper with a pattern of rosettes, and could hardly be distinguished in the gloom. There were three double doors; one, the middle one, opening on to the landing, the other two, one at each end, to the doctor's and Clotilde's rooms. The woodwork of these doors and of the cornice around the smoke-stained ceiling dated back to Louis XV.

An hour passed, without a sound. Then, Pascal put aside his work and unwrapped a newspaper which had been lying on his table, a copy of the *Temps*, and exclaimed:

"Listen to this! Your father has been appointed director of the *Epoque*, the republican paper, with such a large circulation, which publishes the communiqués from the Tuileries!"

The news seemed unexpected. He chuckled, somewhat ruefully, and added, quietly: "If I were to try and invent news, it would be less interesting .. I find this article engrossing."

Clotilde did not answer. Her thoughts were hundreds of miles away. Her uncle finished reading the article, took up a pair of scissors, cut it out and glued it to a sheet of paper. He wrote a heading in his large irregular writing and returned to the cupboard to file it away. Tall as he was, he had to stand on a chair to reach the top shelf on which stood a row of bulging files. These were made of thick blue paper and were classified methodically in alphabetical order. They contained all sorts of documents, sheets of manuscript, official stamped papers and newspaper cuttings. Each bore a label with a name in large letters. This was the only part of the cupboard which had been kept tidy. It was obvious that these documents had been carefully arranged, were frequently consulted and scrupulously put back in their proper places.

Pascal stepped on the chair, picked out one of the thickest files marked "Saccard", inserted the new cutting and replaced the file. After stacking up a pile of papers which had been about to collapse, he jumped down: "Do you understand, Clotilde? When you tidy up, you must not touch the files on the top shelf."

"Very well, uncle!" she replied for the third time, with her usual docility.

Pascal laughed, in his cheerful and infectious fashion, as he added: "Taboo!"

"I know, uncle!"

He closed the cupboard, locked it and threw the key in the back of the table drawer. The young woman knew enough about his work to be able to put his manuscripts in some sort of order; he often made use of her as a secretary to copy his notes, when a colleague and friend, like Doctor Ramond, asked him to write a paper. But she was no scholar. He had, quite simply, forbidden her to read anything he considered inadvisable for her to know.

Nevertheless, on this occasion, her absorption was so complete that he was disconcerted: "What is the matter? Why won't you answer? Are you so passionately interested in copying those flowers?"

This was another way in which she had made herself invaluable to him; she made drawings, water-colour paintings and pastels, which he used to illustrate his books and articles. For the previous five years he had been carrying out intricate experiments on hollyhocks. He had succeeded, by artificial fertilization, in producing a whole series of new colours. She was able to reproduce both shapes and colours with extraordinary precision. He never ceased to be astonished by her ability, and complimented her by saying that she had "an excellent little headpiece on those shoulders".

This time, as he looked at the drawing, he uttered a loud cry of protest: "Ah! I am ashamed of you! Off again into dreamland! .. Please oblige me by tearing that up, at once!"

She drew herself up, her cheeks flaming, her eyes flashing with enthusiasm for what she had been drawing, her slender fingers stained with red and blue crayon: "Oh! Uncle!"

For the first time there was an accent of revolt in the affectionate submissiveness with which she was in the habit of pronouncing the word "uncle"; a note of independence, a hint of self-affirmation.

It had been almost two hours since she had pushed aside her faithful copy of the hollyhocks and had been drawing a cluster of imaginary flowers; dream flowers, extravagant and superb creations. Often, in the middle of making an exact reproduction, she felt a sudden urge to escape into the world of pure fantasy. It was too strong to resist and each time she returned with avidity to her dream world of extraordinary flowers. So powerful was the impulse, so inexhaustible her imagination, that she never repeated herself; roses with bleeding hearts weeping tears of sulphur, lilies like crystal urns, even non-existent flowers with weird shapes; stars with their points protracted, leaving the petals to droop like falling cloudlets. On that day she had drawn a shower of pale stars against a background of bold crayon strokes; a downpour of infinitely soft petals; in one corner a bud was unfolding its diaphanous wings and seemed to be raising them to the sky.

"Another one to nail on that wall!" continued the doctor, pointing to the line of equally fantastic pastels. "But, if I may ask, what have you been trying to express?"

"I don't know, it is my idea of beauty."

At this moment Martine, their only servant, came into the room. She had been in the doctor's service for more than thirty years and had become the real mistress of the household. She too had retained an air of youthfulness, though she was over sixty. Soft-footed and silent, she was constantly scurrying from task to task. In her eternal black dress and white cap she looked like a nun. The grey eyes in her small face, which was pale and serene, were like the ashes of an extinguished fire.

She did not speak, but sat down on the floor, pulled out a needle and a skein of wool from her pocket and proceeded to mend a tear in the worn-out upholstery of an armchair, through which the hair stuffing was escaping. She had been obsessed for three days by her inability to find an odd hour for this purpose.

"While you are at it, Martine," cried Pascal with a twinkle in his eye, "you might sew up the holes in this noddle", and he took hold of Clotilde's averted head with both hands."

Martine raised her pale eyes and looked at her master with

her usual expression of adoration: "Why does monsieur say that?"

"Because, my good woman, I think that you, with your fanatical devoutness, are the one responsible for introducing ideas of the other world into this thick little round head."

The two women exchanged a glance of complicity.

"Oh, monsieur, religion has never done anyone any harm .. And if two people cannot agree about ideas of that kind, it is better not to talk about them, I am sure!"

There was an embarrassed silence. This was the only subject on which these three people disagreed. Otherwise they were singularly united in their quiet and restricted lives. Martine had been twenty-nine, one year older than the doctor, when she had started working for him. He had just set up practice at Plassans, in a gay little house in the new town. Thirteen years afterwards, Saccard, one of Pascal's brothers, had sent his seven-year-old daughter Clotilde down from Paris, after his wife's death and just before his remarriage. It was Martine who had brought up the child, taken her to church regularly and imparted some of her own religious fervour. The doctor had been too tolerant to interfere. He did not feel justified in forbidding the child to attend religious services, if faith made her happy. He contented himself with taking charge of her education. He had done his best to give her a balanced view of life and make her share his conception of the importance of thinking accurately and sanely about everything. The three of them had been living in this retreat at the Souleiade for nearly eighteen years. The property was on the outskirts of the town, a quarter of an hour's walk from Saint-Saturnin, the cathedral. The even flow of their lives, dedicated to ceaseless and unselfish endeavour, had been troubled of late by the increasing divergence of their opposing beliefs, though, hitherto, an open clash had been averted.

Pascal was bitterly annoyed. He restrained himself for a moment but, finally, could not help blurting out: "You see, my dear, this obsession of yours with the great mysteries has clouded your brain .. Your precious God does not need you and it would have been far better for both of us if I had kept you to myself."

Clotilde was quivering with suppressed emotion. She was not in the least intimidated and answered him boldly:

"It is you, uncle, who would benefit if you were to stop closing your eyes to everything which transcends the flesh .. There is so much more, why will you not admit it?"

Martine came to Clotilde's assistance in her own idiom: "It is true, monsieur, that you are a saint, as I tell everybody. You should come with us to church .. Then God would save you. I feel all of a tremble when I think that you will not go straight to Paradise."

Pascal was amazed. Both these women, usually so tenderly affectionate, so docile, were in open rebellion. He was about to lash out at them with his tongue, when he realized the futility of arguing: "Stop! Leave me alone. I had far better get to work .. Under no circumstances am I to be disturbed."

Pascal's room had been fitted up as a sort of laboratory. He shut the door behind him and breathed a sigh of relief. As he was compounding a new preparation according to his own secret formula, he had made a strict rule that no-one was to be admitted. Soon afterwards, the sound of a pestle grinding something in a mortar could be heard.

"He is at his devil's brew again, as grandmother calls it," said Clotilde with a smile. She returned to her drawing of the hollyhocks. Her copy was marvellously lifelike. She drew with mathematical precision and accuracy and had succeeded in reproducing the whole range of colours with every variation in tone and shade.

"Ah!" murmured Martine, sitting down on the floor again to finish mending the armchair, "what a misfortune for a saintly man like that to lose his soul! .. There is no denying (and I have known him for more than thirty years) that he has never harmed a living soul. A real heart of gold! He would take the bread out of his own mouth .. And kind too, always in good health and spirits, a real blessing! .. It is terrible to think that he will not make his peace with our good Lord. We shall have to force him, mademoiselle."

Clotilde, astonished by this unusually long speech, answered quite seriously: "Certainly, Martine, we must swear it. We will force him."

The ensuing silence was shattered by the sound of the front-door bell. It rang just inside the door, where it could be heard all over the house, which was too large for the three people who lived in it. The servant seemed surprised and muttered: "Who can it be, out in this heat?" She got up, opened the door, leaned over the banisters and called out: "It is Madame Felicité."

Old Madame Rougon swept briskly into the room. In spite of her eighty years, she had climbed the stairs with the agility of a young girl; she was still the same dark-skinned, thin and strident grasshopper. She was stylishly dressed in black silk. From behind, with her slender waist, she might have been taken for a young woman hurrying to keep an appointment with her lover. From the front, the folds of the parchment-like skin of her face betrayed her age, but her eyes were as bright as ever and, when she wanted to, she was still capable of captivating with her smile.

Clotilde crossed the room to meet her, crying: "You should not be out in this terrible heat, you must be boiled alive!"

Felicité kissed her on the forehead and laughed: "Oh! I love the sun. It never does me any harm." Then, tripping daintily across to one of the windows, she started undoing the rope fastening to the blind: "You must raise this a little! It is too depressing to spend your time in the dark .. At home I let the sun flood through the house."

Blazing sunshine poured in through the opening, like a shower of dancing embers. A vast expanse of countryside could be seen, under a violet-blue sky. The fields were burnt brown by the sun and seemed as if they were sleeping, exhausted by the baking heat; to the right, above the pink roof-tops, towered the steeple of Saint-Saturnin, gilded by the sun, with its groins like blanched bones.

"Yes," continued Felicité, "I shall probably be going on to the Tulettes and I wanted to know if Charles was visiting you, so that he could come with me .. I see that he is not here. I will take him some other day."

As she made this pretext for her visit, her eyes darted around the room. She let the subject drop and proceeded to talk about her son Pascal, whom she could hear grinding away at his mortar in the next room: "Ah! he is still at his devil's brew .. Do not disturb him, I have nothing special to say to him."

Martine continued mending the chair and shook her head, as if to imply that she had no wish to disturb her master; the room was silent once more. Clotilde was wiping the crayon stains from her fingers and Felicité trotted around the room on a tour of investigation.

Old Madame Rougon had been a widow for almost two years. Her husband had grown so fat that he could not move. He had succumbed to a violent attack of indigestion on the night of September 3rd, 1870, after hearing the news of the catastrophe of Sedan. He had been shattered by the collapse of a form of government, for the establishment of which he considered himself partly responsible. As for Felicité, she had taken no further interest in politics and lived henceforth like a queen who had abdicated her throne. It was an open secret that the Rougons had saved Plassans from anarchy in

1851, by contributing to the successful overthrow of the previous government on December 2nd. Again, some years later, they had been mainly instrumental in the defeat of the legitimist and republican candidates. It was due to their efforts that a Bonapartist deputy had been elected. Until the war the empire had remained all-powerful, so popular that a plebiscite had given it an overwhelming majority. Ever since the disaster, however, republican sentiment were rapidly gaining ground in the town. The Saint-Marc quarter remained the centre of sordid royalist intrigues, but the older part of the new town had elected a liberal representative to the chamber. He was faintly tainted with Orleanism and ready to rally to the republic, once firmly established. Felicité was too intelligent to ignore the evidence of her own eyes, hence her loss of interest in politics and her willingness to be relegated to the rôle of a dethroned queen.

Her authority and influence had been so great that her present position was tinged with an element of poetic melancholy. Her undisputed reign had lasted for eighteen years. The legend of her two salons had been embellished by the passage of time; the yellow salon, where the plot for the *coup d'état* had been hatched and, later, the green salon, which had been neutral and where the conquest of Plassans had been completed. Besides, she was very wealthy and universally admired for her dignity in adversity; she kept her regrets to herself and had never been heard to utter a word of complaint. Her appetites had been insatiable, she had considered no intrigue beneath her, however sordid, if it led to their gratification. Nowadays, she had to be content with the peaceful enjoyment of her wealth and the memories of her former royalty. Her one remaining passion was to defend the sanctity of her own past history, by removing every possible source of future calumny. Her pride, nourished by her two signal exploits, which were still topics of everyday conversation in the town, kept a jealous watch on everything which was written. She was determined that only laudatory documents should survive and that her reputation, which caused everyone to bow down before her whenever she passed through the town, should be kept unsullied.

She crossed to the door of Pascal's room and listened to the sound of his pestle. Then she turned to Clotilde with a frown: "What, in heaven's name, is he making? You know, I presume, that his new drug is seriously jeopardising his reputation. I was told, the other day, that he nearly killed another of his patients with it."

"Oh! grandmother!" protested the young woman.

14

coincided with his preliminary studies on heredity. As they developed, he had been fascinated by typical examples in his own family, which confirmed laws he had established as the result of his own researches. Was it not a natural field for his observations, conveniently at hand and one with which he was thoroughly familiar? And, with the ruthlessness of a scientist, he had accumulated a host of intimate details about his relatives over a period of thirty years; recording and filing everything, using it as material for his genealogical tree of the Rougon-Macquart family, to which the voluminous files were only an appendage, a commentary, bulging with evidence of unmentionable anomalies.

"Most certainly," continued old Madame Rougon, emphatically, "all those papers, which will ruin our reputation, must be burnt, thrown into the fire!"

The servant, seeing that the conversation was becoming heated, rose to her feet and was about to leave the room. Madame Rougon stopped her with a peremptory gesture: "No, no! Martine, don't go! I want you to hear what I have to say. After all, you are practically a member of the family." Then she added, venomously: "A mass of falsehoods, malignant gossip, stale lies invented by our enemies, jealous of our success! .. Think of that, my child. About all of us, about your father, your brother, about me, horrible lies!"

"Horrible lies, grandmother, how do you know?"

Her grandmother hesitated for a moment: "Oh! I have my reasons! .. Can you think of a family which has not had its misfortunes, which could not be distorted and magnified? Even my own mother, that dear and venerable aunt Dide, your great grandmother, has she not been in the lunatic asylum at the Tulettes for the last twenty-one years? Though God has graciously allowed her to live to the age of a hundred and four, he has cruelly punished her by depriving her of her reason. There is certainly nothing shameful about that; but what exasperates me, what must be avoided at all costs, is that people should say that we are all mad .. Another instance: deplorable rumours have been circulating about your great uncle Macquart! Macquart certainly had his faults, I am not defending him. But to-day, can anyone deny that he is living, modestly and virtuously, in his little property at the Tulettes, a stone's throw from my unfortunate mother, whom he cherishes like a good son? .. And as a final example, your brother Maxime was undoubtedly very wrong to have had a son by a servant, to beget that poor little Charles, and it is equally certain that the wretched

But the old lady was well away on her hobby-horse: "Yes it is quite true! Some of the women are spreading even worse stories. Go and ask them, out in the poorer quarters. They will tell you that he is pounding up dead men's bones in the blood of a new-born baby."

This time, even Martine was stung to protest and Clotilde, wounded in her affections, became really angry: "Oh! grandmother, you should not repeat such abominations! .. Uncle is so kind, all he thinks of is helping humanity!"

Felicité realised that she had been tactless and became persuasive: "But, my little pet, it is not I who say these horrible things. I am only repeating the stupid remarks I have heard, to make you understand that Pascal cannot afford to ignore public opinion .. He thinks that he has discovered a new remedy. Nothing could be more desirable! I am even willing to admit that he has found a universal remedy, as he hopes. But, why must he be so mysterious about it? Why not proclaim it openly? Above all, why must he test it on the scum of the old quarter and on peasants, instead of trying to effect spectacular cures on respectable people, which would make him famous? .. No, my dear, your uncle has never been able to do anything like other people."

She lowered her voice, as if to reveal a shameful secret: "God be praised, eminent men have not been lacking in our family. My other sons have been a credit to me! Your uncle Eugène was a minister for twelve years, almost as powerful as the Emperor! Countless millions have passed through your own father's hands and he played a prominent part in the great work of reconstruction which made Paris a new and greater city! Not to speak of your brother Maxime, so rich, so distinguished, or your cousins, Octave Mouret and our dear Abbé Mouret, a saint if ever there was one! .. You see what I mean. Why does Pascal, who is equally gifted, obstinately bury himself in this hole and behave like an eccentric old fool?"

As the young woman was showing renewed signs of indignation, Felicité put her hand affectionately over her mouth: "No, no! Let me finish .. I know that Pascal is far from stupid, that he has written some remarkable books and that his papers to the Academy of Medicine have earned him a great reputation among scientists .. But what is all that compared with the brilliant future I had visualized, my dreams for him—a fashionable practice in the city, a great fortune, honours, and a position worthy of our family. Do you know I used to say to him, when he was a little boy: 'Where have you come from? You are not one of us!' As for myself, I have sacrificed everything for the family. I would gladly let myself be hacked into little pieces, if it would lead to a great and glorious future for the family!"

She drew her small body up to its full height and managed to look almost tall, as if inflated by pride in her own achievements. She resumed her restless prowling. Suddenly, she gave a start. She had caught sight of the number of the *Temps*, which the doctor had thrown away. She noticed the gap in the page and drew the obvious conclusion. She sank into a chair. She had finally found what she was looking for.

"Your father has been appointed director of the *Epoque*," she continued.

"Yes," answered Clotilde calmly, "uncle told me. It was in the paper."

Felicité stared at her, searchingly. Saccard's appointment, the very fact of his rallying to the republic, had dismayed her. After the Emperor's disappearance from the political stage, he had been bold enough to return to France, in spite of his condemnation as director of the Universal Bank, which had failed in the most spectacular fashion just before the fall of the government. Thanks to influential supporters and his own genius for intrigue, his position had been re-established. He had not only been pardoned but was already manipulating large sums of money, acquiring influence in the newspaper world and had a hand in every shady transaction of any magnitude. She remembered the old quarrel between Saccard and his brother Eugène Rougon, whom he had so often compromised in the past.

Now, by the irony of fate, Saccard would probably become his brother's protector, seeing that the ex-minister was henceforth no more than a simple deputy, and confining his activities to defending his fallen master, with the same obstinacy with which his mother defended her family. She still blindly obeyed the orders of her eldest son, the eagle, whose wings had now been clipped; but she could not help having a soft spot in her heart for Saccard, in spite of her disapproval of his conduct, because of his relentless pursuit of a successful career. She was also proud of Maxime, Clotilde's brother who, after the war, had taken up residence again in his house in the Avenue du Bois-de-Boulogne and was squandering his late wife's fortune. Recently he had reduced his scale of expenditure, as he was suffering from some disease of the spine and was terrified of becoming completely paralysed.

"To be director of the *Epoque*," she repeated, "is almost like a minister. It is a great triumph for your father .. And, I fo tell you, I have written to your brother, urging him to come a us. It would take his mind off his illness. Then there is that that unfortunate Charles .."

She did not pursue the subject, which she considered incomp with her conception of family pride; a son born to Maxime by vant girl, when he had been a mere boy of seventeen. The chil now fifteen and feeble-minded. He lived at Plassans, was p from one member of the family to another and was a burden of them.

She paused, hoping that Clotilde would say something to hel broach the subject which was on her mind. She saw that the yc woman, who was busy tidying the papers on her desk, was pa little attention to the conversation. She glanced at Martine, who still sewing up the armchair and seemed both deaf and dumb, continued: "Was it your uncle who cut out the article from *Temps*?"

Clotilde smiled equably: "Yes, uncle filed it away. What a lo notes he buries in that cupboard! Every birth, every death, any event of interest to our family, it is all filed away. Our genealogical tree is in there too, you know, our famous genealogical tree, which he keeps up to date!"

Old Madame Rougon's eyes flashed. She stared at the young woman: "Do you know exactly what is in those files?"

"Oh! no, grandmother! Uncle never talks about them and he has forbidden me to touch them."

Felicité was incredulous: "Come! You have them right under your nose, you must have looked at them."

Clotilde simply smiled again and answered: "No, when uncle forbids me to do something, he must have a good reason for it and I obey him.

"Very well, my child!" cried Felicité vehemently. "Pascal is fonde of you than anybody and he might listen to you. You must persuad him to burn all that rubbish. If he died and all the horrible thing in there were disclosed, we should all be dishonoured!"

Those abominable files. Felicité had nightmares about them; sh saw the grisly facts written in letters of fire, the physiological defect the reverse side of the family glory, which she would have liked bury, like her dead ancestors. She knew the doctor's motive assembling these documents. In the beginning, the collection ha child is not normal in the head. Never mind! Would you be pleased if somebody told you that your nephew was degenerate, that he was following in the footsteps of his great-grandmother, three generations back, that dear woman, whom we take him to visit and to whom he is so devoted? .. No! All family life would become impossible, insufferable, if one started dissecting everything and everybody. It would make life disgusting!"

"That is science, grandmother."

"Science!" exclaimed Felicité, "a fine thing this science they talk about. It goes against everything that is sacred in the world! When they have demolished everything, what will that benefit them? .. They kill respect, they kill the family, they kill God himself .."

"Oh! do not say that, madame!" interrupted Martine piteously, shocked to the core of her simple faith. "Do not say that the master kills God!"

"Yes, my poor girl, that is just what he is doing. And, you see, our religion teaches us that it is a crime to allow him to incur his own damnation. I am afraid that you cannot really love him, you two who are fortunate enough to believe in the true faith, if you do nothing to lead him back to the path of righteousness .. Ah! If I were you, I would hack this cupboard to bits with an axe, I would make a fine bonfire of all the insults to the Almighty which it contains!"

She stood in front of the huge cupboard, gazing at it with blazing eyes, measuring it, as if she intended to take it by assault, sack it, annihilate it, despite the frailty of her age. Then, with a gesture of ironical disdain: "As though, with all his science, he could know everything!"

Clotilde was absorbed, a far-away look in her eyes. She had forgotten the other two and was muttering to herself: "It is true, he cannot know everything .. There is always something else, over there .. That is what makes me indignant, that is the cause of our quarrels; I cannot forget the mystery of the impalpable, as he can; I worry about it, to the point of torture .. Over there, somewhere, everything which is groping and striving in the chill world of shadows, all those unknown and perhaps unknowable forces .." She spoke increasingly slowly and her voice finally faded into an indistinct murmur.

Martine was becoming more and more concerned and agitated: "If it is really true, mademoiselle, that the master is damning himself with all those nasty papers! Are we right to let him? I don't care about myself. If he were to tell me to throw myself down from the balcony, I would shut my eyes and jump, because I know that he is always right. But, to save him, if I only could, I would do anything, even against his wishes. It is too cruel to think that he will not be in heaven with us."

"Excellent sentiments, my girl," approved Felicité. "You at any rate love your master in a sensible fashion."

Clotilde was not yet convinced. She had faith, but had never conformed to the strict rules of the dogma. Her religious beliefs did not include the hope of a paradise, a concrete haven of delight, where her loved ones were waiting for her. In her case, it was simply the need for believing in a "beyond", a certainty that the vast world could not be confined to physical sensation, that there was another world of the unknown, which should not be neglected. But her grandmother, who was so old, and the servant, who was so devoted, were winning her over by playing upon her anxiety for her beloved uncle.

Did they, perhaps, love him more deeply and wisely, seeing that they wanted to free him from his preoccupation with science, to make him perfect—pure enough to belong to the elect? She remembered phrases in the sacred manuals, the everlasting battle against the spirit of evil, the glory of conversions achieved against great odds. Should she undertake this holy task? Save him in spite of himself? The idea appealed to her lively sense of adventure and she felt filled with exaltation.

"Certainly," she said in the end, "I would prefer him not to waste his time and energy collecting these bits of paper and come to church with us."

Realizing that she was on the verge of consenting, Madame Rougon insisted on immediate action. Martine supported her. They gathered around Clotilde. They gave her instructions, lowering their voices like conspirators in a plot to achieve a miracle, a divine joy which would perfume the whole atmosphere of the house. What a triumph to reconcile the doctor with God! And afterwards, what bliss to live together in the celestial communion of a common faith!

Clotilde was subjugated, won over: "What do you want me to do?"

The sound of the doctor's pestle, its regular rhythm, seemed intensified by the silence. Felicité, exulting in her victory, was about to speak, but glanced apprehensively towards the door of the next

But the old lady was well away on her hobby-horse: "Yes it is quite true! Some of the women are spreading even worse stories. Go and ask them, out in the poorer quarters. They will tell you that he is pounding up dead men's bones in the blood of a new-born baby."

This time, even Martine was stung to protest and Clotilde, wounded in her affections, became really angry: "Oh! grandmother, you should not repeat such abominations! .. Uncle is so kind, all he thinks of is helping humanity!"

Felicité realised that she had been tactless and became persuasive: "But, my little pet, it is not I who say these horrible things. I am only repeating the stupid remarks I have heard, to make you understand that Pascal cannot afford to ignore public opinion .. He thinks that he has discovered a new remedy. Nothing could be more desirable! I am even willing to admit that he has found a universal remedy, as he hopes. But, why must he be so mysterious about it? Why not proclaim it openly? Above all, why must he test it on the scum of the old quarter and on peasants, instead of trying to effect spectacular cures on respectable people, which would make him famous? .. No, my dear, your uncle has never been able to do anything like other people."

She lowered her voice, as if to reveal a shameful secret: "God be praised, eminent men have not been lacking in our family. My other sons have been a credit to me! Your uncle Eugène was a minister for twelve years, almost as powerful as the Emperor! Countless millions have passed through your own father's hands and he played a prominent part in the great work of reconstruction which made Paris a new and greater city! Not to speak of your brother Maxime, so rich, so distinguished, or your cousins, Octave Mouret and our dear Abbé Mouret, a saint if ever there was one! .. You see what I mean. Why does Pascal, who is equally gifted, obstinately bury himself in this hole and behave like an eccentric old fool?"

As the young woman was showing renewed signs of indignation, Felicité put her hand affectionately over her mouth: "No, no! Let me finish .. I know that Pascal is far from stupid, that he has written some remarkable books and that his papers to the Academy of Medicine have earned him a great reputation among scientists .. But what is all that compared with the brilliant future I had visualized, my dreams for him—a fashionable practice in the city, a great fortune, honours, and a position worthy of our family. Do you know I used to say to him, when he was a little boy: 'Where have you come from? You are not one of us!' As for myself, I have sacrificed everything for the family. I would gladly let myself be hacked into little pieces, if it would lead to a great and glorious future for the family!"

She drew her small body up to its full height and managed to look almost tall, as if inflated by pride in her own achievements. She resumed her restless prowling. Suddenly, she gave a start. She had caught sight of the number of the *Temps*, which the doctor had thrown away. She noticed the gap in the page and drew the obvious conclusion. She sank into a chair. She had finally found what she was looking for.

"Your father has been appointed director of the *Epoque*," she continued.

"Yes," answered Clotilde calmly, "uncle told me. It was in the paper."

Felicité stared at her, searchingly. Saccard's appointment, the very fact of his rallying to the republic, had dismayed her. After the Emperor's disappearance from the political stage, he had been bold enough to return to France, in spite of his condemnation as director of the Universal Bank, which had failed in the most spectacular fashion just before the fall of the government. Thanks to influential supporters and his own genius for intrigue, his position had been re-established. He had not only been pardoned but was already manipulating large sums of money, acquiring influence in the newspaper world and had a hand in every shady transaction of any magnitude. She remembered the old quarrel between Saccard and his brother Eugène Rougon, whom he had so often compromised in the past.

Now, by the irony of fate, Saccard would probably become his brother's protector, seeing that the ex-minister was henceforth no more than a simple deputy, and confining his activities to defending his fallen master, with the same obstinacy with which his mother defended her family. She still blindly obeyed the orders of her eldest son, the eagle, whose wings had now been clipped; but she could not help having a soft spot in her heart for Saccard, in spite of her disapproval of his conduct, because of his relentless pursuit of a successful career. She was also proud of Maxime, Clotilde's brother who, after the war, had taken up residence again in his house in the Avenue du Bois-de-Boulogne and was squandering his late wife's fortune. Recently he had reduced his scale of expenditure, as he was suffering from some disease of the spine and was terrified of becoming completely paralysed.

"To be director of the *Epoque*," she repeated, "is almost like being a minister. It is a great triumph for your father .. And, I forgot to tell you, I have written to your brother, urging him to come and see us. It would take his mind off his illness. Then there is that child, that unfortunate Charles .."

She did not pursue the subject, which she considered incompatible with her conception of family pride; a son born to Maxime by a servant girl, when he had been a mere boy of seventeen. The child was now fifteen and feeble-minded. He lived at Plassans, was passed from one member of the family to another and was a burden to all of them.

She paused, hoping that Clotilde would say something to help her broach the subject which was on her mind. She saw that the young woman, who was busy tidying the papers on her desk, was paying little attention to the conversation. She glanced at Martine, who was still sewing up the armchair and seemed both deaf and dumb, and continued: "Was it your uncle who cut out the article from the *Temps?*"

Clotilde smiled equably: "Yes, uncle filed it away. What a lot of notes he buries in that cupboard! Every birth, every death, any event of interest to our family, it is all filed away. Our genealogical tree is in there too, you know, our famous genealogical tree, which he keeps up to date!"

Old Madame Rougon's eyes flashed. She stared at the young woman: "Do you know exactly what is in those files?"

"Oh! no, grandmother! Uncle never talks about them and he has forbidden me to touch them."

Felicité was incredulous: "Come! You have them right under your nose, you must have looked at them."

Clotilde simply smiled again and answered: "No, when uncle forbids me to do something, he must have a good reason for it and I obey him.

"Very well, my child!" cried Felicité vehemently. "Pascal is fonder of you than anybody and he might listen to you. You must persuade him to burn all that rubbish. If he died and all the horrible things in there were disclosed, we should all be dishonoured!"

Those abominable files. Felicité had nightmares about them; she saw the grisly facts written in letters of fire, the physiological defects, the reverse side of the family glory, which she would have liked to bury, like her dead ancestors! She knew the doctor's motive in assembling these documents. In the beginning, the collection had coincided with his preliminary studies on heredity. As they developed, he had been fascinated by typical examples in his own family, which confirmed laws he had established as the result of his own researches. Was it not a natural field for his observations, conveniently at hand and one with which he was thoroughly familiar? And, with the ruthlessness of a scientist, he had accumulated a host of intimate details about his relatives over a period of thirty years; recording and filing everything, using it as material for his genealogical tree of the Rougon-Macquart family, to which the voluminous files were only an appendage, a commentary, bulging with evidence of unmentionable anomalies.

"Most certainly," continued old Madame Rougon, emphatically, "all those papers, which will ruin our reputation, must be burnt, thrown into the fire!"

The servant, seeing that the conversation was becoming heated, rose to her feet and was about to leave the room. Madame Rougon stopped her with a peremptory gesture: "No, no! Martine, don't go! I want you to hear what I have to say. After all, you are practically a member of the family." Then she added, venomously: "A mass of falsehoods, malignant gossip, stale lies invented by our enemies, jealous of our success! .. Think of that, my child. About all of us, about your father, your brother, about me, horrible lies!"

"Horrible lies, grandmother, how do you know?"

Her grandmother hesitated for a moment: "Oh! I have my reasons! .. Can you think of a family which has not had its misfortunes, which could not be distorted and magnified? Even my own mother, that dear and venerable aunt Dide, your great grandmother, has she not been in the lunatic asylum at the Tulettes for the last twenty-one years? Though God has graciously allowed her to live to the age of a hundred and four, he has cruelly punished her by depriving her of her reason. There is certainly nothing shameful about that; but what exasperates me, what must be avoided at all costs, is that people should say that we are all mad .. Another instance: deplorable rumours have been circulating about your great uncle Macquart! Macquart certainly had his faults, I am not defending him. But to-day, can anyone deny that he is living, modestly and virtuously, in his little property at the Tulettes, a stone's throw from my unfortunate mother, whom he cherishes like a good son? .. And as a final example, your brother Maxime was undoubtedly very wrong to have had a son by a servant, to beget that poor little Charles, and it is equally certain that the wretched child is not normal in the head. Never mind! Would you be pleased if somebody told you that your nephew was degenerate, that he was following in the footsteps of his great-grandmother, three generations back, that dear woman, whom we take him to visit and to whom he is so devoted? .. No! All family life would become impossible, insufferable, if one started dissecting everything and everybody. It would make life disgusting!"

"That is science, grandmother."

"Science!" exclaimed Felicité, "a fine thing this science they talk about. It goes against everything that is sacred in the world! When they have demolished everything, what will that benefit them? .. They kill respect, they kill the family, they kill God himself .."

"Oh! do not say that, madame!" interrupted Martine piteously, shocked to the core of her simple faith. "Do not say that the master kills God!"

"Yes, my poor girl, that is just what he is doing. And, you see, our religion teaches us that it is a crime to allow him to incur his own damnation. I am afraid that you cannot really love him, you two who are fortunate enough to believe in the true faith, if you do nothing to lead him back to the path of righteousness .. Ah! If I were you, I would hack this cupboard to bits with an axe, I would make a fine bonfire of all the insults to the Almighty which it contains!"

She stood in front of the huge cupboard, gazing at it with blazing eyes, measuring it, as if she intended to take it by assault, sack it, annihilate it, despite the frailty of her age. Then, with a gesture of ironical disdain: "As though, with all his science, he could know everything!"

Clotilde was absorbed, a far-away look in her eyes. She had forgotten the other two and was muttering to herself: "It is true, he cannot know everything .. There is always something else, over there .. That is what makes me indignant, that is the cause of our quarrels; I cannot forget the mystery of the impalpable, as he can; I worry about it, to the point of torture .. Over there, somewhere, everything which is groping and striving in the chill world of shadows, all those unknown and perhaps unknowable forces .." She spoke increasingly slowly and her voice finally faded into an indistinct murmur.

Martine was becoming more and more concerned and agitated: "If it is really true, mademoiselle, that the master is damning himself with all those nasty papers! Are we right to let him? I don't care about myself. If he were to tell me to throw myself down from the balcony, I would shut my eyes and jump, because I know that he is always right. But, to save him, if I only could, I would do anything, even against his wishes. It is too cruel to think that he will not be in heaven with us."

"Excellent sentiments, my girl," approved Felicité. "You at any rate love your master in a sensible fashion."

Clotilde was not yet convinced. She had faith, but had never conformed to the strict rules of the dogma. Her religious beliefs did not include the hope of a paradise, a concrete haven of delight, where her loved ones were waiting for her. In her case, it was simply the need for believing in a "beyond", a certainty that the vast world could not be confined to physical sensation, that there was another world of the unknown, which should not be neglected. But her grandmother, who was so old, and the servant, who was so devoted, were winning her over by playing upon her anxiety for her beloved uncle.

Did they, perhaps, love him more deeply and wisely, seeing that they wanted to free him from his preoccupation with science, to make him perfect—pure enough to belong to the elect? She remembered phrases in the sacred manuals, the everlasting battle against the spirit of evil, the glory of conversions achieved against great odds. Should she undertake this holy task? Save him in spite of himself? The idea appealed to her lively sense of adventure and she felt filled with exaltation.

"Certainly," she said in the end, "I would prefer him not to waste his time and energy collecting these bits of paper and come to church with us."

Realizing that she was on the verge of consenting, Madame Rougon insisted on immediate action. Martine supported her. They gathered around Clotilde. They gave her instructions, lowering their voices like conspirators in a plot to achieve a miracle, a divine joy which would perfume the whole atmosphere of the house. What a triumph to reconcile the doctor with God! And afterwards, what bliss to live together in the celestial communion of a common faith!

Clotilde was subjugated, won over: "What do you want me to do?"

The sound of the doctor's pestle, its regular rhythm, seemed intensified by the silence. Felicité, exulting in her victory, was about to speak, but glanced apprehensively towards the door of the next

had wounded and exasperated him. For another moment their eyes remained interlocked, neither of them giving way to the other.

"You, you!" he repeated in a voice vibrant with feeling.

"Yes, I! .. Why, uncle, should I not be capable of loving you as much as you love me? And why, if I am convinced that you are in danger, should I not try to save you? Your first concern has always been to control my thoughts, you want to force me to think as you do!"

Never before had she defied him in this manner.

"But you are still a child, you cannot understand!"

"No, I have a soul and you know no more about it than I do!"

He released her arm and made a vague sweeping gesture towards the sky. A heavy silence fell on the room, pregnant with unspoken thoughts and grave issues which he was reluctant to raise. He moved restlessly over to the middle window and pulled up the blind. The sun was sinking and the room was full of shadows.

Clotilde felt that she needed air and space. She leaned out of the open window. The shower of burning embers had ceased. From above, there fell only the last quiver from the overheated sky, which was growing pale; warm odours rose from the hot earth, which seemed to be breathing in the evening air with relief. She could see the railway lines, then the buildings near the station. A line of trees, crossing the vast arid plain, showed the course of the Viorne river, surmounted by the hills of Sainte-Marthe; terraces of reddish earth planted with olive trees, shored up by walls of dry stones and crowned by woods of sombre pine trees; a great desolate amphitheatre, baked by the sun to the colour of weathered brick and fringed by the dark trees above it. To the left, there were the open gorges of the Seille, vast heaps of yellow stones, crumbled rocks on ground as red as blood, dominated by an immense barrier of rocks, like the wall of a gigantic fortress. Towards the right, at the entrance to the valley of the Viorne, the town of Plassans could be seen, with its overlapping layers of faded pink roof-tiles, the serried medley of an ancient town, pierced by the tops of its immemorial elms and by the lofty tower of Saint-Saturnin, solitary and serene, at this hour, in the limpid golden glow of the setting sun.

"Dear Lord!" said Clotilde slowly, "what arrogance to believe that we can grasp everything, know everything!"

Pascal had climbed on a chair to inspect his files and reassure himself that none of them were missing. He then picked up the fragments of marble and replaced them on the shelf; after which, he locked the cupboard and put the key in his pocket.

"Yes," he said, "one must attempt to know everything and, above all, one must never be dismayed by what one does not know and what will probably never be known!"

Martine had come close to Clotilde, as a gesture of solidarity. This time, the doctor noticed her and sensed that they were united against him and equally determined to get the better of him. At last, after years of latent conflict, open war had been declared. His was the invidious position of the scientist who sees his own people turn against his ideas and threaten them with destruction. There is, perhaps, no torment greater than treachery in one's own household. To feel harassed, dispossessed, annihilated by those you love and who love you!

Suddenly an idea struck him, in all its naked horror: "But, you both love me all the same!"

He saw the tears rise to their eyes and was filled with sadness at this tranquil end of a fine day. He was shattered by the realization that all his gaiety, all his kindness, both expressions of his passionate love of life, counted for nothing.

"Ah! my dear and you, my poor girl, you are convinced that you are doing this for my happiness, are you not? But, alas, we are all going to be profoundly unhappy!"

CHAPTER TWO

THE next morning Clotilde was wide awake at six o'clock. The night before they had both gone to bed bitterly angry with each other. She still felt depressed and unhappy and could think of nothing but the necessity for an immediate reconciliation.

She flung the covers off, leapt out of bed and opened the shutters. The sun was high enough to fling two bars of gold across the middle of the room, in which the atmosphere was heavy with sleep and the faint, heady perfume of her person. The morning breeze stole softly into the room, as Clotilde sat down on the edge of her bed and fell into a daydream. In her scanty and tight-fitting chemise, her slenderness seemed accentuated, with long tapering legs, slim but well-developed torso, small rounded breasts, round and supple neck and arms. The skin of her adorable shoulders was as white as milk, silky and infinitely soft. For a long time, from the age of twelve to eighteen, she had looked too tall, awkward and gawky, clambering up trees like a boy. Then, the sexless tomboy had turned into this exquisite creature, full of charm and grace.

Still dreaming, she stared at the walls of the room. Although the Souleiade dated back to the previous century, it had been re-decorated under the First Empire. The walls had been hung with a cotton print of sphinx busts linked in circles like wreaths. Originally bright red, the print had become rose coloured, a faded pink verging on orange. The window and bed curtains were of the same material and repeated washings had made them still paler. The effect was delightful, like the first delicate flush of dawn. The bed, with its pink hangings, had become so dilapidated that it had been replaced by another bed from a neighbouring room. This too was Empire, low and wide, made of heavy mahogany and ornamented with copper. Its four pillars were topped with sphinx busts of the same design as the hangings. The rest of the furniture was of the same period; a massive cupboard with columns, a chest of drawers with a white marble top and raised shelf, a monumental cheval-glass, a couch with wooden legs, and some lyre-backed straight chairs. A counter-pane, made of an old Louis XV silk skirt, made a cheerful splash of colour on the majestic bed and was draped over the middle panel, facing the windows; a jumble of cushions tempered the austerity of the hard couch; pieces of old silk embroidered with flowers, unearthed from the bottom of a cupboard, covered two shelves and a table.

Clotilde finally roused herself and pulled on stockings and a white, quilted dressing-gown, slipped her feet into grey linen mules and ran into her dressing room, which was behind the bedroom and was on the other side of the house. The walls were covered with plain unbleached ticking with blue stripes; the furniture, a dressing-table, two cupboards and some chairs, was of plain varnished pine. But, it had an atmosphere of refinement and reflected her taste, subtle and very feminine, which had developed at the same time as her beauty. She still showed traces of the obstinate tomboy, but, on the whole, she had become submissive and affectionate, pathetically anxious to be lovable. The fact was that her development had been an entirely spontaneous process. Her education had been anything but comprehensive or even systematic. She had merely been taught to read and write. While helping her uncle she had taught herself, imbibing all the elements of a broad culture. She had become well versed in natural history, and thus thoroughly familiar with all the facts of life. Her virginal modesty, however, was still intact, doubtless because of an unconscious aspiration towards a perfect union; she was, so to speak, keeping herself in trust to lay herself, unsullied, at the feet of the man of her choice.

She pinned up her hair and washed herself, splashing vigorously; then, feeling she could wait no longer, she went back into her room, quietly opened the door and tiptoed noiselessly across the study. The shutters were still closed, but she could see well enough not to collide with the furniture. When she reached the doctor's door, she held her breath and leaned forward to listen. Was he up yet? What could she do? She heard him walking around his room, probably dressing. She never ventured into his sanctum, which was kept locked like a tabernacle. Suddenly she was seized with panic. He would open the door and find her standing there! She was profoundly agitated, torn between her pride and her desire for a reconciliation at any price. For a moment her impulse to submit to him was so powerful that she was about to knock on the door. Then, when she heard his footsteps approaching, she took fright and fled, incontinently, back to her room.

From then until eight o'clock Clotilde was in a fever of impatience. She kept glancing at the clock on the mantelpiece, an Empire clock of gilded bronze depicting a milestone with a smiling Cupid and a sleeping Father Time. It was at eight o'clock that she usually joined the doctor for breakfast in the dining room. She sat down at her dressing table, made an elaborate and lengthy toilet and brushed her hair. Then, she put on her shoes and a linen dress, white with red polka dots. As she still had a quarter of an hour to spare, she was able to do some sewing, which she had long been intending to do; attach a piece of imitation Chantilly lace to her black overall, which, she now felt, looked too boyish, not feminine enough. When she heard eight o'clock striking, she dropped the overall and hurried downstairs.

"You are going to be alone for breakfast," said Martine placidly, when she reached the dining room.

"How is that?"

"Monsieur called me and opened his door just wide enough for me to pass him his egg. He's busy now with his mortar and his filter funnel. We shan't see him before lunch."

This was such an unexpected blow that Clotilde blanched. She drank her milk standing up and took her roll with her, as she followed the servant into the kitchen. Apart from the dining room and the kitchen there was a disused drawing room on the ground floor, now used for storing potatoes. The doctor had once used it as a consulting room, when he had been seeing patients at home; but, many years ago, the desk and armchair had been carried up into his bedroom. The only other room, at ground level, was the old servant's bedroom, spotlessly clean, with a walnut chest of drawers and a monastic bed, draped with white curtains.

"Do you think he has started making his brew again?" asked Clotilde.

"Of course! You know how he forgets to eat and drink when the fit takes him."

Clotilde's disappointment burst out in a low cry:

"O God! Dear God!"

Martine went upstairs to do the rooms, Clotilde took a parasol from the stand in the hall, meaning to eat her roll out of doors. She was desperately racking her brains to decide how to fill in the time until midday.

It was now nearly seventeen years since Doctor Pascal, determined to move away from his house in the new town, had bought the Souleiade for twenty thousand francs. He had wanted more privacy for himself, more space and a more cheerful environment for the little girl whom his brother had just sent him from Paris. The

Souleiade was on the outskirts of the town, on a plateau overlooking the plain. At one time, it had been a large estate, but successive sales had reduced it to less than four acres; the building of the railroad had involved sacrificing the last two fields fit for ploughing. The house itself had been partially destroyed by fire, leaving only one of the two wings standing; a square building, with four "pane-sides" as they say in Provence, five windows in front and roofed with heavy pink tiles. The doctor had bought it furnished and he had contented himself with repairing and completing the garden wall, in order to make sure of complete privacy.

Clotilde had become passionately attached to this solitary realm, small enough to explore in ten minutes, but which still retained traces of its pristine grandeur. But that morning, it clashed with her mood. She started walking along the terrace which had an ancient cypress tree, as sentinel, at each end, both so tall as to be visible three leagues away. From there, the garden sloped down to the railroad, dry stone walls shored up the red earth, in which the last vines had been planted and perished; all that now grew on these giant steps were rows of sickly olive and almond trees. The heat was already intense. She watched the tiny lizards running over the cracked flag-stones, between the tufts of caper.

Then, as if irritated by the vastness of the horizon, she hurried through the orchard and the kitchen garden, which Martine, in spite of her age, insisted obstinately in looking after by herself, except for a man who came twice a week to do the heavy work; she turned to the right and climbed to a clump of pine trees, all that was left of a superb pine wood which had covered the plateau. She was still restless and discontented; the dry pine needles crackled under her feet and the heavy scent of resins fell from the branches. She skirted the garden wall, past the entrance gate, which gave on to the Fenouillères road, five minutes from the first houses of Plassans, and reached the yard, which was very large, some forty yards in diameter, and bore witness to the original size and importance of the property. Ah! that ancient yard, with its round pebbles in the old Roman pattern, it was a sort of esplanade, covered with closely-cropped, dry grass, golden in colour, as if with a thick carpet of wool! What wonderful games she had played there, running, tumbling, rolling and lying idly on her back for hours, until the stars came alight in the limitless dome of the sky!

She opened her parasol and walked, more calmly, across the grass. The terrace was now to the left of her and she had completed her round of the property. She then made her way to the back of the house, under a row of enormous plane trees, overlooked by the two windows of the doctor's room. She raised her eyes in the hope of catching sight of him. But his windows were closed and she felt almost as if he had deliberately slighted her. It was only then that she noticed that she was still holding the roll, which she had forgotten; she stood under the trees and devoured it with youthful zest.

It was delightful under these old plane trees, which were another relic of the past splendour of the Souleiade. Only a faint green light filtered through the foliage of these gigantic trees, with their monstrous trunks, and it was wonderfully cool there, even on the hottest summer day. This had once been the site of a formal French garden, of which nothing remained except the box hedges, which had flourished in the shade and grown as tall as small trees. The special attraction of this shady corner was a fountain, a simple lead tube inserted into the shaft of a stone column from which flowed a perpetual stream of water, no thicker than your little finger. It plashed into a large basin overgrown with moss, which was only cleaned out every three or four years. Even when all the neighbouring wells were dry, the Souleiade kept its spring, which must, hundreds of years ago, have given birth to the great plane trees. For centuries, night and day, this trickle of water, never varying, sang the same pure song, like the vibration of a crystal glass.

Clotilde brushed past the box hedges, which came up to her shoulder, and went indoors to fetch her embroidery. She came out again and sat down in front of a stone table beside the fountain. It was surrounded by garden chairs, as they often came out there to drink their coffee. As if absorbed in her needlework, she appeared not to raise her head. From time to time, however, she seemed to glance, through the trees, towards the burning distance, the baking yard flaming like a brazier in the dazzling sunshine. But, in fact, her eyes, under their long lashes, were rivetted on the doctor's windows. Nothing, not even his shadow! She became increasingly depressed and annoyed. It was insufferable of him to abandon her, pay no attention to her after their quarrel of the previous day. What a contrast to her own overwhelming impulse, that morning early, to make her peace with him! Was he in no hurry for a reconciliation, had he no love for her, seeing that he seemed to be content to live on bad terms with her? Her mood became increasingly sombre. She began to think of renewing the conflict, determined not to give way, on principle.

Martine joined her about eleven o'clock, before starting to cook the meal. She was carrying her eternal stocking, knitting even as she walked when she had no housework to do: "Do you know that he is still shut up in there, like a wolf, making his nasty brew?"

Clotilde shrugged her shoulders without raising her eyes from her needlework.

"And, mademoiselle, if I were to repeat to you the stories that are being told! Madame Félicité was right, yesterday, when she said that it was enough to make you blush with shame .. They threw it in my face, yes in *my* face, that he had killed old Boutin, you remember, that poor old man who had fits and who died in the street."

There was a short silence. Then, noticing Clotilde's gloomy expression, the servant continued, her needles clicking even more rapidly: "*I* do not understand what he is trying to do, but it makes me so angry .. Do *you* approve of what he is doing?"

Suddenly, Clotilde raised her head, swept by a flood of passionate resentment: "Listen, I have no wish to understand any more than you do, but I am convinced that he is storing up serious trouble for himself .. He doesn't love us .."

"Oh! you are wrong, mademoiselle, he loves you dearly!"

"No, no, not as we love him! .. If he really loved us, he would be here with us, instead of shutting himself up, jeopardising his soul, his happiness and ours, trying to become a universal saviour!"

The two women looked at each other, their eyes burning with tenderness, in a tempest of jealous concern for him. Then, without saying anything further, they resumed their work in the deep and peaceful shade of the trees.

Above, in his room, Doctor Pascal was working with the serenity of perfect contentment. He had practised medicine for only about a dozen years, from the time he had left Paris to his retirement at the Souleiade. He was satisfied with the hundred odd thousand francs he had earned and invested with prudence and foresight. Since then he had devoted himself to his favourite studies, keeping a few friends as patients, never refusing to go to the bedside of a sick person, but never sending a bill. If he was given a fee, he threw the money at the back of one of his desk drawers. He looked on it as pocket money, for his experiments and his whims, quite outside his income, which was sufficient for his needs. He was quite indifferent to the fact that he was considered an eccentric. He was only happy when he was busy with his research on the subjects in which he was passionately absorbed. Many of his friends were surprised that a scientist of his calibre—almost a genius but for his too-vivid imagination—should stay in Plassans; a deserted provincial town that could hardly offer him the facilities necessary for his work. But, as he explained, he had found it particularly convenient; first of all because of its tranquillity and secondly because it was an unrivalled field for the continuous study of heredity, which was his favourite theme. In this neglected corner of the world, in which he knew every family, he could follow, over two or three generations, phenomena which are usually kept hidden. Besides, it was near the sea. He went there almost every summer, to study the infinite variations of primitive life at the bottom of the ocean, where it burgeons and multiplies. Finally, there was a post-mortem room at the Plassans hospital, of which he had the virtual monopoly, a large, light and quiet room in which, over a period of more than twenty years, he had been able to dissect all bodies unclaimed by relatives. He was shy too, and he was content to correspond with his old teachers and a few new friends, on the subject of the remarkable papers which he contributed periodically to the Academy of Medicine. He was entirely lacking in worldly ambition.

In the beginning, it was his work on gestation which had caused Doctor Pascal to take a special interest in the laws of heredity. As always, it was partly chance, which had provided him with a series of cadavers of pregnant women, victims of an epidemic of cholera. Later he had been on the look-out for suitable bodies, to complete his series, to fill in missing details and arrive at an understanding, first of the formation of the embryo and then the development of the foetus, day by day throughout intra-uterine life. From that time onwards, he had been preoccupied with the basic problem of conception in all its irritating mystery. Why and how did a new being come into the world? What were the laws of life, this never-ending stream of new creatures who made up the world? He did not confine himself to dead bodies, he completed his dissections by investigations on the living, struck by the persistent repetition of certain phenomena in his patients; much of his attention was concentrated on his own family, which soon became the principal field for his experiments, as it provided him with clear and conclusive evidence. As he accumulated facts and classified them in his notes, he was able to make his first attempt at elaborating a general theory of heredity which would explain the whole gamut of the facts. An arduous problem, on the solution of which he had been ruminating for many years.

31

He had started from the principle of invention and the principle of imitation, heredity or reproduction of similar characteristics, the inborn factor or the reproduction of dissimilar characteristics. As for heredity, he was only prepared to accept four possible forms: direct heredity, a representation of the father and the mother in the physical and mental make-up of the offspring; indirect heredity, a representation of collateral members, uncles and aunts, male and female cousins; latent heredity, a representation of ascendants, at a distance of one or more generations; finally the heredity of influence, a representation of couples in the more remote past, for example the first male who had so impregnated the female as to influence any future conception of her, even if he himself were not responsible for it. As to the inborn factor, this was the new being, or the seemingly new being, in whom the physical and mental characteristics of the parents are intermingled, although in a superficially unrecognizable form. He had then proceeded to subdivide the hereditary and inborn factors into various categories; he distinguished two hereditary alternatives, either the election of the father or the mother by the offspring, the choice, the individual predominance or the mixture of one with the other, and a mixture which could take three forms, either by linkage, dissemination or fusion, in an ascending order from the less desirable to the more perfect; whereas, on the other hand, the mechanism of the transmission of inborn characteristics could only be that of combination, analogous to the chemical combination of two substances which constitute a new substance totally different from either of its constituents. These hypotheses were arrived at as the result of a large number of observations, not only in the field of anthropology, but also in those of zoology, pomology and horticulture. This was only the beginning of his difficulties; to make a synthesis of the multiple data accumulated during the process of analysis and formulate the theory which would explain them all. Here, he felt himself on the shifting ground of hypothesis, transformed by each new discovery; and, although he could not refrain from attempting to find a solution, such is the human compulsion towards some sort of conclusion, he was sufficiently objective to leave the problem open. Starting from Darwin's pangenesis, with his gemmules, he had switched over to Haeckel's perigenesis, via Galton's stirpes. Then, in a flash of intuition, he had foreshadowed Weismann's theory, which was to become generally accepted, and had postulated the existence of an extremely delicate and complex substance, the germinative plasma, a part of which is always handed on, unchanged, from generation to generation, from each individual to each new individual. This seemed to explain everything; but what infinite mysteries still unexplained in this world of resemblances transmitted by the spermatozoon and the ovum, in which the human eye can distinguish nothing, even under the highest power of the microscope! He was well aware of the fact that his theory would be disproved in time, its value was transient, adequate to explain the facts in the actual state of scientific knowledge, that, however intensive and continuous our investigation of the phenomena of life, its actual source would always escape us. Was it not both unexpected and amazing that the resemblance between parents and offspring was never complete, mathematical? In the case of his own family, he had begun by drawing up a hypothetical family tree, allotting parental influence half to the mother and half to the father, generation by generation. But, on almost every occasion, the living reality contradicted theory. Heredity, instead of being resemblance, was merely an attempt at resemblance, thwarted by circumstances and the environment. He had ended up by formulating what he called his hypothesis of the miscarriage of cells. Life is movement and, as heredity is propagated movement, the cells, during the process of multiplication, jostled each other, were in constant conflict with each other, until they eventually reached their final positions determined by the individual hereditary impulse; thus, if, during the struggle, the weaker cells were to succumb, the end result would be serious disturbances of function and totally different organs. Was not this the cause of inborn characteristics, an ever-recurring device of nature, though repugnant to it? Was not the fact that he himself was so different from both his parents due to some such accident, or to the effect of larval heredity, in which he had, at one time, believed?

As every genealogical tree has roots which plunge deep into the human race, down to the first man, we cannot trace our descent from a single ancestor, we may always resemble some remote, unknown ancestor. Nevertheless, he was doubtful of the validity of the theory of atavism; in spite of a striking example in his own family, he believed that resemblances cease at the end of two or three generations because of accidents, interference, a thousand possible combinations. Thus, there was a perpetual process of becoming something different, a constant transformation of this transmitted force, agitation which is responsible for imbuing matter with life and which is its essence. Innumerable questions clamoured for an answer. Had there, in fact, been any physical and intellectual progress through the ages? Was the human brain improving, pari passu with the increase in our knowledge? Was it legitimate to hope that, in the long run, human conduct would become more reasonable and that the sum total of happiness would increase? Then there were special problems, such as the one he found particularly puzzling: Why a male, why a female, at conception? Would there ever be an accurate scientific method for prophesying sex, or even explaining it? He had written a curious paper on this subject, crammed with facts, but concluding that his ignorance remained complete in spite of all the data, compiled so laboriously. Finally, his recent, extensive study of the heredity of phthisis had reanimated his wavering faith in the possibility of finding a cure for the disease and had kindled a spark of hope in him, as mad as it was noble, of being able to regenerate mankind.

Essentially, Doctor Pascal's only faith was his faith in life. Life was the unique manifestation of the divine. Life was God, the great motive power, the soul of the universe. And the sole instrument of life was heredity, which made the world; so that if one could only understand it, master it and make it do one's bidding, one could remake the world at will. Owing to his familiarity with disease, suffering and death, he felt inundated with pity, the militant pity of the professional healer. Ah! no more illness, no more suffering, to be able to limit the causes of death! His hope was that the advent of universal happiness, a new world of perfection and felicity would be hastened by active preventive measures which would make everyone healthy. When all were healthy, strong and intelligent, the human race would be a superior race, infinitely wise and happy. In India, had they not been able to make a Brahman out of a Sudra in seven generations, thus using scientific methods to raise the lowest of creatures to the highest level of human achievement? And, as his work on phthisis had taught him that the disease was not hereditary, but that every child of an adult suffering from phthisis was born with impoverished tissues in which phthisis was able to develop unchecked, his one thought was to enrich this soil impoverished by heredity, to give it strength to withstand parasites, or rather the destructive ferments which he suspected to be the causal agents of the disease, long before the microbial theory had been established. The essence of the whole problem was to give people strength; and to give physical strength was also to reinforce will-power, to increase the efficiency of the brain by consolidating the other organs of the body.

34

At this stage of his career, the doctor had read an old fifteenth-century medical treatise and had been greatly impressed by a form of treatment called the "medicine of signatures". In order to cure a diseased organ, the method was to take the same organ from a healthy sheep or ox, boil it and give the broth to the patient. The theory was that like cured like and, according to the old treatise, the cure was almost infallible, especially in diseases of the liver. The doctor's imagination was stimulated. Why not try? As his object was to regenerate patients whose nervous systems were hereditarily defective or weak, all he would have to do was to give them normal, healthy nervous tissue. The broth method, however, seemed to him primitive, and he proceeded to devise his own technique; he pounded up sheep's brains with a little distilled water in a mortar, then decanted and filtered the thick semi-liquid mixture. He tried the end-product, a liquid, mixed with Malaga wine, on some of his patients, without any appreciable result. Suddenly, as he was about to abandon the method, he had an inspiration; on that particular day, he happened to be giving an injection of morphia to a female patient, using a small hypodermic syringe. Why not try hypodermic injections of his liquid? He began by trying injections on himself, night and morning for several weeks. The first doses, a mere gramme on each occasion, had no effect. He doubled and then tripled the dose and was delighted, one morning, to find himself feeling as light and energetic as he had been in his youth. He gradually pushed the dose up to five grammes at a time. As a result, he was breathing more deeply and working with greater ease and lucidity than he had done for years. His energy was enormously increased and he felt literally rejuvenated. He had a special syringe made in Paris, with which he could inject a dose of five grammes and was astonished by the effect on his patients; not only were their symptoms cleared in an incredibly short time, but the treatment seemed to give them a new lease of life. He realized that his method was still empirical and primitive and feared that it might cause undesirable side-effects, in particular an embolus, if the liquid was not perfectly clear and devoid of particles. Then he began to suspect that the revivifying action of the remedy on his convalescent patients might be due to suggestion, his own faith in it. But his rôle was simply that of the pioneer, the method would be perfected later. Besides, was it not amazing, verging on the miraculous to be able to make the ataxic walk, resuscitate the phthisic, grant a few hours of lucidity to the insane? He allowed his imagination to be overstimulated by this discovery of

35

twentieth-century alchemy; he deluded himself that he had discovered the universal panacea, the elixir of life which would do away with weakness, all debility, the sole cause of all maladies, a veritable scientific fountain of eternal youth, which, by conquering strength, health and will-power, would result in a new and better race.

That morning, in his room, which faced north, rather dark because of the giant plane trees, simply furnished with an iron bedstead, a mahogany desk and a big table on which stood a mortar and a microscope, he was carefully pouring his liquid into a flask. He had pounded up some sheep's nerve tissue in distilled water and had then decanted and filtered the liquid. The end-result was a small flask of a cloudy, opalescent fluid, with a bluish irridescence. He held it up to the light and admired it for a long time, as if he were holding up a specimen of blood which was to regenerate and save the world.

He was aroused from his reverie by a tap on the door and Martine's voice: "Monsieur! Do you know that it is a quarter past twelve? Don't you want any lunch?"

Lunch was ready downstairs in the cool dining room. One of the shutters had just been partly raised, but the others were down. It was a cheerful room. The walls were panelled with wood, painted a pearly grey colour picked out with blue lines. The table, the sideboard and the chairs were a part of the empire furniture which had at one time been installed throughout the house. The sombre mahogany glowed, a rich red, against the light background. The brass hanging lamp was polished so often that it shone like a sun; four flower pastels hung on the walls, a display of wallflowers, carnations, hyacinths and roses.

Doctor Pascal hurried in, radiant: "Ah! I'm sorry! I was immersed in an experiment, I wanted to finish it .. Here you are, a new batch, highly purified this time. I expect it to work miracles!"

He held up the flask which, in his enthusiasm, he had brought with him. He glanced at Clotilde and saw that she was sitting stiff and silent, with a sullen expression on her face. She felt a recrudescence of bitter resentment. He had kept her waiting too long. She, who only that morning had been longing to throw her arms around him, was now glued to her chair, withdrawn and hostile.

"Very well!" he continued, unperturbed, "so we are still sulking. Very wrong of you! .. So you don't think much of my sorcerer's brew, which can wake the dead?"

They drew up their chairs and the young woman, who was sitting opposite to him, could not avoid an answer:

"You know very well, uncle, how much I admire your work .. But, I want everybody else to admire you as well. Now there is poor old Boutin's death and .."

"What!" he interrupted, "an epileptic who succumbed to an attack of congestion! .. Come! As you are in a villainous mood, we had better change the subject; you would only upset me and spoil my day."

There were boiled eggs, some cutlets and a custard. During the prolonged silence which followed, Clotilde, in spite of her mood, did full justice to the meal, and Pascal remarked, dryly:

"It is reassuring to know that there is nothing wrong with your stomach, at any rate. Martine, give mademoiselle some more bread!"

Martine, as usual, was serving them and watched them eating. She even joined in the conversation from time to time, with easy familiarity.

"Monsieur," she said, when she had sliced the bread, "the butcher had brought his bill, shall I pay it?"

He raised his head and looked at her with astonishment:

"Why do you ask me that? Don't you usually pay without consulting me?"

It was in fact Martine who held the purse strings. The money deposited with M. Grandguillot, a notary at Plassans, yielded an income of six thousand francs. Every quarter, fifteen hundred francs were paid to the servant, who used it for the household expenses, bought and paid for everything with the strictest economy, as she was very stingy, in fact they were always teasing her about her miserliness. Clotilde, who was the reverse of extravagant, had no money of her own. As for the doctor, he took what he needed for his experiments and for pocket money out of the three or four thousand francs which he still earned every year and which he threw into a drawer of his desk; it was his private hoard, in coins and bank notes, though he never knew the exact amount.

"Certainly, monsieur, I pay," continued the servant, "but only for what I buy myself; and, this time, the bill is so large, because of all the brains the butcher has delivered ..

The doctor interrupted her abruptly:

"Come now, are you going to start attacking me, you too? No, no! That would be the last straw! .. Yesterday you both made me very angry. But it has got to stop, I am not going to have my home turned into a miniature hell .. Two women, the only ones who

37

claim to be fond of me, turning against me! I tell you, I would far rather walk out of the house, this very minute!"

He was not in a temper, he was laughing though his voice was not quite even and a note of genuine distress could be detected. But he was still feeling elated and added, cheerfully:

"If you are worrying about the end of the month, my girl, tell the butcher to send me a separate bill .. You need have no fear that you will be asked to contribute any of your own money. Your savings can go on sleeping in peace!"

He was referring to Martine's little personal fortune. Over a period of thirty years, with an annual wage of four hundred francs, she had earned twelve thousand francs and spent almost nothing; to-day, thanks to the interest, her savings had almost tripled in value and totalled about thirty thousand francs, which she had refused to invest with M. Grandguillot because she liked the idea of having a private hoard of her own, a hoard of gilt-edged securities.

"Money that is sleeping is honest money," she replied sententiously. "But monsieur is right, I will tell the butcher to send a separate bill, as all the brains are for monsieur's kitchen and not for mine."

The conversation had brought a smile to Clotilde's face; she was always amused by jokes about Martine's stinginess. By the end of lunch she was almost her old self again. The doctor asked Martine to serve the coffee under the plane trees, saying that he needed air after being shut up all morning. The coffee tray and the doctor's flask were both put on the stone table near the fountain. How pleasant it was there, in the shade, how cool the gentle, insistent murmur of the water, whilst, all around them, the pine trees, the lawn, the whole property were baking in the early afternoon sun!

The doctor gazed meditatively at his flask of nerve extract: "So, mademoiselle," he resumed, half in jest, half in earnest, "you refuse to believe that my elixir can resurrect the dead, but you do believe in miracles."

"Uncle," answered Clotilde, "I think that human knowledge is limited, that we do not know everything."

He interrupted her impatiently: "But we shall and must know everything .. Try and get it into your obstinate little noddle that there had never been proof, scientific proof, of a single interference with the immutable laws which govern the universe. To this day, human intelligence reigns supreme, the sole force capable of such a feat, I defy you to find any evidence of a real will, or even of any purpose, outside human life .. That is what I am driving at, that, in the whole wide world, there is no other will than this powerful drive, which is like a whirlwind, sweeping all life along with it, towards a higher and better form of life."

He had risen to his feet and opened his arms, like a prophet inspired by his faith in life:

"Shall I explain my own Credo, as you accuse me of rejecting yours .. I believe that the future of mankind lies in the progress of reason through science. I believe that the pursuit of truth is the divine purpose to which man should devote himself. I believe that man now possesses a treasure house of truths, slowly and painfully acquired, imperishable, and that everything else is illusion and vanity. I believe that the sum total of these truths will go on increasing and will eventually endow man with incalculable power and with serenity, if not happiness .. Yes, I believe in the final triumph of life."

Flinging his arms out wider still, as if to embrace the whole hot, rich countryside, he continued:

"It is life, my child, which is the ever-recurring miracle .. open your eyes and look!"

She shook her head:

"I am looking, and I still cannot see everything. It is you, uncle, who are obstinate because you will not admit that there is, somewhere over there, an unknown into which you will never be able to penetrate. Oh! I know that you are too intelligent to ignore it, but you refuse to take it into account; you push the unknown aside because it would interfere with your work .. It is all very well for you to tell me to disregard mystery, to master the known before attempting to grasp the unknown, but I simply cannot do it! It is the mystery of life which attracts and fascinates me."

He listened with a smile, pleased to see her so animated, and ran his hand affectionately over her rebellious curls:

"Yes, yes, I know, you are like the rest of them, you cannot live without illusions and lies .. Never mind, we shall come to some sort of understanding in the end. In the meanwhile, just be sure to keep your magnificent health, which is half the battle for wisdom and happiness." Then, changing the subject:

"I presume that you are coming with me on my round of miracles .. It is Thursday, my visiting day. We will wait until the heat is less fierce and then go out together."

She demurred at first, in order not to appear to surrender without a struggle, but, when she saw how disappointed he was, she consented. She usually accompanied him on these occasions. They remained in the shade of the plane trees for a long time, until it was time for the doctor to go up and change his clothes. When he reappeared, very correct in his tight-fitting frock-coat and wide-brimmed hat, he suggested harnessing Bonhomme, the horse which had taken him on his visits for a quarter of a century. But the poor old beast was going blind and no longer fit to pull a carriage. They were too fond of him and too grateful for past services to make him work. That evening he was barely conscious, his eyes filmed over and his legs crippled by rheumatism. The doctor and Clotilde had been to see him in his stable, planted a kiss on each side of his muzzle and told him that they wanted him to have a good rest on a truss of clean straw, which the servant had brought him. And they decided to walk.

Clotilde, still in her white linen dress with red polka dots, covered her head with a large straw hat crowned with a spray of lilacs; she was charming, with her big eyes and pink cheeks in the shadow of the wide brim. When they set off together, arm in arm, Clotilde so slender and supple and alive, Pascal so erect and proud, his white beard seeming to illuminate his face, still strong enough to pick her up and lift her over the streams, everybody smiled at them, they were so handsome and radiant. That day, as they came to the end of the Fenouillères road, at the gate into Plassans, a group of old women, who were gossiping, stopped talking, abruptly. He looked like one of those ancient kings in an oil painting, one of those powerful and gentle kings who never grow old, with one hand on the shoulder of a child, beautiful as the day, whose submissive and resplendent youth irradiates and sustains them.

They were walking along the lane of the Sauvaire towards de la Banne street, when they were stopped by a tall dark young man in his thirties.

"Ah! doctor, you have forgotten me. I am still waiting for your paper on phthisis."

It was Doctor Ramond, who had put up his plate in Plassans two years ago and had already worked up a flourishing practice. He had a fine head, was superbly virile and invariably cheerful. And he was extremely intelligent and his judgement was excellent.

"Fancy, Ramond! Good day to you! .. You are quite wrong, my friend, I have not forgotten my promise. It is Clotilde's fault. I gave her my manuscript to copy yesterday."

The two young people shook hands cordially.

"Good afternoon, Mademoiselle Clotilde."

"Good afternoon, Monsieur Ramond."

The year before, Clotilde had contracted a bad cold, with a high temperature, which had proved to be of no consequence. But Doctor Pascal had been in a panic and distrusted his own judgement; he had called in his young colleague to reassure him. This had been the beginning of a friendship, a sort of comradeship, between the three of them.

"You will have my paper to-morrow morning, I promise you", resumed Pascal with a laugh."

But Ramond walked along with them for several minutes, to the end of de la Banne street, which marked the beginning of the old quarter and was their destination. It was obvious, as he bent over Clotilde with smiling solicitude, that he was in love with her. But she was quite unaware of his feelings, as he was content to wait patiently for the moment, he hoped inevitable, when she would show that she reciprocated them. He also listened respectfully to Doctor Pascal, whose work he sincerely admired.

"In fact, my dear friend, this is quite a coincidence. I am just going to visit Mme. Guiraude, you know the woman, whose husband, the tanner, died of phthisis five years ago. She has two children: Sophie, who is nearly sixteen, whom I was able to arrange to send to one of her aunts, in the country near here, four years before her father's death; and a son, Valentin, who is just twenty-one and whom his mother refused to part with, in spite of all my efforts to persuade her. I warned her solemnly of the inevitable and dreadful consequences. Well! you can see how right I am in claiming that phthisis is not hereditary, but that tuberculous parents hand down a predisposition, a degenerate soil, in which disease flourishes at the slightest contagion. To-day, Valentin, who was in daily contact with his father, is phthisic, whereas Sophie, who has grown up in the sun, is in excellent health."

He was delighted with himself and added, laughingly:

"In spite of everything, I may still be able to save Valentin. He is obviously recovering, he has put on a lot of weight since I started giving him my injections .. Ah! Ramond, you will come round to them, you will have to try my treatment!"

The young doctor shook hands with both of them:

"I do not deny it. As you well know, I am always ready to follow your example."

41

When he had left them, they hurried along until they reached Canquoin street, one of the narrowest and darkest of the old quarter. Even in this ardent sunshine, the light was dim and it was as cool as a cellar. Mme Guiraude with her son Valentin lived on the ground floor of one of these houses. She opened the door to them. She looked ghastly. She was suffering from some obscure blood disease which was slowly undermining her. From early in the morning until late at night she cracked almonds, with the head of a sheep's thigh-bone, against a stone gripped between her knees; this was her only means of supporting the pair of them, as her son was not fit for work. On this occasion, however, Mme Guiraude smiled when she saw the doctor; Valentin had just eaten a cutlet, with enjoyment, a real feast for him, as he had been completely without any appetite for months. He was a lean and sickly young man, almost hairless, with a rosy flush on his prominent cheek bones, contrasting with the waxy pallor of the rest of his face. He was out of bed and had dressed himself to show how much better he felt. Clotilde herself was moved by the gratitude of these humble folk. They welcomed him like a saviour, the expected Messiah. They grasped his hands and would have kissed his feet! Their eyes shone with devotion. To them he was omnipotent, he was God, who resuscitates the dead! The doctor himself was encouraged by the astonishing progress in his patient's condition. He was not cured, of course; perhaps it was only a temporary stimulation, as he seemed ominously excited and feverish. But, was it nothing to be able to retard the disease, even by a few days? He gave him another injection. Clotilde went over to the window and turned her back; when they left, she saw that he laid twenty francs on the table. It was not unusual for him to pay his patients, instead of being paid by them.

They made three further visits in the old quarter, then went to see a lady in the new town; and, when they were back in the street:

"If you have no objection, Clotilde, we could go and see Sophie at her aunt's before paying our visit to Lafouasse. Nothing would give me greater pleasure."

It was less than two miles away, it would be a pleasant walk in such admirable weather. Clotilde agreed. Her mood had changed, she squeezed his arm affectionately, happy to be near him. It was five o'clock and the slanting sun made the countryside look like a great cloth of gold. But, as soon as they left Plassans, they embarked on the vast, desiccated and bare plain to the right of the Viorne. The new canal, which was still under construction and which was to irrigate and transform the arid countryside, had not yet reached this district; there was an endless vista of reddish and dirty yellow earth, in a state of gloomy prostration under the sun. This was only relieved by a few stunted almond and olive trees, continually cut back and pruned with the result that their short branches twisted upwards and seemed to be gesturing to the sky in attitudes of suffering and revolt. Above, on the barren slopes, formal lines of cypress trees surrounded white patches, which, on closer inspection, proved to be country houses. The immense treeless expanse was not without a certain severe grandeur, thanks to the classical lines of the rolling hills, standing out desolate and clear in the dazzling sunshine. A layer of snow-white dust, nearly ten inches thick, covered the road. The slightest breeze raised large clouds, which looked like smoke and powdered the fig trees and bramble bushes at the side of the road.

Clotilde who, like a little girl, was playing at making the dust crackle under her feet, wanted Pascal to share her parasol:

"The sun is in your eyes. Come over to my left side."

But, in the end, it was Pascal who took the parasol away from Clotilde: "You are not holding it properly, besides it tires you .. We are nearly there."

In the distance they could now see an island of foliage in the midst of the burnt plain, a thicket of enormous trees. It was the Seguiranne, where Sophie lived, with her aunt Dieudonné, the tenant farmer's wife. Wherever there was a spring, however small, or a stream, this sun-drenched earth sprouted a luxuriant vegetation. Thanks to these trees, the lanes which wound through the property were shady and delightfully cool. Plane, chestnut and young elm trees flourished and grew vigorously. They walked up an avenue of admirable oak trees in full leaf.

As they reached the farm, a girl, who was haymaking in a meadow, dropped her fork and ran towards them. It was Sophie, who had recognized the doctor and "the young lady", as she called Clotilde. She worshipped them and was speechless with emotion. She was very like her brother Valentin, short, with fair almost colourless hair and prominent cheek bones; but living in the country had made her strong and healthy; her cheeks were full and her hair was thick and abundant. She had beautiful eyes, which were shining with health and gratitude. Aunt Dieudonné had also been haymaking and called to them from afar in her loud peasant's voice, cracking simple jokes in a Provencal accent:

"Ah! Monsieur Pascal, we don't need you here! Nobody is ill.!"

The doctor, who had come simply to feast his eyes on a picture of bucolic health answered in the same tone:

"I should hope not. But does not mean that this little girl should forget her debt to you and me!"

"That is the solemn truth! And she knows it, Monsieur Pascal, not a day passes without her saying that, if it were not for you, she would be like her poor brother Valentin at this minute."

"Bah! We shall save him too. Valentin is much better. I have just been to see him."

Sophie seized the doctor's hands. Tears rolled down her cheeks and she could only stammer: "Oh! Monsieur Pascal!"

How they loved him! Clotilde felt her own affection reinforced by all the affection he aroused in others. They chatted for a few moments, lingering in the beneficent shade of the oak trees. Then they returned to Plassans, having one further visit to make.

It was at the corner of two roads, in a tumble-down pothouse, white with flour dust. A steam mill had been installed opposite, in the old buildings of the Paradou, which had been built in the previous century. Lafouasse, the owner of the pothouse, had benefited by the custom of the workmen from the mill and the peasants who brought their wheat. On Sundays, he was also patronized by the few inhabitants of the Artaud, a neighbouring hamlet. But he had had a stroke of bad luck; for the last three years he had been dragging himself about, complaining of severe pains in his limbs. The doctor had finally diagnosed the initial stages of ataxia, but he obstinately refused to engage a servant. By clinging to the furniture he managed somehow to serve his customers. After about ten injections, he had improved so much that he boasted to everyone that he was cured.

He was standing in his doorway, tall and heavily built, his face flushed crimson underneath a mop of carroty hair.

"I was expecting you, Monsieur Pascal. Do you know that I was actually able to bottle two barrels of wine yesterday, without feeling tired!"

Clotilde sat on a stone bench, outside, while Pascal went in to give Lafouasse his injection. She could hear their voices; the man, oversensitive to pain in spite of his powerful muscles, was complaining that the injections hurt him; but agreed that a little pain was a small price to pay for regaining his health. Then he insisted on the doctor drinking a glass of something. He also forced Clotilde to have a glass of syrup. He carried a table outside. He was determined that they should drink each other's health.

"Your very good health, Doctor Pascal, and health to all the poor devils you are treating!"

Clotilde smiled, thinking of all the malicious gossip which Martine had repeated to her, about old Boutin, whom the doctor was accused of having killed. He certainly was not killing all his patients. Perhaps his new treatment really was as effective as he claimed. Her faith in her uncle was being restored, a flood of exuberant feeling, a torrent of love for him, flooded through her heart. When they left, she felt entirely at his mercy, she would have gladly let him take her, carry her away, dispose of her as he wished.

But, a few minutes ago, on the stone bench, as she looked at the steam mill, she had been dreaming about a strange story. Had not those buildings, now black with soot and white with flour, been the scene of a dark and violent drama of passion, a long time ago? And she had tried to piece the story together from the details given her by Martine, from the doctor's hints: the tragic love story of her cousin, the Abbé Serge Mouret, then Curé of Artaud, with an adorable creature, savage and passionate, who lived at the Paradou.

As they retraced their footsteps, Clotilde stopped and pointed to the vast gloomy plain, some cottages, flat ploughed fields and large patches of waste ground overgrown with weeds:

"Didn't you tell me, uncle, that all this was once a big park?"

Pascal, who had thoroughly enjoyed their afternoon together, started and smiled affectionately, but with an expression of infinite sadness:

"Yes, yes, the Paradou, an immense garden, woods, meadows, orchards, flower-beds, fountains and streams which flowed into the Viorne .. A garden which had been abandoned for a century, the garden of the sleeping beauty, left to be reconquered by nature .. And, you see, they have cut down all the trees, cleared it, levelled it and divided it into lots which they are putting up for sale. Even the springs have dried up, there is nothing over there except that poisonous swamp .. Ah! whenever I pass this spot, I feel overwhelmed by an intolerable sense of depression."

She hazarded another question:

"Was it not at the Paradou that my cousin Serge had a love affair with his great friend Albine?"

Pascal had become oblivious of her presence, he was looking into the distance, reliving the past:

"Albine! I can still see her, in the sun-drenched garden, like a living bouquet perfumed with her own scent, her head thrown back, laughter bubbling up from her throat, revelling in her flowers; wild flowers in her fair hair, twined around her neck, stuck in her blouse, around her arms, those thin, bare, sun-tanned arms .. And, when she smothered herself, I can see her lying dead, very white, her hands folded, sleeping with a smile, on her couch of hyacinths and tuberoses .. She died of love, and how passionately Albine and Serge loved each other in that great garden! The temptation was too great, with all that wild beauty around them. It was life, pulsating triumphant life, that swept away all false standards and ties!"

Clotilde stared at him, perplexed and disturbed by this flood of impassioned eloquence. She had never ventured to speak to him about another story she had heard about: the story of his own solitary love affair, conducted with the greatest of discretion, with a lady who was also now dead. The story went that he had looked after her devotedly without even kissing the tips of her fingers. Up to now, when he was nearing sixty, his work and his bashfulness had kept him away from women. But one felt that he was keeping his passions in leash, that his heart was still young, his pent-up feelings clamouring for an outlet.

"And the woman who died, who is mourned .."

She hesitated, her voice was trembling and her cheeks were flushed:

"How could Serge let her die, did he not love her?"

Pascal seemed to be waking out of a dream. He shuddered and seemed surprised to see her by his side, so young with such lovely eyes, gleaming brightly under the brim of her hat. Something had happened to them, they both felt as if a warm breath of romance had been wafted over them. They were faintly embarrassed and did not link arms, but walked on side by side.

"Ah! my dear, it would be too wonderful if human beings did not always spoil everything. Albine is dead and Serge is now Curé at Saint-Eutrope, where he lives with his sister Désirée, who is a good soul but lucky enough to be half mad .. He is a saintly man, I have never denied it .. Even a murderer can serve God."

He went on talking, expounding his views on life, on humanity, which he found execrable and irretrievably sullied, with a cheerful smile still on his face. He loved life, he persisted in admiring mankind's incessant and valiant struggle towards the light, in spite of all its evils and frightful tragedies. Life might seem horrible, but it must

46

be great and good seeing that, inherent in all of us, there is such a tenacious will to live, with, apparently, no other object than the will itself and the great, though unrecorded deeds which we have accomplished. Certainly, he was a scientist, an enlightened man, he had no illusion about human life being an idyll amidst the unspoiled beauty of nature, quite the contrary; he saw its evils and defects only too clearly, he had exposed them, investigated them and catalogued them for over thirty years; and his passion for life, his admiration for the powers of life were strong enough to send him into ever-recurring transports of delight. Hence his love for all his fellows, a fraternal tenderness, a warm sympathy which one sensed beneath the hard surface and the apparent impersonality of his studies.

"Bah!" he concluded, turning for a last look at the vast gloomy fields, "the Paradou is no more, they have sacked, soiled, destroyed it; but, what matter! Vines will be planted, wheat will grow, there will be a new harvest; and people will love each other again in the distant future, when the grapes are gathered and the corn garnered .. Life is eternal, it always grows again and goes on expanding."

He took her arm again and they went home, pressed against each other, good friends, in the twilight dying slowly out of the sky, in a lake shimmering with every shade of purple and pink. And seeing them pass, the old king, powerful, and gentle, leaning on the shoulder of the charming and submissive child, whose youth sustained him, the women of the suburb, sitting on their doorsteps, followed them with their eyes and a smile of understanding.

Martine was waiting for them at the Souleiade. She waved at them impatiently from afar. Had they forgotten their dinner? When they had reached the house, she greeted them with:

"There now! You will have to wait for at least a quarter of an hour. The leg of lamb is not in the oven yet. I did not want to risk spoiling it."

They stayed out of doors, enchanted by the falling dusk. The pine trees, drowned in shadows, exhaled the powerful scent of their resins; and, from the lawn, which was still smoking with heat, there arose a faint murmur. It was like a sigh of relief, the whole garden settling down to its rest, including the thin almond trees and the twisted olive trees, under the great, serene sky which was growing pale; whilst, behind the house, the thicket of plane trees was nothing but a mass of darkness, black and impenetrable and one could hear the fountain with its eternal crystal note.

"Well!" said the doctor, "Monsieur Bellombre has had his dinner; he is out in his garden."

He pointed to a bench in the adjoining property, on which a thin old man of seventy was sitting; he had a long, wrinkled face, with large expressionless eyes and wore an elegant tie and frock-coat.

"He is a wise man," murmured Clotilde. "He is happy."

Pascal protested violently: "Heavens! I sincerely hope not!"

He was incapable of hatred, but Monsieur Bellombre, of all men, had the gift of exasperating him almost beyond measure; he was a retired schoolmaster, who lived alone in his little house, without any other company than that of his gardener, who was deaf and dumb and older than he was.

"That's a fellow who is frightened of life! Frightened of life, do you hear! Selfish, hard and mean! If he has kept women out of his life it was because he was terrified of having to buy them boots. The only children he has known have been other people's children and they baited him; that is why he hates children and thinks of them as units of flesh for him to beat .. Fear of life, fear of responsibilities and duties, worries and catastrophes! When a man fears life and shrinks from its afflictions, he is debarred from enjoying it! Such cowardice revolts me, I cannot excuse it .. It is our duty to live, to live fully, to live every moment of life; and suffering, a life of nothing but pain, would be preferable to renunciation, which involves the death of everything that is alive and human in us!"

Monsieur Bellombre had risen to his feet and was walking along a path, taking slow, small, deliberate steps. Clotilde was watching him and said: "But even renunciation has its compensations. To renounce, not to live, to keep oneself for the great mystery, has not that been the supreme happiness of the saints?"

"If they did not live," cried Pascal, "they could not have been saints."

But he felt that she was rebelling against him again, that she was escaping from his influence. Underlying any preoccupation with the after life, there is always a fear and hatred of life. He became tender and conciliating and laughed softly:

"No, no! That is enough for to-day, no more quarrelling. We must concentrate on loving each other—very dearly .. Come, Martine is calling, let us go in to dinner."

CHAPTER THREE

Throughout the following month, the situation steadily grew worse. Clotilde felt particularly distressed when she saw that Pascal kept his table drawer locked. To feel that he no longer trusted her incensed her so much that, if she had found the cupboard door open, she would have thrown his files in the fire, as grandmother Felicité was always urging her to do. And the quarrels became more frequent and so bitter that they often did not speak to each other for two days on end.

One morning, when they had not been on speaking terms for nearly two days, Martine said, as she served the breakfast:

"Just now, as I was crossing the square of the Sous-Préfecture, I saw a stranger going into Madame Felicité's house who seemed familiar .. I think it was your brother, mademoiselle, if I am not mistaken."

The ice was broken and Pascal and Clotilde started talking to each other:

"Your brother! Was your grandmother expecting him?"

"No, I don't think so .. She has been expecting him for more than six months. I know that she wrote him another letter, a week ago."

They asked Martine for her opinion.

"Gracious, Monsieur, I can't say, because it is four years since I saw Monsieur Maxime. He was here only two hours, on his way to Italy and he may have changed .. But I did think that I recognized his back."

They went on talking. Clotilde was pleased that something had happened which at last put an end to the brooding silence, and Pascal concluded: "Anyway, if it was Maxime, he will come and see us."

It had in fact been Maxime. After some months, old Madame Rougon's insistence had finally overcome his reluctance to travel. She was determined to solve his problem, which represented yet another threat to the family honour. It was an old story and the threat was becoming more urgent day by day.

It had happened fifteen years ago, when Maxime had been seventeen. He had had a child by a servant whom he had seduced.

Saccard, his father, and Renée, his stepmother, who had merely been annoyed at his having chosen such an unworthy partner, had been vastly amused by this stupid adventure of a precocious adolescent. The servant, Justine Mégot, happened to come from one of the neighbouring villages, a docile, gentle blonde, the same age as Maxime; they had sent her back to Plassans, with an income of twelve hundred francs, to bring up the little boy, who was called Charles. Three years later, she had married a local harness-maker, Anselme Thomas, a good workman and a thrifty fellow, who had been attracted by her income. Henceforth, her conduct had been exemplary, she had grown plump and seemed cured of a cough which had been suspected to be hereditary, due to a long line of alcoholic ancestors. The two children of the marriage, a boy of ten and a little girl of seven, both fat and rosy-cheeked, were in excellent health; she would have been the most respected and happiest of women if it had not been for Charles. Thomas, in spite of the income, hated this son of another man and bullied him, which worried and grieved his mother, though she was too submissive a wife to say anything. For this reason, although she adored the boy, she would gladly have sent him back to his father's family.

Charles was now fifteen, but he looked no older than the average boy of twelve, and his mental development was that of a child of five. He was extraordinarily like his great-great-grandmother, Tante Dide, the mad woman at the Tulettes. He was slender and graceful, as refined and delicate as one of those bloodless boy-kings who are the last of an ancient dynasty, crowned with long fair hair, as fine as silk. His large pale eyes were vacant and there was the shadow of death over his uncanny and disquieting beauty. He had no brain and no heart; no more feeling than a little dog, that rubs up against people, to gratify itself. His great-grandmother Felicité, captivated by his physical beauty, which she attributed to her own side of the family, had sent him to a private school, but he had been expelled at the end of six months, accused of unspeakable vices. She had been obstinate enough to change his school three times, each time with the same ignominious result. Then, as he neither wished nor was able to learn anything and as his habits were becoming increasingly repulsive, they had been forced to keep him at home and he was passed from one member of the family to another. Doctor Pascal had taken pity on him, hoping to cure him, and had only abandoned the impossible task after having had him in his house for nearly a year, unwilling to prolong the ordeal for Clotilde. And now, when he was not with his mother, whom he rarely visited, he could be found at Felicité's or some other relative's house, elaborately dressed, surrounded by toys, living like a little effeminate prince of an ancient and degenerate race.

This bastard, who looked like a prince, was a thorn in old Madame Rougon's flesh and her plan was to deprive the malicious tongues of Plassans of a subject for gossip by persuading Maxime to take him and keep him in Paris. Thus, another family scandal would be buried in oblivion. For a long time Maxime had turned a deaf ear to her arguments, terrified of taking any step which might interfere with the even tenor of his existence. His wife's death had made him a rich man. After the war he had returned to his hotel in the Avenue du Bois-de-Boulogne and was spending his wealth judiciously; his precocious experience of debauchery had given him a healthy fear of enjoyment, his main object was to avoid excitement and responsibilities, in order to live as long as possible. He had been suffering for some time from severe pains in his feet, due to rheumatism, as he thought; he was already visualising himself as an invalid, immobilized in an armchair; and his father's sudden return to France, Saccard's new activities, had thrown him into a panic. There was nothing he did not know about this devourer of millions and he trembled when his father showered him with attentions, smiling his jovial and hypocritical smile. Some day, now that the pains were spreading up his legs, he would be a cripple and entirely at Saccard's mercy. He became so frightened of being alone that he actually considered paying a visit to his son. If the little fellow seemed amenable, intelligent, healthy, why not bring him back? He would then have a companion, an heir who would protect him against his father's machinations. Little by little he persuaded himself that this might fulfil his selfish dream of being loved, pampered, defended; but, he might never have embarked on such a journey, if his doctor had not ordered him to take the waters at Saint-Gervais. Thus, it had only been a question of going a few leagues out of his way and he had arrived, unexpectedly, at old Madame Rougon's that morning, determined to catch a train, that same evening, after seeing and talking to the boy.

At about two o'clock, Pascal and Clotilde were still sitting near the fountain, under the plane trees, where Martine had served the coffee, when Felicité arrived with Maxime.

"What a surprise, my dear! I have brought your brother."

The young woman got up, bewildered by this emaciated and

jaundiced stranger, whom she hardly recognized. Since they had been separated, in 1854, she had only seen him twice, once in Paris and once at Plassans. She remembered him as an elegant and lively young man, but his cheeks were now hollow and his hair thinning and growing grey. Yet she saw that his fine head with its delicately chiselled features was still the same and that there were still traces of feline, almost feminine grace in this man who bore all the stigmata of premature old age.

"How magnificently healthy you look, at any rate!" was his only comment as he kissed his sister.

"For a very good reason," she answered, "because I live in the sun .. Ah! I am delighted to see you again!"

Pascal examined his nephew with a piercing professional eye and embraced him:

"Good day to you, my boy .. She is right, you know, human beings thrive in the sun, just like the trees!"

Felicité had trotted back to the house in a hurry and returned, crying:

"Isn't Charles here? I was sure that he would be."

"No," said Clotilde. "He came here yesterday. Uncle Macquart took him away to spend a few days at the Tulettes.

Felicité was in despair. She had only brought Maxime because she had been sure of finding Charles. What was to be done now? The doctor placidly suggested writing to his uncle and asking him to bring the boy back the following morning. Then, when he was told that Maxime was bent on leaving by the nine o'clock train, without spending the night, he made another suggestion. He would hire a carriage and they would all four go and see Charles, at Uncle Macquart's. An opportunity for a very pleasant excursion. Plassans was less than three leagues away from the Tulettes; an hour's drive and an hour for the return journey. Martine would cook a meal for them. Maxime would have plenty of time for dinner before catching his train ..

But, Felicité was in a state of nerves, obviously uneasy about this visit to Macquart.

"Come, you do not think that I am going all that way, in this uncertain weather .. It would be much simpler to send someone to fetch Charles."

Pascal shook his head. It was not always easy to make Charles obey. He was not amenable to persuasion. Sometimes, for no apparent reason, he rushed off, like an untamed animal. Old

Madame Rougon found herself in the minority, angry with herself because she had not made her plans more carefully, and had no choice but to consent:

"Very well, just as you like. But it really is a stupid business!"

Martine ran to fetch the carriage and, before the clock had struck three, the two horses were on the Nice road, trotting down the slope to the bridge over the Viorne. Then, the road turned left and ran parallel with the wooded banks of the river for about a mile and a half, then plunged into the Seille Gorge, a narrow defile between two gigantic walls of rocks baked a golden brown by the fierce sunshine. Individual pine trees had taken root in crevices; bushes and stunted trees, looking, from below, no larger than tufts of grass, fringed the crests, poised over the void. It was chaos, a ravaged countryside, a gateway to hell, with its agonizingly twisted contours, the jagged landslides of blood-red earth, a desolate solitude.

Felicité, immersed in her reflections, preserved an obstinate silence. It was very hot, the sun was blazing behind a thick veil of livid clouds. Pascal, alone, kept up a flow of conversation, voicing his passionate admiration for this aspect of nature, teeming with life, hoping that his nephew could be induced to share his enthusiasm. But it was no use showing him the life of the rocks, demonstrating the obstinacy with which the olive trees, fig trees and brambles managed to grow in them, against all odds, dilating on this colossal and powerful carcass of earth, which seemed to breathe with an intimate rhythm of its own; Maxime remained indifferent, intimidated by the savage majesty of these great blocks, so huge as to accentuate his own insignificance. He preferred looking at his sister, who was sitting opposite him. He found an increasing attraction in her health and good spirits, her lovely round head, the straight forehead, her serenity. From time to time she gave him an affectionate smile, which soothed him.

But the countryside was now no longer wild; the two rocky walls gradually flattened out and were replaced by rolling country, verdant slopes dotted with thyme and lavender bushes. For a while, it was still deserted, bare spaces, greenish and violet in colour, swept, when there was the slightest breeze, by an acrid scent. Then, all of a sudden, they drove around a curve and were rolling through the valley of the Tulettes, fertile because of its many springs. Down below they could see the emerald green of the meadows, darkened here and there by great trees. The village was half way down the slope,

among the olive trees and Macquart's country house was by itself, to
the left, facing south. To reach it, the carriage had to take the road
which led to the lunatic asylum, the white walls of which they could
see in front of them.

Felicité's expression became increasingly gloomy; she disliked
having to exhibit Uncle Macquart. Another good riddance to the
family, when he was out of the way! It would have been better for
all of them, if he had been under ground years ago. But, the old
drunkard went on, obstinately, saturating himself in strong drink;
he was now eighty-three, it was if he were preserved in alcohol. He
had an appalling reputation in Plassans as an idler and a bandit, and
the old men whispered a horrible story of corpses, which had em-
broiled him with the Rougons, at the time of the riots in December
1851, when he had treacherously led his comrades into an ambush
and left them, their bellies slashed open, on the blood-spattered
pavement. Later, when he had returned to France, instead of taking
up a good post which he had been promised, he had preferred this
little estate at the Tulettes, which Felicité had bought for him. And
he had lived there comfortably ever since. His only ambition was
to round off the estate, and he watched like a spider for any opportunity to do so. He had even managed to acquire a field which he
had long coveted, by making himself useful to his sister-in-law, when
she had been engaged in reconquering Plassans from the legitimists.
That was another terrifying story that had passed from ear to ear, of
a lunatic escaping from the asylum, galloping wildly through the
night, bent on vengeance and setting fire to his own house, with four
people inside. But, fortunately, all this was ancient history, and
Macquart, now a respectable citizen, was no longer the alarming
bandit who had been such a source of anxiety to the family. His
manners were now irreproachable, almost like those of a subtle
diplomat, except for his old bantering laugh which betrayed his
low opinion of his fellow men.

"Uncle is at home," said Pascal, as they approached the house.

The country house was built like a Provencal *mas*, all on one
floor, covered with faded tiles and its walls painted a vivid yellow.
In front was a narrow terrace shaded by ancient mulberry trees,
whose long and twisted branches had been trained and trimmed to
make a trellis. It was here, in summer, that Uncle Macquart sat and
smoked his pipe. The noise of the carriage wheels had brought him
to the end of the terrace. He was standing erect, drawn up to his full
height, neatly dressed in blue cloth, his head covered with his

eternal fur cap, which he wore from one end of the year to the other.

When he had recognized his visitors, he gave a mocking laugh and cried:

"What a select company! .. I am highly honoured. We must have a little drink to celebrate!"

But Maxime's presence disconcerted him. Who was he? What had he come for? When he was introduced by name and they were beginning to explain his exact relationship, he cut them short:

"I know, Charles' father! .. My nephew Saccard's son, to be sure! The one who made a wealthy marriage and whose wife died .."

He stared at Maxime, beaming with malicious pleasure when he recognized all the signs of premature old age in this man of thirty-two.

"Of course," he added, "we are all getting old .. But I cannot complain, myself; there is nothing much wrong with me."

His flaming red face, which looked as if it had been boiled, oozed self-satisfaction. He had long ago given up drinking ordinary spirits which had no more effect on him than water; double-strength brandy, which he now drank, barely impinged on his hardened gullet; he drank such enormous quantities, that he had become saturated with it, his flesh soaked in it like a sponge. Alcohol oozed like sweat from his pores. When he breathed or spoke, he puffed a thick cloud of alcohol from his mouth.

"Yes indeed, you seem in fine condition, uncle!" said Pascal. "But, as you have done nothing to deserve it, quite the contrary, you are justified in poking fun at the rest of us, who are less fortunate .. I have only one fear, that one day, when you light your pipe, you will set yourself alight, like a bowl of punch."

Macquart, flattered, protested loudly:

"You can joke as much as you like, my young friend! A glass of brandy is worth more than all your nasty drugs .. And you will all join me, won't you, so that no one can say that I am not a credit to you. People can say what they like about me. I have as much wheat and land and as many olive and almond trees and grape-vines as any gentleman needs. In the summer, I smoke my pipe in the shade of my mulberry trees; in the winter I smoke it there, against the wall, in the sun. Well? Need you be ashamed of an uncle like that? .. Clotilde, I have some syrup for you. As for you, Felicité my dear, I know that you prefer anisette. I have everything, everything that you could possibly want!"

He made a wide gesture with both arms, the reformed rake complacently displaying the advantages of a hermit's life; whilst Felicité, dismayed by this catalogue of his possessions, stared at him, waiting for an opportunity to interrupt him:

"Thank you, Macquart, but we have no time for refreshments .. Where is Charles?"

"Oh, Charles! I see! All in good time, all in good time! I have it now: Papa has come to see his son .. But why should that stop us having a drink?"

When they persisted in refusing, he became angry and said, with a sneer:

"Charles is not here, he is at the asylum with the old lady."

Then, taking Maxime by the arm and walking to the end of the terrace, he showed him the vast white buildings with its gardens, which looked like prison yards:

"There, nephew, you see the three trees in front of us. Well, above the one on the left, there is a fountain in a courtyard. Look along the ground floor, and the fifth window on the right is Tante Dide's. That is where you will find the little boy .. I took him there just now."

It was a concession on the part of the administration. Throughout the twenty-one years she had been an inmate of the asylum, the old lady had given her nurse no trouble. Very calm and gentle, she sat for days, motionless in her armchair, looking in front of her; and, as the child liked being there, as she seemed to take a faint interest in him, this breach of the rules was overlooked; sometimes he spent two or three hours with her, busily cutting out pictures.

This further disappointment was almost too much for Felicité. When Macquart proposed that all five of them, together, should go and fetch the boy, she snapped:

"What an idea! Go by yourself and be quick about it .. We have no time to waste."

Macquart, seeing her quiver with repressed fury and sensing how she dreaded such a visit, was amused and insisted in his usual bantering manner:

"Come, my children, it will be a good opportunity for seeing our old mother at the same time. There is no getting away from it, you know; she is mother to all of us; we have all come out of her and it would be hardly polite not to go and bid her good day—particularly as my great-nephew, who has come from so far, has probably never seen her .. I'm not the one to disown her! No, forsooth! She may be mad, but you do not often see an old mother who has passed the century mark. It is worth treating her with some consideration."

There was a short silence. Clotilde, like the others, felt a cold shiver run down her back and was the first to speak:

"You are right, uncle, we will all go."

Even Felicité had to agree. They took their places in the carriage again, Macquart sitting next to the coachman. The increased pallor of Maxime's drawn features betrayed his uneasiness; and, during the drive, he asked Pascal questions about Charles, with a pretence of fatherly solicitude which masked his increasing apprehension. The doctor, intimidated by his mother's threatening glare, compromised with the truth. The child was not exactly strong, that is why it had been considered good for him to spend several weeks at a time with his uncle in the country; however, he was not suffering from any particular disease. Pascal did not add that he had, for a while, dreamed of strengthening his brain and his muscles, by injecting him with his nervous tissue extract; but there were continual accidents, each injection causing a local haemorrhage which required compression with a bandage to staunch it; it was a degenerative process of relaxation of the tissues, a shower of little haemorrhages under the skin, and, above all, such sudden and abundant bleeding from the nose, that it was dangerous to leave him alone, for fear of his bleeding to death. The doctor concluded by saying that, though his intelligence might be a little backward, he hoped that it might develop in an atmosphere of greater intellectual activity.

When they arrived at the asylum, Macquart, who had been listening intently, climbed down from his seat, saying:

"A very gentle little fellow, very gentle. Besides, he is so handsome, a real angel!"

Maxime, pale and shivering, in spite of the suffocating heat, asked no more questions. He was gazing at the enormous building, the wings for the different departments, separated by gardens, for men and women; for the quiet lunatics and the violent ones. Everything was immaculately clean. The gloomy silence was only broken by the sound of footsteps and the rattling of keys. Old Macquart knew all the porters. Besides, all doors were opened for Doctor Pascal, who had been authorised to attend some of the inmates. After walking through a long corridor, they turned into a courtyard; here was the room, on the ground floor, with light wallpaper, a bed, a cupboard, an armchair, a table and two straight chairs. The nurse, who was never supposed to leave her patient, had just gone out. The only occupants, one at each end of the table, were the mad woman, rigid in her armchair and the child, on a chair, absorbed in cutting out his pictures.

"Come in, come in! There is nothing to be afraid of, she is quite harmless!"

Their common ancestor, whom her great grandchildren, all her innumerable offspring, called by the affectionate nickname of Tante Dide, did not even turn her head to look at them. She had been subject to all sorts of hysterical disturbances from her youth upwards. Ardent, always madly in love with some male or other, buffeted by an endless series of tragic and gruesome events, she reached the great age of eighty-three, when an appalling bereavement, a terrible mental shock had deprived her of her reason. Since then, throughout a period of twenty-one years, her mind had ceased to function, a sudden and irreparable mental breakdown. To-day, at a hundred and four, life still flowed slowly through her veins. She was like a forgotten woman, in a state of calm dementia, her brain ossified; her madness might well remain stationary for an indefinite period, and her condition involved no threat to her physical survival. Senile changes had, however, supervened and her muscles had gradually atrophied. Age had, as it were, eaten away her flesh, she was a bag of skin and bones, which had to be carried from the armchair to the bed. She was like an ancient tree, yellow and sere, with nothing but the bark remaining, but she held herself erect against the back of the armchair, with only the eyes living in the thin and elongated face. She was gazing fixedly at Charles.

Clotilde, feeling faintly tremulous, went up to her:

"Tante Dide, we were anxious to pay you a visit .. Don't you recognize me? I am your grandchild, who comes to see you from time to time."

But the mad woman did not seem to hear. Her eyes remained riveted on the child, who had just finished cutting out a picture, a king clothed in a golden mantle.

"Come, mother," Macquart intervened, "Don't pretend that you do not know us. You might at least look at us. Here is one of your great-grandchildren, who has come from Paris especially to see you."

His voice made her turn her head, in the end. Her empty, light eyes travelled slowly over all of them and then returned, inexorably, to Charles. No further attempt at conversation was made.

"She has been like this ever since her terrible shock," explained Pascal in a low voice; "all intelligence, all memory seem to have been abolished. As a rule, she never speaks; sometimes she utters a stuttering flood of indistinguishable words. She laughs and cries for no apparent reason, nothing impinges on her .. And yet, I would not venture to say that she lives in a complete state of darkness, that there are no memories stored up in some remote recess of her being .. My poor old mother, how I pity her, perhaps final annihilation would be preferable! What has she thought about all these twenty-one years, if she has remembered anything?"

He made a gesture, as if to push aside that dreadful past, with which he was intimately acquainted. He remembered her as a young woman, a tall, thin, pale creature, even then with a wild light in her eyes, widowed almost immediately after her marriage to Rougon, the slow-witted gardener whom she had insisted on marrying; then, before she was out of mourning, throwing herself into the arms of the smuggler Macquart, whom she loved with the abandon and ferocity of a she-wolf and whom she never even married. That had been her life for fifteen years, with one legitimate child and two bastards, a turbulent and fantastic existence; she had disappeared for weeks at an end, returning just as suddenly, her arms covered with bruises. Then, Macquart had been killed, shot down like a dog by a policeman; at first, she had been paralysed by the shock. Her eyes, the colour of spring water, were the only features which seemed to retain any vitality; she had retired from the world, cowering in a corner of the hovel her husband had left her, living the life of a nun for four years, with periodic attacks of frightful nervous excitement. The next shock was to be her last, unhinging her reason. Pascal remembered the atrocious scene, to which he had been an eye-witness. Her grandson Silvère, a victim of the hatreds and sanguinary feuds inside the family, was brought into the house with his head smashed by a pistol shot at the hands of another policeman during the fighting in 1851, when the insurrection had been suppressed. It was her fate, it seemed, to be spattered by the blood of her family.

Felicité, in the meanwhile, had trotted up to Charles, who was so absorbed in his pictures that he had paid no attention to the visitors.

"This gentleman is your father, my little darling .. give him a kiss."

They all turned to concentrate on Charles. He was beautifully dressed in a black velvet jacket and trousers. As pale as a lily, he looked exactly like the son of one of the kings he had been cutting out, with his large pale eyes and his fair silky hair rippling down to his shoulders. But at that moment, his most striking feature was his extraordinary resemblance to Tante Dide, a resemblance which had surmounted three generations, which leapt from the old lady's desiccated features, worn and wrinkled, to that delicate child's face; her own faded likeness to her old self, a sort of duplication of the effete appearance of this young scion of an old and exhausted race. As they faced each other, the idiot child, with the beauty of the dead, was like an ending to his old, forgotten ancestor.

Maxime bent over to plant a kiss on the little boy's forehead; he felt no stirring of any feeling for the boy, not even affection, his very beauty frightened him; he felt increasingly disturbed in this cold madhouse cell, into which a breath of human misery had been wafted from afar.

"How handsome you are, my dear little fellow! .. Have you a little love for me in your heart?"

Charles looked up at him. His eyes were blank, as if he had not understood a word, and then he returned to his cutting out.

But they were all startled. Without any change of expression, Tante Dide was crying, a flood of tears rolled from the living eyes over the dead cheeks. She was still staring at the child, and she was weeping quietly, interminably.

Then, Pascal was gripped by a powerful emotion. He had taken Clotilde's arm and was pressing it violently. Clotilde could not understand what was happening to him. But there, in front of his eyes, was a representation of the whole line, both the legitimate and the bastard branch, which had grown from this old trunk, so profoundly affected by hereditary neurosis. Five generations were gathered together there, the Rougons and the Macquarts, Adelaide Fouque at the root of them all, then the old bandit of an uncle, then himself, then Clotilde and Maxime and, finally, Charles. Felicité represented her dead husband. Not a single gap, the chain was complete, the chain of logical and implacable heredity. A whole century spread out in retrospect, in this tragic room, with its breath of misery from afar, so dreadful that all of them were shivering, in spite of the oppressive heat.

"What is it, uncle?" whispered Clotilde, trembling.

"Nothing, nothing!" murmured the doctor. "I will tell you later."

Macquart, who alone had retained his joviality, was scolding his old mother. What an idea, to welcome people with tears, when they have put themselves to considerable inconvenience to pay you a visit! It was hardly polite. Then he reverted to Maxime and Charles:

"Well, nephew, now that you have seen the little rascal, don't you find him a real picture, a credit to you after all?"

Felicité hastened to interrupt them, most dissatisfied with what had happened, her only concern being to get them all out of the room as quickly as possible:

"He is certainly a handsome child and less backward than one would think. Look how clever he is with his hands .. Besides, when you have put some polish on him in Paris .. It won't be the atmosphere as Plassans."

"No doubt, no doubt," murmured Maxime. "I am not saying no, but I must think it over." He seemed embarrassed and added:

"You understand, I only came to have a look at him. .. It is impossible for me to take him now, as I have to spend a month at Saint-Gervais. But, as soon as I am back in Paris, I will think about it and write to you."

Then, pulling out his watch:

"Confound it, it's half past five .. You know I must not miss the nine o'clock train."

"Quite, quite! Let us go," said Felicité. "There is nothing to keep us here."

Macquart made a vain attempt to delay them, by telling all sorts of stories. He told them about occasions on which Tante Dide had become talkative and claimed that he had even found her singing a ballad of her youth, one morning. Besides, he had no need of the carriage, he would walk back with the boy, as the others were leaving.

"Kiss your father, my child, you have got him here now, but heaven knows when you will see him again!" With the same surprised and indifferent movement, Charles raised his head and Maxime gingerly planted a second kiss on his forehead.

"Be a good boy, keep your looks, my little darling .. And try to love me a little bit."

"Come, come, we have no time to lose," repeated Felicité.

But the nurse had come back into the room. She was the old lady's private nurse, a buxom and vigorous woman, who got her up, put her to bed, fed her and washed her like a child. She lost no time in starting to talk to Doctor Pascal, who in any case wanted her to answer a few questions. One of the doctor's cherished dreams was to treat and cure lunatics by his method, by his injections. As it was lunatics' brains that were in danger of ceasing to function, was it not logical that injections of nerve tissue should increase their resistance and their will-power, by repairing the breaches in that organ? He had even played with the idea of trying his remedy on his old mother; then he had been overcome by his scruples, a sort of holy terror; in any case, dementia, at her age, meant total and irreparable ruin. He had picked out another subject for the experiment, a journeyman hatter, Sarteur, who had been in the asylum for a year; he had actually come forward of his own accord and begged to be admitted, in order to avoid committing a crime. He suffered from attacks, during each of which he was overwhelmed by such ungovernable homicidal mania, that he was liable to murder anybody he met in the street. He was short, very dark, with a receding forehead; he looked like a bird, with his beaklike nose and almost no chin. His left cheek was appreciably larger than his right. The doctor's treatment was having miraculous results on this case of impulsion mania. He had been free of attacks, now, for a whole month. The nurse was telling Pascal that Sarteur was quite calm and improving all the time.

"You hear, Clotilde!" cried Pascal delighted. "There is no time for me to see him this afternoon, we must come back to-morrow. My visiting day .. Ah! if I only dared, if she were younger .."

He looked back at Tante Dide. But Clotilde, who was smiling at his enthusiasm, said softly:

"No, no, uncle, even you cannot make her life over again .. Come, we are keeping them waiting."

The others had already gone out of the room. Macquart, at the door, was watching Felicité and Maxime walk away, with his usual cynical expression. And Tante Dide, pitifully thin, remained motionless, her eyes once again fixed on Charles, with his bloodless face under the regal crown of hair.

During the return journey, the atmosphere was strained. Hot clouds billowed up from the overheated earth and seemed to weigh on the carriage and make it roll along heavily. It was a stormy sky and the twilight was falling like a shower of copper-coloured ashes. At first, a few desultory words were spoken; then, as soon as the walls of the Seille Gorge closed in, all conversation ceased as the gigantic rocks lowered menacingly over them. Was it the end of the world? Were they driving towards some unknown abyss, which would swallow them up? An eagle flew past, uttering its loud raucous cry.

They had reached the banks of the Viorne again and were bowling past willow trees, when Felicité returned to her argument, without warning, as if she were continuing a conversation which had already been started:

"You need have no fear that the mother will object. She is very fond of Charles, but she is an eminently reasonable person and understands perfectly that it is greatly to the child's benefit that you should take him back. I must confess that the poor boy is never very happy when he is at home, because, naturally, the father prefers his own son and daughter. It is only right that you should be told the whole story."

And she went on and on, trying to make Maxime commit himself and make a definite promise. She went on talking until they reached Plassans. Then, all of a sudden, as the carriage rattled over the cobbles of the suburban street:

"Look, there is his mother . . That fat, fair woman, at the door."

It was the door of a saddler's shop, outside which hung harness and halters. Justine was outside, sitting on a chair, knitting a stocking, with a little girl and boy playing at her feet; behind them, in the comparative gloom of the shop, one could just see Thomas, a large dark man, sewing up a saddle.

Maxime had turned around to look, without any emotion, simply out of curiosity. He was disconcerted when he saw this stout woman of thirty-two, looking so staid and respectable, with no traces of the wild adolescent with whom he had had his first thrilling love affair, when both of them were entering on their seventeenth year. Perhaps, ill and prematurely aged as he was, he felt a twinge of melancholy nostalgia.

"I should never have recognized her," he said.

The coachman now turned the carriage into Rome street. Justine, a vision from the past, faded into the twilight, with Thomas, the children and the shop.

At the Souleiade, the table was set. Martine had cooked an eel from the Viorne, rabbit and roast beef. Seven o'clock was striking. There was plenty of time.

"Do stop worrying," repeated Doctor Pascal to his nephew. "We will take you to the station, which is only a short ten minutes' walk. . As you left your trunk there, all you will have to do is buy your ticket and jump into the train."

Then, as he joined Clotilde in the hall, where she was hanging up her hat and parasol, he said in a low voice:

"I am not at all happy about your brother, you know."

"Why?"

63

"I had a good look at him; I don't like the way he walks. It is a symptom which, in my experience, is always conclusive .. In short, the young man is threatened with ataxia."

She grew pale and repeated: "Ataxia!"

The word was associated in her mind's eye with the painful memory of a gentleman, a neighbour of theirs, whom for ten years she had seen drawn by a servant in a little carriage, though he was still a young man. Was it not the worst of all human evils, to be infirm, to be, as it were, severed from life by the blow of an axe?

"But," she murmured, "he is only complaining of rheumatic pains."

Pascal shrugged his shoulders; and, putting a finger to his lips, went in to the dining room, where Felicité and Maxime had already taken their seats.

The atmosphere throughout dinner was cheerful and friendly. Pascal's warning, out of the blue, had made Clotilde feel affectionate towards her brother, who was sitting next to her. She looked after him, teased him and made him take the choicest morsels of food. On two occasions, she called Martine back, because she had served a dish too quickly. And Maxime fell increasingly under her spell, she was so kind, so radiant with good spirits, so thoughtful and so wistfully charming. So much so, that a plan, nebulous at first, gradually assumed concrete form in his mind. As his son, little Charles, had made such a bad impression on him, because of his effete good looks, his royal airs coupled with a pathological imbecility, why should he not take Clotilde back to Paris with him? The idea of a woman in his house terrified him, as he distrusted them all, owing to his disastrous experience of them as a young man; but this one had something maternal about her. Besides, to have an honest woman in his house would be a refreshing change and might be very pleasant. It would at least prevent his father from sending him any more young women, who were almost certainly depraved, in order to finish him off so that he could lay his hands on his son's money. It was his terrified hatred for his father which finally made him come to a definite decision.

"Have you no intention of getting married?" he asked, feeling his way.

The young woman laughed: "Oh! I am in no hurry."

Then, in a bantering tone of voice and looking at Pascal, who had raised his head:

"How can one tell? .. Perhaps I shall never marry."

But Felicité protested vehemently. Clotilde's devotion to the doctor was not at all to her liking. She often wished for a marriage, which would separate her from him and leave her son isolated, in a household become rudderless, in which Felicité herself could become the all-powerful and undisputed mistress. And she appealed to her son: "Did he not agree that a woman should marry, was it not unnatural to allow oneself to become an old maid?" He nodded his head, gravely, and kept his eyes fixed on Clotilde.

"Yes, yes, of course she should marry .. She is much too sensible, she will soon find a husband .."

"Bah!" interrupted Maxime, "would it really be so sensible? .. It might well lead to unhappiness, there are so many unsuccessful marriages!"

And then, nerving himself to make the plunge:

"Do you know what you ought to do? .. You ought to come to Paris with me .. I have been thinking, in my state of health I am reluctant to take on the responsibility for looking after a child. After all, I am almost like a child myself, I badly need somebody to look after me .. You could be there to take care of me, if I were finally to lose the use of my legs."

His voice broke; he had lashed himself into an acute state of self-pity. He visualised himself as an invalid, with Clotilde at his bedside, like a sister of charity; and, if she were willing to remain unmarried, he would gladly leave her his money to prevent his father from laying his hands on it. It was pitiful to see how terrified he was of loneliness, how convinced he was that he would probably soon need a nurse to look after him.

"It would be a charitable act on your part and, for my part, I promise you that you would never regret it."

But, Martine, who was serving the roast, stood transfixed with astonishment; and the others were equally surprised by this unexpected proposal. Felicité was the first to express her approval, realizing that Clotilde's departure would further her own plans. Clotilde was too stunned to say anything and Pascal, very pale, waited anxiously for her answer.

"Oh! brother, brother," stammered the young woman, incapable, as yet, of coherent speech.

Then, her grandmother spoke:

"Is that all you have to say? Your brother's idea is an excellent one. If he is reluctant to take Charles for the present, there is nothing to prevent your going; and, later, you can send for the little boy ..

Come, come, it would be a splendid arrangement. Your brother is appealing to your better feelings .. Pascal, don't you think that she should consent?"

The doctor had made a great effort and now had his feelings well under control, but it was obvious that Maxime's offer had shocked him to the core. He answered, with studied objectivity:

"I repeat that Clotilde is eminently sensible and that if she feels she should go, she will accept the offer."

Clotilde was so agitated and disappointed that she protested:

"Oh! uncle, are you really anxious to send me away? .. Of course, I appreciate Maxime's offer. But to leave everything—my home, my loved ones—everything that I have loved up to now!"

She made a despairing gesture, including both people and the familiar objects around her, embracing the whole of the Souleiade.

"And," continued Pascal, gazing sternly at her, "what about Maxime, who claims he needs you?"

Tears came into her eyes, she gave a shiver of dismay, she felt that she was the only one of them all who had fully grasped the situation. What a dreadful prospect; Maxime, an invalid, pulled in a little carriage by a servant, just like the neighbour whom she had watched for so many years. But her instinct revolted against this appeal to her emotions. Why were they trying to make her feel dutiful towards a brother who had lost contact with her for fifteen years? Duty! Was it not her duty to consider herself first, her own deepest feelings?

"Listen, Maxime," she said in the end, "I too shall have to think it over. I will see .. I can only say that I am very grateful to you. And, if, some day, you should really need me, well, you may be sure that I would not fail you."

She was determined not to commit herself any further. Félicité, with her invariable lack of tact, persisted in trying to persuade her, without success; whereas the doctor's attitude implied that if she had come to a definite decision, it was no further concern of his. Martine brought in the dessert and made no attempt to hide her feelings; she was both delighted and relieved. Would they take her Mademoiselle away! What an idea, to leave Monsieur all alone, it would be the death of him! This incident had prolonged the meal. Half past eight struck and they were still eating. Maxime started fussing and fidgeting, worried about missing his train.

They all accompanied him to the station and, as he said goodbye to his sister, Maxime added: "Don't forget."

"Don't worry," declared Felicité, "we shall be here to remind her of her promise."

The doctor smiled ,and all three of them waved their handkerchiefs, as the train puffed away.

When they had dropped Grandmother at her door, Pascal and Clotilde strolled back to the Souleiade and spent a delightful evening together. The sense of strain, the cloud of brooding antagonism, which had made their lives intolerable for weeks, seemed to have been blown away, like a puff of smoke. They felt as if they were recovering from a long illness and were filled with relief and confidence in themselves. They had never felt such happiness at just being together, closely united, inseparable. For a long time they lingered outside in the warm night, under the plane trees, listening to the faint crystal note of the fountain. They had no need of words, they were steeped in the peace of perfect understanding.

CHAPTER FOUR

A WEEK later, the storm clouds had already gathered again inside the house. Once again, for long periods, Pascal and Clotilde glared at each other in offended silence; and their resentment against each other flared up periodically into bitter quarrels. Even Martine was goaded into a state of irritation. Life became an inferno for the three of them.

Then, all of a sudden, something happened which aggravated the situation to an extent which became almost intolerable. A Capuchin friar, reputed to be a very saintly man had come to visit Plassans. He was travelling from town to town in the south, preaching. His voice thundered from the pulpit of Saint-Saturnin. He was a sort of apostle, with the kind of eloquence which appealed to simple people, abounding in flowery and picturesque verbal images. He preached in an emotional state of extraordinary mystical fervour, anathematising modern science, denying the reality of this world, exalting the unknown—the mystery of the other world. The more devout members of the town congregation were enthralled and uplifted.

When Clotilde and Martine returned from hearing the friar's first sermon, Pascal noticed that Clotilde was in a state of feverish exaltation. They had to wait for her as she had lingered in the cathedral for an hour after the service, praying in a dark corner of one of the chapels. She could not tear herself away from the church and came out exhausted, her eyes shining with visionary ecstasy; she was haunted by the friar's burning words. She seemed to be filled with anger and contempt for everybody and everything.

Pascal became seriously worried and decided to remonstrate with Martine. He came down early one morning, when she was sweeping the dining room:

"You realise, I hope, Martine, that I have never made any objection to your taking Clotilde to church with you. I do not believe in interfering with other people's beliefs .. But I do object to your making her ill."

The servant, without interrupting her sweeping, answered in muffled tones:

"Sometimes people who don't even know that they are ill are the worst."

She had expressed herself with such conviction that he could not help smiling: "Yes, I know, I am the one with all the infirmities and you keep praying for my conversion, you and Mademoiselle have a monopoly of good health and wisdom in this house .. Martine, I warn you, if you persist in torturing me and torturing yourselves, I will show you what it means when I really lose my temper."

He was so obviously in despair and had spoken so roughly to her that the servant was dumbfounded, stopped sweeping and stared at him. An expression of infinite tenderness and immense sadness flitted over her face, which was like a mask of grief, faded and lined by years of selfless devotion. Tears began to roll down her cheeks and she ran out of the room, stammering:

"M-Monsieur, you do not love us."

He was left with his thoughts, so gloomy that he gradually became abysmally depressed. He bitterly regretted his past weakness; he had been much too tolerant, he should have kept Clotilde's training and education solely and firmly in his own hands. On the theory that trees grow straight, if they are not interfered with, he had left her free to develop at her own sweet will and had confined himself to teaching her to read and write. It had been according to no plan, but simply as a result of the ordinary routine of their joint lives that she had become a voracious reader. It had been due to her work with him, helping him with his experiments, correcting his proofs, copying and filing his manuscripts that she had, quite spontaneously, become passionately interested in the natural sciences. How he now regretted having left her to her own devices! How easy it would have been to teach that clear brain, thirsting for knowledge, to think logically and scientifically, instead of letting its thoughts wander and lose themselves in an empty mystical waste, at the instigation of Felicité and the good Martine! Whilst he had succeeded, thanks to scientific discipline, in basing all his thinking on established facts, never venturing beyond the phenomenon, he had watched her becoming increasingly preoccupied with the unknown, the mystery. It was an obsession with her, an instinctive curiosity, so imperious that it tortured her if she could not satisfy it. It was an insatiable appetite, an irresistible urge towards the inaccessible, the unknowable. Even when quite small, and more so as she became adolescent, her first question had always been why and how, she was determined to be told the ultimate cause for everything. When he had shown her a flower, she had asked him why it produced seeds and why the seed germinated. Then, it had been the mystery of conception, of sex, birth and death, of the unknown forces, of God and every thing.

Three or four such questions had always been enough, each time, to make him admit his ignorance; and, when he had been at a loss for an answer and had tried to brush her questions aside with a gesture of comic rage, she had laughed triumphantly, gone back to her day-dreaming, her endless speculations about what was not and could not be known. He had often been astounded by her extraordinary imagination. As she had learnt a certain amount of science, she usually based her arguments on established truths, but then her thoughts suddenly leapt right out of the material world straight into the world of legend. She evoked mediators, angels, saints, super-natural forces, modifying matter and imbuing it with life; sometimes she confined her imagination to a single force, the soul of the world, striving to fuse the animate and the inanimate in a final loving em-brace—in fifty centuries. She claimed to have arrived at this figure by calculation!

Clotilde's state of mind was disturbed to an unprecedented extent. The friar had now been preaching every day for a week. She spent her days, impatiently waiting for the moment when she could go to the cathedral to hear the evening sermon; then, she hurried there, abstracted and exalted, like a young girl on her way to her first meet-ing with her lover. The next day, her whole attitude proclaimed her detachment from everyday life, from her accustomed existence, as if the visible world, the necessary routine of life, were nothing but a snare and a delusion. She no longer helped either Martine or Pascal, overcome by an invincible distaste for movement or activity, sitting for hours with her hands on her lap, her eyes vacant and lost in some distant dream. Usually an early riser, she now stayed in bed late, getting up barely in time for lunch; all these hours alone in her bed-room were certainly not spent at her dressing table, because she was losing her innate feminine vanity and came down with her hair untidy, in any old dress with its fastening askew, but still looking adorable because of her radiant youth. She no longer went out; she abandoned her morning rambles through the gardens of the Souleiade, down the terraces planted with olive and almond trees, up to the pine trees, fragrant with balsam, the prolonged sunbaths in the yard, which had been her favourite form of relaxation; she preferred staying shut up in her bedroom, with the shutters closed, doing nothing. Her afternoons were spent in the study, in a state of languid idleness, flopping down first on one chair and then another, tired, bored and irritated with everything which had interested her in the past.

She was of no use to Pascal. A paper, which he had given her to copy, lay on her desk for three days. She filed nothing, would not even stoop to pick up a manuscript which had fallen on the floor. She had even given up her pastels and some drawings of flowers, which were needed to illustrate a book on artificial fertilization. Some large mallows, a new and most unusual blend of colours, had faded in their bowl before she had finished drawing them. She spent one whole afternoon, in a sudden fever of enthusiasm, on one of her mad drawings of dream flowers. Extraordinary blooms expanding in a miraculous light, golden rays in the shape of spikes seemed to be gushing upwards, amidst large purple corollae, with, instead of pistils, jets of stars, billions of little worlds streaming up towards the sky like a milky way.

"Ah! my poor girl," was the doctor's comment, "what a waste of time! And I have been patiently waiting for you to copy those mallows you have allowed to die! .. You will end up by making yourself really ill. Neither health nor beauty can possibly thrive except in the soil of reality.

Usually, she did not answer him, so as to avoid any possibility of an argument, but he had touched a sore spot:

"There is no reality," she declared with a sort of crushing finality.

Pascal, amused by such solemn philosophical statements coming from an overgrown child, burst out laughing:

"Yes, I know .. Our senses are fallible, our only knowledge of the world is through our senses, therefore there is a possibility that the world does not exist .. So, let us open the door wide and welcome madness, agree that the most preposterous fancies are possible, wallow in a nightmare world of the imagination, and reject all laws and all facts .. But can't you see, if you abolish nature, any form of order becomes impossible, that the only reason for living is to love life, to love it, to concentrate all the forces of our intelligence on arriving at a better understanding of it."

She shrugged her shoulders to express her indifference and the conversation was dropped. She was now slashing the pastel with heavy lines of blue crayon, emphasizing the flaming foreground against a limpid summer night.

But two days later, after another argument, there was a further painful scene. After dinner, Pascal had gone back to work in the study and Clotilde stayed out of doors, sitting on the terrace. When he heard midnight striking, he was surprised and a trifle worried because he had not heard her go back to her room. She would have had to come through the study and he was certain that she could not have done so behind his back. He went downstairs and satisfied himself that Martine was in bed and asleep. As the front door was locked, Clotilde was surely still out in the garden. On hot nights, she sometimes lingered out of doors, but never as late as this.

When he found that she was not sitting on the chair, where he had left her, he began to become seriously alarmed. He had hoped to find her asleep in the chair. Why had she not gone to bed? Where could she be at this late hour? It was a lovely September night, still hot, with the immense dome of the sky a dark velvety blue and dotted with an infinity of stars; there was no moon, but the glow of starlight was so bright that the garden seemed aglitter with light. First, he leaned over the balustrade of the terrace and scanned the slopes, the stone steps down to the railway line; no sign of a moving shape, he could see nothing but the round and motionless heads of the young olive trees. It then occurred to him that she might be under the plane trees, near the fountain. He ran to the back of the house and was then plunged into complete darkness, so black, that even he, who was familiar with each tree trunk, had to walk with his arms stretched out in front of him, to avoid colliding with them. Then, he walked up to the thicket of pine trees, through which he felt his way, without meeting anyone. He ended up by calling, in a voice which he kept low:

"Clotilde! Clotilde!"

Nothing, but the deep silence of the night. He gradually raised his voice:

"Clotilde! Clotilde!"

Not a soul, not a breath. His voice was echoed feebly and died away, drowned in the depths of the infinitely smooth lake of dark blue shadows. Then he shouted, he was becoming frantic, he searched the plane tree thicket again and the pine thicket, ran, staggering and stumbling, all over the garden. Suddenly, he found her, in the yard.

At this hour, the immense yard, the vast circle of pebbles, was sleeping too. Once, its pebbled surface had been used for threshing corn. For many years, it had been left undisturbed and grass had grown, baked a golden colour by the sun, as if shaved by it, it was like the thick wool of a carpet. And, between the tufts of this soft vegetation, the round pebbles never grew cold, after twilight a cloud of steam arose from them, exhaling into the night the heat they had stored up in the course of an endless succession of flaming days.

The round expanse of grass and pebbles, naked, deserted, covered by a faint, tremulous haze, gleamed under the calm starlit sky and Pascal was crossing it to run to the orchard, when he nearly fell over something thick and soft; it was a human figure lying stretched out at full length. He gave a startled exclamation:

"Is that you, Clotilde?"

Clotilde did not even condescend to answer. She was lying on her back, her hands clenched behind her head, her face upturned to the sky; in the pale shadow of her face, only her large eyes could be seen shining.

"And I, who have been worried to death and calling you for a quarter of an hour! .. You must have heard me!"

Finally, she managed to mutter:

"Yes."

"Well then, that was stupid! Why didn't you answer?"

But she had lost the use of her tongue once more, she refused to explain, there was an obstinate frown on her forehead, her eyes were gazing steadily upwards.

"Come to bed, you are just like a naughty child! You can explain to-morrow."

She went on lying as motionless as a log; he begged her, repeatedly, to come into the house, with no result. He ended up by squatting down on the grass beside her, feeling the warmth of the pebbles underneath.

"But you cannot sleep here .. You might, at least, answer me. What are you doing here."

"I am looking at the sky."

Her large eyes, wide open, unwinking, seemed to be searching, higher and higher, among the stars. She seemed to be completely absorbed in the infinite purity of this summer sky, lost amidst the stars.

"Oh! uncle," she continued in a low, even murmur, "how mean and shallow everything you know seems, compared with what I am sure there is up there .. I did not answer you, because I was thinking about you and it made me very sad .. You must not think that I am ungrateful."

Her voice was alive with so much sincere and tender feeling that he was deeply moved. He stretched himself out at her side, also on his back. Their elbows were touching. They talked:

73

"What I am afraid of, my dear, is that you are torturing yourself unreasonably, unnecessarily .. You say that thinking about me makes you sad. Why?"

"Oh! for reasons which I would find it difficult to explain. I know so little. Though, you have taught me a great deal and living with you has taught me other things. Besides, my reasons are sort of instinctive .. Perhaps I will try to tell you, as we are here, quite alone together and it is such a beautiful night!"

Her heart was full to overflowing, after hours of reflection, in the unutterable peace of the admirable night. He was careful not to interrupt her.

"When I was a little girl and I heard you talking about science, I thought you were talking about God, you were so full of hope and faith. You seemed to think that nothing was impossible. Scientists were going to be able to discover the secret of the world and there would be perfect happiness on earth .. According to you, they were making giant strides. Every day brought a new discovery, increased knowledge. Another ten years, another fifty years, a hundred years perhaps, the sky would be wide open and we should see truth face to face .. Well, the years go by, and nothing opens and the truth is farther away than ever."

"You are too impatient," he replied. "A thousand years may be necessary; we shall just have to wait."

"It's true, I cannot wait. I want to know, to be happy now, at once. And know everything in a sudden flash, be absolutely, completely happy! .. You see, that is what causes me such anguish, not to grasp all knowledge at a single bound, not to be able to sink down into complete happiness, without scruples or doubts. Do you call that living, to grope forward slowly in the darkness, not to have even one little hour of contentment, without trembling at the prospect of future unhappiness? No, no! All happiness and all knowledge in one day! .. Science promised to give them to us and, if it does not fulfil its promise, it is worthless."

Pascall felt impelled to protest, energetically:

"But, what you are saying is madness, my dear! Science is not revelation. Its pace is governed by scientists, who are human beings, its glory is in the struggle itself, the straining towards new knowledge .. And besides, it is not true that science has promised happiness."

She interrupted him, heatedly:

"What, not true? Open your own books, up there. You know that

74

I have read them. They are crammed full of promises! To read them, you would think that we were marching forward towards the conquest of the earth and the heavens as well. They demolish everything and swear to replace everything; and that by pure reason, soundly and wisely .. No doubt, I am like a child. When I have been promised something, I want it to be given to me. My imagination gets to work, the object has to be a very fine one, to satisfy me .. It would have been so simple, not to promise me anything! And above all, just now, when my longing is exasperated and painful, it would be wrong to tell me that I was not promised anything."

He made another gesture of protest, in the serenity of the night.

"In any case," she continued, "science has made a clean sweep, the earth is naked and the sky empty, and what is to become of me, even if, as you claim, science is not responsible for making me hopeful? You cannot expect me to live without faith and without happiness. What solid ground have I on which to build my house, now that they have demolished the old world and are in no hurry to make a new one? The whole of the old city is in ruins, thanks to all that investigation and analysis; nothing is left but a panic-stricken population roaming the ruins, not knowing what stone it can lay its head on, cowering in the storm, demanding a solid and stable refuge, where it can start life again .. So you must not be surprised at our discouragement and impatience. We cannot wait any longer. As science is too slow and has gone bankrupt, we prefer to rely on the past, yes, the beliefs of the past, which, for centuries have given happiness to the world."

"Ah! there we have it," he cried, "that is the curse of our times, this end of the century; so many people are exhausted, disorientated by the incredible, frighteningly huge mass of new knowledge which has been unearthed .. And it is the eternal craving to be told lies, the eternal craving for illusions which torments and pulls it backwards, towards the delusive charm of the unknown .. As everything will never be known, why bother to know anything? Because the fact of conquering truth does not mean achieving immediate and certain happiness, why not be satisfied with ignorance, that miserable bed in a cave on which mankind slept heavily throughout the pre-scientific ages? .. Yes! yes it is a return to the mystery, the reaction to a century of experimental enquiry. It was inevitable, one must expect desertions, when one cannot satisfy everybody's needs simultaneously. But it is only a pause, the march forward will continue, out of our sight, in the infinity of space."

They remained silent and without movement, for an instant, gazing at the billions of worlds, glittering in the black sky. A shooting star flashed across the constellation of Cassiope. And the illuminated universe, up there, turned slowly on its axis, in holy splendour, whereas, from the shadowy earth around them, rose only a faint breath, the respiration, soft and warm, of a sleeping girl.

"Tell me," he asked in a lighter tone, "is it your friar who has turned your head?"

She answered frankly:

"Yes, some of the things he says from the pulpit fill me with consternation. He thunders against everything you believe in. He makes me feel that science, the knowledge I owe to you, has turned into a poison which is destroying me .. Oh God, what is to become of me?"

"My poor child! .. I cannot bear to see you tormenting yourself like this. But, I still feel confident that you will recover; you have a good solid little round head on your shoulders, as I often tell you. You will calm down .. But what a devastating effect the man must have on people's brains, if you, basically sound and balanced, have been nearly unhinged by him! Tell me, are you really a convinced believer?"

She did not answer, she sighed and he added:

"If you are only concerned with happiness, there is no doubt that faith is a comforting support, like a stout walking stick which makes walking easier and less tiring, if you are fortunate enough to possess one."

"Oh! I simply don't know any more. Some days my faith seems as firm as a rock, other days I agree with you and your books. But, if anyone has unhinged my brain, it is you, you are the cause of my self-torment. And all my sadness and bitterness, perhaps, is due to my rebellion against you and your ideas, you whom I love and admire so much .. No, no! Don't say anything, don't say that I shall calm down in time. Just at this moment, I would find that unbearably irritating .. You deny the supernatural. Surely you agree that the mystery is simply what has not yet been explained? You even admit that everything will never be known; and that, therefore, the only reason for living is to go on endlessly acquiring more knowledge about the unknown, to go on straining eternally to know more .. Ah! I already know too much to be able to abandon myself blindly to faith; I am too much under your influence, and sometimes I feel that it will kill me."

He had taken her hand in his and was clasping it, very tightly:

"But what you are afraid of, child, is life itself! .. And you are so right when you say that our only hope of happiness lies in the continual struggle to achieve! because, henceforth, to rest, to remain content with ignorance is impossible. No more stopping by the wayside, no hope of achieving tranquillity by voluntarily blinding yourself to the truth. One must go on marching, marching all the same, with life, which is always marching on. Everything they propose and dangle in front of your eyes, turning backwards, the dead religions, the religions which have been refurbished to meet the requirements of the present, all a snare .. So learn to know life, love it, live it as it should be lived; there is no other wisdom."

She snatched her hand away from his, irritably and her voice shook with passionate scorn:

"Life is abominable, how can you expect me to live it in peace and happiness? .. Your science throws a terrible dazzling light on the world, your analysis probes into man's wounds, pitilessly and impersonally, and exposes them in all their naked horror. You speak out, explaining everything in terms of searing crudity and leave us shivering in our nakedness, with nothing to console us."

He interrupted her with a cry of burning conviction:

"Yes, 'speak out'. Exactly! In order to know everything and find a remedy for everything!"

Her reaction was so violent that she sat up abruptly:

"As if equality and justice existed in nature! But, you admit yourself, life is for the strong, the weak perish inevitably, just because they are weak. No two people are equal, either in health, or beauty, or intelligence; it is a question of pure luck, it depends on chance, like a gamble, governed by some accidental incident .. and, if we admit that your great and glorious justice does not exist, our whole world collapses around us!"

"It is true," he murmured, as if to himself, "there is no justice. A society based on justice could not survive. For centuries, attempts have been made to remedy abuses and suffering by charity. But the world is collapsing and, to-day, justice is put forward as the panacea .. Is nature just? I prefer to believe that nature is logical. Perhaps logic is a natural and superior form of justice, the key to the sum total of our common endeavours, including the labour at the end of them all."

"Ah, then!" she cried, "you mean the justice which crushes the individual for the benefit of the race, which destroys the weaker species in order to fatten the strong and triumphant species. Is that what you mean? .. No, that is the crime of crimes! It is a horrible idea, which condones obscenity and murder! He was right, this evening in the cathedral; the earth has been corrupted, all that science can do is to expose its rottenness, and what *we* must all do is to take shelter up above, on high .. Uncle, I beg and pray of you, let me save myself—and let me save you too!"

She was weeping, uncontrollably, and the sound of her sobbing was infinitely desolate in the limpid silence of the night. He tried to soothe and comfort her, unavailingly, but she managed to control her voice:

"Listen, uncle, you know I love you, that you are everything to me .. And yet, you are the cause of my suffering. The thought that we do not share the same belief, that we should be separated for all eternity, if we were both to die to-morrow, is intolerable. It is like an agonizing stab right through my heart .. Why do you persist in rejecting the true faith?"

He tried, once more, to reason with her:

"Come, my dear child, this is madness .."

But she was now on her knees in front of him, had grasped his hands and was clinging to him, feverishly. She was imploring him, in a loud voice, so vibrant with despair that the shadowy countryside, far away, sobbed in sympathy.

"Listen, he said it in church .. we must change our lives and repent, we must burn everything that reminds us of our past sins, yes! your books, your files, your manuscripts .. I beg of you on my knees, make this sacrifice, uncle. And you will see what a wonderful life we shall lead together."

This was too much! He protested violently:

"No! you forget yourself, be quiet!"

"You must listen to me, uncle, you must do what I want .. I assure you that I am horribly unhappy, in spite of my great love for you. There is something missing in the fond love we have for each other. Up to now, it has been empty and useless, and I ache with longing to make it complete, to fill it with everything that is divine and eternal! What can be lacking, if it is not God? Kneel down, pray with me!"

He pulled away from her, in his turn, intensely irritated:

"Be quiet, you are raving. I have not interfered with your liberty; you must not interfere with mine."

"Uncle, uncle! It is our happiness that I long for! .. I will take you away, far away. We will go to some solitary place and live in God!"

"Be quiet! .. No, never!"

They were glaring at each other, silent and hostile. The Souleiade, lay placidly slumbering all around them, in the silence of the night, broken only by the faintly melancholy voice of the spring, guarded by the olive trees with their light shadows, and by the pines and plane trees, like dense black smudges against the silvery background; and, above their heads, the vast sky, thickly powdered with stars, quivered, as if struck by a sudden flash of lightning, though dawn was still far away in time.

Clotilde raised her arm, as if to emphasize the infinity of the shimmering sky. But Pascal had quickly grasped her arm and, holding her hand in his, brought it down towards the ground. Not a word was spoken, they were both simmering with resentment, worlds apart.

She tore her hand away, like an animal resisting capture, fierce, proud and untameable; then she fled swiftly, across the night, towards the house. The loud sound of her heels clattering across the pebbles of the yard faded out along a sandy path. He, conscience-stricken and filled with forebodings, called out to her, begging her to come back. She was already too far away to hear him. In a turmoil of anxiety, he started running, to intercept her, but he reached the plane tree thicket, just in time to see her flying skirts disappear through the front door. He hurled himself after her, hurtled up the stairs and flung himself against her bedroom door, only to hear her locking and bolting it with unnecessary violence. He stood there, mastering his impulse to shout, to make another appeal to her, to break down the door and seize her, convince her, keep her entirely to himself. He could not hear a sound. No doubt, she had thrown herself on the bed and was stifling her cries and sobs in the pillow. He finally bestirred himself sufficiently to go down and shut the front door and went up again on tip-toe, to listen outside her room; the sun was rising, when he went to bed, in despair, choked with tears.

From then onwards, it was war to the death. Pascal felt himself spied on, tracked, threatened. He was homeless, the house was no longer his; the enemy was everywhere, behind every door, forcing him to fear the worst, to lock up everything. On two occasions, one after the other, he found a vial of his nerve extract on the floor, smashed to smithereens; he was driven to barricading himself in his room, muffling the sound of his pestle, and not coming down even at meal times. He no longer took Clotilde with him on his visiting days, because she discouraged his patients by her attitude of aggressive incredulity. Every time, no sooner had he left the house than his one thought was to hurry back, haunted by the fear of finding his locks forced, his drawers ransacked, on his return. He no longer used the young woman for filing or copying his papers, after finding several of them missing, as if carried away by the wind. He no longer even risked letting her correct his proofs as, on one occasion, she had cut out a long passage from an article, because the ideas expressed in it offended her Catholic faith. Thus, she was left without anything to do and spent her time prowling around the rooms, lying in wait for an opportunity to put her hands on the key to the big cupboard. This was her great ambition, the plan she was turning over and over in her mind, hour after hour, as she prowled or sat, not speaking, her eyes glittering, her hands tremulous and hot; to hold the key in her hand, open the cupboard, take everything, destroy everything in an autodafé which would please and placate God. One day, he left a few pages of a manuscript on the corner of the study table; before he had had time to wash his hands and put on his frockcoat they had disappeared, leaving a few ashes in the fireplace. One evening, he had been delayed at a patient's bedside, as he was walking back through the twilight, he was seized with panic at the sight of a heavy cloud of black smoke swirling upwards towards the pale evening sky. Was it the Souleiade burning? If she had made a bonfire of all his papers it was enough to set the whole house ablaze! He raced home, only to be reassured, on the way, by the sight of a pile of roots smouldering by the roadside.

Nothing could be more dreadful than this torment of a scientist who feels his brain, his work, his writings perpetually attacked and threatened with destruction! The results of his experiments, the manuscripts he had intended to leave for posterity, these are his pride, his life's blood, his children, to destroy them, to burn them, was like burning his own flesh. Almost the most distressing feature of this never-ending onslaught on his opinions, ideas and thoughts was his realisation that Clotilde, now his bitter enemy, lurking in ambush, was enshrined in his heart, permanently, that he loved her and would always love her, whatever happened. Hence, he was too vulnerable, could not defend himself, was not willing to take action against her and had no resource other than perpetual vigilance. He felt himself increasingly threatened from all sides, his reaction became obsessive, he imagined that he could feel her little thieving hands slipping into his pockets, he did not even feel safe behind his own locked door, terrified that she might be able to rob him through the cracks.

"But, you wretched child," he cried one day, "you are the only person I love in this world and it is you who are killing me! .. And you love me, you are doing all this precisely because you love me, it is abominable, we might as well end it all at once by throwing ourselves into the water with a stone tied to our necks!"

Her lips remained obstinately closed, but her smouldering eyes showed that she would welcome death, now, instant death, if they could die together.

"Tell me, if I were to die to-night, suddenly, what would happen to-morrow? .. Would you empty the cupboard, empty the drawers, make a great pile of all my books and papers and burn them? You would, wouldn't you? .. Do you realize that it would be murder, the same as assassinating a fellow human being? And what abominable cowardice, to kill thought!"

"No!" she said in a muffled voice, "kill evil, prevent it from spreading and being reborn!"

All their arguments ended in increasing their raging resentment against each other. Some of them were terrifying. And, one evening, when old Madame Rougon had called in the middle of one of their quarrels, Clotilde had escaped to her room and Pascal was left alone with his mother. At first, there was a heavy silence. In spite of her hypocritical pretence of sympathy, her bright eyes gleamed with unholy joy.

"Life in this house must be like living in hell!" she cried.

The doctor made a gesture, but avoided answering. He had always sensed his mother behind Clotilde, encouraging her religious beliefs, using this ferment of rebellion in order to disorganize his household. He had no illusions, he knew for a fact that the two women had met that same day, and that it was his mother's perfidious advice which had been responsible for the appalling scene which had left him still trembling with rage and dismay. Doubtless, his mother had come to gloat over the havoc and see how near he was to the breaking point.

"You cannot go on like this," she resumed. "Why don't you separate, as you no longer agree with each other? .. You should send her away to her brother Maxime, who wrote again a few days ago, asking me to persuade her to come."

He had drawn himself up, pale and determined:

"Leave each other while we are at loggerheads! Oh, no, no, I should never forgive myself, it would become a festering wound, impossible to heal. If, at some future time, she must go away, I want to be sure that we shall go on loving each other at a distance .. But why go? We are not complaining of any grievance against each other."

Felicité felt that she had been premature:

"No doubt, if you enjoy quarrelling, it is nobody's business .. Only, my poor boy, allow me, in that case, to tell you that I am inclined to sympathize with Clotilde. You force me to confess that I saw it just now; yes, you had better know it, in spite of my promise not to tell. Well, she is not happy, she complained bitterly about your attitude towards her, and you can imagine my feelings. I gave her a good scolding and told her that her duty was to be completely submissive .. But I must say that I find it very difficult to understand you. You seem to me to be doing everything you can to make yourself unhappy."

She had taken a chair and had obliged him to sit down with her in a corner of the study. She was obviously delighted to have him to herself, at her mercy. She had, in the past made several attempts to force him to discuss his relationship with Clotilde, but he had succeeded in evading her. Although she had harried and distressed him for many years and he was well aware of her intrigues against him, he still behaved with the deference he considered a mother's due from her son .. He had sworn to himself that, come what may, he would never deviate from this attitude of filial respect. For this reason, as soon as she broached certain subjects, he took refuge in obstinate silence.

"Come," she continued, "I can understand your not wanting to give in to Clotilde; but to me? .. If I begged you to sacrifice those abominable files, which are there, in that cupboard, for my sake! If you were to die suddenly and those papers were to fall into the hands of strangers, we should all be dishonoured .. Surely, you don't want that to happen? Well then, what is your object, why do you persist in playing with fire? .. Promise me to burn them."

He did not want to answer, but had to say something:

"Mother, I have already asked you, many times, not to bring up that subject .. You know very well that it is impossible for me to consent."

"But you might, at least," she cried, "give me a reason. One would think that you are as indifferent towards your family as you are to that herd of cows over there. But you belong to it .. Oh, I know, you do everything you can to be different. I am astonished myself, sometimes. I ask myself where you could have sprung from. I find it so unfeeling of you to risk smirching us, without stopping to think how much you are distressing your own mother .. In plain words, your behaviour is unforgivable."

He was so indignant that he gave way for a moment to the impulse to defend himself, in spite of his determination not to break silence:

"You are being very hard on me, unjustifiably so .. I have always believed in the utter sanctity of truth. It is a fact that I do not conceal anything either about other people or myself; and it is because I firmly believe that in revealing everything I am taking the only possible course open to an honest man of science, in the interests of the community .. Besides, those files are not for public consumption, they are personal notes, which I should be very sorry to part with. Further, I quite understand that you would not stop at burning my files; you would throw all my other writings in the fire, would you not? And that is what I am determined to prevent .. As long as I live, not a single line will be destroyed."

But he was already regretting his impulsiveness; he had been too outspoken. His mother was quick to take advantage of that fact and was trying to coax him into continuing the painful discussion.

"Go on, then, tell me what your grievances are against us .. Yes, take me for example, what do you object to? You can hardly reproach me with having brought you all up with the greatest of care and trouble. Ah, it took me a long time to establish our position! If we enjoy a little happiness to-day, we thoroughly deserve it. As you have seen it all and write it all down in your papers, you should be able to bear witness that the family has done far more for others than the other way round. Twice, we saved Plassans from a miserable fate. And, as was to be expected, our great services have only been rewarded by ingratitude and envy, to such an extent that to-day the whole town would like nothing better than to see us spattered with mud by a scandal .. You cannot want that to happen and I am sure that you must approve of the dignity of my behaviour since the fall of the Empire and the dire misfortunes from which France will probably never recover."

"Leave France alone, mother!" he began again, so successful had she been at goading him, by attacking every subject about which she knew him to be particularly sensitive. "France is tough and I believe that she is astonishing the world by the rapidity of her convalescence .. Certainly, there are many corrupt elements. I have never concealed them; perhaps I have exposed them too clearly. But you are very much mistaken if you think that I believe that the edifice is ultimately bound to collapse, because I point out its flaws and cracks. I believe in life, which ceaselessly eliminates harmful substances, makes new tissue to heal wounds, which is always on the march towards health and is continually fulfilling its function of renovating, even amidst putrefaction and death."

He suddenly realized that he was warming to his pet subject and getting excited, made an angry gesture and stopped talking. His mother was now shedding tears of self-pity, minute tears, squeezed out with difficulty, which dried on her face almost as soon as they were shed. She reverted to her fears, which haunted her old age and, she too, began to beg him to make his peace with God, if for no other reason, out of respect for his family. Was it not true that she had given a demonstration of courage? Had not Plassans in its entirety, the Saint-Marc quarter, the old quarter and the new town, rendered homage to her proud resignation? All she asked for was to be helped; she expected all her children to make the same effort as she had herself. She went on to quote the example of Eugène, the great man, now fallen from his eminence, and who was content to be nothing more than a simple deputy, defending, to his last breath, the system of government which had been overthrown and to which he owed his own past glory. She was also full of praise for Aristide, the indomitable fighter, who was climbing back, under the new government, to a position of great influence, in spite of the unjust catastrophe which had buried him temporarily amidst the ruins of the *Union universelle*. And Pascal himself, would he persist in keeping himself apart from the family, would he do nothing to make her last years happy ones, so that she could die in peace, certain of the final triumph of the Rougons? He was so intelligent, so affectionate, so kind! He must understand. Surely he would go to Mass the next Sunday and burn those horrid papers, the very thought of which made her ill. She begged, ordered, threatened. But he could not be induced to answer. Now that he had calmed down, he reassumed his attitude of deference. He was determined not to be drawn into another argument; he knew his mother too well to hope to convince her.

"I knew it!" she cried, when she realized that he was unshakeable, "you do not belong to us; I have always said it. You are no credit to us."

He bowed:

"Mother, on reflection, you will forgive me."

That day, Felicité went away in a state of boiling indignation; and, as she met Martine at the door of the house, in front of the plane trees, she unburdened herself, without knowing that Pascal, who had gone into his bedroom, could hear everything through his open windows. She gave vent to her resentment, swore to lay her hands on his papers, by fair means or foul, and destroy them, as he refused to hand them over of his own accord. But it was Martine's attitude to his mother which particularly depressed the doctor, she was placating her in a soothing monotone. She was, only too evidently, his mother's accomplice, she counselled patience; she said that it was unnecessary to consider any premature action, as Mademoiselle and herself had sworn to overcome Monsieur, by not giving him an hour's peace. They had sworn to reconcile him with the Almighty, because it was not possible to let a saintly man like Monsieur risk his soul by being without religion. Then the two women lowered their voices, soon he could only hear whispering, a muffled murmur of gossip and conspiracy, and he could only distinguish occasional words, each an encroachment on his personal liberty. When his mother finally left, he saw her trotting off, with her light step and her young girl's figure, looking very pleased with herself.

For an hour, Pascal felt hopeless and utterly desperate. What was the good of struggling, fighting for his conviction if all his loved ones were united against him. Martine who, at a word from him, would cheerfully throw herself into the fire, was betraying him, for his own good! And Clotilde, in league with the servant, plotting in corners, enlisting her help in order to lay traps for him! Now he was all alone, surrounded by traitresses, tainting the very air he breathed. If it had only been these two, who loved him, he might, perhaps, have been able to overcome their hostility in the end; but, now that he knew that his mother was behind them, he understood their implacability and abandoned any hope of being able to regain the old footing. A semi-monastic life of study had made him timid with women and he was crushed by the idea that the three of them were against him, trying to break his will. He felt that one of them was always dogging his footsteps; when he shut himself up in his room, he felt sure that they were flattened against the wall in the next room; they haunted him, filled him with a strange fear of being robbed of his thoughts, if he allowed them to be glimpsed at the bottom of his cranium, even before he had formulated them.

It was certainly the most unhappy period of Pascal's life. The perpetual state of defence, in which he had to live, shattered him; and, sometimes, it seemed to him that the very foundations of his house were crumbling away under his feet. It was then that he regretted, bitterly, not having married and not having had children. Had he himself been frightened of life? Was he not being punished for his own selfishness? Sometimes his longing for a child became poignant, his eyes were often wet with tears, when he passed little girls on the road, with their eager and enchantingly innocent expressions as they smiled at him. Undoubtedly he nourished the same sentiments for Clotilde, but now, it was a different kind of tenderness, ruffled by storms, not a calm tenderness, infinitely gentle and soft, the tenderness of a child, which he craved as a balm for his wounded heart. What he longed for now that he was in his declining years was continuity, the child who would perpetuate him. The more he suffered the more consoling would it have been, in the light of his boundless faith in life, to have been able to hand down that suffering. He considered himself immune from the physiological defects of the family; but even the thought that heredity sometimes jumped a generation and that the disabilities of his ancestors might reappear in his own son, did not deter him; he continued to wish for a son, as one wishes for an unexpected windfall, an unusual stroke of luck, the undreamed of happiness which consoles and enriches one's life for ever after, in spite of the old and decadent stock and in spite of the long sequence of execrable relatives. In the midst of the storm which threatened to uproot and destroy the little affection vouchsafed to him in the past, he was swept by a wave of unutterable sadness because he realized that he had waited too long. Surely, it was now too late!

One night at the end of September, the air was so heavy and the heat so stifling that Pascal could not sleep. He opened a window. The sky was black, there was a storm in the distance and he could hear a continuous rumbling of thunder. He could barely distinguish the sombre mass of plane trees, except, from time to time, when a flash of lightning flared across the sky and detached them from the surrounding darkness and each leaf stood out green in colour. He felt as if his heart was bursting with unhappiness, he was reliving in his mind the last few days, which had been intolerable, more quarrels, the tortures of treachery and increasing suspicion, when, all of a sudden, he remembered something, a frightful thought which made him quiver with anxiety. He had been so afraid of being robbed that he always carried the key of the big cupboard around with him, somewhere on his person. But, that afternoon, he had been too hot and had taken off his jacket, and he remembered seeing Clotilde hang it up on a nail in the study. If she had felt the key at the bottom of his pocket, she would certainly have stolen it. He ran across the room and searched the jacket, which he had thrown over the back of a chair. The key had vanished. A definite feeling came over him that the cupboard was being ransacked at that very moment. It was two o'clock in the morning. The clock was just striking; he did not wait to put on his clothes, he was in his trousers, his feet were in slippers, without socks, and his chest was bare under his unbuttoned nightshirt; he pushed open the door, violently, and strode into the room, candlestick in hand:

"I knew it," he cried. "You thief! You murderer!"

It was true, Clotilde was there, half dressed like himself, her bare feet in the linen mules, her legs bare, her arms and shoulders bare and the rest of her body just covered by a short petticoat and a chemise. In order to avoid arousing his suspicions, she had not brought a candle with her and had merely opened the shutters of one of the windows; the storm which was passing over the sky, to the south, had provided enough light, thanks to the frequent flashes of lightning, which bathed the room in a livid phosphorescence. The old cupboard with its large flanks, was wide open. She had already emptied the top shelf, had carried the files down in armfuls and piled them up on the long table in the middle of the room. And, fearing that she would not have time to burn them, she was sorting them into bundles, with the intention of hiding them and then sending them to her grandmother. Pascal's candle threw a bright light over her slender figure, standing, motionless, in an attitude of surprise and defiance.

"You are robbing and murdering me," repeated Pascal, in a blind rage.

She was still holding one of the files under her bare arm. He tried to snatch it from her, but she held on to it with all her might, still obstinately determined to continue her work of destruction, without embarrassment, relentlessly, like a warrior convinced that his cause is a just one. Then, distracted and blinded by rage, he threw himself at her; he dug his hands into her bare flesh and was bruising her.

"Go on, kill me then!" she stammered. "Kill me, or I shall tear them to shreds.!"

But he was squeezing her so tightly that she could hardly breathe.

"When a child steals, she has to be punished!"

He had lacerated the thin and delicate skin of her shoulder, a few drops of blood appeared and trickled down towards the armpit. She was panting and he, disturbed by the almost unearthly beauty of her slender virginal body, released her; as he did so he managed, with a final effort, to wrench the file away from her.

"And you are going to help me put them back on the shelf, to-morrow, I swear it, by your almighty God! Come here, begin by putting them in order on the table .. Obey me, please, at once!"

"Yes, uncle!"

She went up to the table and started helping him; she was sub-jugated, broken by such a brutal embrace which had seemed to penetrate her whole body. The candle, flaming steadily in the heavy night, threw a bright light over them both; the distant rumbling of thunder had not stopped, the window open to the storm seemed to be on fire.

CHAPTER FIVE

PASCAL stood looking at his files, which had been thrown on the long table in the middle of the study, in an untidy heap, which looked enormous. Many of the thick blue paper files had opened as they fell, spilling out letters, newspaper cuttings, documents on official stamped paper and notes written by hand.

In the process of bringing order out of chaos, he was looking through the names written, in large letters, on the files and, suddenly straightened up, made a gesture as if to shake off his sombre and discouraged mood. And, turning to Clotilde, who was standing erect, silent and white, waiting for him to speak:

"Listen, up to now, I have always forbidden you to read these papers and I know that you have obeyed me .. Yes, I had scruples. It is not that you are ignorant, like so many young women. I allowed you to learn all about the human male and female, knowledge which cannot be harmful in itself and could only harm naturally prurient natures .. But why plunge you prematurely into the morass of human infirmity? I kept the history of our family from you, which like the history of all families, of all mankind, is made up of much that is bad and much that is good .."

He stopped, suddenly quite calm and radiant with energy:

"You are twenty-five, you should be told .. Besides, we cannot go on living together like this; you are living and you are making me live in a nightmare world, all because of the fact that you are possessed by your impossible dreams. I am going to give you a glimpse of reality, naked and unashamed. It may shock you, but it will open your eyes and may even have the effect of helping you to grow up and become the woman I have always wanted you to be .. Let us put these files in order again together, look through them and read them; you will learn something about the hard facts of life, which you may find terrifying."

Then, as she still stood there without moving:

"We must have plenty of light; you had better light the two other candles."

His new mood demanded light, floods of light everywhere and over everything, best of all blazing sunlight; the light of the three candles seemed much too dim; he fetched the two double candle sticks from his own room. The seven candles flickered over the table, over Pascal and his bare chest, and over Clotilde, with her bare arms and neck, the bloodstains on her left shoulder. But, they were too engrossed to look at each other. Two o'clock was striking. They were oblivious of time. They were united in this passion for knowledge, to which they were going to dedicate the night, heedless of sleep, outside space and time. The storm was raging more violently, through the open window they could hear the loud rumblings of thunder and see the lightning flicker on the horizon.

Clotilde had never seen Pascal in such a fever of enthusiasm. During the last few weeks, he had been overworking, the atmosphere of discord and suspicion in the house had made him irritable. But now, he seemed to be filled with infinite tenderness, his immense compassion for suffering mankind was aroused by the prospect of revealing the painful truth to Clotilde; he was almost sublime in his complete forgetfulness of self and his olympian pity for his fellows, which made it easier for Clotilde to face the gruesome facts. He had decided that he would not conceal anything; he felt that it was a question of kill or cure. Was the history of their common relatives, so near to them both, not the inevitable evolution, the supreme argument? That was life and it should be faced. Surely she would emerge from such an ordeal tempered, full of tolerence and courage.

"They have turned you against me and made you treat me abominably. I want to arouse your conscience, restore your sense of values. When your eyes have been opened, you will be in a position to judge and act accordingly .. Come closer, we will read them together."

She obeyed. She could not help shrinking from these files, which her grandmother denounced with such vehemence; but her curiosity was now aroused and becoming intense. Besides, tamed though she had been and her will broken by his virile brutality, she was not entirely dominated and still capable of making up her own mind. Why not listen to him, read with him? Did not that still give her the right to agree or disagree, afterwards? She was ready.

"Come, have you any objection?"

"No, uncle, I am quite willing!"

He began by showing her the genealogical tree of the Rougon Macquarts. It was not usually kept in the cupboard, but in the desk in his bedroom, where he had taken it when he had fetched the candles. He had kept it up to date for more than twenty years, entering births and deaths, marriages and anything of importance that happened to the family, wording his short notes according to his theory of heredity. It was a large sheet of paper, yellow with age, with deep folds from constant use, on which a symbolical tree was drawn in heavy lines, with outspread branches, subdivided and ending in five rows of large leaves; inside each leaf he had written, in minute letters, a name and a biography, the summary of a single hereditary case history.

The doctor was uplifted, almost transformed by the fervour of a scientist when he contemplates the result of twenty years' work, which in his case, constituted a clear, complete demonstration of the laws of heredity, established by his own efforts.

"Look at this carefully, my dear child! You know enough, you have copied so many of my manuscripts, to understand .. Don't you find it fascinating, this expression in diagrammatic form and in miniature covering a vast field and yet final and complete, with nothing missing? It is as conclusive as a laboratory experiment, like a problem set and solved on a blackboard .. You see, down here, the trunk, the common stock, Tante Dide. Then, the first three branches, the legitimate son, Pierre Rougon and the two bastards, Ursule and Antoine Macquart. Then, we have the new branches and their ramifications; on the one side, Maxime, Clotilde and Victor, Saccards three children and Angélique, Sidonie Rougon's daughter; on the other side, Pauline, the daughter of Lisa Macquart and Claude, Jacques, Etienne, Anna, Gervaise's four children, Lisa's sister. There, Jean, their brother, right at the end. And you notice here, in the middle, what I call the node, the legitimate and illegitimate derivatives uniting in Marthe Rougon and her cousin François Mouret, to give birth to three new branches, Octave, Serge and Désirée Mouret; and here we have the offspring of Ursule and the hatter Mouret, Silvère, the tragic circumstances of whose death you already know, Hélène and her daughter Jeanne. Finally, right up there, we have the last twigs, the son of your brother Maxime, our poor Charles, and two other little fellows, both dead, Jacques-Louis, the son of Claude Lantier and Louiset, the son of Anna Coupeau .. Five generations in all, a human tree, which has already seen five springs, five renewals of humanity and thrust out branches, filled with the sap of life, eternal life!"

He pointed to the cases on the old yellow-tinged piece of paper, as animated as if he were demonstrating an anatomical chart.

"And, I repeat, nothing has been left out .. Look at the elections in the direct line of heredity; those that take after the mother,

Silvère, Lisa, Désirée, Jacques, Louiset, yourself; after the father, Sidonie, François, Gervaise, Octave, Jacques-Louis. Next, there are the three forms of mixture: by linkage, Ursule, Aristide, Anna Victor; by dissemination, Maxime, Serge, Etienne; by fusion, Antoine, Eugène, Claude. I even had to specify a fourth form, most remarkable, balanced mixture, Pierre and Pauline. And there is endless variety, taking after the mother for example often goes with a physical resemblance to the father, sometimes it is the other way round; similarly, in the mixture, the physical and mental predominance may go with the one or the other factor, according to circumstances . . Next, here is the indirect line of heredity, the collaterals; I have only a single well-established example, the striking physical resemblance of Octave Mouret to his uncle Eugène Rougon. I also have only one example of heredity by influence: Anna, the daughter of Gervaise and Coupeau, had an astonishing resemblance, especially during her childhood, to Lantier, her mother's first lover, as if he had impregnated her, so to speak permanently . . But where I have abundant material is latent heredity; the three most striking cases Marthe, Jeanne and Charles, resembling Tante Dide, the resemblance thus skipping one, two and three generations. A most exceptional phenomenon, as I am very reluctant to believe in atavism; it seems to me that the new elements contributed by the partners, accidents and the infinite variety of possible mixtures must very soon obliterate the particular characteristics, with the result that the individual reverts to the general type . . We are left with the inherent factor, represented by Hélène, Jean, Angélique. That is the mixture, the chemical combination whereby the physical and mental characteristics of the parents are inextricably intermingled, and it is impossible to find any of the features of either parent in the new offspring."

There was a short silence. Clotilde had listened with the closest attention, determined to understand. And he, now, was absorbed, his eyes still fixed on the Tree, in an attempt to arrive at an objective judgement of his own work. He continued slowly, as if talking to himself:

"Yes, I have tried to be as scientifically methodical as possible . . I have only dealt, on the Tree, with the members of the family, I should have paid equal attention to the partners, to the fathers and mothers, from outside, whose blood has been mixed with ours and thus inevitably modified it. I did, in fact, draw up a mathematical tree, with half of the father and the mother handed on to the child, from generation to generation; in such a way that, in Charles for instance, Tante Dide's contribution was only a twelfth; which was absurd, as the physical resemblance is complete. I therefore considered it sufficient, for practical purposes, to indicate the elements which had been derived from external sources, making due allowance for the marriages and the new factor introduced by them on each occasion .. Ah! these sciences which are in their infancy, these sciences in which even rudimentary hypotheses are difficult to elaborate and in which the imagination still runs riot, they are fields which are as appropriate for poets as they are for scientists! Poets are pioneers, an advance guard, and they often discover virgin territories and point the way to future investigators. To them a marginal zone belongs, between definitely ascertained truth and the unknown, from which the truth of to-morrow will be wrested .. What an immense fresco to paint, what masterpieces of human comedy and tragedy to write, on the subject of heredity, which is the very genesis of families, societies and the world!"

His eyes were gazing into the distance, he was following his wandering thoughts. But, he shook himself and returned to the files, throwing the Tree on one side, saying:

"We will go back to that later; I cannot expect you to understand, properly, unless I give you the full sequence of events, so that you can see the actors playing their parts, all of which is merely summarized on the Tree .. I will call out the files and you can pass them to me one by one; I will show you the contents and make my comments, before we put them back, up there, on the shelf .. I shall not be guided by the alphabetical order, but the order of the facts. I have been intending, for a long time, to establish such a classification .. Come, look at the names on the files. Tante Dide, first."

At that moment, a corner of the storm which was flashing on the horizon, slanted across the Souleiade and descended on the house in a deluge of rain. But they did not close the window. They were as oblivious of the flashes of lightning as they were of the rain beating on the roof. She had passed him the file marked Tante Dide, in large letters; from the medley of papers which it contained, he extracted some old notes, in his own handwriting and proceeded to read them.

"Give me Pierre Rougon .. Give me Ursule Macquart .. Give me Antoine Macquart .."

She followed his instructions, in silence, painfully affected by what was being revealed to her. And the files followed each other, displayed their documents and were returned to the shelf in the cupboard.

They started from the beginning, Adelaide Fouque, that distracted young woman, already half crazy, the primary nervous lesion, giving birth to the legitimate branch, Pierre Rougon and to the two bastard branches, Ursule and Antoine Macquart; that blood-stained tragedy played out in city and town, in the framework of the *Coup d'Etat* in December 1851, the Rougons, Pierre and Felicité, restoring order to Plassans, spattering their rising fortunes with the blood of Silvère, whilst Adelaide, now aged, the miserable Tante Dide, was shut up at the Tulettes, like a spectral figure of expiation and suspense. Then, the riot of appetites was unleashed, the sovereign appetite for power in Eugène Rougon, the great man, the eagle of the family, disdainful, immune from any vulgar interest in profits, loving power for the sake of power, conquering Paris in old boots, with the adventurers of the empire which was to come, becoming Prime Minister and then a minister in the Cabinet, raised to power by an unsavoury crew of place-hunters who carried him on their shoulders and fed on him, his career temporarily checked by a woman, the beautiful Clorinde, for whom he had conceived a mad passion, but so essentially strong, so burning with a thirst for power, that he was able to climb back to it by an act which contradicted the principles to which his whole life had been dedicated, onwards to the triumphant semi-royal position of vice-emperor. In Aristide Saccard, the appetite was for the basest forms of enjoyment and self-indulgence, for money, women, luxury, a devouring hunger, which had thrown him penniless on the streets, when the lean period started, in the tornado of unbridled speculation which swept through the city, pulling down whole quarters and rebuilding them, ill-deserved fortunes made in six months, spent and remade, an orgy of gold in an ever-mounting drunken tempo which carried him away to the extent of selling his name, when his first wife Angèle's body was still warm, in order to put his hands on the indispensable first hundred thousand francs, by marrying Renée, and which induced him later, because of a temporary financial crisis, to tolerate incest, to shut his eyes to his son Maxime's love affair with his second wife, in the mad whirl of a delirious Paris. And it was Saccard again, some years later, who controlled the gigantic Universal Bank, Saccard the unconquerable, Saccard increased in stature, raised to the level of intelligence and courage of the great financier, understanding the over-riding importance and the civilizing rôle of money, engaging in, winning and losing battles on the stock exchange, like Napoleon at Austerlitz and at Waterloo, swallowing up a host of pitiful small investors in the disaster of a world, letting his natural son Victor slip away from him into some unknown den of vice, disappear, on the run through the night, and he himself, under the impassable protection of unjust nature, beloved of the adorable Madame Caroline, doubtless as a reward for his execrably misbegotten life. Next, an immaculate lily grown on this compost heap, Sidonie Rougon, who obligingly abetted her brother Saccard, the procuress with a hundred suspicious side-lines, bore to an unidentified lover the pure and divine Angélique, the little embroidress with the fairy fingers who lost herself in dreams of a prince charming as her golden threads wove through the chasubles, her thoughts so wedded to her companions the saints, so little suited to the hard reality of life, that she was vouchsafed the grace of dying for love, the very day of her marriage, as Félicien de Hautecoeur kissed her for the first time, to the clash of the bells ringing the glory of his royal wedding. The node of the two branches followed, the legitimate and the bastard, Marthe Rougon married her cousin Francois Mouret, a peaceful household which slowly disintegrated, ending up in the most dire catastrophes, a gentle and sad woman, taken, used, broken and smashed by the vast war machine set up for the conquest of a city, her three children as if torn away from her, and her spirit broken by the fierce Abbé Faujas, and the Rougons saved Plassans a second time, while she was on her death bed, in the light of the fire in which her husband, mad with accumulated rage and thirsting for vengeance, was flaming together with the priest. Of the three children, Octave Mouret was the bold conqueror, with his clear brain, resolved to use women in order to master Paris, thrown into a spoiled middle class, being given the most painful kind of sentimental education, passing from the capricious denial of the one to the tame abandon of the other, having to suffer the most degrading inconveniences of adultery, still, fortunately, full of energy, a worker and a fighter, extricated little by little, tempered and increased in stature, above the base intrigues of this rotten world, the foundations of which could be heard cracking. And Octave Mouret victorious proceeded to revolutionize big business, to smash the timid little shops in which the traditional rules of trade were followed, to erect, in the centre of Paris, the colossal palace of temptation, blazing with a thousand lamps, overflowing with velvet, silk and laces, to make a fortune equal to a king's ransom by exploiting women, to live smilingly contemptuous of women, until the day when the avenging female, in the person of a young woman, the simple and prim Denise, tamed him, had him at her feet frantic with unsatisfied longing, because she had not been willing, for all her poverty, to marry him, at the height of the success of his Louvre, under the golden rain of the takings. This left the two other children, Serge Mouret, Désirée Mouret, the latter innocent and healthy as a happy young animal, the former, refined and mystical, becoming a priest by accident, due to the nervous heritage of his race, repeating old Adam's adventure, in the legendary Paradou. He is reborn to love Albine, possess her and lose her, with the complicity of mother nature; is taken back into the church, fights to kill his sexual instincts, casting on the body of the dead Albine the handful of earth of the officiating priest, whilst, at the same hour, Désirée, the child-like animal lover, is filled with simple joy, amidst the warm fertility of her farm-yard.

Later on, there was the beginning of a gentle and tragic interlude: Hélène Mouret living peacefully with her little girl Jeanne on the heights of Passy, dominating Paris, the limitless and bottomless human ocean, the site of this sad story; a sudden infatuation for a passer-by, a doctor brought by Hélène at night, by chance, to the bedside of her daughter; Jeanne's unhealthy jealousy, the jealousy of an instinctive lover fighting to keep her mother away from love, already so ravaged by sick passion, that she died, a terrible price for one hour of desire in a blameless life, poor dear little dead one lying alone up there, under the cypresses of the hushed cemetery, above Paris the eternal. Lisa Macquart was the first of the bastard branch, in her it was fresh and ebulliently healthy, flaunting the prosperity of the full belly. On the threshold of her pork-butcher's shop, she smiled at the central markets, where famine and plenty were flaunted side by side, the battleground for the age-old battle between the Fat and the Lean, the lean Florent, her brother-in-law, execrated, hunted down by the fat fishwives and whom the fat Lisa, herself rightous and upright, but merciless, caused to be arrested as a republican who had broken his parole, convinced that by so doing she was furthering the peace of mind of all honest folk. From this mother sprang the best, the most human of daughters, Pauline Quenu, balanced, rational, the virgin who understood and accepted life, with such a passionate love of her fellows, that, thwarting all her healthy natural instincts, she surrendered her fiancé Lazare to a friend, then saved the child of the ill-fated union, became its real mother, perpetually sacrificing herself, ruined, but ever triumphant and cheerful, buried in a solitary village, facing the great sea, in the midst of a human microcosm, composed of a group of sick people bemoaning their sufferings and pains but unwilling to die.

Next came Gervaise Macquart with her four children and her bandy legs, pretty and hard working, thrown into the gutter by her lover Lantier, picked up by the zinc-worker Coupeau, good workman and sober to boot, whom she married, so happy at first, established in her own laundry employing three women, then gradually and inevitably sinking with her husband to the degrading level of their environment, he becoming more and more addicted to drink, eventually to the point of violent maniacal outbursts and an unspeakably sordid death, she herself becoming perverted, idle, finished off by the reappearance of Lantier, amidst the tranquil ignominy of a three-cornered household, the pitiful victim of increasing poverty and finally utter destitution, in which state she succumbed one evening, hungry and in despair. Her eldest son Claude had the invidious distinction of being a great though uneven painter, maddened almost to the point of lunacy by the consciousness of being capable of painting a great masterpiece, if only his clumsy fingers had not rendered the practical execution of such a feat impossible, an indomitable fighter foredoomed to failure, a martyr crucified by his art, with a devouring passion for women, sacrificing his wife Christine, so loving, so loved for an all too brief period, to his uncreated ideal woman, whom his brush was impotent to portray in all her sovereign nudity, eaten up by his insatiable passion for creation, which leads to unutterable anguish and despair, when it cannot be satisfied, and which had driven him to suicide, ending his tormented life dangling at the end of a rope. Jacques, for his part, was an example of the hereditary defect canalized into crime, an instinctive appetite for blood, fresh young blood flowing from the bare breast of a woman, any woman, the first comer, casually met on the pavement, abominable vice against which he struggled, which mastered him again in the course of his love affair with Séverine, the submissive, the sensual, herself the trembling victim of a prolonged and tragic story of murder, and he stabbed her one evening in an uncontrollable fit of mania, maddened by the sight of her white breast, and then, this savage beast's headlong flight amidst the trains streaming past at full speed, his wild leap on the footplate of the engine amidst the hissing of steam and the grinding of the wheels, that beloved engine, which was to crush him one day, left to career blindly, without a driver, towards unknown disasters on the horizon. Etienne in his turn, hunted and lost, arrived in the mining country on a freezing March night, descended into the voracious maw of the pit, loved the sad Catherine who was taken away from him by a sordid brute, shared the miners' dismal lives of poverty and base promiscuity, until the day when hunger, the mother of rebellion, incited a howling mob of poverty-stricken workers to march across the bare plain demanding bread, leaving ruins and blazing houses behind them, ringed by soldiers whose rifles seemed to fire of their own accord, a terrible convulsion heralding the end of a world, blood of the Maheus soon to be revenged, Alzire killed by hunger, Maheu killed by a bullet, Zacharie killed by an explosion of fire-damp, only the Maheude left as sole survivor, forced to go back to the pit to earn her thirty sous, whilst Etienne, the men's defeated leader, obsessed by the justice of his cause, walked away one warm April morning, listening to the faint crackle of the seeds of the new world swelling under the ground, which when germinated, would splinter the earth. Next, Nana, revenge incarnate, the born prostitute, thrust up from the social dregs of the suburbs, the golden fly which had taken its flight from the foulest refuse, which one tolerates and hides, each flutter of its wings spreading the ferment of destruction, climbing up to and corrupting the aristocracy, infecting every man on whom it lighted, flying into palace windows, a busy and unconscious carrier of ruin and death, the stoical last blaze of passion in Vandeuvres, the despair of Foucarmont seeking surcease by cruising the China seas, the disaster of Steiner reduced to living like an honest man, the smug imbecility of de la Faloise, the tragic collapse of the Muffats, and the pale corpse of Georges, watched over by Philippe, himself liberated from prison but the day before, a contagion such, in the tainted amosphere of this period of history, that she contracted and died of virulent smallpox, caught at the deathbed of her son Louiset, whilst, beneath her windows, the whole of Paris marched, intoxicated, carried away by enthusiasm for the war, hurling itself towards universal ruin. Finally, here was Jean Macquart, the workman and the soldier returned to the land, wrestling with the hard earth which has to be paid by a drop of sweat for each grain of corn, wrestling, above all, with the people of the countryside, burning with a ceaseless hunger for more land, because of their lives of unending toil, the long and arduous conquest of the soil, the ageing Fouans parting with their fields as if they were parting with their own flesh, the Buteaus, ex-asperated, to the point of committing parricide to hasten the in-heritance of a plot of lucern, the obstinate Françoise mowed down and killed by a scythe, without uttering a word, unwilling to be the cause of the loss to the family of a single clod of earth, all this drama of simple folk governed by their instincts, not far removed from the savagery of their remote ancestors, all this human filth on this great earth, which alone remains immortal, the mother from which we spring and to which we return, which we love to the point of com-mitting crimes for her, which goes on continually renewing life for its unknown ends, even at the expense of untold human misery and suffering. And here was Jean again who, now a widower and having joined up at the first rumours of war, contributed the inexhaustible reserve, the material for eternal rejuvenation which the earth keeps for itself, Jean the humblest, the staunchest of soldiers, involved in the ultimate collapse, swept along by the frightful and inevitable tempest which, from the frontier to Sedan, destroyed the empire and came within an ace of destroying France, always sober, cool, never losing hope, loving, with tender fraternal affection, his comrade Maurice, this half-mad son of the middle class, the sacrificial goat, weeping tears of blood when inexorable fate chose him to be the executioner of his worthless friend, then, after it was all over, the unbroken sequence of defeats, the atrocious civil war, the lost provinces, the billions to be paid, going forward, imperturbable and serene, returning to the soil which was waiting for him, to the great and arduous task of raising a fallen France to its feet again.

Pascal paused, Clotilde had passed him all the files, one by one, and he had perused the contents, taken them out, put them back in order and replaced them on the top shelf of the cupboard. He was out of breath, exhausted by his tremendous feat of exposition; the young woman was incapable of uttering a word or even making a gesture, stunned by this turbulent torrent of life, still in a state of suspense, unable, as yet, to reflect on or to attempt an interpretation of what she had heard. The storm was still deluging the dark countryside with pelting rain. A tree in the vicinity had just been struck by lightning and collapsed with a tremendous crash. The candles flickered wildly in the wind which streamed in through the wide-open window.

"Ah!" he continued, pointing to the files, "a whole world, a society, a civilization, the whole of life, are all in there, with their good and evil manifestations, in the fire and the travail of the smithy which carries off everything .. Yes, our family alone would suffice, as a scientific example for those scientists who hope to be able to define one day, mathematically, the laws which govern the nervous defects and obscure blood diseases which manifest themselves in a given race, as the result of a primary organic lesion, and which determine, according to the environment, the sentiments of each individual of that race, as well as his desires, passions, all human manifestations, whether natural or instinctive, the end-products of which are called virtues and vices. It all also constitutes a complete historical record, it tells the story of the second empire, the *coup d'état* at Sedan, for the members of our family came from the people and then spread throughout all the strata of contemporary society, they climbed to the highest positions, driven by their insatiable appetites, by that essentially modern urge, the whiplash which drives the lower classes towards self-indulgence, on their way through the body politic .. I have told you their origins; they came from Plassans; and here we are again at Plassans; we have travelled a full circle."

He paused again, he was falling into a reverie, which slurred his speech:

"What a frightful heap of facts we have stirred up, what adventures, both sublime and terrible, what joys, what suffering thrown on to the heap in shovelfuls! .. We have pure history, the empire founded on blood, pleasure loving at first, though unduly authoritative, conquering rebel towns, then slowly disintegrating, collapsing in blood, in such a sea of blood, that the whole nation was nearly drowned in it .. We have social studies, petty trade and big business, prostitution, crime, the soil, money, the middle classes, the people, which rots in its suburban cesspit, which revolts in the great industrial centres, all that increasing pressure of socialism, pregnant with the new century .. We have simple human studies, intimate vignettes, love stories, the war waged by hearts and brains against unjust nature, the crushing of those who groan under loads too heavy for them, the cry of virtue which immolates itself and conquers pain .. We have fantasy, the imagination soaring to realms outside reality, immense gardens, in which flowers bloom all the year round, cathedrals with their delicate tracery in stone, marvellous tales fallen from paradise, idyllic sentiments wafted up to the sky in a kiss .. We have everything, from extreme virtue to the basest vice, from the vulgar to the sublime, flowers, mud, sobs, laughter, humanity endlessly drifting along the river of life!"

He reverted to the genealogical Tree, which was still on the table, spread it out, ran his finger over it, pointing to the members of the family who were still alive. Eugène Rougon, fallen from power, was now in the Chamber of Deputies, indefatigable defender of the old world which had collapsed in ruins. Aristide Saccard, after shedding his old skin, had fallen on his feet again as a republican, director of a great newspaper, in the process of making fresh millions; whilst his son Maxime was living on his income in his little hotel in the avenue of the Bois-de-Boulogne, suspicious and prudent, threatened by a dreadful disease, and his other son Victor had not reappeared, presumably still lurking in the shadow of crime, seeing that he was not in jail, spurned by the world and preordained to finish on the scaffold. Sidonie Rougon, after a long absence, tired of a life spent in shady transactions, had just retired to the cloistered security of some sort of religious institution, treasurer of the Charity of the Sacrament, the object of which was to help unmarried mothers to find a husband and was henceforth to live a life of nun-like austerity. Octave Mouret, proprietor of "Au Bonheur des Dames", a gigantic department store, which was earning increasingly fabulous profits, had had, towards the end of the winter, a second child by his wife Denise Baudu, whom he adored, although he was beginning to develop strange habits. The Abbé Mouret, curé at Saint-Eutrope, at the bottom of a marshy gorge, was cloistered there with his sister Désirée, so permeated with sincere humility that he would not accept advancement at his bishop's hands, waiting patiently for death, more of a saint than a man and refusing any form of treatment, although he was suffering from the early stages of pulmonary tuberculosis. Hélene was living very happily, in an isolated spot, idolized by her new husband, M. Rambaud, in a small property owned by them near Marseilles, by the sea; she had no children of the second marriage. Pauline Quenu was still at Bonneville, at the other end of France, facing the vast ocean, alone with little Paul, ever since the death of Uncle Chanteau, determined not to re-marry and to devote herself entirely to the son of her cousin Lazare, who, now a widower, had gone to America hoping to make a fortune. Etienne Lantier, back in Paris after the strike at Montsou, had compromised himself, later, in the Commune uprising, the ideas of which he had hotly defended; he had been condemned to death, then pardoned and deported, so that he was now at Noumea; it was believed that he had married soon after his arrival and that he had had a child, although the sex of the child was not known. Finally,

Jean Macquart, discharged after that week of bloodshed, had come back to settle near Plassans, at Valqueyras, where he had had the opportunity of marrying a stout wench, Mélanie Vial, the only daughter of a prosperous peasant, whose land he was cultivating; and his wife, impregnated the night of their wedding, after producing a boy in May, was now once more two months pregnant, one of those cases of superabundant fertility in which the mothers have no time to suckle their offspring in between pregnancies.

"It is an undoubted fact," he murmured, "that races degenerate, it is a question of real exhaustion, a rapid process of decadence, as if the members of our own family, after wallowing in self-indulgence, after gluttonously satisfying their appetites, had burned themselves out too quickly. Louiset dead in his cradle; Jacques-Louis, almost an idiot, carried off by a disease of the nervous system; Victor reverted to a state of primitive savagery, roaming through God knows what dark by-ways of crime; our poor Charles, so handsome and so fragile; these are the top branches of the Tree, the last etiolated twigs into which the powerful sap of the large branches seems unable to penetrate. The worm was in the trunk, it is now in the fruit and is devouring it .. But it is wrong to give way to despair, families are an eternal becoming. They plunge, through innumerable layers of past races, right down to the first man; and they will grow endlessly, they will spread out their branches and ramify *ad infinitum*, to the far end of future ages .. Look at our Tree; it only records five generations, it has no more significance than a single blade of grass, as compared with the human forest, which covers the earth, the people of which are represented by the great centuries-old oaks. But, think of the immense roots burrowing through a vast area of soil, think of the continuous unfolding of the top leaves which mingle with the other leaves, of the ever rippling sea at the summits of the trees, all due to the eternal fertilizing breath of life .. Well! that is our great hope, we must pin our faith on the day by day reconstitution of the race thanks to the new blood which comes from outside. Every marriage brings new elements, good or bad, the effect of which, nevertheless, is to prevent mathematical and progressive degeneration. The breaches are repaired, the defects are effaced, an inevitable equilibrium is re-established at the end of a few generations, and the end-result is always the average man, ordinary humanity, obstinately bent on its mysterious labour, marching towards an unknown objective."

He stopped and sighed:

"Ah! our family, what is going to become of it, what kind of being will it eventually produce?"

And he continued, paying no further attention to the surviving members he had mentioned, those had been classified, as he knew all about their potentialities, but he was still full of curiosity about the children who were still pre-adolescent. He had written to a colleague at Noumea, asking for exact information at to Etienne's wife and the child to whom she had almost certainly already given birth; there had been no answer and he was afraid that the Tree would remain incomplete because of these missing data. He was better informed as to Octave Mouret's two children, as he still corresponded with the father; the little girl was sickly, a source of worry to the parents, whereas the little boy, who took after his mother, was magnificently healthy. His main hope, however, was in Jean's children, whose first born, a bonny lad, seemed to be the product of a rejuvenating element, the young sap of a race which had re-steeped its roots in the soil. He sometimes visited Valqueyras, and he always returned delighted with this islet of fertility, with the father, so calm and rational, always at the plough, with the mother, so simple and full of spontaneous gaiety, with her wide hips, capable of giving birth to a multitude. Who could know from what source the healthy branch would arise? Perhaps the awaited sage, the man of power would germinate from there? Unfortunately for his Tree, these little lads and lassies were too young for classification. And he grew enthusiastic as he talked about this hope for the future, these blonde little heads, the more so, perhaps, because of his unacknowledged regret at his own celibacy.

Pascal went on gazing at the Tree spread out in front of him and cried:

"But, all the same, how complete and decisive it is. Just look at it! .. I repeat that you can find in it all forms of heredity. In order to establish my theory, all I had to do was to base it on the sum total of these facts .. What is marvellous, what you can touch with your finger, is how these creatures, born from the same stock, can appear radically different, although they are the only result of certain logical modifications of our common ancestors. The trunk explains the branches which, in their turn, explain the leaves. In your father, Saccard, as in your uncle, Eugène Rougon, so opposite in temperament and in mode of life, there is the same urge, which accounts for the disordered appetites of the one, the sovereign ambition of the other. Angélique, that pure lily, offspring of the equivocal Sidonie, has saintly aspirations which lead to becoming either a mystic or a great lover, according to environment. The three Mouret children, all from the same source, have a very different fate; Octave, the intelligent one, becomes a millionaire rag-seller; Serge, the devout one, a poor country curé; Désirée, the stupid one, a fine happy girl. But even more striking is the case of Gervaise's children; the neurosis passes, and Nana sells herself, Etienne rebels, Jacques commits murder, Claude is a genius, whereas Pauline, their first cousin, a close relation, is an example of honesty victorious, the woman who fights and immolates herself .. It is heredity, life itself, which gives rise to idiots, madmen, criminals and great men. Some cells abort, others take their place, and one has a rascal or a homicidal maniac instead of a man of genius or simply an honest man. And mankind rolls on sweeping everything before it!"

Then, his thoughts took a new twist:

"And the problem of the animals, of the beast which suffers and loves, which is like a primitive sketch of man. All those animals who live a life so like our own! .. Yes, I should have liked to let them into our ark, to leave some room for them in our family, and show them ceaselessly mixed up with us, completing our existence. I have known cats conferring a mysterious charm on a house, adorable dogs, whose death left us in a state of inconsolable mourning. I have known goats, cows, asses, with strong personalities, so important to us that their history should be written up .. And take Bonhomme, our poor old horse, who served us faithfully for a quarter of a century, are you not prepared to believe that he has mingled his blood with ours, and that he is, therefore, or has become, a member of our family? We have modified him, and he has had some influence on us; we end up by being fashioned in the same image; and that is so true, that now, when I see him half blind, with his wandering eye, his legs crippled by rheumatism, I kiss him on both cheeks, like a poor old relative, whom I have undertaken to support .. Oh animals! everything which drags itself along and laments its lot under the domination of man, what sympathy we have for them, what a big place we should reserve for them in a history of life!"

This was his last cry, in which Pascal expressed the exaltation of his affection for all living creatures. He had gradually whipped himself into a state of excitement; he was now proclaiming his confession of faith, in the continuous and victorious labour of living nature. And Clotilde, who had not spoken up till now, dismayed and pale because of the catastrophic rain of facts which had been poured upon her, was finally able to ask:

"Well! uncle, and what about my place in all that?"

She had put the tip of one of her slender fingers on the spot marked with her name, her leaf on the Tree. He had persistently avoided this leaf. She was insistent:

"Yes, me, where do I fit in? .. Why did you avoid reading the contents of my file?"

He did not answer for a moment, as if surprised by her question:

"Why? no special reason .. In any case, I have no wish to hide anything from you .. You can see what I have written here: "Clotilde, born in 1847. Takes after her mother. Latent heredity, with physical and mental predominance of her maternal grandfather .." Nothing could be clearer. You are your mother's daughter, you have her healthy appetite, and also a bit of her vanity, sometimes something of her indolence, her submissiveness. Yes, you are all woman, like she was, without your knowing it. I mean that you have a craving to be loved. Besides, your mother was a great novel reader, a dreamer who loved lying for days on end dreaming over a book; she doted on old wives tales, had the cards read for her, consulted fortune tellers; and I have always thought that your preoccupation with mystery, your yearning towards the unknown, came from her .. But what put the finishing touch to your character, was the influence of your grandfather, Commander Sicardot. I knew him, he was no eagle, but he had integrity and energy. If it were not for him, frankly, I do not think that you would be worth much, because the other influences are hardly favourable. He is responsible for the best part of you, the fact that you are a brave fighter, your pride and your sincerity."

She had listened to him attentively and gave a slight nod to signify that she agreed, that she was not offended, despite the slight painful tremor which these new details about her relatives, about her mother, had brought to her lips.

"Well!" she then asked, "what about you, uncle?"

This time, without the slightest hesitation, he cried:

"Oh, me, why talk about me? I have no part in it, in the family! .. You can see what I have written there: "Pascal, born in 1813. The innate factor. Combination, in which the physical and mental characteristics of the parents are confused, without any apparent resemblance to be found in the offspring .. My mother has repeated

to me often enough that I did not belong, that she could not understand where I had sprung from! It was a cry of relief, an exclamation
of involuntary joy.

"You see, the common people are never wrong. Have you ever
heard them call me Pascal Rougon, in the town? No! Everybody
always calls me Doctor Pascal, just that. It is because I am a part. .
It may not be very nice of me, but I am delighted, because some
hereditary burdens are too heavy to bear. I may love them all, but
feel unutterably relieved when I feel myself different, with nothing
in common with them. Not to be of them, not to belong to the
family, my God! It is a breath of fresh air, which gives me the
courage to put them all there, to strip them naked in those files and
still have the courage to go on living!"

He stopped speaking. There was a silence. The rain had stopped,
the storm was moving away, the rumblings of the thunder became
more and more distant; whilst, from the countryside, still wrapped
in darkness, but refreshed, there arose through the open window the
delightful fragrance of wet earth. In the stilled air, the candles were
burning low, with long, steady flames.

"Ah!" exclaimed Clotilde, with a gesture of despondency, "what
is to become of us?"

It was the same cry of anguish, which she had uttered, one night,
on the lawn; life was abominable; how could one live it in peace and
happiness? Science threw a terrifyingly bright light on the world, its
analysis probed into all the wounds of mankind and displayed them
in all their naked horror. And now he had spoken in even more
crude terms, increasing the feeling of nausea which both the animate
and the inanimate aroused in her, throwing her family, exposed to
its very marrow, on the amphitheatre floor. The river of mud had
rolled over her, for nearly three hours, the revelations were unspeakable, the utter and terrible truth about her relatives, her dear ones,
those whom it was her duty to love; her father sullied by his criminal
lust for money, her brother incestuous, her grandmother without
any scruples, covered in the blood of the righteous, the others almost
all tainted, drunkards, vicious people, murderers, the monstrous
flowering of the human tree. The shock was so brutal that she felt
lost, in a painful stupour at learning all about life, all at once. But,
the very violence of the lesson had been softened by something great
and good, a breath of profound humanity, which had blown over it.
She was left with no impression of having learnt something evil, she
had felt herself whipped by a bracing wind from the sea, a storm

wind, which refreshes and deepens one's breathing. He had told her everything, talking freely about her own mother, preserving his attitude of deference towards her, the attitude of the true scientist who never dogmatizes about his facts. To say everything, in order to know everything, cure everything, had he not said that, on that lovely summer night? She remained shaken by the vast implications of all that she had learnt, blinded by a light which was too dazzling, but understanding at last, ready to admit that he was attempting to solve a gigantic problem. In spite of everything, it was a cry of health, of hope in the future. He spoke as a benefactor, who, in view of the fact that heredity was responsible for the world, considered it essential to discover its laws in order to make use of them and make a happier world.

Besides, was there nothing but mud, in this turbulent flood, to which he had opened the flood-gates? How much gold there was, mingled with the weeds and the flowers on its banks! She could see all these hundreds of creatures flitting past her eyes and she remained haunted by the charming and kind figures, exquisite profiles of young girls, the serene beauty of some of the women. The very essence of passion had been displayed to her, an inspiring demonstration of the finer feelings in both men and women. There were so many of them, the Jeannes, the Angéliques, the Paulines, the Marthes, the Gervaises, the Hélènes. There was a wonderful element of fraternal humanity about them and the others, even the less attractive of them, even the terrible men, the worst of the lot. And it was precisely this breath of humanity she had felt passing over her, this current of all-embracing sympathy which flowed, underneath the didactic tones of his lesson in science. She had seen no trace of any sentimental emotions in him; his was the impersonal approach of the scientist making an academic demonstration; but, underneath it all, what wounded gentleness, what a fever of devotion, what an outpouring of all his being for the sake of the happiness of others! His work, the whole of it, conducted with such mathematical precision, was always permeated with the same fraternal compassion, even when his irony was at its most biting. Had he not spoken about animals, as being elder brothers to all those miserable beings who are in pain? Suffering exasperated him, his anger was due to the rare quality of his dreams, he was brutal only in his hatred of what was artificial and transient, aspiring to work for the benefit not of the polite society of the moment, but of all mankind, at the most trying period of its history. Perhaps it was even this revolt

against current banality, which had made him so defiantly auda-
cious in his theories and in their application to practical problems.
He remained profoundly human, overflowing with pity for everything that lived or was on this earth.

Besides, was that not life? There is no absolute evil. There has
never been a man who is all bad, the worst of men is capable of
conferring happiness on someone; with the result that, if one avoids
a rigidly unitary point of view, one ends up by realizing that every
man has his uses. Those who believe in a God should say to themselves that, if God does not strike down the wicked, it is because he
sees his creation as a whole, and does not descend to the particular.
All labour finishes and starts again; it is impossible to avoid admiring the courage and indefatigability of mankind; and the love of
life is stronger than anything. This gigantic labour of man, this
clinging to life, is its excuse, its redemption. Thus, from a high
vantage point, one would see nothing but this continual struggle,
and much good, in spite of all the evil. One became infinitely in-
dulgent, one pardoned, one was filled with overwhelming pity. This
is surely the haven, awaiting all those who have lost faith in dogmas,
who want to understand why they are alive, amidst the apparent
iniquity of the world. To live for the sake of the struggle, to add one
stone to the distant and mysterious edifice, and the only joy possible
on this earth is the joy of sustained effort.

Another hour had gone by, the entire night had been devoted to
this terrible lesson on life, without Pascal or Clotilde noting either
the passage of time or where they were. And he, who had been overworking for several weeks and who had already been ravaged by his
life of suspicion and vexation, gave a shudder, as if suddenly awakening from sleep:

"Now you know everything, do you feel stronger, tempered by
the truth, full of understanding and hope? .. Are you on my side?"

But she was still quivering from the appalling shock to her
innocence, unable to marshal her thoughts. It had all involved such
a collapse of her old beliefs, such a step forward towards a new
world, that she hardly dared to question herself and come to any
conclusion. She felt that, from now onwards, she had become a de-
votee of the truth, all powerful. It had flowed into her, but she was
neither emotionally nor intellectually convinced.

"Uncle," she stammered, "uncle .."

For an instant they stared at each other. Daylight was breaking,
a dawn of exceptional purity, in the great light sky, washed by the

storm. Not a single cloud veiled the pale azure, tinted with pink. The merry sounds of awakening life in the sodden countryside came in through the window and the candles, almost consumed, became almost invisible in the waxing light of the day.

"Answer me, do you still want to destroy, burn everything here? .. Are you with me, altogether, unreservedly, with me?"

He thought for a moment that she was going to throw her arms around his neck and sob her heart out. The impulse to do was self-evident. But they saw each other, for the first time, in their semi-nudity. She became conscious of wearing only a simple petticoat, with shoulders and arms bare, the latter partially veiled by her unbound hair; and there, near the left armpit, when she looked down, were the few drops of blood, where he had lacerated her, during their struggle. She became, then, extraordinarily confused and agitated as if his brutal embrace had made him her master, in everything and for always. This sensation remained with her, she was transfused with it, carried away beyond any possibility of control, swept by an irresisitible urge to give herself to him.

Clotilde, swiftly, drew herself up, striving to regain control of herself. She had folded her arms over her bare neck and breasts. All the blood in her body seemed to be under her skin, a scarlet flood of modesty. She turned on her heels and fled, with all the divine grace of her slender figure.

"Uncle, uncle, leave me alone .. I will see .."

Like a startled virgin, she had taken refuge in her bedroom, as on other occasions in the past. He heard her quickly double-locking her door. He was left alone and, overtaken all of a sudden by discouragement and an immense sadness, he asked himself if he had been right in revealing everything, whether the truth would germinate inside this dear creature, whom he adored, and would grow, one day, into a harvest of happiness.

CHAPTER SIX

SOME days passed. October, that year, was a peculiar month. At first it was hot, a real Indian summer without a cloud in the sky, then the weather changed; gales of wind howled around the Souleiade, a violent storm wrecked the garden. As the winter set in, a mournful cloud seemed to settle down over the gloomy house.

The gulf between Pascal and Clotilde had, if anything, widened; the conflict was as atrocious as ever, but had entered into a new phase; there were no more open quarrels, no slamming of doors, no shouting and Martine no longer had to rush upstairs several times a day to separate them. Now, they hardly ever spoke to each other and not a word had been said about the scene in the yard that night. On his part, it was because he was over-scrupulous and he shrank from bringing up the subject again. On her part, it was because, after such a sudden and violent mental shock, she was still ruminating and hesitating; the instinctive rebel, loath to surrender without a final struggle. And the gulf of misunderstanding widened in the desolate silence of the house from which happiness had fled.

This was an agonizing period for Pascal, which he was compelled to put up with in silence. They wanted him to believe that it was a period of truce, but he was not at all reassured, quite the contrary. He became more suspicious than ever. He imagined them lurking in ambush around every corner; their pretence of leaving him in peace covered incessant plotting, which would involve even greater danger to his future peace of mind! He feared the worst, any day now he expected to find that his papers had been swallowed up in some abyss, that the Souleiade would be razed to the ground, carried away, crumble into nothingness. This underhand persecution of his very thoughts, his spiritual and intellectual life, was becoming intolerable; such was his state of nervous agitation that he actually felt feverish when he went to bed at night. Often, for no reason, he started and even jumped, turned around suddenly, expecting to surprise the enemy behind his back, in the act of betraying him; and there was nothing, nothing but the shadow of his own fear. On other occasions, filled with morbid suspicion, he lay in wait for hours, hidden behind the curtains or concealed in some dark corridor; but not a soul was stirring, he could hear nothing but the pounding of blood in his temples. He became frantic and searched every room each night before going to bed. He stayed awake for hours and, when he finally dozed off, awoke at the slightest sound, panting with terror, ready to leap out of bed and defend himself.

And what made Pascal's ordeal increasingly and atrociously unbearable was the thought, which never left him, that his sufferings were due to the only creature in the world whom he loved, Clotilde whom he adored, whom he had watched for twenty years growing more beautiful, more charming every day, expanding like a marvellous flower, filling the whole house and his own life with an ineffably delicate perfume. Clotilde, heavens! who filled his heart with quintessential tenderness, the only human being whom he had never subjected to any form of scientific analysis! his joy, his courage, his hope, the new generation, resplendent and unspoiled youth, in which he had felt himself revived and rejuvenated! When she passed him, the sight of her slender neck, so round and delicately modelled, refreshed him and bathed him in well-being and happiness. It was not surprising that he had become possessed, obsessed by this child, who had crept into his affections as a child and who, as she grew older, had monopolized them. Ever since he had settled in Plassans he had led the life of a Benedictine monk, cloistered amidst his books, with no women friends. He had fallen in love, once, with the lady who had died and whom he had never touched, whose finger-tips he had not even kissed. It is true that he sometimes spent a night in Marseilles; but these were brief and sordid escapades with the first loose woman he met. In fact he had never lived. He had stored up all his reserves of virility, which, now that he felt that he would soon be growing old, were threatening to break through and overwhelm him. His pent-up emotions would have responded to an animal, any mongrel picked up in the street, if it were to lick his hand; and it was Clotilde, the little girl, miraculously transformed into the most desirable of women, who was torturing him and had been turned into his worst enemy.

Pascal, usually so kind and considerate and cheerful, was now unbearably cantankerous, always frowning and depressed. When he was addressed he flew into a rage and swore at Martine, who was unfailingly astonished and looked up at him with the expression of a beaten dog. He stalked around the house looking so bad-tempered that they did not dare to speak to him. On his visiting days he never took Clotilde with him. One afternoon, he came back his mood even blacker than usual; he had the death of a patient on his conscience. He had given Lafouasse his injection. This man's ataxia had been progressing, recently, at a frightening rate and Pascal considered his condition desperate. But he was determined to keep on with the treatment; and it was just his luck that, on that particular day his syringe had sucked up some particles which had managed to find their way through the filter and were lying at the bottom of the flask. The final stroke of bad luck had been that, as he made the injection, he had seen blood seeping under the skin, he had penetrated a vein. The man had gone as white as a sheet, his breathing had become laboured and he had broken out into a cold sweat. Death had been instantaneous, the lips had gone blue and the face black. Pascal realized that he had caused an embolism, because his extract had not been sufficiently purified, his method was still too primitive, almost barbarous. No doubt, Lafouasse was a hopeless case. Without treatment the most he could have hoped for would have been another six months of life, in constant, racking pain; but this did not alter the brutal fact of his horrifying death; his faith in himself had been shaken. He even raged against science, it was still at an impotent and murderous stage! He had come home livid and had not reappeared until the next day, after remaining shut up in his room for sixteen hours, where he had thrown himself, fully-clothed, on his bed.

The next afternoon in the study, Clotilde, who was sewing, ventured to break the heavy silence. She had been watching him nervously turn over the leaves of a book, looking for a reference he could not find.

"Uncle, are you ill? .. Why don't you tell me? I could look after you."

He kept his eyes glued to the book and muttered:

"Ill, why should you care? Besides, I hate having anyone fuss over me."

Clotilde continued, in a conciliatory tone of voice:

"If you are upset about something, it might make you feel better if you were to tell me about it .. You looked so sad yesterday when you came home! You must not let yourself get depressed. I was worried about you all night. I got up three times and listened at your door, tormented by the idea that you might be in pain or unhappy."

She had chosen her words with the greatest of care and had

expressed her sincere feelings, but it was enough to make him fly into a sudden rage. He threw the book across the room and drew himself up quivering:

"So you have been spying on me, I cannot even go to my room without your gluing your ear to the walls or to the door .. Yes, you even listen to the beating of my heart, you are waiting for me to die so that you can ransack and burn everything .. !

His voice rose and he gave vent to his intolerably wounded feelings by a flood of accusations and threats:

"I forbid you to keep track of my movements .. Have you anything else to say? Have you thought it over, can you put your hand in mind, loyally, and tell me that you agree with me?"

But she had lost her voice, she could only stare at him, wide-eyed, not yet ready to surrender; and he, exasperated beyond measure by her attitude, could only stammer, waving her away with an angry gesture:

"Go away! Go away! .. I don't want you near me! I will not have my enemies near me! If you stay here, I shall go mad!"

She had risen to her feet, very pale. She walked away, erect, without turning around, taking her sewing with her.

Throughout the following month, he threw himself into his work in an attempt to forget his troubles. He did not leave the study for days on end, he even spent whole nights reading over old documents, revising his manuscripts on heredity. He seemed determined, at any cost, to convince himself that his hopes were legitimate, to wring from science an absolute assurance that mankind could be made over in a better and finer mould. He never left the house, lived with his papers, without air and without exercise. And, at the end of this month of almost demented overwork, which overstrained him without relieving the tension between Clotilde and himself, he fell into a state of complete nervous exhaustion; he had, for a long time, been riding for a fall, he had been asking the impossible of himself and his health broke down.

When he got up in the morning, he felt so weak that he could hardly stand, heavier and more tired than he had been on going to bed. He was so ill that his legs gave way after walking a few steps. His whole body trembled at the slightest effort. He was in constant pain, accentuated by any movement. Sometimes he felt the floor heaving beneath his feet. There was a continuous buzzing noise in his ears, and he had increasingly frequent attacks of giddiness. He had always liked drinking wine, but now it revolted him, he lost his appetite and could not digest the little food he ingested. He fell into a state of apathy, broken by sudden excesses of purposeless and feverish activity. Periods of prostration alternated with periods of nervous irritability. The slightest emotion brought tears to his eyes. In the end he locked himself in his room and his attacks of despair were so violent that he wept interminably with great tears rolling down his cheeks, for no immediate reason, just feeling crushed by the immense sadness of human life.

His condition became aggravated by a visit to Marseilles, one of his usual bachelor flights from celibacy. He had hoped that some violent distraction, a fit of debauchery, might bring him some relief from his symptoms. He only stayed away two days and came back, infinitely worse, with the haunted expression of a man who has lost his most treasured possession, his virility. It was a disgrace which could not be acknowledged and which sent him into a frenzy of terror and further repeated attempts had merely accentuated the clumsy brutality of his inhibited love-making. He had never attached any importance to this simple act, but he was now obsessed by it, crushed, plunged in misery, to the point of considering suicide. He told himself that it could only be a symptom of his bad physical condition and therefore transient, but he was none the less abysmally depressed; his impotence put him on the same level as an adolescent neophyte trembling with fright during his first experience of sex.

Towards the first week of December, Pascal was attacked by intolerable neuralgia in various parts of the body. The scalp manifestations were the worst, he felt as if his skull were going to crack open at any minute. Old Madame Rougon had been told about his illness and came to enquire about him. She trotted into the kitchen, wanting to talk to Martine first before seeing her son. The servant, looking frightened and miserable, said that monsieur was certainly going mad; and she described his peculiar symptoms, his constant shuffling around his room, locking all the drawers, searching the house even at two o'clock in the morning. With tears in her eyes, she declared that monsieur must be possessed by a devil and that they would be well advised to call in the curé of Saint-Saturnin.

"Such a good man," she repeated, "for whom I would gladly let myself be cut up in four pieces! What a misfortune that we cannot persuade him to come to church, that would certainly cure him!"

They were joined by Clotilde, who had heard Felicité's voice.

She also now spent most of her time roaming through the empty rooms and sitting in the abandoned drawing-room on the ground floor. She said nothing, but merely listened with a thoughtful and expectant expression on her face.

"Ah! it is you, my darling. Good day to you! .. Martine was telling me that Pascal has a devil in him. I am inclined to agree; but his particular devil has a name, pride. He thinks that he knows everything, he is pope and emperor all in one, so naturally, anyone who disagrees with him exasperates him."

She shrugged her shoulders disdainfully:

"It would make me laugh, if it wasn't so tragic .. A man who knows precisely nothing, who has never lived, who has remained shut up with his books. Put him in a drawing-room and he is as innocent as a new-born baby. As for women, he knows less than nothing about them .."

Forgetting that she was talking to the young woman and a servant, she lowered her voice confidentially:

"Gracious! being too virtuous can do a man a lot of harm. No wife, no mistress, nothing. That is what has turned his brain, in the end."

Clotilde did not move. Only her eyelids closed, like shutters, over her wide-open thoughtful eyes. Then she raised them, but her expression remained blank and did not betray what was going on in her mind.

"Is he upstairs?" asked Félicité. "I must see him, all this has got to stop, it is too stupid!"

She walked out, towards the stairs, whilst Martine went back to her saucepans and Clotilde to her prowling around the empty rooms.

Upstairs, Pascal was sitting at his table, an open book in front of him, with a stupefied expression on his face. He could no longer read, the words escaped him. They were all jumbled together and made no sense. But he went on trying, in despair at not being able to work, at losing his one passion, his life. His mother proceeded to scold him, took away his book and threw it on the other table, crying that one had to be looked after when one is ill. He staggered to his feet, made an angry gesture, about to send her out of the room, as he had sent Clotilde away. Then, with a great effort, he controlled himself and reverted to his usual deferent attitude towards her:

"Mother, you know that I have always avoided arguing with you .. Please leave me alone."

She stood her ground and started reproaching him for his unfounded suspicions. It was all his own fault, he was making himself ill by thinking that he was surrounded by enemies, who were laying traps for him in order to rob him. Could any man in his senses believe in such nonsense? He was suffering from a persecution mania. Then she accused him of having allowed himself to be carried away by his enthusiasm for his precious new treatment, his injections, his discovery which he believed to be such an infallible cure for all human ills. It was all false pride! Did he think himself God? What did he expect! He was sure to be cruelly disappointed! She mentioned Lafouasse, the man whom he had killed; naturally, she understood what a blow it must have been to his pride, enough to make him take to his bed.

Pascal still had himself well in hand. He stared at the floor and merely repeated:

"Mother, I beg of you, leave me alone."

"Oh! no, I am not going to leave you," she cried, with her usual impetuosity. "That was exactly why I came, to give you a little jolt, to stop you brooding over your fancied grievances .. No, it has got to stop, I have no intention of letting the whole town start gossiping about us again, about you and your precious new treatment .. I want you to be properly looked after."

He shrugged his shoulders and said, in a low voice, as if trying to reassure himself:

"I am not ill."

Felicité reacted, immediately and violently:

"What, not ill! not ill! .. No one but a doctor could possibly be so blind .. My poor boy, it sticks out a mile, you are going mad, mad with pride and fear!"

This time she had managed to jolt Pascal into raising his head, and he looked her straight in the eye, as she continued:

"That was what I wanted to say, had to say, seeing that no one else was willing to face you. Do you understand? you are old enough to know what to do .. You must pull yourself together, think about something else, not let yourself be dominated by one fixed idea, especially as you belong to a family like ours .. You know what I mean, nobody knows our hereditary tendencies better than you do. You must be careful and look after yourself."

He had grown pale, he kept staring at her, as if he were searching her, to ferret out any hidden resemblances. All he said was:

"You are right, mother .. Thank you."

Then, when she had gone, he fell back in his chair and tried to read his book. But, as before, he was unable to concentrate, to understand the words, which seemed one long blur. His mother's words still rang in his ears. She had brought a frightful thought to the surface which he had pushed down into his sub-conscious mind. It became conscious, only too definite. He was now haunted by a fear too terrible to be faced. Was this not the crowning irony of his life, was he, who had boasted, two short months ago, that he did not belong to the family, to be proved wrong, spectacularly, horrifyingly wrong? Would the taint be revived in his own marrow, was he to be clawed alive by the dreadful hereditary monster? His mother had said that he was going mad because of his pride and his fears. If that were so, his exalted faith in his power to abolish suffering, to endow man with greater determination, to make it healthier and finer, all these were merely early symptoms of acute megalomania. Further, it was painfully obvious that his fear of being ambushed, the fact that he had been morbidly watching for his enemies to fall upon him, were symptoms of common persecution mania. The family history showed several terrible examples of such cases; rapidly progressive insanity, then general paralysis and death.

From that day onwards he became possessed by the one thought, he fell an easy prey to this haunting terror of madness and death. All his symptoms, the immense tiredness on waking, the buzzing in the ears, the attacks of giddiness, even his bad digestion and his fits of weeping, were definite proofs of gradual mental deterioration. He was convinced that he was going mad .. When it came to his own case, all his powers of observation and the diagnostic subtlety of the trained observer, failed him; if he used his reasoning powers at all, it was to confuse and pervert the issue, overwhelmed by physical and mental depression. He felt that he no longer controlled his own fate, it was only a question of hours or, at most days, before the final collapse of all reason!

He spent whole days of this pale December in brooding over this supposedly inevitable decline into madness. Every morning, he tried to shake off this obsession; but, when he returned to the study, he invariably succumbed to it again. His prolonged studies of heredity, his researches and experiments on that subject, now merely served to warp his mental processes and cause him further worry about his own case. There was more than abundant proof in his all too voluminous files. If he had been wrong in his assessment of himself, if he could not be excluded from the family, as a remarkable instance of predominance of the inborn factor, should he consider himself a case of latent heredity, skipping one, two, or even three generations? Or was his case, more simply, one of larval heredity, which provided further proof of his theory of the existence of a germinative plasma? or should he not consider himself as a case illustrating singular successive resemblances as he declined in years? From that moment onwards he was unable to rest, he felt impelled to go on examining all the data which might have a bearing on his own case, scanning his notes and re-reading his books. And he analysed himself unceasingly and minutely, watching for any facts which might clinch the diagnosis. Some days, when his brain worked more sluggishly than usual, when he believed that he could detect new visual symptoms, he believed that these were conclusive signs of the predominance of the original nervous lesion; other days, when the leg symptoms were prominent, with his feet feeling heavy and painful, he imagined that these proved that he was under the indirect influence of some antecedent who had come from outside the family. His imaginary symptoms multiplied and became the source of unutterable confusion. And, every evening, the conclusions were the same, the same knell tolled inside his skull: heredity, terrifying heredity, the fear of going mad.

At the beginning of January Clotilde was an involuntary witness to a scene which she found excruciatingly painful. She had been sitting reading in front of one of the study windows, hidden from the room by the high back of her armchair; Pascal who had been invisible, cloistered in his room since the day before, came in, carrying, unfolded, a sheet of paper yellowed by age, which she recognized as the genealogical Tree. He was so absorbed that he would not have seen her, even if she had been standing in front of him. He spread the Tree out on the table, scanning it with a despairing expression, as if he were begging for an answer to an insoluble dilemma, and the tears were pouring down his cheeks. Why, my God! would the Tree not answer and tell him which ancestor he took after so that he could write his own accurate case history inside his leaf? If he was to go mad, why would the Tree not give him a definite answer, he would feel so much better if his doubts could be cleared up? But his tears blurred his vision, he was pitifully disappointed. Clotilde had to hide when she saw him go to the cupboard and throw both doors wide open. He pulled down all the files, threw them on the table and leafed through them with feverish haste. It was a repetition of that awful stormy night, nightmare unleashed, with the phantoms gibbering at him from the papers. He seemed to see them clearly and was muttering to each one of them, as it arose and then flitted away out of sight, then his voice became more distinct and Clotilde could hear whole phrases:

"Is it you? .. Or you? .. Or you? .. Or you, age-old mother, mother of us all, is it you who are driving me insane? .. Is it you, drunken old uncle, old bandit of an uncle, must I pay for your drunken orgies? .. Is it you, ataxic nephew, or you, the mystical nephew, or you, idiotic niece, who will tell me the truth and explain what form of lesion I am suffering from? .. Or is it you, little cousin, who committed suicide by hanging yourself, or you, little cousin, with a lust for murder, or you, little girl, little cousin, who rotted away until nothing was left of you? Which of your tragic ends will be mine?"

And the procession continued, they kept crowding up from the pages and were swept away, as rapidly as if they had been leaves whirled away by a storm-wind. The files were now alive with these members of his family, all suffering mankind. He saw them in the flesh.

"Ah! Which of you will tell me? Which of you will tell me? The one who died insane? The one who died paralysed? The young girl who was starved to death in her prime? Which is it, hysteria, alcoholism, tuberculosis, scrofula? And what will it do to me, make me an epileptic, an ataxic or a lunatic? .. A lunatic! who says a lunatic? They are all saying it, a lunatic, a lunatic, a lunatic!"

A fit of sobbing overcame him. He let his whirling head drop and rest on the files scattered over the table and went on sobbing, his whole body shaken by a sort of convulsive tremor of grief. And Clotilde, filled with awe, just as if she had been taking part in a religious service, held her breath and tiptoed away; well aware that he would feel unbearably ashamed were he to suspect that he had been seen and overheard.

A long period of prostration followed. January was very cold. But a cold winter sun shone steadfastly from the clear blue, cloudless sky; and at the Souleiade, the windows of the study, which faced south, turned it into a conservatory and kept it delightfully warm. It was not even necessary to light the fire, the sun kept pouring in, filling it with a pale gold mote-cloud, in which hovered torpidly, such flies as had survived the winter. The faint buzzing of their wings was the only sound in the room. It was a somnolent and cosy warmth, like a fragment of springtime hoarded up in the old house.

It was here, one morning, that Pascal overheard, in his turn and equally involuntarily, a conversation which aggravated his mental turmoil. He now rarely left his room before lunch. Doctor Ramond had come to visit Clotilde and they were chatting peacefully in the study, sitting close together and enjoying the warmth of the sun.

This was Ramond's third visit in a week. He had reached a point in his career, at which it was essential for him to stabilize his position and his practice in Plassans; the question of his marriage could no longer be left in suspense. He would have to ask Clotilde for a definite answer. Twice he had been balked by the presence of a third person. This time she was alone and he was determined to speak with complete frankness. They had always been such good friends, they were both such eminently sensible human beings that he anticipated no difficulty in persuading her to come to a decision. And gazing into her eyes he finished by saying:

"I assure you, Clotilde, that you would not be making a mistake, that you would be coming to a wise decision .. You must have known, for a long time past, that I am in love with you. I love you tenderly and have the most profound respect for your character .. But, even that, perhaps, would not be enough. We are also temperamentally suited to each other, we understand each other and I am certain that we should be very happy together."

She had not lowered her eyes, she, too, was looking at him, openly and frankly, with a friendly smile:

"Why," she asked, "don't you marry Mademoiselle Lévêque, the solicitor's daughter? She is better looking and richer than I am and I know that she is in love with you .. My good friend, I am afraid you may be making a serious mistake."

He showed no signs of impatience, he was too sure of his own feelings and the wisdom of his decision:

"But I do not happen to be in love with Mademoiselle Lévêque and I do love you .. Besides, I have taken everything into consideration, I repeat that I know what I am doing. Say yes, if you have no alternative in mind."

Then, her expression changed, became serious and a shadow passed across her face, the shadow of the troubled thoughts, the almost unconscious internal struggles, which had been bothering her for a long time and to which she had never, as yet, given voice:

"Well! my friend, as you seem to be in earnest, allow me to reserve my decision, not to give you an answer to-day, grant me a few weeks to think about it .. Uncle is really very ill. I myself am in a disturbed mental state, full of anxiety and forebodings; and I know that you would not like me to say yes on a sudden impulse, which I might regret later, when I am in a calmer frame of mind .. I can assure you that I have a great deal of affection for you. But it would be wrong to decide at this moment, when we are all so seriously worried about Pascal .. You understand, I hope? I shall not keep you waiting for long."

And to change the subject, she added:

"Yes, Uncle's condition is most disquieting. I wanted to see you and talk to you about him .. The other day I caught sight of him weeping bitterly. I am certain that he is haunted by the fear of going mad .. The day before yesterday, when you were talking to him, I noticed that you were trying to sum up his condition, professionally. Tell me, frankly, what did you think of him? Is he in any danger?"

Doctor Ramond protested, without hesitation:

"Oh, no! He is overworked, that has disturbed his mental balance, that is all! .. How can a man like him, who is an expert on diseases of the nervous system, be so mistaken about himself? It distresses me to think that our best and clearest brains can be subject to such lapses from sanity! .. In his case, his own injections, his own discovery, might provide the ideal solution. Why does he not try his injections on himself?"

And, when the young woman made a despairing gesture, implying that Pascal no longer listened to her, that he would not even let her speak to him, he added:

"Very well! I will speak to him myself."

It was at this juncture that Pascal came out of his room, attracted by the sound of voices. But, when he saw them close together, talking in such an animated fashion, so young and so handsome, as if clothed in sunshine, he stopped on the threshold. His eyes widened, his pale face twitched and he winced, as if in pain.

Ramond had taken Clotilde's hand, wishing to keep her sitting with him for a while longer:

"I have your promise, have I not? I would like our marriage to take place this summer .. You know how much I love you and I shall have to wait, patiently, for your answer."

"Agreed," she answered. "Everything will be settled within a month from now."

Pascal felt giddy and staggered. Here was another one, a friend and a pupil, insinuating himself into the household in order to rob him! He should have expected it, but this sudden news of a possible marriage astounded him, crushed him like an unexpected catastrophe, which was the final blow to all his hopes. Was this creature of his own making, whom he had always considered devoted to him going off without a backward glance and leaving him all alone to die in some solitary corner of the house? She had upset him so much the previous day, that he had even thought of a separation, sending her to her brother, who was still anxious to have her come to Paris. He had been nerving himself to decide on such a step, in their mutual interest. But to find her there with Ramond, without warning, hear her promising an answer, to think of her getting married, leaving him so soon, was like having a knife thrust through his heart.

He walked forward into the room, stepping heavily on purpose. The two young people turned around and felt faintly embarrassed:

"Ah! sir, we were talking about you," said Ramond cheerfully. "We were conspiring against you, I must confess .. Come, why will you not treat yourself? There is nothing seriously wrong with you, you could be fit inside a fortnight."

Pascal, who had let himself sink into a chair, just went on staring at them. By now his feelings were well under control and his face showed no sign of the shock they had given him. He was convinced that he would die of it and not a soul would know why. But, it was a relief to be able to appear to lose his temper, to refuse emphatically to consider the idea of even drinking a cup of herb-tea:

"Treatment! What for? .. My old carcass is played out, finished!"

"Not at all! You are as sound, if not sounder than the rest of us. All this is purely accidental and the remedy is in your own hand .. Inject yourself .."

He hesitated. Pascal understood and protested violently. Did they want him to kill himself as he had killed Lafouasse? His injections! a fine idea, something to be really proud of! He was through with medicine, he swore that he would never see another patient. A man who no longer fulfilled any useful function in the community, should be allowed to croak and good riddance to him. That, in fact, was what he intended to do, as quickly as possible.

"Rubbish!" concluded Ramond, thinking it wiser to go, for fear of exciting Pascal still further; "I will leave you in the best of hands .. I am sure that Clotilde will be able to persuade you."

But this final blow had been too much for Pascal. He took to his bed that afternoon and remained locked up in his room until the following evening. Clotilde, increasingly worried, went and pounded on his door with her fist; not a breath, no answer. She was joined by Martine, who begged him through the keyhole to answer her and say whether he needed anything. There was complete silence, as if the room were empty. The following morning Clotilde, quite by chance, tried the handle and the door opened. Perhaps he had unlocked it hours before. This was the first time she had ever been in his room, which faced north. There was an iron bedstead, without curtains, a shower in one corner, a long black wooden table, some chairs and, on another trestle table along the wall, a lot of apparatus which looked to her as if it were a complete alchemist's equipment; mortars, incubators, machines and several doctor's bags. Pascal was dressed and sitting on the edge of his bed, obviously exhausted by making it himself.

"Don't you want me to look after you?" asked Clotilde, both moved and apprehensive, not daring to move forward into the room.

He made a weary gesture:

"Oh! you can come in, I shan't attack you. I have no strength left."

Henceforth he tolerated her presence in his room and allowed her to wait on him. He still had his whims; he did not want her to come in when he was in bed, overwhelmed by a prurient sense of modesty and insisted on her sending Martine. Besides, he rarely stayed in bed, dragged himself from chair to chair, quite unable to settle down to any form of work. His condition deteriorated steadily, he was crucified by blinding headaches accompanied by nausea, too weak, as he said himself, to put one foot in front of the other. He was convinced, every morning, that he would sleep that night at the Tulettes, a raving lunatic. He was becoming emaciated, his face became a tragic mask of singular beauty, underneath his shock of white hair, which he continued to comb; his only remaining gesture of personal vanity. And, though he was now willing to be waited on, he refused categorically to take any form of medicine, he had become a therapeutic nihilist.

Finally, Clotilde became his devoted slave. She thought of nothing else; to begin with she had attended low mass, then she stopped going to church altogether. In her impatient search for a sign and for immediate happiness, she seemed to be finding some degree of contentment in devoting every minute of the day to her beloved uncle, doing her best to restore him to his usual health and good spirits. It was a form of self-surrender, or rather self-forgetfulness; a need for finding happiness in someone else's happiness; it was an automatic reaction, owing simply to the goodness of her heart, in spite of the crisis in their more profound relationship. She still kept silent about the disagreement which had separated them, she had no intention, as yet, of throwing her arms around his neck, crying that she was at his disposal, that he could come to life again, seeing that she was ready to surrender herself to him. She simply thought of herself as a sort of nurse, nursing him as any other relative might have done. It was all very pure and rather childlike, her life was completely filled by her delicate attentions, her absorption in attending to his comfort, forestalling his every whim, the days flew past, free from any thought of the "beyond" and filled with her single-minded determination to nurse him back to health.

She found him docile, except when it came to persuading him to try his own injections on himself. He fought her tooth and nail. He denied the validity of the treatment and called himself a fool. She had to pretend to lose her temper and raise her voice. She was now the one who had faith in science, who was indignant with him for doubting his own genius. For a long time he persisted in his refusal; then, his resistance weakened, she had begun to dominate him and finally he gave way in order to avoid quarrelling with her. After the first few injections he began to feel much better, although he refused to admit it. She was overjoyed, took him to task because he would not agree that his method was marvellous; he should have been immensely proud of having thought of such a wonderful new remedy which could perform untold miracles. He began to smile and to consider his own case with sober objectivity. Ramond must have been right, it was merely a question of nervous exhaustion. Perhaps, after all, he might get better.

"Ah! It is you, dear child, who are responsible for my improvement," he said, though not prepared, as yet, to admit that he was beginning to feel optimistic. "All remedies, you see, depend on the hand that administers them."

Convalescence was prolonged throughout the month of February. The weather remained clear and cold. Every day the sun warmed the study with its pale rays. Inevitably, there were relapses, fits of black depression, hours when his fears returned and overwhelmed him; whilst Clotilde, much distressed, went to sit at the other end of the room in order to avoid irritating him. On these occasions he was convinced, once more, that he would never recover. He became bitter and aggressively ironical.

It was on one of these bad days that Pascal, looking out of the window, saw his neighbour, M. Bellombre, the retired teacher, inspecting his fruit trees to see whether the flowers were likely to give him plenty of fruit. The sight of the old man, so correct and erect, so serene in his egoism, which seemed to render him immune from ill-health, sent Pascal into a transport of rage:

"Ah!" he growled, "there is a fellow who will never suffer from the consequences of overwork, who will never be in danger of losing his health through worry!"

And he proceeded to embark on an ironical eulogy of selfishness. "To be alone in the world, not to have a single friend, no wife, no child, what supreme happiness!" This implacable miser who, after forty years of smacking other people's children, had retired, without a dog, with a deaf and dumb gardener, even older than himself, did he not represent the greatest sum total of felicity possible on this earth? No responsibilities, no duties, preoccupied with nothing except his own health! What a wise man, he would live to be a hundred!

"Ah! fear of life! decidedly, the finest form of cowardice .. To think that I have sometimes regretted not having a child of my own! Have we the right to bring more miserable creatures into the world? We should kill bad heredity, kill life .. The only honest man, believe me, is that old coward!"

M. Bellombre, quietly enjoying the March sun, continued to inspect his pear trees. Every movement was restrained, he was economizing his green old age. When he found a stone on the path, he pushed it aside with the tip of his walking stick and then walked on at his usual unhurried pace.

"Look at him! .. How well preserved he is, how handsome. All the blessings of heaven in one person! He is the most fortunate of men."

Clotilde said nothing, she was distressed by Pascal's irony, behind which she sensed his despair. As a rule, she defended M. Bellombre, but, this time, she felt like protesting. Her eyes were wet with tears and she answered in a low voice:

"Yes, but no one loves him."

This put an immediate end to the painful scene. Pascal turned around, as if he had received a shock, and looked at her. A sudden rush of emotion brought the tears to his own eyes and he walked away to regain control of himself.

During the next few days bad periods alternated with good ones. He was slow to regain his strength and what exasperated him was that he could do no work without breaking out into abundant perspiration. This was, doubtless, a warning, to continue working would have made him faint. It was a vicious circle; he knew that he would have recovered more rapidly, if he had been able to do a little work. He was, however, able to take an interest in and make plans for continuing his experiments, he re-read what he had been writing before his illness; and, as his interest in science revived, he began to lose his self-confidence again. His fears and suspicious recurred. At one time he had been so prostrate that the house itself might have disappeared; they could have sacked it, taken and destroyed everything and the disaster would have left him cold. Now, he was on the watch again, he kept feeling in his pocket to make sure that the key of the cupboard was still there.

One morning, he had been luxuriating in his bed later than usual and came out of his room at about eleven; he found Clotilde in the study, busy making an exact crayon copy of a spray of almond blossoms. She looked up, smiled at him, picked up a key from the desk and handed it to him: "Here you are, uncle!"

At first he looked at it uncomprehendingly:

"What is it?"

"It is the key of the cupboard. It must have dropped out of your pocket yesterday. I picked it up this morning."

Pascal took the key, extraordinarily shaken. He looked at it and looked at Clotilde. Was it really all over? No more persecution, no more plots to steal his papers and burn them? And, when he saw that she, too, was much moved, he felt immensely relieved and elated.

He put his arms around her and kissed her:

"Ah! if we could only stop making each other unhappy!"

Then he walked to his table, opened the drawer and threw the key into it, as he had done in the past.

This seemed to hasten his recovery and he soon began to look like his old self. He had a few relapses, but they were short and of no consequence. He was able to write again and the days seemed shorter. The weather grew warmer. The sun threw deep golden rays into the study and it was so hot that the shutters had to be pulled down half way. Pascal would not see any visitors, he barely tolerated

Martine and his mother was told that he was sleeping when she called from time to time for news of him. He was basking in this delightful solitude, cherished by the one-time rebel, his enemy of yesterday, now his submissive pupil. There were long comfortable silences between them. They were thinking and dreaming in a state of infinite languid contentment.

One day Pascal surprised Clotilde by his unusually serious expression. He was now convinced that his illness had been purely accidental and that heredity had played no part in it. But he was, none the less, extremely humble:

"My God!" he murmured, "what insignificant creatures we are! I considered myself eminently rational, I was so proud of my reasoning powers. And then, a few worries and a little overwork were enough to make me almost go raving mad!"

He stopped and reflected for a moment. His eyes lit up, he was in full command of himself again. He felt clear-sighted and full of courage:

"I feel so much better and if it means that I have really recovered, it is for your sake, entirely for your sake, that I am pleased."

Clotilde, puzzled, raised her head:

"What do you mean?"

"Why, because of your marriage, of course .. Now you will be able to fix the date."

She was astonished:

"Ah! that's true, my marriage!"

"Shall we decide today and make it the second week in June?"

"Yes, the second week in June, that would be excellent."

They stopped talking, she kept her eyes down on her sewing and he sat, without moving, gazing mournfully into the distance.

CHAPTER SEVEN

THAT day, when she arrived at the Souleiade, old Madame Rougon caught sight of Martine in the kitchen garden, planting leeks; she trotted up to the servant, knowing that she could count on hearing some tit-bits of gossip from her before going into the house.

As time passed, she was increasingly embittered by what she called Clotilde's desertion. She realized that there was now no hope of persuading her to steal the files. She had gone over to the enemy. She was not only reconciled to Pascal, but ever since she had nursed him back to health far more intimate with him and his work than before; she had been corrupted, so much so that she no longer went to church. For these reasons, she had reverted to her first idea of sending her away and asserting her influence over her son, when he was alone and at her mercy. As she had not been able to persuade Clotilde to go to her brother, she was now all in favour of marrying her off. She was impatient of the continual delays and would have liked to throw her into Doctor Ramond's arms, the very next day. And she had come, that afternoon feverishly determined to bring matters to a head.

"Good afternoon, Martine .. How is everybody here?"

The servant, on her knees, her hands covered in earth, raised her pale face, which was protected from the sun by a handkerchief knotted over her cap:

"As usual, madame, quite well."

And they chatted. Felicité confided in her, treated her as a devoted friend, part of the family, to whom she could speak freely. She started by asking her whether the doctor Ramond had been to see Clotilde that morning. He had, in fact, called but they had only talked about matters of general interest. Felicité was in despair, she had seen the doctor herself that morning and he had confessed to her that he was disappointed at not being given a definite answer. He was now anxious to force Clotilde to come to a final decision. The matter could not be left in suspense any longer, the young woman must be manoeuvred into committing herself.

"He is weak, too full of scruples," she cried. "This morning once again I told him that I was sure that he would not be firm, and that he would not force the issue .. But I shall take a hand in it, myself. We shall see if I don't succeed in making the little fool come to her senses."

Then, more calmly:

"My son has quite recovered, he no longer needs her."

Martine, who had resumed her planting, bent double, straightened herself up with a jerk:

"Yes, yes indeed, madame, I am sure that you are right!"

A little flame flickered in her faded eyes. She bitterly resented the fact that her master no longer relied upon her services, in fact, hardly allowed her to come near him. He had kept her at a distance throughout his illness, gradually dispensing with her services and finally barring his door to her. She was subconsciously aware of what was happening and was tortured by an instinctive jealousy:

"For sure, we don't need mademoiselle! .. I can manage without her."

Then she began to talk about her gardening, explained that she was able to find time to grow vegetables and save the wages of a man. The house was big, that was true; but if you were not afraid of work, it was surprising how much you could manage. And, if mademoiselle were to leave them, it would be one person the less to wait on. And her eyes glistened at the thought of the pleasant solitude, the happy, peaceful existence the two of them would lead, after mademoiselle had gone.

She lowered her voice:

"I shall be sorry, because monsieur will be broken-hearted. I should never have believed that I would welcome a separation .. Only, madame, I think like you do, that it would be better, because I am afraid that mademoiselle will end up by being spoiled here and that she will be another soul lost to God .. It is very sad. When I think of it, my heart swells so that I sometimes think it will burst!"

"Are they both upstairs?" asked Felicité. "I will go up and see them and you can count on me to see that Clotilde stops dithering."

An hour later, she came out again and found Martine still on her knees, about to finish the row of seedlings. Upstairs, as soon as she had told them that she had seen Doctor Ramond and found him impatient for an answer, she saw that Pascal agreed with her; his expression was serious and he nodded his head, as if to imply that he found such impatience natural. Clotilde herself, no longer smiling, had listened to her with deference. But she seemed surprised. Why were they pressing her for an answer? Uncle had decided that the marriage should take place in the second week of June, so she had two full months ahead of her. In the near future she would have a talk with Ramond. Marriage was such a serious matter that they might well allow her time for reflection. Why commit herself until the last moment? She spoke with an air of precocious wisdom and seemed to know her own mind. And Felicité had been forced to be content with the fact that both of them seemed determined that events should take their course in the most reasonable manner possible.

"To tell you the truth, I think that she has made up her mind to marry him. Pascal seems to have no objection and she merely seems anxious to consider every aspect of the matter, before committing herself for life .. I will let her think about it for another week."

Martine, squatting on her heels, stared steadily at the ground, her face veiled in shadows:

"Yes, yes," she murmured, "mademoiselle is very absent-minded these days .. She is always in some corner or other. When I speak to her, she does not answer. She is like a person who is sickening for something and has her eyes turned inwards .. Something is happening, she is not the same, not at all the same as she used to be.."

She picked up her dibble and planted another leek seedling, bent upon finishing yet another job; whilst old Madame Rougon went off, considerably easier in her mind. She was sure that Clotilde would marry ..

Pascal did seem to take Clotilde's marriage for granted. He had avoided mentioning it; if they alluded to it at all, in the course of conversation, they were quite calm about it; they acted as if the two more months of living together were endless, an eternity. Clotilde, in particular, smiled at him and refused to worry about the future. With a pretty, vague gesture she waved aside the unpleasant necessity of having to come to a decision and reverted to the real delights of the present. He was now completely recovered and was getting stronger every day. It was at night, when he was facing the solitude of his room after Clotilde had gone to bed, that he allowed himself to become a prey to gloomy thoughts. He felt cold and shivered when he remembered that a time was coming when he would be all alone. Was it because he was growing old that he shivered like that? It was a hideous prospect which filled him with dismay. It was then that he felt the old longing for a wife, for a child of his own; he felt that his life was empty, a sensation of indescribable anguish.

He had never lived! Some nights he even went so far as to curse science, which he accused of having deprived him of the best years of his manhood. He had allowed himself to be swallowed up by his work, which had consumed his brain, his heart and his muscles. And all this solitary, unremitting labour had produced was books, black marks on paper, which would be blown away by the wind. The pages felt icy cold when he touched them. And no living breast to press against his own, no silky child's hair to kiss! He had lived alone in the cold and bloodless fastnesses of science, selfish and alone, and he would die alone. Was it really true, was that to be his fate? Would he die without experiencing the simple happiness of ordinary men, yes, even street-porters and the carters, whose whips cracked under his windows? He became frantic at the thought that he would have to hurry, it would soon be too late. All his youth wasted, he felt all his repressed desires reviving and sweeping through him in a tumultuous flood. He swore to himself that he would not let himself be extinguished without having loved. He was still vigorous enough to slake his unsatisfied passions, to allow them all to run riot, before he was too old. He would knock at doors, accost people in the street, scour the countryside and the town. Then, the next day, when he had splashed himself all over with cold water and was leaving his room, the fever left him, the voluptuous visions were obliterated and he became his usual timid self again. Then, the following night, his fear of loneliness prevented him from sleeping, fanned his smouldering discontent into a blaze and he fell victim to the same despair, the same rebellious thoughts, the same craving to fulfill his passion for women before he died. When he lay awake, his eyes wide-open in the darkness, he fell to dreaming and it was always the same dream. A young girl, a young peasant woman of twenty was passing by, surpassingly beautiful; she came and knelt down in front of him and looked up at him with submissive adoration and he married her. She was one of those pilgrims of love, so well described in ancient tales, who had followed a star, beckoning her to come and restore health and strength to an old king, very powerful and covered in glory. He, Pascal, was the old king and she adored him and made him the miraculous gift of her youth. Her embraces gave him back his courage and his faith in life. He owned a fifteenth-century Bible, illustrated by naive wood cuts. One of these had always fascinated him, the old king David going into his room, his hand on the bare shoulder of Abishag, the young Shunammite. He proceeded to read the text on the opposite page: "Now King David was old and stricken in years; and they covered him with clothes but he gat no heat. Wherefore his servants said unto him: Let there be sought, for my lord the king, a young virgin; and let her stand before the king and let her cherish him and let her lie in thy bosom, that my lord the king may get heat. So they sought for a fair damsel throughout all the coast of Israel and found Abishag, a Shunammite and brought her to the king. And the damsel was very fair and cherished the king and ministered to him .." Was it not the old king who shivered when his own body felt icy cold, in his lonely bed, under the dismal ceiling of his bedroom? And the peasant girl, the pilgrim of love who visited him in his dream, was it not Abishag, devoted and docile, the subject who passionately surrendered herself to her master, intent upon serving him? He could still see her, clearly, in front of his eyes. She was his slave, his creature, glorying in self-abnegation, attentive to his slightest whim, so dazzlingly beautiful that he was content to spend the rest of his life feasting his eyes on her, so gentle that, in her presence, he felt anointed with perfumed oils. He often leafed through the old Bible, looked at the other wood-cuts and allowed his imagination to stray in this vanished world of patriarchs and kings. What faith in the longevity of man, in his creative powers, in his sovereign lordship over his women; these extraordinary stories of centenarians still able to fertilize their wives, taking their servants into their beds as well or the young widows and even virgins met with in the streets! Then there was the story of Abraham, another centenarian, father of Ishmael and Isaac, his sister Sarah's husband, the master of her servant Agar, who obeyed him. Then, too, there was the delightful idyll of Ruth and Boaz; the young widow, arriving at Bethlehem, at the time of the barley harvest, prostrating herself at the feet of the master one warm night, demanding her rights. And he marries her, as his relative by marriage, according to the law. There was this astonishing, untrammelled growth of a strong and vital race, whose offspring were to conquer the world, these men with their inexhaustible virility, women for ever fertile, this obstinate continuity of proliferation, through crimes, adulteries, incest, and lust everlasting, throughout life and beyond reason. And, as he sat in front of these old and naive wood-cuts, his dream began to come to life. Abishag herself came into his room, dispelling its gloom with her radiance and filling it with the sweet scents of the East, opening her bare arms, her bare flanks, all her divine nudity, to bestow her resplendent youth upon him.

Ah! youth, this passionate hunger for youth, as his powers declined, was an expression of rebellion against the threat of old age, a desperate longing to be able to turn back, start again. This need for a renewal of opportunity did not only reflect his resentment at having missed the fulfilment of his own youth. There was an element of regret for his dead past. And, even more, there was a determination to enjoy his health and strength to the full, this time to drink the cup of loving to the dregs. Ah! youth, how he would have plunged his teeth into it, with what wild abandon he would have thrown himself into it, his appetite so voracious that he would have swallowed it all up, drunk it all down, before growing old. A pang of poignant nostalgia shot through him when he remembered himself as he had been at the age of twenty; thin and wiry, vigorous and healthy as a young oak, with dazzling white teeth and thick black hair. If only he could have the qualities of his youth back again, with what zest he would lavish them on living! And in the street the sight of young girls and young women brought sentimental tears to his eyes. It was often not the individual, not the concrete person who stirred his senses, it was his mental image of feminine youth in the abstract, evoked by a faint perfume, a radiant personality, limpid eyes, fresh young lips, above all a delicately modelled neck shadowed at the back by curls; and youth, in women, always appeared to him in the guise of a tall and supple figure, divinely slender. To him, youth became the symbol of everything that was good and desirable, the end and be all, the essence of perfect beauty, the only joy and, together with health, the only gift of inestimable value which nature could bestow on man. Ah! to be young again, to possess all womankind, young and palpitating, in one wild and passionate embrace!

Pascal and Clotilde, now that the fruit trees were flowering in the warm April sun, had resumed their morning walks through the grounds of the Souleiade. These were his first attempts at walking again since his illness. She supported him and led him to the yard, with its pebbles which were already almost too hot to touch, then up to the pine trees and back to the terrace, across the long shadows of the two ancient cypress trees. The sun was baking the old paving stones and the immense horizon spread out, endlessly, under the scintillating sky.

One morning, Clotilde had been running and came back to the

house unusually animated, brimful of laughter, so exhilarated that she ran up the stairs to the study without taking off her hat or the filmy square of lace which she had knotted around her neck.

"Ah!" she said, "I'm too hot! .. How silly of me not to have taken my things off downstairs! I will take them down later."

She had thrown the lace on a chair. Her hands were fumbling, impatiently with the ribbons of her large straw hat, knotted under her chin.

"There! Now I have tightened the knot. I shall never be able to undo it, you will have to help me."

Pascal, who had also been stimulated by the outing, was delighted to see her flushed and happy. He went over to her and she bent her head back. They were very close, almost touching each other.

"Raise your chin .. Oh! you keep moving, how do you expect me to manage?"

She burst out laughing irrepressibly, he could see her throat swell with the sound. His fingers, involuntarily, touched the satin-smooth skin just under her chin. She was wearing a dress which was cut very low. She was still a little out of breath, her breasts were moving in time with her respiration, her skin was still hot from the sun and moist with perspiration. The sight and scent of her maddened his senses. Suddenly he felt giddy and faint:

"No, no! I cannot do it, if you will not keep still!"

His blood was beating in his temples, his fingers were fumbling helplessly. She arched her body still further backwards, as if offering herself, unconsciously, tempting him. She was like a flower unfolding in front of his eyes. He had never seen her so alive, so young, so beautiful!

"There, at last!" she cried.

He had managed to undo the knot, heaven knows how. His fingers were trembling, the walls seemed to be revolving. She was shaking her head with its rippling golden hair and her face was a blur! He suddenly became afraid of losing control of himself, giving way to a wild impulse to crush her in his arms and press his lips to that adorable neck. He rushed out of the room, her hat still in his hand, stammering:

"I will hang it up in the hall .. Wait for me, I must speak to Martine."

Downstairs, he locked himself into the abandoned drawing-room, terrified that she might become uneasy about him and come downstairs to look for him. He was distracted and haggard, as if he had just committed a crime. He found himself crying aloud: "I have always loved her, wanted her desperately!" Yes, ever since she had grown up, he had worshipped her. Why delude himself? She was a woman now, no sexless hoyden. She was infinitely desirable.

Then Pascal burst into tears, sitting with his head between his hands, as if to keep out the light. Dear God, what was to become of him? A little girl, entrusted to him by his brother, whom he had always treated like a daughter and who was, to-day, this temptress of twenty-five, the embodiment of all that was desirable! He felt as weak and helpless as a child.

And, over and above his physical hunger for her, he loved her with an immense tenderness, he loved her spirit and her brain, her integrity, her courage and determination. The cruel conflict which had recently made them hostile to each other, his impatience with her persistence in brooding about the mystery, had made her even more dear to him, had made him realize that she was a different kind of human being, more spiritual, perhaps better than he was. He admired her when she rebelled against him and defied him. She was his companion and his pupil. He saw her as he had helped to make her, with her great heart, her passionate frankness, her subtle and enquiring mind. She had become as necessary to him as the air he breathed. It was essential for his peace of mind to have her near him, hear the rustling of her skirts, feel enveloped by her thoughts and her affection, her smile, to know that she was somewhere in the house, busy with some task which was part of the daily ritual of their lives together. She could not be so cruel as to take all this away from him! At the thought that she was going to leave him, he felt as if the sky were collapsing about his ears. It would be the end of everything, like being swallowed up in the utter blackness of night. Why then, seeing that he worshipped her and that he was her master, did he not go back upstairs and take her in his arms? They were both free agents, she was no longer an ignorant child. It was time for her to become a woman in the full sense of the word. It would mean happiness for both of them.

Pascal, who was no longer weeping, rose to his feet with an effort and tried to walk towards the door. But, he fell back on the chair, his body wracked by great shuddering sobs. No, no! it was abominable, impossible! He put his hand to his head, brushed his hair back and remembered that his hair was white; he was horrified at the realization of his age, fifty-nine, as compared with twenty-five!

He felt utterly dismayed, she had taken possession of his senses and his mind. Would he have the strength to resist temptation day after day? He visualized her, asking him, once again, to undo the knot in her hat-ribbon, calling to him, making him bend over her, or behind her, to correct some mistake in a manuscript; and he saw himself, blinded, uncontrollably infatuated, devouring her neck with his kisses. Or, worse still, some evening, when they were both reluctant to have the lamps brought in, languid but throbbingly aware of each other as the wings of night slowly closed about them, suddenly falling into each other's arms, and then the melting fusion, exquisite but irreparable. He became savagely angry with himself and determined to make this inevitable consummation impossible by an immediate separation. It would be a crime on his part, a betrayal, a base seduction. His revulsion had been such that, this time, he had no difficulty in getting up and he went upstairs, resolutely determined to put an end to an impossible situation.

Clotilde had quietly resumed her drawing. She did not even turn her head, but merely remarked:

"You have been a long time! I began to think that you must have found a mistake of at least five pence in Martine's accounts."

This familiar joke about the servant's avarice made him laugh. He sat down calmly at his table. They worked, in a companionable silence, until lunchtime. He felt soothed and tranquillized by her very presence. He stole a glance at her and was moved almost to tears by seeing her frown of concentration, just like a big girl at her lessons. Had he been in the grip of a nightmare, down below? Was it going to be easy, after all?

When Martine called them, he cried out: "I am as hungry as an ogre! you will soon be able to see my muscles bulging through my clothes!"

Gaily he took her arm and walked towards the door.

"That's right, Uncle! I want you to be cheerful and strong!" But that night, in his room, he relapsed into despair. At the idea of losing her he had been forced to bury his face in the pillow to smother his cries. He visualized her in another man's arms, giving herself to Ramond and he was tortured by atrocious pangs of jealousy. He would never consent to such a sacrifice. He conceived one plan after another in his poor head, which felt on fire; put a stop to the marriage, keep her near him, making sure that she would never suspect his guilty passion, go away with her, travel from city to city, keep her and himself engrossed in study, an endless series of projects, so as to make sure that their old footing of comradeship, as master and pupil, would be maintained; or even, if it became essential, send her to her brother, rather than hand her over to a husband. And, as each plan passed through his head, he felt an agonizing sense of loss. He could not bear the thought of sharing her with anyone! He was no longer content with her mere presence. He wanted to monopolize her, to feel that she was his alone, part of himself, he wanted the whole of her, he could see her white body, naked, gleaming in his dark room, pure and indescribably lovely, with nothing but her hair, her glorious hair, falling down over her perfect shoulders. He held out his arms and grasped nothing but the empty air, he jumped out of bed and staggered, like a drunken man; it was only in the darkness of the quiet study, his feet bare on the parquet floor, that he recovered from this sudden fit of madness, as if waking out of a nightmare. Where had he been going? To knock at the door of this sleeping child? break it down, perhaps, with his shoulder? He thought he could hear her gentle breathing, which swept through him like a sacred wind. He went back to his room and fell on his bed, overwhelmed with shame and agonizing despair.

Next day, when he got up, Pascal, exhausted by a sleepless night, was sure of himself. He took his usual shower and felt refreshed and clearer in his mind. He had come to a decision. He would force Clotilde to commit herself. When she had formally promised to marry Ramond, his problem would be solved finally, irrevocably, it would be almost a relief to him. It would erect an insurmountable barrier between her and himself. Henceforth, he would be armoured against his own passion. It would mean suffering the tortures of the damned, but even that was better than the horrible fear of behaving like a brute and a monster, getting up again one night and taking her, before the other man.

Later on that morning, when he pointed out that it was unfair to keep Ramond waiting any longer, that it was her duty to give him a definite answer without any further delay, she seemed, at first, to be astonished. She looked him straight in the eye; and he had sufficient command of himself not to betray his feelings. He even managed to look as if he was bored at having to repeat what should have been obvious to her. In the end, she gave him a wan smile and turned her head away:

"So, uncle, you actually want me to leave you?"

His answer was an indirect one:

"I assure you, my dear, it is ridiculous to go on like this. Ramond would have every right to be angry with you."

She went over to her desk and started putting some papers in order. Then, after a silence:

"I cannot understand it. You, of all people, talking like grandmother and Martine. They have been nagging me, urging me to decide .. I thought that I had a few days more. But, really, if all three of you are pressing me .."

She broke off and he did not insist upon her continuing:

"Well," he asked, "when do you want me to tell Ramond to come?"

"He can come whenever he likes, I have never objected to his coming to see me .. Don't worry, I will send him a message, to say that we shall be expecting him, one of these days."

Two days later, there was another scene. Clotilde had done nothing and Pascal, this time, was violently angry. He was on edge. He was bitingly emphatic, he demanded, ordered her to stop behaving irresponsibly and to stop trifling with an honourable man who was in love with her.

"The devil take it! As the matter must be settled, let us settle it! I warn you that I shall write to Ramond and he will be here to-morrow at three o'clock."

She had listened to him in silence without raising her eyes. Neither of them seemed willing to broach the subject as to whether the marriage was really to take place; they seemed to take it for granted that some kind of decision had already been arrived at. When he saw her raise her head, he trembled, he felt, all of a sudden, that he could see into her mind that she was on the point of telling him that she could not bring herself to leave him and that she was going to refuse Ramond's offer. What would he do? He was both immensely relieved and, at the same time, terrified. But she was looking at him, smiling her discreet and affectionate smile, and answered, as if anxious to obey him:

"As you wish, uncle. Tell him to come to-morrow, at three o'clock."

Pascal spent such an abominable night that he stayed in bed late, on the pretext that he had had another bad attack of his blinding headaches. The icy water of the shower revived him to some extent. Then, at about ten o'clock, he went out. He told Clotilde that he was going to give Ramond the message in person. But, he had no such intention. He had seen a shawl of French point lace in the window of a Plassans shop, an exceptionally fine and costly piece of work, which had been lying in the window for a very long time, waiting to be bought by some wealthy and generous lover; it had occurred to him during the night, as he was tossing in agony, that it would make a perfect wedding present for Clotilde, who could use it as part of her wedding dress. In his state of self-sacrificial exaltation he felt inspired by the idea of making her even more beautiful for another man's enjoyment. She had seen the shawl and been enraptured by it, one day when they had been out walking together. She had coveted it, not for herself, but to be able to take it to Saint-Saturnin and drape it over the shoulders of the Virgin, a very old wooden Virgin, worshipped with particular fervour by the faithful. He had asked them to pack the shawl in a small cardboard box, which he had carried home in his pocket and then concealed at the back of his desk.

At three o'clock, Doctor Ramon duly presented himself. Pascal and Clotilde were waiting for him in the study, in a state of repressed nervous agitation and welcomed him with exaggerated cordiality.

"But you are a new man, sir!" said the young man. "I have never seen you looking so well."

Pascal shook his head:

"Oh! oh! physically, perhaps! but, the mainspring is broken."

This spontaneous and involuntary confession startled Clotilde. She stared at him and then at Doctor Ramond. She felt compelled to compare them. Ramond looked what he was; the successful physician, idolized by his patients, especially the women, handsome and smiling, with his fine head of black hair and immaculately groomed beard, young, resplendent with vitality and self-confidence. And Pascal, his face, under the thick white hair, like a snow-white fleece, was like a beautiful tragic mask, as the result of these last six months of mental torture. His features were drawn and he looked older. Only the eyes were as before, wide-open brown eyes, clear and limpid as those of a boy. But, at that moment, he seemed to radiate a sort of noble selflessness, his expression was so infinitely gentle and kind that she felt irresistibly drawn towards him. There was a short expectant silence.

"Well! my children," continued Pascal heroically, "you must want to have a talk .. There is something I have to attend to, downstairs, I will come back later."

He left them, with a smile.

139

No sooner alone with him than Clotilde turned towards Ramond, took his hands in hers and held them as she spoke:

"Listen, my friend, I am going to make you unhappy .. I hope that you will not be angry with me. I swear to you that I have a profound respect for your great qualities and a deep affection for you."

He blanched and hastened to say:

"Clotilde, I beg of you, do not answer me now, take your time, you may not know your own mind yet."

"Useless, my friend, my decision is final."

She looked at him with gentle and affectionate compassion. She had not released his hands, she wanted him to feel that they were not feverish and that she was calm and determined. It was Ramond who continued, in a low voice:

"So, it is 'no'?"

"I am afraid so and I assure you that it grieves me deeply to have to say it. Please, do not ask me to give my reasons, you will understand in due course."

He sat down, he could not take such a blow, the most crushing in his life, standing up. But his strength of character and natural poise were such that he was able to repress his feelings. But he was speechless and Clotilde, who was standing over him, continued:

"Above all, my friend, do not think that I have been trifling with you .. The reason that I allowed you to go on hoping and made you wait so long for my answer, was, genuinely, because I had not made up my own mind .. You have no idea of the excruciating nature of the ordeal through which I have been passing. I feel as if I had been swept by a hurricane in the middle of the night and I am only just beginning to feel my way back to solid ground."

He had now found his tongue:

"As it is your wish that I should not ask for any explanation, I shall only ask one question. You do not love me?"

Clotilde answered without a moment's hesitation, with such an obvious desire to avoid hurting his feelings that he could not resent her frankness:

"No, I do not love you, my feelings towards you are those of a sincere and affectionate friend."

He stood up and put out his hand to stop her trying to soften the blow with more pretty speeches:

"Please do not say anything else. The subject is closed, we must never refer to it again. I wanted you to be happy. Do not worry about me. Just at present I feel like a man who has been hit on the head with a sledgehammer but I have no doubt that I shall survive it."

His face, which had been so white, became suffused with blood, he seemed to be choking, he went to the open window, took several deep breaths, turned around, walked back towards her, almost staggering, but gradually regained control of himself. He was still breathing heavily. Through the painful silence they heard Pascal walking upstairs. He was making as much noise as possible, anxious not to take them unawares.

"Please," murmured Clotilde hastily, "don't say anything to uncle. He does not know what I have decided, I want to tell him myself, tactfully. He wanted me to say 'yes'."

Pascal stopped in the doorway. He was swaying, out of breath, as if he had been running up the stairs. He managed a wan smile:

"Well! children, have you settled your little problem?"

"Yes—yes, of course," answered Ramond, no less agitated than Pascal.

"That's a good thing. Quite settled, I hope?"

"Completely," answered Clotilde, who, suddenly, felt as if she was about to faint.

Pascal dragged himself towards his table, holding on to the furniture and let himself drop into his chair:

"Dear me! you see, my legs are not any too strong yet. That old carcass of mine! .. Never mind! I am very pleased, delighted, my children, your happiness will hasten my recovery."

Then, after a few more minutes of casual conversation, Ramond left. Pascal, alone with the young woman, became agitated again:

"Is it settled, really settled, do you swear it?"

"Absolutely settled."

He made no further comment, he nodded his head, as if to imply that he was delighted, that nothing could be more perfect, that life would be tolerable again. His eyes were closed, as if asleep. But his heart was pounding and tears were gathering beneath his obstinately closed eyelids.

That night, at about ten o'clock, Clotilde had gone downstairs to give Martine some instructions. Pascal took the opportunity of slipping into her room and putting his little parcel on the bed.

On her way back to her room, she said good-night to Pascal, as usual; he had been in his bedroom for twenty minutes and was in his shirtsleeves when he heard her laughing and shouting outside his door. She was hammering it with her little fist and crying:

"Come out, come and see!"

She sounded so happy and light-hearted, that he could not help responding to her mood and felt almost cheerful himself.

"Oh! come along, come and see what the bluebird has dropped on my bed!"

She pulled him along into her room, still laughing and chattering. She had lit both her candles; the old room, with its soft faded pink hangings, seemed transformed into a chapel; and, on the bed, like a sacred vestment displayed before a worshipping congregation, she had spread out the little French point lace shawl.

"You have no idea! .. Just imagine, I did not look at the bed, at first, so I did not see the parcel. I brushed my hair and did all the things I usually do, then I undressed and it was only when I was about to get into bed that I saw your present .. Ah! What a surprise, I was dumbfounded! I felt I just could not wait until tomorrow, so I slipped on my petticoat and ran to fetch you .."

Then he noticed that she was half-naked; exactly the same as on that unforgettable, stormy night, when he had surprised her in the act of stealing his files. She looked like a young goddess, like Diana, with her lovely slender, virginal body.

She had grasped his hands and was pressing them in a spontaneous access of warm affection:

"How thoughtful of you, how kind, thank you a thousand times! And what a present, much too magnificent for an insignificant little person like me! .. Fancy your remembering; I admired it as an antique, a priceless work of art, I told you that only the Virgin of Saint-Saturnin could be worthy of wearing it on her shoulders .. I am so pleased, oh! so pleased! You know, that is one of my faults, I am really a coquette. I am incorrigibly vain. I sometimes have a mad longing for dresses made of impossibly filmy materials, impalpable veils made of bits of the blue sky .. How beautiful I shall look in that lace! How beautiful!"

She was radiant, she felt so grateful to him that she was pressing herself against him, gazing, all the time, at the shawl, inviting him to admire it with her. Then, a sudden thought struck her:

"But, it never occurred to me, why—what made you give me such a sumptuous present?"

Ever since she had hurled herself at his door, like a merry madcap, Pascal had felt as if he was living a dream. He was moved to tears by her transports of gratitude. He felt as if relieved of a great weight of anguish, soothed, exalted, as if he were poised on the threshold of some great and wonderful adventure. This room, which he never entered, was like a holy shrine in which mankind could slake its unquenchable thirst for the impossible.

He looked surprised, however, and answered:

"The present, my dear, why, it is for your wedding dress, of course."

She looked equally surprised and seemed, for a moment, unable to grasp his meaning. Then, with the gentle and enigmatic smile, which had so often been on her face during the last few days, in a fresh outburst of merriment:

"Of course, my wedding!"

Then, composing her features with an effort, she asked in a serious tone of voice:

"Then, you are determined to get rid of me, that is why you were so anxious to marry me off .. Do you still think of me as an enemy?"

A black flood of depression surged over him again, he dared not look at her. He made another heroic effort:

"Yes, do you deny it? We have made each other so intolerably unhappy these last few months! A separation, perhaps, is the only solution .. Besides, I still do not know what you have been thinking, you have never answered the question I put to you some time ago. I have been expecting an answer."

She tried, unsuccessfully, to make him look at her. She began talking about that terrible night, when they had gone through the files together. It was true, she had been so profoundly shaken that she had not yet told him whether she was for or against him. He was right to demand an answer.

She grasped his hands again and forced him to look at her:

"And is it because I am your enemy that you are sending me away? .. Listen to me! I am not your enemy, I am your servant, I am what you have made me and I am your property, to dispose of as you wish .. Do you hear? I am with you and for you, entirely yours and only yours!"

His eyes were flaming with unspeakable relief and joy.

"I will wear that lace, oh yes! I will wear it on my wedding night, because I want to be beautiful, very beautiful, for you .. Don't you understand? You are my master, it is you that I love with all my heart .."

Distracted, he tried to put his hand over her mouth, but she pulled her head away and cried:

"And I want you, want you desperately!"

"No, no! Stop talking like that, you will send me off my head! . . You are engaged to another man. You have pledged your word. Fortunately for you all this extravagant nonsense can lead to nothing."

"The other man! I compared him with you and I made my choice. I chose you . . I sent him away, he has gone out of my life and he is never coming back . . You and I are together now. I love you and you love me, I have known it for a long time, I am all yours . ."

He was trembling all over, there was no fight left in him, he was carried away by his eternal longing to clasp her madly in his arms, to lose himself in the softness of her, to inhale the ineffable scent of her, the perfume of the flower of her womanhood unfolding in the warmth of his love.

"Take me then, can't you see and feel that I want you!"

It was no downfall, they were uplifted by the glory of living. They took each other in a mad whirl of happiness. The warm room, with its antique furniture, seemed to be encouraging them and to be filled with light. There was no more fear, no suffering, no scruples; she gave herself, knowingly, willingly, and he accepted the sovereign gift of her body, as a priceless possession, conferred on him or rather wrested from life by the irresistible power of love. Place, time, the ages, no longer existed for them. All that remained was immortal nature, passion which possesses and creates, happiness clamouring to be fulfilled. She, in a daze of delight, surrendered herself to him in silence, except for a soft faint cry as her virginity left her; and he, with a sob of rapture, was crushing her, enveloping her, straining to make her understand his immeasurable gratitude to her for restoring his manhood.

Pascal and Clotilde were in each other's arms, drowned in ecstasy, divinely happy and triumphant. The night air was soft and sweet-smelling. The silence enfolded them like a soft warm cloak. So steeped in the joy of each other were they that the hours flowed by unnoticed. She had been murmuring words of endearment into his ear, in a caressing voice, a long, endless murmur of words:

"Master, O my master, my master . ."

And this word, which she had so often used in the past, sounded very different now, taking on a more profound, wider and more permanent significance, as if it expressed an ungrudging and complete surrender of herself. She repeated it in a fervour of thankfulness, like a woman who understands her mission and yields herself freely. Was she not proclaiming that mysticism had been vanquished, that reality had triumphed, life had been glorified, now that love had, at last, been revealed to her and satisfied?

"Master, my own master, I am thinking of the past. I feel that I must tell you, confess myself to you .. It is true that I went to church in search of happiness; I was determined to understand, too much perhaps! Their dogmas revolted my reason, their paradise seemed to me incredibly puerile .. Nevertheless, I believed that the world we can see and touch and hear and taste is not the only world, that there is an unknown world, infinitely greater, which should be taken into account; it is the idea of the beyond; and that is still my belief which is not shaken, even by the happiness I have found in the shelter of your arms .. But, how I suffered from that craving for happiness, immediate happiness, for reassurance! I went to church because I felt that something was missing and I could not help going on searching for it. It was agonizing to think that I should never be able to satisfy that irresistible longing .. You remember what you called my eternal thirst for illusion and lies. One night, in the yard, under that great star-studded sky, do you remember? I was horrified by your science, I was exasperated by its devastating consequences, I wanted to turn away from the dreadful wounds and sores it has uncovered. And I wanted, my master, to take you away with me into a solitary place, far from the world, where we could be alone together and live in God .. Ah! what torture, to be thirsty, and to struggle and not to be satisfied!"

Very gently, without a word, he kissed her eyes, one after the other.

"Then, my master, you remember," she continued in a voice light as a sigh, "you caused a great mental and spiritual upheaval inside me, that night of the storm, when you taught me that terrible lesson about life, when you emptied the files in front of me. I remember your words: 'Learn to understand life, love it, live it as it should be lived.' But what a frightful and overwhelming flood, rushing inexorably towards a human sea, which goes on increasing in volume, all for some unknown future! .. And you see, my master, that was the beginning of an insensible change, a sort of spiritual germination inside me. From that the bitter knowledge of reality was born inside my heart and my flesh. At first, I felt annihilated.

The blow was so shattering. I could not find myself. I said nothing because I had nothing definite to say to you, as yet. Later, little by little, I experienced a process of evolution, I had a few last flickers of revolt, because I did not want to admit that you had defeated me .. But every day, I became more conscious of the truth. I realized that you were my master, that my only hope of happiness was in you, in your science, in you as a great and good man. You were life itself, tolerant and wise, concealing nothing, accepting everything, in your single-minded passion to promote health, your belief in endeavour unremitting, for its own sake, and in the work of the world, giving a meaning and purpose to our ceaseless and passionate labour, urging us on to live, to love, to remake life, and yet more life, in spite of our abominations and our miseries .. Oh! to live, live, that is the great thing, to go on accomplishing more and more, until some evening, perhaps, all life ends, for ever!"

Still silent, he smiled and kissed her on the mouth.

"And, my master, although I have always loved you, for as long as I can remember, it was on that terrible night that you finally stamped me with your convictions, your own brand and made me all yours .. You remember when you laid violent hands on me and nearly choked me. I had blood on my shoulder. I was half-naked, I felt as if your body had penetrated mine. We fought, you proved the stronger and, ever since, I have felt the need of your support. At first, I felt humiliated; then, I realized that it was only a form of submission, infinitely gratifying .. I was never without that peculiar sensation of you inside me. When you lifted your hand, even at a distance, I trembled, because it seemed to be touching my skin. I wanted your arms around me again, I wanted you to go on crushing me until the whole of me melted into you for ever. And I had a sort of sixth sense, I knew that you felt the same towards me, that the violence which made me yours had also made you mine. I knew that you were continually struggling not to lose control, that you wanted to pounce on me, whenever you passed near me, to hold me and keep me .. When you were very ill, the very act of looking after you soothed me to some extent. It was then that I understood, all in a flash. From that time onwards, I stopped going to church. I began to feel happy whenever I was near you, you were my sign and my certainty .. Remember, I cried out to you in the yard that something was missing in our tender affection for each other. It was empty and I wanted to fill it. What could be missing, if not God, the motive power of the world? And, in fact, it was

146

something divine, complete possession, the act of love and life."

Her voice faded into an indistinct murmur. He laughed exultantly; they took each other again. The whole night was a miracle of beatitude, in that happy room, redolent of youth and passion. When the first faint flush of dawn began to light the sky, they opened the windows wide to let in the spring. The fertilizing April sun rose slowly in the immensity of the heavens, in a cloudless sky and the earth, aquiver with germinating life beneath it, celebrated their wedding.

CHAPTER EIGHT

THEN followed the blissful possession, the happy idyll. Clotilde was Pascal's belated second spring, a tardy renewal in the declining years of his life. She brought him the sun and flowers, her wedding gown overflowing with them; and she bestowed this precious gift of second youth upon him after thirty years of unremitting toil, when his energy was flagging and his face had grown pale at the sights revealed by probing the hideous depths of human depravity. Her clear eyes watched and her pure breath was wafted over his rebirth. He had regained his faith in life, in health, in strength and in the eternal beginning again.

That first morning, after their wedding night, Clotilde was up and dressed before Pascal, though it was nearly ten o'clock. When she opened the door of the study she saw Martine standing there, stock still, gaping at her. The night before the doctor had left his door open when he had followed the young woman to her room; and, the next morning the servant had walked in through the open door and found that the bed had not been slept in. Then she had heard voices coming from the other room. She was still so stupefied that she looked ludicrous.

And Clotilde, highly amused, but bursting with happiness to such an extent that she felt impelled to share it, ran towards her crying:

"Martine, I am not going away after all! .. The master and I have been married."

The news was a staggering blow to the old servant. A horrible expression of distress and disgust contorted her features, so pale and worn with toil and nun-like resignation. Not a word came from her lips, she turned, went downstairs to the kitchen and collapsed on a chair, her elbows on the chopping board, her face between her hands and her body shaken with sobs.

Clotilde, disconcerted and worried, followed her downstairs. She tried to understand what thoughts were passing through her muddled old mind and tried to console her:

"Come, you are being stupid! What has come over you? The master and I will love you just the same as before, we want you to stay with us for as long as you like, for always .. Our being married will not make you unhappy. Quite the opposite, because now the master will be light-hearted and cheerful, from morning to night."

But Martine was sobbing more violently, desperately.

"Answer me, at any rate. Tell me why you are upset and why you are crying .. Aren't you pleased to know that the master is happy, so happy! .. I shall call him, because I know that he can force you to answer."

At this threat the old servant jumped up and ran into her room, which opened out of the kitchen; and she slammed the door shut behind her and proceeded to lock it, angrily and noisily. For a long time the young woman went on calling to her and knocking, without the slightest result.

In the end, Pascal came down, to find out what all the noise was about: "Well! What is the matter?"

"It is that obstinate old mule of a Martine! Think of it, she started sobbing when I told her about our happiness. And now, she has barricaded herself inside her room and won't budge."

There was no appealing to her. Pascal called and knocked, in his turn. He raged at her and then he wheedled. They went on trying, turn and turn about. No answer, nothing but a deathly silence in that little room. They could visualize it, kept maniacally clean, with its walnut chest-of-drawers and its monastic bed hung with white curtains. It was on this bed, no doubt, in which the servant had slept throughout her long old maid's life, that she had thrown herself and was biting the bolster to stifle her sobs.

"It can't be helped," said Clotilde, finally, in the egoism of her own elation, "let her sulk!"

Then, putting her own cool palm on Pascal's hand, lifting her adorable head towards him, still burning with the urge to blot herself out against him, to be his creature:

"You know, master mine, what I am going to do to-day, you are going to have me as your servant."

Thrilling to her enthusiasm, he kissed her eyes; and she started at once preparing the lunch, turning the kitchen upside down. She had draped an enormous white apron around her and looked enchanting, sleeves rolled up, showing her delicate forearms, as if she were about to undertake some task involving enormous physical strength. Fortunately, the cutlets were already on the table and she cooked them to a turn. She then proceeded to scramble some eggs and even managed to fry some potatoes, very nicely, all crisp and golden brown. And it was a delightful meal, interrupted twenty times by her eagerness to please, her insistence on running to fetch bread, water, a fork. To please him, she would have knelt at his feet. Ah! to be alone, just the two of them, in the shelter of this great house which seemed to have some share in the warmth of their love for each other, to feel far away from the world, to be free to laugh and make love in peace!

All afternoon they lingered over the housework, swept and made the beds. He had insisted upon helping her. It was a game, they joked and laughed, for no reason, like children playing on the beach. But, from time to time, they went back and knocked on Martine's door. Come! it was sheer madness, was she going to starve herself? What a stubborn mule, when nobody had done anything or said anything to her! But, every time, their blows echoed through the gloomy emptiness of the room. Night fell, they had to cook the dinner, to eat it from the same plate, squeezed up against each other. Before going to bed, they made a last effort, threatened to break down the door; they glued their ears to the door, but not a sound, not even a quiver. And, next day, when they came downstairs, they became seriously worried, when they found that nothing had been moved and that the door remained hermetically shut. The servant had given no sign of life for twenty-four hours.

Then, after going upstairs for a short while, they were astounded, when they came back to the kitchen, to see Martine sitting at the table peeling some sorrel for their lunch. She had quietly gone back to her work.

"But, what was the matter with you?" cried Clotilde. "Will you talk to us, now?"

Martine lifted her sad face, ravaged by tears. But her features had resumed their usual expression of dull, apathetic resignation. She gave the young woman a look of infinite reproachfulness from her mournful eyes; then she lowered her head again, without uttering a word.

"Is it because you have some grievance against us?"

Still no answer, and Pascal intervened:

"Are you vexed with us, Martine?"

Then the old servant looked up at him with her old expression of dumb worship, as if she loved him enough to put up with everything and still go on working for him. At last she spoke:

"No, I have no grievance, I am not vexed with anybody .. The master is free to do as he wishes. It is all right as long as he is pleased."

Thus, the new life was established. Clotilde, for all her twenty-five years, had been a child and was now developing and expanding, like a flower in the warmth of love, which had transformed her from a boy with round head and short curly hair into a woman, supremely feminine, whose sole ambition was to be loved. Her great charm, in spite of her book learning, had been an ingenuous simplicity as if, unknowingly, she had been keeping herself intact, mentally as well as physically, until she could surrender herself, completely, to the man she was to love. Ultimately she had done so, it is true, as much from gratitude and admiration as from love, primarily intent upon making him happy, rejoicing in the feeling of security he gave her when she was in his arms, in being his creature, worshipped by him, like a graven image, before which he prostrated himself in a state of semi-religious exaltation. Her own religious training predisposed her to a docile abandon of self to the master, mature in years and all-powerful, consoled and uplifted by his strength and, even in her physical relationship with him, experiencing a thrill of religious veneration, due to the associations of her devout past. But above all, this woman in love, so sensual, passionate to the point of almost swooning, had lost nothing of her super-abundant vitality, if anything it was enhanced; she was bursting with health and bubbling over with gaiety, her appetite was prodigious, she filled the house with her flying limbs, the radiance of her skin, the grace of her movements, there was something reminiscent of the gallantry of her grandfather, the soldier, in the way she flung her adorable young body into the fray of everyday life.

And Pascal too was transformed, outwardly as well as inwardly; there was a serene beauty about this man, with his crown of white hair, who seemed to be in the prime of life, with all its zest and vigour. His face was no longer covered with a tragic mask, as it had been after those terrible months of mental agony; with its fine features and the bright, childishly innocent eyes, it was the face of a kind, gentle and happy man, once more; even his white hair and beard had grown thicker, with leonine abundance, like a bright halo of snow which made him look younger. He had lived the life of a scholarly hermit for so long, with no vices, with no outlet for his passions, that his neglected virility, resuscitated, was clamouring for satisfaction at last. It was a reawakening. He was as impetuous as a young man, always on the move, breaking out into loud laughter, he had a craving for noise and constant activity, he felt an urge to use up every ounce of energy, to enjoy every minute of life. He seemed to see everything through different eyes, everything was new and enchanting; even the familiar view from the garden shimmered with magic, the sight and smell of a simple flower enraptured him, an ordinary term of endearment, hallowed by usage, moved him to tears, as though just invented for his benefit and not profaned by millions of indifferent mouths. Thus, "I love you" from Clotilde's lips was a password to magical realms of sensation, accessible to him alone. He had regained not only his health and his looks, but also his tranquil good humour, due, in the past, to his passion for life, and now enhanced by his passion for Clotilde, who had transformed his life.

The two of them, flowering youth and mature strength, both radiant with vitality, gaiety and happiness, made a magnificent couple. For a whole month, they shut themselves up in the Souleiade and did not once leave the grounds. At first Clotilde's bedroom was their whole world. They were enveloped in warm faded pink, those cotton-print hangings, so old and so soothing to the eyes and surrounded by the familiar empire furniture, the enormous rigid couch and the monumental cheval-glass. And they could not look at the clock, the gilded bronze milestone, against which Cupid leaned and smiled at slumbering Father Time, without laughing. Was it not singularly appropriate? They sometimes teased each other about it. All these inanimate objects were like old friends, who had watched other lovers in the past, with the same mute approval, forget themselves in each other. One evening, she maintained that she had seen a beautiful lady in the cheval-glass, undressing, certainly not herself; and, allowing her fantastic imagination to run away with her, she prophesied that, in a hundred years, she herself would be seen in the same mirror, by another woman as blissfully in love as herself. He was now so attached to this room, saturated in memories of Clotilde, that he had abandoned his own room, which now seemed to him gloomy, cold and soulless. On the rare occasions he visited it, he left it as quickly as possible, with a shiver of distaste. They were almost equally fond of the vast study, the scene of their labours in common and their past affectionate intimacy. They sat there for days on end, wrapped in contentment, not even working. The great oak cupboard slumbered with its doors closed, as did the bookcases. They allowed papers and books to pile up on the tables, untouched and unheeded. Like newlyweds, oblivious of their surroundings, they were so steeped in each other that they had forgotten their old habits. The hours were all too short to savour the charm of being physically close to each other, often sitting in the same big old armchair, under the fine old ceiling of this their retreat, dedicated solely to their enjoyment of each other, simple and unpretentious, cluttered with familiar objects and brightened, from morning to night, by the renascent warmth of the April sun. When, conscience-stricken, he spoke of his work, she twined her arms around him, held him to her with gentle force, laughed and scolded him; too much work would make him ill again! Next, in order of preference, was the dining room, so cheerful with its light panels, framed with thin blue lines, its furniture of old mahogany, the flower pastels and the brightly polished copper hanging-lamp. They devoured their meals with juvenile relish, lingered over them and tore themselves away from the table, only to return to their cherished and solitary retreat upstairs.

Then, when they began to feel themselves a little cramped in the house, their realm became the garden, the whole of the Souleiade. The spring vegetation climbed with the sun, at the end of April the early roses were in bloom. How they enjoyed wandering through the property, with its high walls, which protected them from the outside world! They spent long lazy afternoons on the terrace, facing the immense horizon, the tree-shaded course of the Viorne and the slopes of Sainte-Marthe, from the rocky barrier of the Seille to the dusty valley of Plassans in the distance. There, the only shade was that of the two towering age-old cypress trees, planted at either end, like two enormous dark-green tapers, visible three leagues away. Sometimes, hand in hand, they ran down the slope and climbed back up the giant steps, clambering over the low stone walls which shored up the earth, to see whether the stunted olive and the meagre almond trees were growing. But, more often, they strolled under the fine needles of the pine trees, drenched in sun, inhaling their resinous fragrance, or along the path which skirted the inside of the wall facing the narrow lane of the Fenouillères, which was usually deserted, except for an occasional farm-cart rumbling noisily by; or, they spent enchanting hours on their backs in the old yard, gazing at the limitless expanse of sky and remembering, with a tinge of melancholy, their tears under the stars. But they always finished up in their favourite spot under the plane trees, in the shade of their dense foliage, which was now a soft green. They wandered through the endless labyrinth of tall box and the

153

weed-grown flower borders of the former formal French garden
and the trickle of water from the fountain, that eternal pure and
crystalline vibration, seemed to be singing in their hearts. They
were wont to sit near the moss-grown basin, watching the twilight,
slowly drowning in the darkness of the trees, no longer able to see
the water, but listening to its sustained flute-like notes. This unbroken
seclusion of Pascal and Clotilde's lives was maintained until the
middle of May. Then, one morning, while she lingered in bed, he
disappeared and came back an hour later; he found her still in
bed, dishevelled, arms and shoulders bare, leaned over her and
slipped two diamond ear-rings through her ears. He had dashed
out to buy them, suddenly remembering that it was her birthday.
She loved jewellery and was surprised and delighted. She refused
to get up, she was so fascinated by the sight of the twin stars flashing
above her bare shoulders. Henceforth, not a week went by without
his escaping in the early morning, at least once or twice, and
bringing back a present. The slightest pretext sufficed, an anniver-
sary, a wish, simply to please her. He chose the days when she was
unusually lazy, always came back before she was up and the ritual
of adorning her with yet another precious stone was repeated. He
brought her, in succession, rings, bracelets, a necklace, a slender
diadem. Then, he pulled out all her jewellery and covered her with
it, with the zest of a child playing at dressing-up, amidst peals of
laughter. She was like an idol, sitting propped up against the
pillows, scintillating with gold, a gold band in her hair, gold on her
bare arms, gold on her wonderful bare neck, a dazzling display of
gold and precious stones. Her vanity was inordinately aroused by
this gorgeous ritual. She allowed him to worship her on his knees,
knowing that he was only expressing his love for her in a temporarily
exalted form. In time, however, she began to scold him, to remonstrate with him, it was becoming absurd, all these expensive presents,
which had to be kept locked in a drawer. She could never wear
them, as she never went out. She was grateful for an hour of intense
pleasure when they were new, but then they were hidden and
forgotten. But he would not listen to her, he was possessed by a real
mania for extravagant gifts and he could not resist buying any
piece of jewellery which caught his fancy. It was an expansive
gesture straight from the heart, an imperious desire to prove to her
that he was always thinking about her, pride, which made him
want to see her the most magnificent, the happiest, the most envied
of women, an even deeper sentiment, which drove him to beggar

himself, to keep nothing, to squander his money, his very flesh, his life and put them at her feet. And, what a thrill of pure joy, when she was more than usually pleased and moved, when she flushed, threw her arms around him and showered him with grateful kisses! Then, after the jewels, there were dresses, silks and satins, toilet accessories. The room became cluttered with them, the drawers were full.

One morning, she was really angry. He had brought another ring:

"But I never wear them! And, look! If I were to wear them all, I should be covered in them, to the finger-tips .. Please, be sensible."

He hung his head:

"Have I not succeeded, then, in giving you pleasure?"

She ended by taking him in her arms and swearing with tears in her eyes that she was the happiest woman in the world. He was so kind, he was so anxious to please! And when, that same morning, he ventured to talk about redecorating the room, new hangings for the walls, a big carpet, she protested violently:

"No, please! .. Don't touch my dear old room, so full of memories, where I grew up and which has been our bridal chamber. If you changed it, I should never feel at home in it again."

In the house, Martine's obstinate silence implied a mute condemnation of all this exaggerated and useless expenditure. Her manner was now less familiar, as if she were no longer the housekeeper, a sort of friend, but relegated to the rank of a servant. She had changed towards Clotilde in particular. She treated her as a young lady, a mistress, to be obeyed rather than loved. When she came into their bedroom to serve their breakfast, her expression was one of submissive resignation, still worshipping her master and indifferent to everything else. On two or three occasions she appeared in the morning, her face ravaged, her eyes reddened with tears, unwilling to give a direct answer to their questions, saying that it was nothing, that she had caught a chill. She never once alluded to the presents, overflowing from the drawers, she seemed not to see them, she dusted them, tidied them, without a word of admiration or reproach. But, she was profoundly shocked by his extravagant folly, so alien to her own instincts. Her protest took the form of becoming even more economical, cutting down on the household expenditure to a ludicrous extent. Thus, she bought a third less milk, never served a dessert except on Sunday. Pascal and Clotilde, without venturing to complain, laughed at her miserliness behind her back, revived the jokes which had amused them for the last ten years, one of them being that, when she buttered the vegetables, she used the cullender, so that she could recover the melted butter.

On quarter day, she insisted upon presenting her accounts. Usually she fetched the quarterly income of fifteen hundred francs from the notary, M. Grandguillot, and spent it as she pleased, jotting down her expenditure in a notebook, which the doctor had refused to look at for more years than he could remember. This time, she made a point of asking him to check the items. He protested and said that he was sure that it was all right.

"But, monsieur," she said, "this time I have been able to save a little money. Yes, three hundred francs . . Here they are."

He looked at her in amazement. In the past she had just been able to make both ends meet. By what miracle of cheeseparing had she been able to save all that money? In the end, he laughed and teased her:

"Ah! my poor Martine, is that why we have eaten so many potatoes? We know that you are a pearl of economy, but I should really prefer you to spoil us a bit more."

This discreet reproach wounded her so deeply that she could not help reciprocating:

"Heavens, monsieur, as you are throwing so much money out of the window, somebody has to be careful."

"Oh, so you are starting to keep an eye on my accounts, are you? But, let me tell you, Martine, that I, too, have savings, which have been sleeping in my drawer!"

He was referring to the fees which his patients sometimes still forced on him, which he threw at the back of one of the drawers of his desk. In this way for more than sixteen years he had been putting roughly four thousand francs a year into the drawer, which should have made a tidy sum, in gold and notes all jumbled together, if he had not been drawing appreciable amounts day by day without counting them, for his experiments and his personal expenses. The money for all his presents had come from there and he was continually opening the drawer for this purpose. Besides, he thought of it as an inexhaustible treasury, he was so used to taking what he needed that it never occurred to him that it might come to an end.

"I might as well enjoy my savings," he continued cheerfully. "The notary must have told you that I also have a private income of my own."

She answered, in the colourless tone of the miser, haunted by the nightmare of an ever-threatening disaster:

"And what if your income stopped?"

Dumbfounded, Pascal stared at her and made a vague gesture of dissent, as the idea of such a misfortune had never entered his mind. He simply thought that her avarice was going to her head; he joked about it that night to Clotilde.

The presents were also the subject of endless gossip in the town of Plassans. This sudden flare-up of passion at the Souleiade was a notable phenomenon, which aroused much interest; in some unaccountable fashion, the news had been spread, over the walls, by some legerdemain only manifested in small towns always eager for something on which to feed their starved curiosity. It was certainly not the servant who had talked; but, perhaps, her manner had been enough to arouse suspicion and the lovers had doubtless been spied on over the walls. His purchase of the presents had been the final proof. When the doctor, early in the morning, hurried through the streets, visited the jeweller, the dressmaker and the milliner, eyes were glued to the windows, his purchases were scrutinized and that evening, the whole town knew that he had bought a silk cape, a lace blouse, a sapphire bracelet. It became an open scandal, this uncle who had debauched his niece, who, with the extravagant folly of a young man in love, covered her in jewels like a holy Virgin. The most extraordinary stories began to circulate. The townspeople nudged each other and pointed when they passed the Souleiade.

But it was old Madame Rougon who was most roused to exasperated indignation. When she had been told that Clotilde had refused to marry Doctor Ramond, she had stopped her usual visits to her son. They were making a public exhibition of her, they were determined not to respect her wishes. Then, after their rupture had lasted a month, during which she had been puzzled by the looks of pity, the discreet speeches of commiseration, the peculiar smiles of her friends, she had suddenly been enlightened and it was a stunning blow to her pride. And she who, when Pascal had been ill, acting like a were-wolf, nursing his pride and his fears, had so vociferously defended him, in order to prevent him becoming the talk of the town! It was worse this time, a crying scandal, a licentious adventure at his age, which was making him a general laughing stock! Once again the legend of the Rougons was in danger, her wretched son was evidently bent on destroying the glory of the family, so painfully acquired. Consumed with rage, in her capacity of guardian of that glory, and resolved to safeguard the legend by any and every means, she put on her hat and ran to the Souleiade, with all the juvenile vivacity of her eighty years. It was ten o'clock in the morning.

Fortunately, Pascal, who had been delighted by the breach with his mother, was out hunting for an old silver buckle for one of Clotilde's belts. Felicité burst in on Clotilde sitting at her dressing table, still in her camisole, arms bared, hair down, as gay and fresh as a rose.

The battle was engaged without any preliminaries. The old lady vented her rage on Clotilde, exhorted her in the name of religion and morality to abjure her evil ways. Finally, she concluded:

"Answer me, why have you behaved in this abominable fashion, in defiance of God and man?"

The young woman listened, very respectfully, but with a smile on her face:

"Because we wanted to, grandmother. We are both adult, surely we have the right to do as we please? Our duty is to ourselves, not to any outsiders."

"You have no duty? What about me and the family? Our name is being dragged in the mud once more, and you think that I should feel pleased!"

All of a sudden her rage left her. She realized that Clotilde looked adorable. After all, what had happened was not so surprising. She was not shocked, merely indifferent, she was simply concerned with the conventional ending, in order to stop the tongue of scandal from wagging. And, she cried, in a conciliatory tone:

"Then, you must get married! Why has there been no wedding?"

Clotilde betrayed her astonishment. Neither she nor the doctor had thought of marriage. She answered, with a smile:

"Would we be any happier, grandmother?"

"I am not considering your feelings, it is a question, rather, of my feelings, the whole family! .. My dear child, how can you joke about such sacred things? Have you no shame?"

. But the young woman, without any sign of indignation, still gentle and serene, threw out her arms in a gesture which implied that she was by no means ashamed of her behaviour. Seeing that life was full of corruption and frailty, what harm had they done, under the dazzling sky, by finding happiness in each other's arms? Besides, she saw no insuperable objection:

"No doubt we shall marry in due course, if that is your wish, grandmother. He will do as I ask him .. But later, there is no hurry."

Her attitude was one of humorous toleration. As they were living outside the world, why worry about the world?

Old Madame Rougon went away, forced to be content with this vague promise. She caused it to be known that she had broken off all relations with the Souleiade, that den of perdition and shame. She refused, ostentatiously, to set foot inside the walls. She mourned this new affliction with her usual air of noble resignation. But she did not lay down her arms, she lay in wait with the tenacity which had been responsible for her many victories, ready to pounce on her son and his paramour at the slightest excuse.

Then Pascal and Clotilde emerged from their isolation. It was not because of any provocation, they had no wish to silence the evil tongues by flaunting their happiness. It was a spontaneous process of expansion. The very intensity of their love for each other had demanded a wider field, more space to expand, first outside the bedroom, then outside the house, now outside the garden, into the town, towards the vast horizon. It filled everything, it delivered the whole world into their hands. The doctor quietly resumed his visits, taking the young woman with him and they strolled together along the walks, along the streets, arm in arm, she in her light summer dress, with a spray of flowers on her head, he buttoned into his frock-coat, with his wide-brimmed hat. She with her fair hair, he with his snow-white mane; they advanced, heads up, erect and smiling, so radiant with bliss that they seemed to be surrounded with a blaze of glory. At first, their appearance caused great excitement. The shopkeepers stood at their doors, women leaned out of their windows, passers-by stopped and stared at them. There was whispering, laughing and pointing. It was to be feared that this surge of hostile curiosity would be communicated to the urchins in the street and that they would start throwing stones. But they were so impressive, he arrogant and triumphant, she so young, so submissive and yet so proud, that the townsfolk, little by little, were reluctantly forced into an attitude of indulgence. So contagious was their happiness that no one could help envying and admiring them. The new town, with its middle class population of civil servants and newly-rich, was the last to be won over. The Saint-Marc quarter, in spite of its tradition of rigid conventionality, welcomed them at once, as they walked along the deserted, grass-grown pavements and passed the buildings which had once housed the nobility and were now shuttered and closed and from which arose a faint perfume of exquisitely dressed men and women who, a long, long time ago, had loved each other in those great houses. The old quarter welcomed them with open arms. It was a quarter lived in by humble folk, whose instincts were unspoiled, who responded to the gracious legend, the mythical quality of this couple, the beautiful young woman sustaining the royal and rejuvenated master. The doctor was universally beloved because of his innumerable acts of kindness. His companion soon became popular, saluted by gestures of admiration and praise as soon as she appeared. They, who had seemed to be oblivious of the initial hostility, were now well aware that they were surrounded by affectionate understanding and friendship; it made their countenances shine with even greater effulgence. Their happiness illuminated the whole town.

One afternoon, when Pascal and Clotilde were turning the corner into de la Banne street, they caught sight of Doctor Ramond on the opposite pavement. It was a coincidence; the evening before, they had heard that he had decided to marry Mademoiselle Lévêque, the solicitor's daughter. It was undoubtedly a wise move on his part, his position would not allow him to wait any longer and the young woman, very pretty and equally wealthy, was in love with him. He, in time, would certainly fall in love with her himself. Hence, Clotilde was glad of this chance meeting, delighted to be one of the first to congratulate him as a sincere friend. Pascal waved to him, affectionately. For a moment Ramond hesitated and seemed perplexed. His first instinct had been to cross the road. Then, he seemed to be overcome by scruples, he feared that it would be brutally unfeeling to interrupt their dream, to interfere with their singularly close communion, which set them apart, even in a crowded street. He contented himself with a friendly salute, which condoned their happiness. It was a moving experience for all three of them.

At about this time, Clotilde had been busily occupied for some days with a large pastel, in which she evoked the scene of the idyll between the old king David and Abishag, the young Shunammite. It was the evocation of a dream, one of those inspired compositions into which her other self, fantastically imaginative, expressed its yearning towards the mystery. Against a background of flowers falling like a shower of stars luxuriantly barbarous, the old king was standing, full-face, with his hand on Abishag's bare shoulder; and the child, dazzlingly white, was naked to the waist. He, sumptuously clothed in a long straight robe, loaded with precious stones, wore the royal frontlet in his snowy hair. But she was even more sumptuous though she wore nothing over the lily-white satin-smoothness of her skin, with her tall willowy figure, her round and slender neck, her firm breasts, her supple arms, divinely graceful. He was the great lord, he, the powerful and beloved master, leaning on his subject, chosen and uplifted, so proud to be selected, so anxious to give her king the revivifying blood of her youth. Her limpid and triumphant nudity expressed the serenity of her submission, the tranquil, absolute surrender of her person, before the assembled populace, in the full light of day. He was the emblem of grandeur, she of purity and both of them irradiated a sort of astral effulgence.

Up till the last moment, Clotilde had left their faces almost a blank, just a faint blurred outline. Pascal was standing behind her, emotionally stirred, but teasing her because he had guessed what she intended to do. And he was right, she finished the faces with a few crayon strokes; the old king David was Pascal and she was Abishag, the Shunammite. But they remained shrouded in a faint haze, the faint blur of dream light etherealized them, with their hair, one white and the other golden, which covered them with an imperial mantle, and their features were elongated and set in lines of ecstasy, uplifted to the beatitude of angels, with a look and a smile of immortal love.

"Ah! dearest one," he cried, "you have made us look too beautiful, another one of your dream flights, yes! you remember the days when I reproached you for drawing all those fantastic and mysterious flowers?"

He pointed to the walls with their fantastic array of her old pastels, that unearthly flora, which had sprung up in the midst of some strange paradise of her imagination.

But she laughed merrily and protested:

"Too beautiful? Impossible! I assure you that is how I feel and see us, how we really are .. Here! look, let me show you."

She picked up the old fifteenth century Bible and showed him the naive wood-cut:

"You see, it is an exact likeness."

He chuckled at this tranquil and extraordinary affirmation.

"Oh! You're laughing, you are picking out insignificant details. It is the spirit that matters .. And look at the other prints, the same likeness! I will draw Abraham and Agar, Ruth and Boaz, I will draw them all, the prophets, the shepherds and the kings, to whom the humble daughters, the relatives and the maid-servants have given their youth. They are all handsome and happy, can't you see?"

Then they stopped laughing and bent over the ancient Bible the pages of which she turned over with her long slender fingers. He was behind her and his white beard mingled with her fair hair. He felt and breathed in the whole of her. He touched the smooth skin of the back of her neck with his lips, with reverence he kissed youth in full flower, as she turned over the pages with their naive wood-cuts, yellow with age, which evoked this biblical world, this free upsurge of a strong and vital race, whose offspring were to conquer the world; these men with their perennial virility, these everlastingly fertile women, this obstinate and proliferating continuity of the race, through crimes, incest, lust without limit and beyond reason. And he was inundated with immense gratitude, because his recurrent dream was being realized, his pilgrim of love, his Abishag, had entered his life when it was slipping away from him towards the grave, reviving it and filling it with her perfume.

Then he whispered into her ear, very close to her, asking her:

"Oh! your youth, divine youth, for which I hungered and which has nourished me! .. But you, so young, do you sometimes hunger for youth, since I have taken you, because I am so old, as old as the world?"

She gave a start of astonishment, turned her head and looked at him: "You, old? .. But you are young, much younger than I am!" And she laughed, so merrily and spontaneously that he could not help laughing himself. But he insisted, in a tremulous voice:

"You have avoided answering me .. You are so young, surely you must sometimes hunger for youth?"

She bent forward and kissed him, in her turn, and murmured:

"I have only one hunger and one thirst, to be loved, to be loved beyond everything and above everything, as you love me."

When Martine saw the pastel nailed to the wall, she stared at it for a moment in silence, then she made the sign of the cross, though nobody knew whether she had seen God or the Devil. A few days before Easter, she had asked Clotilde to go to church with her. Clotilde's categoric refusal had jolted her out of her present, habitual, mute deference. Of all the new phenomena which amazed her in the house, the one which she found most intolerable was her young mistress's sudden lapse into irreligion. Hence, she allowed herself to revert to her old tone of remonstrance, to scold her as she had done when she had been a little girl and refused to say her prayers. Had she no fear of the Lord? Did she not tremble with terror at the idea of going to hell and boiling for all eternity?

Clotilde was unable to repress a smile:

"Oh, you know that I have never worried my head about hell .. But you are wrong if you think that I have abandoned my religion. If I have stopped going to church, it is simply that I prefer to worship elsewhere."

Martine gazed at her uncomprehendingly, with open mouth. It was the end, mademoiselle was lost. She never again asked her to go to Saint-Saturnin. But she herself become even more devout, it became a mania. She was no longer to be seen knitting her eternal stocking in her few spare moments. As soon as she was free, she hurried to church and remained there, immersed in endless prayers. One day when old Madame Rougon had found her behind a pillar, an hour after first catching sight of her, she blushed and proceeded to make excuses like a servant caught idling by her mistress:

"I was praying for monsieur."

Pascal and Clotilde were now launching out more boldly. They gradually lengthened their walks, outside the town into the vast countryside. And, one afternoon on the way to the Séguiranne, a pang of melancholy shot through them both, when they passed the neglected and mournful stretch of country, which had once been the site of the enchanted gardens of the Paradou. They had a vision of Albine, as Pascal had seen her, smothered in wild flowers like a meadow in spring. Never, in that distant past, would that little boy, who considered himself practically a man and who had ventured inside the gardens to smile at that little girl, have believed that she would predecease him by so many years and that life would vouchsafe to him this second springtime to gladden his declining years. Clotilde, who had also seen the vision, lifted her face towards him wanting to be reassured by the warmth of his affection. She was Albine, the eternal lover. He kissed her on the lips; and, though no word passed between them, the flat lands quivered in sympathy, sown as they were with wheat and oats, underneath the erstwhile gardens of the Paradou, where all that prodigious wealth of greenery had been wont to ripple in the breeze.

Now, Pascal and Clotilde were walking across the dessicated and naked plain in the crackling dust of the road. They were fond of this stretch of ardent nature, these fields planted with slender almond trees and dwarf olive trees, these denuded slopes, dotted with white country houses, their whiteness accentuated by the dark silhouettes of the centuries old cypresses. They were like antique landscape paintings, classical landscapes, as one sees them depicted in old-fashioned oil paintings, with their hard colouring, their balanced and majestic lines. Innumerable days of blazing sunshine seemed to have baked this countryside, flowed, as it were, in its veins, which made it alive and beautiful under the everlasting blue sky, from which darted the pure, perpetually passionate flame. She, in the relative shade of her parasol, was revelling in this bath of light, like a plant adapted to a southern exposure; whilst he, reflorescent, felt the burning sap of the soil rise up through his limbs in a flood of exultant virility.

This excursion to the Séguiranne had been the doctor's idea, as Aunt Dieudonné had announced Sophie's projected marriage to a young man who worked for a neighbouring miller; and he wanted to see if all were well and happy in that corner of the world. When they reached the avenue of tall green oaks, their heated brows were fanned by a deliciously cool breeze. Along both sides, the springs, mothers of these shade-giving leaves, trickled away into the distance. Then, as they approached the farmer's house, they caught sight of the lovers, Sophie and her miller in each other's arms, kissing, near the well; as her aunt had just left them to go to the washhouse behind the willows of the Viorne. The couple were much embarrassed and covered in blushes. But the doctor and his companion laughed heartily and the lovers, reassured, told them that the marriage had been fixed for Saint-Jean's day, which was a long time to wait, but something definite to look forward to, all the same. Sophie was the picture of health and buxom beauty, preserved from the hereditary taint, as solid as one of those trees, their feet in the moist spring-fed grass and their heads exposed to the beneficent rays of the sun. Ah! that ardent and immense sky, what life it infused into living and inanimate nature! Sophie was distressed only by one thing, tears welled up under her eyelids when she spoke of her brother Valentin, who was not likely to survive for another week. She had been told, the previous day, that his life was despaired of. And the doctor was forced to tell a white lie to console her, as he was expecting the inevitable ending, from one hour to the next. When Clotilde and he left the Séguiranne, they loitered, half-ashamed, but savouring the bliss of being lovers in the best of health, brushed by a breath from the grave.

In the old quarter, a woman whom Pascal was treating told them

164

that Valentin had just died. Two neighbours, women, had had to drag Madame Guiraude away, as she had been clinging to the dead body of her son, shrieking, half-demented. In the end, they resumed their walk towards the Souleiade in silence. He had recommenced his visits, purely because of his sense of professional duty and he no longer expected miracles from his injections. But, he was astonished that Valentin's death had been retarded for so long, he was convinced that he had prolonged the life of the sick man by at least a year. In spite of his extraordinary results, he knew very well that death was the inevitable, ineluctably final victor. Nevertheless the fact of having kept it in check for months should have flattered him, compensated for Lafouasse's sudden death which still weighed heavily on his conscience. But these were obviously not his sentiments, because a deep frown creased his forehead, as they regained their solitary retreat. But there, his feelings were to be harrowed again; he recognized, outside under the plane trees, where Martine had left him, Sarteur, the journeyman hatter, the inmate of the Tulettes, to whom he had given a prolonged course of his injections; and the fascinating experiment seemed to have been crowned with success. The injections of his nerve extract had reinforced the man's will-power. The madman was here, his own living proof, discharged from the asylum that very morning, swearing that his attacks had ceased, that he was completely cured of those sudden accesses of homicidal mania in the course of which he was liable to throw himself upon and strangle the first person who crossed his path. The doctor looked at him, short, very dark, his face like a bird's beak, the receding forehead, with one cheek appreciably larger than the other, perfectly restored to reason and very gentle, brimming over with gratitude. Pascal ended up by feeling moved himself and sent him away with a few affectionate words, advising him to take up his work again, which was the best mental and physical tonic for him. After the man had gone, he seemed relieved, sat down to the meal and began to chat cheerfully about some other subject.

Clotilde looked at him, astonished, still feeling somewhat upset:

"But, master, aren't you more pleased with yourself?"

He replied in jest:

"Who, me? I am never pleased with myself! .. Medicine depends on the day and the mood!"

That night, in bed, they had their first quarrel. They had blown out the candle. The room was in profound darkness. She was pressed against him and he was clasping her in an all-enveloping embrace, her head against his heart. She was annoyed with him for not having more pride in his handiwork, she repeated her grievances, reproaching him for not feeling triumphant because of having cured Sarteur and having prolonged Valentin's agony. She was now the one to be jealous of his glorious reputation. She reminded him of his successes; had he not cured himself? could he deny the efficacity of his method? Her whole body trembled with enthusiasm when she evoked his splendid dream of the past; to combat debility, which was at the root of all disease, cure suffering humanity, make it healthier and better, to hasten the advent of universal happiness, the future city of perfection and bliss, by his treatment, bestowing health on everybody! He held the elixir of life in his hands, the universal panacea, which would consummate his wildest dreams!

Pascal, kept silent, his lips pressed on Clotilde's bare shoulder. Then he murmured:

"It is true, I cured myself, I have cured others, and I still believe that my injections are effective, in many cases . . I do not condemn my treatment. Remorse for an unfortunate accident, for what happened to Lafouasse, does not cloud my judgement . . Besides, my work has been my great passion, it has consumed me, it was striving to prove the possibility of making worn-out humanity vigorous and intelligent again which brought me to the point of death, recently . . It was a dream, a beautiful dream!"

In her turn, she wound her supple arms about him, fused herself in him, penetrated his body:

"No, it was a reality, the reality of your genius, my master!"

Then, intertwined as they were, he lowered his voice still further. His words were an almost silent avowal, a mere fluttering breath:

"Listen, I am going to tell you what I would not tell anybody else in the world, what I have never said, aloud, to myself . . Correct nature, interfere, modify it and venture to disturb its balance, can one justify such an objective? Cure, retard death at one's own whim, prolong life at the expense of damaging the species, no doubt, is that not undoing what nature wants to do? And, have we any right to dream about making humanity healthier, stronger, modelled according to our idea of health and strength? What are we doing, what can our object be in interfering with this labour of life when we know nothing about its means and its final purpose? Perhaps it is right and we who are on the wrong track. Perhaps we are running the risk of killing love, genius, life itself . . You understand, I am confessing myself to you alone, I am full of doubts, I tremble at the idea of my twentieth century alchemy. I am beginning to think that it would be better and far wiser to allow evolution to go its own way."

He paused and added, so softly that she could hardly hear him:

"I must tell you that all I have injected, for some time past, is plain water. You yourself have noticed that you never hear me using my pestle and mortar and when you spoke to me about it, I told you that I had a reserve supply of my extract .. Water relieves them, doubtless a simple mechanical effect. To relieve, to prevent suffering and pain, that is certainly still an obsession with me! That is, perhaps, my only remaining weakness. I cannot stand seeing people suffer, it drives me to distraction, it is monstrously cruel and contrary to nature .. Nowadays, I only treat in order to prevent pain."

"Then, master," she declared, "if you are making no further attempts to cure, you no longer have the right to speak out, to reveal everything. The only possible excuse for the horrible necessity of baring those sores is the hope of being able to heal them."

"Yes, yes. Knowledge is essential, to know all that can be known and conceal nothing; to admit everything about inanimate nature and all living things. Ignorance makes happiness impossible, facing facts with one's eyes open is the only way to ensure tranquillity. When we know more, we shall certainly accept everything .. Don't you understand that to want to cure everything, regenerate everything, is a false ambition, inspired by our own egoism, a rebellion against life, which we declare to be evil, because our judgement is falsified by self-interest? I am convinced that I am more serene, that my vision covers a wider field, that my brain works better, since I have learned to respect evolution. It is my passion for life which has triumphed, to the extent of not meddling with its purpose, yielding myself utterly to it, losing myself in it, without wanting to remake it according to my own conception of good and bad. Life alone is sovereign, life alone knows what it is doing and where it is going. All I can do is to strive to understand it, to live it, as it asks to be lived .. And, you see, understanding has come to me only since you have been mine. Before I had you, I was searching elsewhere for truth, I was struggling in the dark, with the fixed idea of saving the world. You came and life is full, the world is being saved, hourly, by love, by the immense travail, the incessant labours of everything which is alive and reproduces itself, through the vast expanses of space .. Life infallible, life all-powerful, life immortal!"

As he ended his act of faith, only a faint vibration, a sigh came from his lips. She also was carried away:

"My master, I want nothing except to do your bidding, take me and make me yours, make me disappear and be reborn, intermingled with you, flesh of your flesh!"

They took each other again. Then they whispered plans for an idyllic existence in the country. This simple prescription was the end result of all his medical experience. He loathed towns. Health and happiness were only possible in the depths of the country, beneath the life-giving sun, if one were willing to abjure money, give up all ambition, even excess of pride, as represented by too intensive intellectual work. To do nothing but live and love, to dig one's own plot of earth and beget beautiful children.

"Ah!" he continued softly, "the child, the child which will be ours one day .."

He was unable to go on. He was overwhelmed by his emotions at the idea of such a tardy paternity. He always avoided talking about it, turned his head away, his eyes moist, when a child smiled at them during their walk.

She merely declared, with tranquil assurance:

"That day will come!"

To her it was the natural and indispensable consequence of the act. All her kisses were impregnated with the thought of a child; because all love which did not culminate in a child seemed to her useless and ugly.

That was one of the main reasons why romantic literature, novels, left her cold. She was not a great reader, like her mother; she preferred the soarings of her own imagination; and she soon became bored with stories in books. But, above all, she was continually astonished and indignant when she found that stories and novels about love were never concerned with the child. No provision was made for him and when, by chance, he came along and complicated the love interest, it was a catastrophe, a cause for dismay and considerable embarrassment. It never seemed to lovers, when they possessed each other, that they were vehicles of life and that a child might be born. Nevertheless, her studies in natural history had taught her that nature was solely concerned with the fruit. It alone was important, it was the sole objective, every precaution was taken to make sure that the seed was not lost and that the mother gave birth. And man, on the contrary, by civilizing and emasculating love, had discarded the very thought of the fruit. The hero's sex drive, in refined novels, was merely a lust-machine. They worshipped each other, took each other, left each other, endured a thousand deaths, embraced, unleashed a tempest of social evils, all just for a few moments of pleasure, violating all natural laws, without even seeming to realize that making love was a preliminary to begetting children. It was indecent and utterly stupid.

She laughed at herself, she repeated, hiding her head in his neck, with the playful audacity of a loving mistress though faintly embarrassed:

"He's sure to come along .. We are doing our level best to make sure of him, why do you doubt his coming?"

He did not answer at once. She felt him grow cold in her arms, overtaken by regrets and doubts. Then he murmured, mournfully:

"No, no! It is too late .. Think, dearest, at my age!"

"But you are young!" she cried once more with passionate conviction, pressing herself against him to warm and comfort him, covering him with kisses.

Later, they went to sleep, still tightly embraced, her arms and legs around him, those supple long limbs, her head on his chest, her hair fanned out, with strands of it caught in his white beard. And in that hushed silence, in the utter darkness of the room, not a sound could be heard but the quiet breathing of the sleeping lovers.

CHAPTER NINE

DOCTOR PASCAL continued his medical visits in Plassans and the surrounding country, usually arm in arm with Clotilde, who accompanied him into the houses of his poor patients.

But as he had confessed to her one night, almost shamefacedly, his only object, nowadays, was to palliate and console. Even in the past, it had been largely owing to the hopeless inadequacy of current methods of medical treatment that he had gradually given up his practice. He abhorred empiricism. Realizing that medicine was still far from being an exact science, he was bewildered by the complexity of disease and the difficulty of adjusting the remedy to the individual case. Methods of treatment and remedies varied according to the theories of the moment; how many people must have been killed by methods which were now discredited! His clinical instinct was all that a doctor had to rely on; if he cured his patients it was because he had a gift for intuitive diagnosis, but he was merely groping and his successes were due as much to luck as to his own ability. This was why, after twelve years of active practice, he had abandoned all but a few of his patients and concentrated his energies on research. Then, for a while, his work on heredity had revived his interest in therapeutics, and, until recently, he had been passionately convinced of the efficacy of his injections; he now no longer believed that he was justified in interfering with nature, even for the purpose of renewing vigour and vitality. His faith in life had become intensified, so much so that he now believed that life was omniscient as well as all-powerful, that it alone, unaided, was able to ensure health and strength. Thus his visits were now confined to those patients who clamoured for him and whose sufferings seemed almost miraculously alleviated. But it was an open question as to whether the result was due to his tranquil smile or his injections of plain water.

Clotilde sometimes teased him. The element of mystery in life still fascinated her; and she said jokingly that he must have some strange power to be able to work such miracles, that he was a real God! This always put him in cheerful mood and he retorted that she was the one responsible for the miraculous success of his treatment, that it was ineffective really, but it was she who contributed the unknown supernatural element. It was true that his wealthy middle-class patients, whom he did not allow her to visit, failed to improve and that he seemed unable to alleviate their sufferings. This affectionate battle of words afforded them great amusement, each visit became an adventure and they exchanged meaning glances over the patient's head. How bitterly they resented pain, now their only enemy. What joy when they were able to overcome it! They felt amply rewarded when the cold sweat of anguish disappeared from a brow, the grimace of intolerable pain from a face, when an expression of dull despair was transformed into a smile. It was the power of their own love, doubtless, which they carried about with them like an aura, which brought such relief to suffering mankind.

"Death is nothing, it is a natural phenomenon," Pascal was in the habit of saying. "But pain, why? it is abominable and senseless!"

One afternoon Pascal and Clotilde were to visit a patient in the little village of Sainte-Marthe; they went by train, to spare Bonhomme. At the station they had a surprise. They were waiting for the train from Tulettes which, on its way to Marseilles in the opposite direction, made its first stop at Sainte-Marthe. The train arrived, Pascal opened the door of a supposedly empty compartment and out stepped old Madame Rougon. She jumped down lightly, looked straight through them and walked away, bristling with offended dignity.

"It is the first of July," said Clotilde, as the train started. "Grandmother was coming back from her monthly visit to Tante Dide at the Tulettes .. Did you see the look she gave me?"

His mother's uncompromising attitude had been welcomed by Pascal, as it saved him from being continually pestered by her:

"Bah! when people cannot agree, they had better keep away from each other."

But the young woman seemed worried and frowned:

"I found her changed, she was paler .. And did you notice? she, always so neat, was only wearing one glove, a green one, on her right hand .. I do not know why, but she looked horribly pathetic."

He, too became anxious and made a vague gesture. His mother was bound to begin showing her age, like everybody else. She was always exciting herself about nothing, had no control over her emotions. He told Clotilde that she was planning to leave her money to the town of Plassans to build an almshouse which would be called by the name of Rougon. This brought a smile back to their faces, but he cried:

"I have just remembered! it is tomorrow that we too have to go to the Tulettes to see our patients. And, as you know, I have promised to take Charles to Uncle Macquart."

Felicité had, in fact, been coming from the Tulettes, where she had been paying her regular monthly visit for news of Tante Dide. For many years she had shown a passionate interest in the mad-woman's health, astounded and indignant at this prodigious longevity. What a relief it would be when she could bury this embarrassing witness of the past, this brooding spectre of expiation, who was a living reminder of the family's worst abominations! And, when so many others had been taken, she, demented and with only a feeble spark of life at the back of her eyes, seemed to have been forgotten. That day, she had again found her in the armchair, dried up and erect, motionless. As her nurse was saying, there was no reason to suppose that she would ever die. She was one hundred and five.

When Felicité came out of the asylum, she was seething. She was thinking of Uncle Macquart. Another one who exasperated her, who clung obstinately to his miserable existence! Although he was eighty-three, only three years older than she was, he seemed to her ridiculously old, beyond all bounds. And a man whose life was one long debauch, who had been dead drunk every night for sixty years! The virtuous and sober died off; whilst he flourished, bursting with health and joyous contentment. When he had first come to live at the Tulettes she had sent him presents of wine, liqueurs and spirits, in the hope of ridding the family of a singularly loathsome specimen, from whom nothing could be expected but degradation and dis-grace. But she had soon realised that all this alcohol had the extra-ordinary effect of making him cheerful, feel and look better; and she had soon stopped these presents as the poison, instead of being lethal, acted as a tonic. For this she bore him an undying grudge, she would have killed him if she had dared, each time she saw him, solidly planted on his drunkard's legs, with his mocking leer, know-ing that she wanted him to die, wickedly triumphant because he was depriving her of the pleasure of burying him, together with the dirty linen of the past, the blood and mud of the two conquests of Plassans.

"You see, Felicité," he often said to her, with gleeful and

laboured irony, "I am here to watch over the old mother, and the day we make up our minds to die, both of us, it will be for your sake, yes! simply to save you the trouble of coming here each month, out of the goodness of your heart."

Usually she now avoided going to see him, they were able to give her the latest news about him at the asylum. But this time she had been told that he was in the middle of an extraordinary bout of drunkenness, had not been sober for a fortnight, doubtless so helplessly drunk that he could not move from his house. She was curious to see what he looked like. So she went the long way round to the station, in order to call at his country house.

It was a magnificent summer's day, hot and clear. To the right and to the left of the narrow path, she gazed, with mounting resentment, at the fields she had been stupid enough to buy for him; all that fertile ground, the price she had paid, in an attempt to ensure his discretion and good conduct. In the sunshine, the house, with its pink tiles, its walls distempered a bright yellow, looked wonderfully gay and attractive. Under the ancient mulberry trees on the terrace she revelled in their delightful coolness and admired the view. What a worthy and perfect retreat, what a blissful spot for an old man to finish a long, good and dutiful life in peace!

She could neither see nor hear him. Nothing but profound silence! Only the faint buzzing of bees around the giant mallows. There was a little yellow dog on the terrace, the kind called *loubet* in Provence, stretched out on the bare earth, in the shade. He had raised his head and started growling, but he knew her, put his head down again and made no further movement.

There was something eerie about this solitude, in spite of the blazing sun she shivered and called:

"Macquart! .. Macquart! .."

The door of the house, under the mulberry trees, was wide open. But she felt too frightened to go in, the entrance was like a gaping maw. And she called out in a louder voice:

"Macquart! .. Macquart! .."

Not a sound, not a breath. There was still that heavy brooding silence, only the bees seemed alive, buzzing around the giant mallows.

In the end, Felicité began to feel ashamed of her fears and boldly went indoors. In the hall, the door on the left opened into the kitchen, where Macquart usually sat. It was shut. She opened it.

At first she could distinguish nothing, he must have closed the shutters to keep out the heat. Her first impression was merely one of being almost suffocated by the smell of spirits which filled the room; even the furniture seemed to be oozing with it, the whole house was impregnated with it. Then, as her eyes became accustomed to the dim light, she finally saw Macquart. He was sitting near the table, on which stood a glass and a bottle of double-strength brandy, completely empty. Hunched up in his chair he was soundly asleep, helplessly drunk. This sight aroused her to a fury of contempt:

"Come, Macquart, it is unreasonable and shameful to get yourself in such a state! .. Wake up, it's disgraceful!"

He was sleeping so deeply that she could not even hear him breathing. She raised her voice, shouted, started beating him with her fists, all to no avail:

"Macquart! Macquart! Macquart! .. You are disgusting!"

She gave up trying to rouse him, but she was no longer apprehensive, she walked about and bumped against the furniture. Her walk along the dusty road from the asylum had made her very thirsty. She took off her gloves and put them down on a corner of the table. Then, she had the luck to find a water jug, washed a glass and filled it to the brim. She was about to drink when an extraordinary sight filled her with such amazement that she put the glass down near the gloves without drinking.

She could now see everything clearly, thanks to a few narrow shafts of sunlight which filtered through the cracks of the old shutters. There was her brother, wearing, as always, his neat blue suit and his eternal fur cap. He had grown much stouter in the last five or six years, he looked monstrously bulky with his folds of fat. She had just noticed that he must have been smoking before lapsing into unconsciousness, because his pipe, a short black pipe, had fallen on his knees. Then she stood transfixed with astonishment; the cloth of his trousers had caught fire from the smouldering tobacco; and through a hole in the material, already as large as a crown piece, his naked thigh could be seen, a red thigh and it was burning with a blue flame.

At first Felicité thought that it was his linen, his underpants or his vest, which was burning. But, there was no doubt about it, it was his flesh, burning with a flickering blue flame, light, dancing, like a flame spreading over the surface of a bowl of alcohol. It was still no higher than the flame of a night-light, so feeble, so unstable that the slightest breath of air made it waver. But it was growing, spreading rapidly and the skin was splitting, and the fat was beginning to melt.

Felicité uttered an involuntary exclamation:

"Macquart! .. Macquart!"

Not the slightest movement from him. He was completely unconscious, he was in a drunken stupor, more like a coma, all sensation paralysed; but he was definitely still alive, she could see his chest heaving in a slow and regular rhythm.

"Macquart! .. Macquart!"

Now the liquid fat was dribbling through the cracks in his skin, feeding the flame which was spreading to his belly. And Felicité realized that he was burning up, like a sponge soaked in alcohol. He had been saturating himself for years in the strongest, most inflammable of spirits. Soon, doubtless, he would be flaming from head to foot.

Then she stopped making any effort to arouse him, he was too deeply unconscious. During the next few minutes she nerved herself to watch him, terrified, but gradually coming to a decision. Her hands were trembling with a light but uncontrollable tremor. She was choking, she seized the glass with both hands and emptied the water down her throat in a single gulp. She was about to creep out of the kitchen, on tiptoe, when she remembered her gloves. She turned back, thought that she had picked them both up, groping cautiously over the table for them. Then she went out, closed the door carefully and quietly, as if afraid of disturbing someone.

When she reached the terrace, in the bright light and the fresh air, facing the immense horizon bathed in sunshine, she gave a sigh of relief. Not a soul was in sight, nobody could have seen her going in or coming out. The only living creature was the yellow dog, stretched out at her feet, who did not even condescend to raise his head. And she trotted off with her usual short steps, faintly swaying her hips like a young woman. When she was a hundred paces away she felt irresistibly compelled to turn around and take a last look at the house, so calm and gay half way up the slope at the end of a fine day. It was only in the train, when she started pulling on her gloves, that she noticed that one of them was missing. But she was sure that it must have fallen on the platform as she stepped up into the compartment. She felt quite calm, but the fact that she was wearing only one glove and that the other hand was bare could, in her, only be interpreted as a sign of powerful perturbation.

Next day Pascal and Clotilde took the three o'clock train for the

Tulettes. Charles' mother, the saddler's wife, had brought the little boy along to the station, seeing that they had been kind enough to offer to take him to the old uncle, who was going to keep him for a week. Fresh quarrels over the boy had broken out in the saddler's household; the husband refused categorically to tolerate the presence of this other man's bastard, this idle and half-witted rich man's son. As it was grandmother Rougon who paid for and chose his clothes, he was dressed that day in black velvet, embellished with a loop of gold cord like a young nobleman or a court page in the olden days. During the train journey lasting a quarter of an hour Clotilde amused herself, as they were the only occupants of the compartment, by taking off his cap and stroking his admirable fair hair, the royal head of hair with its curls falling to the shoulders. But she was wearing a ring, and as she passed her hand over the back of his neck she was astonished to find that it left a thin trail of blood. The slightest touch caused drops of blood, like red dew, to ooze from his skin; it was a process of tissular relaxation so aggravated by his state of degeneration that even light rubbing caused a haemorrhage. This at once aroused the doctor's suspicions and he asked the boy whether he still suffered from frequent nose-bleeding. Charles was in a daze and found it difficult to answer; first he said no, then he remembered that he had bled a lot the other day. He seemed, in fact, weaker; he was reverting to early childhood instead of progressing as he grew older, his intelligence, which had never been awakened, was even duller. He was fifteen but looked ten, so handsome, so girlish, with the complexion of an etiolated flower. Shaken and full of affectionate pity Clotilde, who had been fondling him on her knees, put him back on the seat when she realized to her horrified amazement that he was trying to slip his hand into the opening of her gown, towards her breast; the precocious and instinctive impulse of a vicious little animal.

At the Tulettes, Pascal decided to take the boy to his uncle' before going to the asylum. They climbed the steep incline. From a distance the house glinted gaily in the sun, as it had done the day before, with its pink tiles, its yellow walls, its green mulberry trees, spreading out their twisted branches and covering the terrace with a thick roof of leaves. This solitary corner was wonderfully peaceful, this sage's retreat, with no sound but the buzzing of the bees around the giant mallows.

"What a lucky old man," murmured Pascal, smiling; "I envy him!"

But he was surprised not to see him in his usual place, standing at the end of the terrace. And as Charles had galloped off, dragging Clotilde behind him, to go and see the rabbits, the doctor finished the climb by himself and was astonished to find no one up there. The shutters were closed, the front door was open, wide open. There was only the yellow dog, on the threshold, his four legs stiffly extended, his hairs bristling, howling softly and continuously. When he saw the visitor, whom he doubtless recognized, he stopped howling, took a few steps and started whimpering and howling again.

Pascal felt unaccountably fear-stricken and could not repress a cry of: "Macquart! .. Macquart!"

There was no answer, the house remained as silent as a tomb, with its only door wide open, a gaping black hole. The dog went on howling.

Impatiently, Pascal called in a louder tone of voice:

"Macquart! .. Macquart!" Nothing moved, the immense serenity of the sky enfolded this solitary corner. He decided to look for the old man. Perhaps he was asleep. But no sooner was the door on the left opened than a horrible smell escaped from the kitchen, the appalling smell of scorching bones and flesh. In the kitchen he could hardly breathe, suffocated, blinded by a sort of thick vapour, a stagnant and nauseating cloud of steam. The few rays of light which came through the cracks were not enough to allow him to distinguish the objects in the room. His first instinct had been to run to the fireplace, but there was no fire and the furniture seemed to be intact, so that a fire could be excluded. He was bewildered and beginning to feel faint because of the awful atmosphere; he ran to the window and pushed the shutters open violently. The kitchen was suddenly flooded in light.

He was astounded by an extraordinary sight. Everything in the kitchen was in its proper place; the glass and the empty bottle of double-strength brandy were on the table; only the chair in which the old man must have been sitting showed traces of fire, the front legs were charred, the straw seat half burnt away. What had happened to Uncle Macquart? Where could he have gone? And in front of the chair all that was to be seen was a pool of liquid fat on the tiled floor and a small heap of ashes, beside which lay the pipe, a black pipe, not even broken by the fall. All that was left of the old man was there, in this handful of finely powdered ashes, in the rust-coloured cloud of vapour escaping through the open window, in the coating of soot which covered the whole kitchen, a horrible greasy film of evaporated flesh, covering everything, oily and foul to the touch.

Pascal was forced to believe that he was observing a case of spontaneous combustion so perfect as to be unique in medical history. He had read about some surprising cases; among others the case of a cobbler's wife who had fallen asleep over a foot-warmer and all they had found had been a foot and a hand. He himself had hitherto been reluctant to admit the old theory that a body, impregnated with alcohol, emitted some unknown gas which blazed up spontaneously and consumed flesh and bones. But he could not deny the evidence of his own eyes. It was easy to reconstruct exactly what had happened; a drunken coma, complete unconsciousness, the pipe falling on the clothes which caught fire, the drink-saturated flesh which burned and split, the fat which had melted, part of it dripping to the floor, the rest of it activating combustion and, in the end, everything, muscles, the organs, bones were consumed, the whole body in a final burst of flames. That was the last of the old man in his blue suit and the fur cap which he wore from one end of the year to the other. Doubtless, as soon as he had started blazing up like a bonfire, he had fallen forwards, which explained why the chair was only slightly charred; and there was nothing left, not a bone, not a tooth, not a nail, nothing but this little heap of grey dust, which the draught from the door was dispersing.

Clotilde had come into the room; Charles was still outside, puzzled by the howling of the dog.

"Oh! my God, what a smell!" she said. "What has happened?"

When Pascal had explained the incredible catastrophe she shuddered violently. She took up the bottle and was inspecting it but she put it down at once, horrified by the wet greasy film from the old man's flesh. Nothing could be touched, everything was covered with this thin layer of yellow grease, which stuck to the hands.

She shivered, almost retching with disgust, burst out crying and stammered:

"What a death! .. A terrible death!"

Pascal had overcome his first reaction to the horrible sight and smell and he was almost smiling:

"Terrible, why? .. He was eighty-four, he felt no pain .. I consider it a splendid death for the old bandit, who lived, by God!

Admittedly it was a somewhat irregular existence! .. You remember his file, he committed many terrible and loathsome crimes, which did not prevent him from settling down later on, from growing old amidst his possessions which meant so much to him, with a twinkle in his eye, rewarded for the great virtues in which he had been singularly lacking .. And now he dies a royal death, like the prince of drunkards, blazing away of his own accord, consumed in the funeral pile of his own body!"

Carried away by his own enthusiasm, the doctor flung out his arms, as if to embrace the imaginary scene:

"Can you see it? .. So drunk that he could not feel himself burning, lighting himself like a Saint-Jean's fire, dispersing himself in smoke, down to the last bone! .. Can't you see the old man disappearing into space, first spread over the four corners of this kitchen, dissolved in and floating in the air, bathing all the objects he owned, then escaping in a cloud of vapour through this window, as soon as I opened it, flying off into the sky, filling the horizon? .. Verily an admirable death! to disappear, to leave nothing of oneself behind, except a handful of ashes and a pipe by one's side!"

He picked up the pipe to keep it, he added, as a relic of the old man; whilst Clotilde, who had thought that she had detected an element of mordant satire in this lyrical outburst, expressed her feelings by another shiver of disgust.

But she had caught sight of something, under the table, perhaps another fragment left over:

"Look, there is something under the table!"

He bent down, and was surprised to find that he had picked up a lady's glove, a green glove.

"Oh!" she cried, "it is grandmother's glove. You remember, the glove that was missing yesterday evening!"

They gazed at each other and the same explanation occurred to them both. Felicité, the day before, had been in this room; and the doctor, in a flash, was convinced that his mother had seen her brother on fire and had made no attempt to extinguish the blaze. The evidence was conclusive, the fact that the room had been quite cold. He saw the same thought in the horrified eyes of Clotilde. But, as it seemed that the real truth would never be known, his imagination got to work and outlined the simplest story:

"Doubtless, your grandmother must have come to say hello to the old man on her way back from the asylum, before he started drinking."

"Let's get away from here! Hurry up!" cried Clotilde. "I am suffocating, I must get away!"

It was Pascal's duty to notify the death. He followed her out, locked the door and put the key in his pocket. Once more outside they could hear the little yellow dog again still howling. He had taken refuge between Charles's legs, and the child, highly amused, but incurious, was poking the dog with his foot.

The doctor went straight to M. Maurin, the notary of the Tulettes, who also happened to be the mayor of the commune. He had been a widower this ten years, living with his daughter, who was also a widow and childless. He had been on good neighbourly terms with old Macquart and had sometimes had Charles in his house for a whole day at a time, as his daughter had taken a kindly interest in the boy who was so handsome and so much to be pitied. M. Maurin was horrified, insisted on going up with the doctor to see the evidence for himself and promised to write out an official death certificate. As for a religious ceremony, a funeral, there seemed to be insuperable difficulties. When they had gone back into the kitchen, the draught from the door had blown away the ashes; and when they tried to collect them, as a pious gesture to his memory, they had only succeeded in picking up floor sweepings which must have contained precious little of the old man. What was there to bury? They decided to give it up. Besides, Macquart had not been a regular churchgoer and the family would have to be content with having masses said for his soul later on.

The notary declared that there was a will, deposited in his office. He gave the doctor an appointment for the next day but one, for the official reading; he had felt justified in revealing that fact that Macquart had made Pascal his executor. And he was good enough to offer to keep Charles until then. He knew that the boy's mother did not want him and that he would be in Pascal's way at the Souleiade. Charles seemed delighted and he was left at the Tulettes.

It was very late before Pascal and Clotilde were able to leave for Plassans. Pascal had to visit his two patients at the asylum, after which they caught the seven o'clock train. Two days later, however, when they were on their way to keep the appointment with M. Maurin, they were disagreeably surprised to find old Madame Rougon waiting for them in the office. She had, naturally, heard about Macquart's death and lost no time in hurrying to the Tulettes, simmering with excitement, vociferous in her expressions of grief. The reading of the will, incidentally, had been a simple affair; Macquart had left all his savings to be devoted to erecting a magnificent tomb, in marble, with two monumental angels, weeping, their wings folded. The idea must have been suggested to him by a similar tomb, seen somewhere abroad—in Germany, perhaps—when he had been soldiering. The will specified that his nephew Pascal should supervise the erection of the monument, because he was the only one in the family who had shown any signs of artistic taste. When Pascal and Felicité reappeared, there was a moment of great embarrassment, as they had not spoken to each other for months. But the old lady was perfectly at her ease and made no allusion to their disagreement, implying that it was desirable to meet occasionally and appear to be united in the eyes of the world without any need for discussion or reconciliation. But she made the mistake of insisting too vehemently on the great grief which Macquart's death had caused her. Pascal was in no doubt about her real feelings. He realized that she was pleasantly surprised and infinitely relieved at the thought that this deep wound to the family pride due to this abomination of an uncle was at last going to be scarred over. Thus he could not help feeling impatient and disgusted. Unconsciously his eyes were fixed on her gloves which were black.

She was in the act of bewailing, in a low voice:

"So unwise, at his age, to insist on living alone like an old wolf. He might at least have kept a servant!"

Then the doctor spoke, without clearly realizing what he was saying:

"But, mother, as you were on the spot, why did you not stop him from burning?"

Old Madame Rougon's face turned deathly pale. How could her son have known? For an instant she looked at him, with her mouth open; Clotilde grew almost equally white in the face, the crime was now proved without the shadow of a doubt. It was a confession, this terrified silence which had fallen on the mother, the son and herself, that quivering silence in which families bury their domestic tragedies. The two women were speechless. The doctor, appalled at having spoken, he who had always so carefully avoided unpleasant and useless argument, was desperately trying to take back his words when a fresh catastrophe dwarfed their embarrassment.

Felicité had decided to take Charles back with her, not wanting to abuse M. Maurin's hospitality; the latter, immediately after lunch, had sent the boy, with an escort, to the asylum to spend an hour with Tante Dide, and he now sent a maid to fetch him back at once. It was at this moment that the maid, whom they were awaiting in the garden, appeared out of breath, covered in perspiration, terribly distressed, crying out as she ran:

"Help! Help! Come quickly .. Master Charles is bleeding to death .."

They were horrified and all three of them started to run toward the asylum.

Tante Dide had been having one of her good days, very calm, very gentle, very straight against the back of the armchair in which she had been sitting for hours at a time for the last twenty-two years, looking fixedly at nothing. She seemed even thinner, her muscles were completely wasted away, her arms and her legs were nothing but sticks of bone covered in parchment-like skin; and her nurse, the buxom blonde wench, had to carry her, feed her, manipulate her like an inanimate object. The ancestor, the forgotten woman, tall, with her knotty fingers, terrifying, remained motionless. Her eyes were the only live thing about her, her clear eyes the colour of spring water in her thin dessicated countenance. But that morning a sudden flood of tears had poured down her cheeks and then she had started stammering a spate of disconnected words and phrases, which seemed to prove that in spite of her senile exhaustion and the inexorable progress of her dementia the hardening of the brain was still not complete; memories remained stored up, gleams of intelligence were conceivable. And her face had reverted to its mute blankness, indifferent to everything, sometimes chuckling at an unfortunate accident, a fall for example, more usually not seeing or hearing anything, intent on contemplating empty space eternally.

When Charles was brought in the nurse installed him at once at his little table, facing his distant forebear. She kept a packet of pictures for him, soldiers, captains, kings, clothed in purple and gold and she handed them to him with his special cutting-out scissors:

"There, have your fun and don't make any noise, be very good. You can see that grannie is very nice today. You must be nice to her, too!"

The child had raised his eyes to the madwoman and they were staring at each other. Their extraordinary resemblance was more striking than ever. Especially their eyes, their vacant and limpid eyes, seemed to be indistinguishable, identical. Then the physiognomy, the faded features of the centenarian, transmitted, at one bound, skipping three generations, to the delicate face of the child, also as if half rubbed-out, prematurely old and faded, the last exhausted remnant of his race. They were not smiling, they were just staring solemnly at each other with idiotic and ludicrous gravity.

"Well!" continued the nurse, who had acquired the habit of talking to herself to keep up her spirits, "they could not deny their relationship. Whoever made the one, made the other. The spit and image . . Come, let's have a smile from both of you, as you are so pleased to be together . ."

But the slightest concentration tired Charles and he was the first to lower his head; whilst Tante Dide, who had astonishing staying power, continued staring at him indefinitely, without once blinking.

For a moment the nurse was busy about the little room, full of sun, gay with its light wall-paper with a pattern of blue flowers. She remade the bed which she had been airing and sorted some linen on the shelves of the cupboard. It was her custom to profit by the little boy's visits and slip out for a little distraction. She was supposed never to leave her charge; but when he was there she ventured to leave the old lady with him.

"Listen," she repeated, "I must go out; if she moves and seems to need me, ring the bell, call me at once, won't you? . . You understand, you are big enough to know how to call me!"

He had raised his head, and made a gesture implying that he had understood and would call her. When he was left alone with Tante Dide he resumed his cutting out very quietly. This continued for a quarter of an hour in the profound silence of the asylum in which only distant sounds, reminiscent of a prison, could be heard; a furtive footstep, the clinking of a bunch of keys, then, sometimes, wild cries, immediately muffled. But on this torrid day the child must have felt tired and he dozed off. Soon his head, lily-white, nodded under the heavy helmet of his royal crown of hair; then it dropped, gently, on top of the pictures, he was sound asleep, one cheek resting on the purple and gold of the kings. His eye-lashes shadowed the other cheek, life ran feebly through the little blue veins under his fragile skin. He was as beautiful as an angel, with the undefinable corruption of a whole race stamped on his countenance. And Tante Dide went on staring at him vacantly, with neither pleasure nor pain, as eternity might look if it stared at the earth.

But at the end of a few minutes her clear eyes showed a faint glimmer of excitement. Something had happened, a red drop was swelling at the tip of the child's left nostril. The drop fell, and another gathered and followed it. It was blood spouting like red dew, noiselessly, with nothing to account for it, no blow this time; it came out of its own accord and dripped away, the sign of degeneration. The drops coalesced to make a thin flow which dripped on to the gold of the pictures. Soon they were obliterated by a pool which spread towards the corner of the table; then the drops gathered more quickly, ran into each other and dropped heavily on to the tiles of the floor. And still he slept on, looking like a divinely calm cherub, without any idea that his life was escaping from him; and the madwoman went on staring at him, looking more excited but with no sign of fear, diverted if anything, her eye caught by the bright colour as it would have been by big flies the flight of which she often followed for hours.

After another few minutes the thin thread of red had widened, the drops followed each other more rapidly and dropped to the floor with an obstinate and monotonous splashing sound. At one moment Charles moved, opened his eyes and saw that he was covered in blood. But he did not take fright, he was used to this red spring which gushed out of him at the slightest blow. He made a faint sound of protest. But then his instinct seemed to come into play and warn him; he looked frightened, made a louder noise and stammered confusedly:

"Mamma! Mamma!"

But he must have been extremely weak, because an invincible lethargy overcame him, he seemed to doze off again, a soft moaning came from his lips, as if his lamentations were continuing in a dream and the sound became fainter and fainter:

"Mamma! Mamma!"

The pictures were drowned in blood, the black velvet of his jacket and breeches, embellished with gold, was covered in blood-stains along the seams; and the little thread of scarlet went on obstinately flowing from the left nostril, without stopping, crossing the scarlet pool on the table, splashing to the floor, which soon became a puddle. A cry for help from the madwoman, a cry of terror, would have been enough. But she made no cry, she did not call out, motionless, with her ancestral eyes staring fixedly at the finger of fate, dried up, knotted, limbs and tongue paralyzed by her hundred years, brain ossified by dementia, incapable of will or movement. And yet, the sight of the little scarlet stream seemed to excite a spark of emotion in her. A quiver had passed over her dead features, a slight warmth rose to her cheeks. Finally, she was aroused by a last plaintive: "Mamma! Mamma!"

Then Tante Dide became visibly and hideously animated. She clasped her temples with her bony claws, as if she felt her skull bursting. Her mouth had opened wide, though it uttered no sound; the tumult seething inside her paralyzed her tongue. She managed to push herself to her feet and tried to run; but she had no muscles and remained nailed to the spot. Her poor old body quivered and shook with the superhuman effort she was making to call for help, without succeeding in breaking the bars of her senility and her dementia. Her face, a ravaged mask of horror, her memory partially restored, she seemed fully aware of what was happening. The end came slowly and almost imperceptibly and lasted long minutes. Charles seemed to have gone to sleep again, did not utter a sound, the blood ran out of his veins and ran away in a slow noiseless, endless, sluggish flood. His blanched, lily-white complexion turned gradually into the pallor of death. His lips changed colour from a pallid pink to white. And, at the last gasp, he opened his eyes wide and fixed them on his great-great-grandmother, who was staring at him, fascinated, and thus saw the last gleam of life flicker out in the depths of those eyes. The waxen face was dead already, only the eyes were still alive. They remained limpid and clear. Suddenly they were emptied of all expression and were extinguished. That was the end, the death of those eyes; and Charles died without a shudder, like a spring emptied of all its water. No more life beat in the veins under his fragile skin, there was nothing but the shadow of his eye-lashes over his white face. But he was divinely beautiful, his head steeped in blood amidst the fair, fanned-out, royal hair, like one of those bloodless princes unable to bear the burden of their execrable heritage who fade away old and feebleminded in their fifteenth year.

He had just exhaled his last faint breath when Doctor Pascal arrived, followed by Felicité and Clotilde. And as soon as he saw all that blood on the tiles of the floor:

"Ah!" he cried, "that is what I had been afraid of. The poor little fellow! no one was there, it finished him!"

But the three of them were even more shocked by the extraordinary spectacle which now met their horrified eyes. Tante Dide, half out of her chair, had almost managed to stand up; and her eyes, fixed on the dead boy, so white and fragile, on the scarlet blood, on the pool of blood which was beginning to clot, were alive with thought after her long sleep of twenty-two years. This terminal lesion of dementia, this night of the brain, irreparable, was not complete; this dreadful blow had doubtless awakened a distant long-stored memory suddenly and terrifyingly. And the forgotten woman was alive again, emerged from her void, rigid and devastated like a spectre of horror and grief.

The effort was inhuman, at first she could only pant. Then she shuddered and managed to stammer one word:

"The policeman! The policeman!"

Pascal, Felicité, Clotilde, all three of them, had understood. They stole horrified glances at each other and shivered. It was an evocation of that long history of violence, the whole life of the old mother, of the mother of all of them, the exasperated and then frustrated passions of her youth, the long Calvary of the years of maturity. Already in the past two emotional shocks had shaken her to the core; the first one, out of the blue, in the full flower of her passionate youth, when a policeman had shot down her lover, the smuggler Macquart, like a dog; the second, many years afterwards, when another policeman, with a pistol shot, had blown out the brains of her grandson Silvère, the rebel, victim of the hatreds and bloody struggles within the family. Always she had been blood be-spattered. A third emotional shock was too much for her, again she was spattered with blood, this impoverished blood of her race which she had watched flowing endlessly away and which was now spread over the floor whilst the dead-white royal child slept on, with no blood in his veins or in his heart.

Thrice more, reliving in her clouded mind the whole of her passionate, tortured and bloody life, dominated by the inexorable law of expiation, she stammered:

"The policeman! The policeman! The policeman!"

She collapsed into her armchair. They thought her dead, a sudden awe-inspiring death, as if struck by lightning.

But the nurse had, at last, ventured back into the room, trying to think up excuses, terrified of an ignominious and immediate dismissal. When Doctor Pascal had helped her to carry Tante Dide on to her bed, he found that she was still alive. She was not to die until the next day, at the age of one hundred and five years three months and seven days, of a cerebral congestion due to this last shock.

Pascal had said at once to his mother:

"She will not last twenty-four hours, she will be dead before tomorrow night .. First, Uncle Macquart, then the old lady and the poor child, one after the other, what dreadful portents!"

He paused to add in a lower voice:

"The family is being thinned out, the old trees are falling and the young trees are being eaten away by decay."

Felicité thought that he was making another ironical allusion .. She was sincerely distressed by the tragic death of little Charles. But all the same, overriding the shiver of dismay was the immense feeling of relief. Next week, when all their tears had been dried, what bliss to know that all this abomination at the Tulettes was no more, that the glory of the family could at last rise again and the legend shine forth unsullied once more!

Then she remembered that she had not replied to her son's involuntary accusation at the notary's; and, as a gesture of bravado, brought up the subject:

"You see, servants are of no use after all. There was one here, but she did nothing to prevent the disaster; even if uncle had had someone to look after him, he would still be in ashes at this moment."

Pascal made a little bow, with his usual deferential air:

"You are right, mother."

Clotilde had fallen to her knees. Her blind faith in the Catholic religion was revived in this room of blood, madness and death. Tears were streaming from her eyes, her hands were clasped in fervent prayer, she was praying for the dear ones who were no more. My God! let their sufferings be finally at an end, let their sins be pardoned, let them be raised again to another life of eternal bliss! And she interceded for them with all her heart, terrified of some sort of hell, which, after such miserable lives, might deliver them over to eternal punishment.

From that sad day onwards, when Pascal and Clotilde sallied forth to visit his patients, they were more loving than ever, pressed closely to each other. If anything, he felt even more helpless than before in the face of disease. The only wise course was to let nature evolve, eliminate dangerous elements, to concentrate on the final goal of health and strength. But one's own relatives, the relatives who suffer and die, make one uncontrollably resentful of disease and feel an irresistible urge to combat and conquer it. Hence, the doctor felt overjoyed when one of his injections succeeded in cutting short an attack and he could see the patient, who had been writhing in pain, alleviated and then fall asleep. When he returned to Clotilde, she worshipped him and was immensely proud of him as if their love was in itself the gift of consolation.

CHAPTER TEN

ONE morning Martine asked Doctor Pascal to sign a receipt for fifteen hundred francs, in order to collect what she called "their income" from notary Grandguillot.

"Another quarter-day already?" he asked. He now paid even less attention to money matters than before and gave Martine a free hand to deal with everything.

Pascal and Clotilde were sitting under the plane trees, lulled by the never-ending song of the spring, when the servant came back, panic-stricken and in an indescribable state of agitation. She was so out of breath that it was a few moments before she could articulate:

"Ah! My God! Ah! My God! Monsieur Grandguillot has gone!"

At first Pascal did not grasp her meaning:

"Well, my good girl, there is no hurry, you can go back another day."

"No, no! He has gone, do you hear, gone away altogether, for good .."

The floodgates opened:

"I arrived in the street, a long way away I saw a crowd in front of the door .. I felt a cold shiver in my spine, I knew something awful had happened. And the front door was closed, not a window blind open, a house of the dead .. They told me at once that he had run away, not left a farthing behind him, that a lot of families were ruined .."

She put the receipt down on the stone table:

"There! That's your paper! We're finished, not a sou left, we shall die of hunger!"

She broke down, wept and sobbed loudly, crushed by this loss of a fortune and terrified at the threat of poverty.

Clotilde was dumbfounded and said nothing, her eyes on Pascal who seemed reluctant to believe Martine's story. He tried to calm her. Come! It was no use upsetting herself. If she had only spoken to people in the street, she was probably only repeating gossip which always magnified everything. M. Grandguillot in flight, M. Grandguillot a thief, it was impossible, monstrous! A man of such universally acknowledged probity! A firm established for more than a century, loved and respected by the whole of Plassans! To invest money with Grandguillot was said to be safer than investing it in the Bank of France.

"Use your brains, Martine, such a catastrophe could not happen out of the blue like a stroke of lightning, there would have been premonitory rumours .. The devil take it! A firm of unimpeachable integrity does not collapse in a night."

She made a despairing gesture:

"Oh! Monsieur, that is what upsets me because, you see, it makes me feel a little guilty .. I have been hearing stories for weeks .. You two, naturally, hear nothing, you do not know that you are alive .."

Pascal and Clotilde smiled, it was very true that their love for each other was out of this world. They were too much wrapped up in each other to hear, much less listen to gossip.

"Only, as these stories were very nasty, I did not want to bother you, I thought they were lies."

But, in the end, she told them the stories that were being circulated; M. Grandguillot had been gambling on the Stock Exchange, or was keeping women at Marseilles, or indulging in orgies and abominable vices. She broke into sobs once more:

"Holy mother of God! What will become of us? We will surely die of hunger!"

Pascal was shaken out of his complacency. He tried to cast his mind back, to remember his old transactions in detail. Some time ago, when he had been in practice in Plassans, he had made a number of payments to M. Grandguillot, the total investment having been the sum of one hundred and twenty thousand francs, the income from which had been keeping them in comfort for the last sixteen years; and, each time, the notary had given him a receipt for the amount deposited. This, doubtless, would enable him to establish his claim to be considered a personal creditor. Then, he had an uneasy feeling that he could remember a long forgotten incident. The memory was so nebulous that he could not even put an approximate date to it; at the request of and after a long explanatory speech from the notary, he had signed a power of attorney authorizing him to invest the whole or part of his money in mortgages; and he felt certain that the name of his proxy had been left blank. But, he had no means of knowing whether this document had ever been implemented. In fact, he had never even bothered to find out how his funds had been invested.

Martine considered this akin to blasphemy and cried:

"Ah! Monsieur, you are being punished for your sins! What a way to neglect one's money! I, for my part, make up my accounts to the last centime, every three months."

In spite of her anguish her faded features were lit up by an unconscious smile. She was thinking of her savings so obstinately and passionately accumulated over the years, her salary of four hundred francs hardly broken into, invested for thirty years, totalling by now, thanks to the interest, the enormous sum of about twenty thousand francs. And this treasure was intact, invested in gilt-edged securities, somewhere unknown and mysterious, a closely kept secret. She felt a marvellous sense of relief, but refrained from saying anything more.

Pascal protested:

"Eh! How do you know that all our money has been lost? Monsieur Grandguillot had a personal fortune, he could hardly have taken his house and his estates away with him. We shall see, the matter will be cleared up. I cannot bring myself to believe that he is really a thief .. The only bother is that we shall have to wait."

He was trying to reassure Clotilde who was looking at him and at the Souleiade around them with a frown. She was concerned solely with Pascal's happiness. This made her more passionately determined than ever to go on living with and loving him in this friendly solitude. Pascal automatically reverted to his usual attitude of lordly indifference to money, which had never been his primary objective. He had always been so secure that he could not imagine being without it nor actually suffering want.

"But I have got some money!" he cried. "So much for Martine's ideas about our being penniless and dying of hunger!"

Once more, he was full of gaiety and insisted upon their both following him.

"Come along, come along! I'll show you the money! And I'll give some to Martine so that she can cook us a good dinner tonight."

He took them upstairs to his room and lowered the flap of his desk with an air of triumph. This was his famous hoard. This was the drawer into which he threw his unsolicited fees. Not once in sixteen years had he counted the gold pieces and banknotes. Up to the last few months he had only drawn insignificant amounts and had come to think of his savings as inexhaustible. He had forgotten his presents to Clotilde, which had been paid for with money from the drawer. He turned to them with a satisfied smile:

"You will see! You will be surprised!"

He was almost ludicrously perplexed when, after a feverish search through an accumulation of bills and invoices, he could only rake up the sum of six hundred and fifteen francs, two notes of a hundred francs, four hundred francs in gold and fifteen francs in change. He shook the papers and poked his fingers into the corners of the drawer, crying:

"But it's not possible! There has always been such a lot, a few days ago there was still a tidy sum! .. I must have mistaken some of these old invoices for banknotes. I swear to you that only a week or two ago, I had my hands on a lot of money."

He was so transparently sincere that Clotilde could not help laughing. What a hopeless business man he was! Then, when she noticed Martine's deep concern, her absolute despair about this small amount of money which was all the three of them had to live on, she felt conscience-stricken. Her eyes were moist, as she murmured:

"My God! you have spent it all on me. I have ruined you, it is my fault that there is nothing left."

Pascal then realized what had happened to the money. It was a relief to be able to account for it And, when full of remorse, she suggested selling everything back to the shopkeepers, he became annoyed:

"Give back what I gave you! But you would be giving back a part of me with them! No, no, even if I have to starve by your side, I want you to look beautiful and radiant."

Then, confidently, and feeling that the future would look after itself:

"Besides, we are not going to start starving tonight, eh, Martine? .. We might be in a much worse plight."

Martine shook her head. She could manage to make the money last for two months, perhaps three, if they did not make too many demands on her:

"Give me the two hundred-franc notes. I will try and make them last for a month. Afterwards, we shall see .. But you must be careful, don't touch the four hundred francs in gold, shut the drawer and don't open it any more."

"Oh! that!" cried the doctor, "you needn't worry! I would rather cut my hand off."

And so the matter was settled. Martine was to have sole charge of their last resources; and she could be relied upon to be economical.

As for Clotilde, she had never had any money of her own and would not know the difference. Pascal would be the principal sufferer as he would no longer be able to draw on his inexhaustible treasure; but he had given his word not to touch the drawer and to allow the servant to pay for everything.

"Ouf! That is an excellent arrangement!" he said, relieved and as pleased as if he had just brought off a business deal profitable enough to keep them in comfort for the rest of their lives.

A week sped by and nothing seemed changed at the Souleiade. Pascal and Clotilde were too immersed in each other to be able to realize that there was a real threat of destitution awaiting them. One morning, when Clotilde had gone to market with Martine, the doctor had a disquieting visitor who, at first, caused him considerable anxiety. It was the saleswoman who had sold him the antique French point lace shawl, that magnificent work of art, the first of his presents. He was genuinely frightened at the idea of any further temptation. Even before the woman had opened her mouth, he started protesting: No! No! he could not, would not buy anything! She merely smiled, fat and affable, very sure of herself and of her victim. In a low, insinuating murmur, she told him the story; yes, a lady whose name could not be mentioned, one of the most distinguished ladies in Plassans, had had a stroke of bad luck and been forced to sell a jewel; then she emphasized the unique nature of the bargain, a most exceptional one, a jewel which had cost more than twelve hundred francs. The lady was reconciled to sacrificing it for five hundred francs. In a casual and leisurely manner, in spite of the doctor's reluctance and increasing anxiety, the saleswoman proceeded to open her bag and pulled out a thin gold necklace with a pendant of seven pearls. It was quite plain but the pearls were perfect. They were round, limpid and glowed with an admirable sheen. He was captivated at once and could visualize it on Clotilde's delicate neck. Any other necklace would have been too pretentious, but these pearls would be perfect on Clotilde's silky skin which felt to his lips like the petals of some marvellous flower. He could not bear the thought of having to give it back. He still tried to make a show of resistance, swore that he did not have five hundred francs, whilst the saleswoman, not untruthfully, continued in her even tone of voice to point out how cheap it was. The conversation went on for another quarter of an hour. Then, sensing he had made up his mind to buy, she suddenly offered to let him have it for three hundred francs; and he agreed, in the grip of his old folly, his mad urge to shower his idol with gifts. When he went to fetch the fifteen gold pieces from the drawer and handed them over to her, he had already persuaded himself that the notary's affairs would soon be settled and that they would have plenty of money.

When he was alone again with the necklace in his pocket, he felt as delighted as a child with a new toy. As he impatiently waited for Clotilde, he was planning the details of his surprise. When he saw her, his heart beat madly. She was as gay as a lark and joked about Martine's latest bargain, two pigeons for eighteen sous. The ardent August sun was blazing in the sky and she wanted to change her dress. He was trembling with excitement as he followed her into the bedroom; and, when she was in her petticoat, arms and shoulders bare, he pretended to see something on her neck.

"Tell me! What have you got there? Let me see."

He was hiding the necklace in his hand but managed to slip it on her, pretending to run his fingers over her neck to make sure that there was nothing there. But she was fighting him off, taking it all as a great joke:

"Stop! I am quite sure that there is nothing .. Come, what are you doing, what have you got in your hand, it's tickling me?"

He pulled her towards him and pushed her in front of the cheval-glass. Then she saw the thin thread of gold around her neck with the seven pearls, like milky stars, nestling against her satin-smooth skin. She made an exclamation of rapture like the cooing of a dove puffing itself out with vanity!

"Oh! master, my master! How good you are! .. You spoil me! .. But you make me so proud and happy!"

Such was her joy, so resplendent was she that he felt that his folly was amply justified.

She was radiant, she threw back her head and offered him her lips. He bent his own head and they kissed.

"Are you pleased?"

"Oh! yes, my master, very, very pleased! I love the feel of pearls and these particular ones seem to be made for me!"

For another minute or two she went on preening herself in front of the mirror. She looked enchanting and the pearls gave a nacreous lustre to her skin. She felt that she had to show them to someone and, hearing the servant moving about in the study, burst in on Martine in her petticoat and bare arms:

"Martine! Martine! Look at what the master has just given me!..
They make me look marvellous!"

She stopped short when she saw the disapproving expression on
Martine's face. She understood, intuitively, what this poor creature
must be feeling; how torn with jealousy, although immured in the
mute resignation of the born servant. But this was merely the
servant's first and unconscious reaction; her basic attitude was one
of bitter disapproval. She deplored and condemned the expensive
present.

Clotilde was dismayed:

"Oh! the master must have been at his desk again .. Are pearls
very expensive?"

Pascal, far from easy in his mind, protested and explained what a
wonderful bargain the necklace had been. In a hasty flood of words
he told the story of the saleswoman's visit. An incredible bargain,
much too good to be missed.

"How much?" asked the young woman, really worried.

"Three hundred francs."

Martine, grimly silent until then, could not refrain from
exclaiming:

"Good heavens! enough to live on for six weeks and we have no
bread!"

Tears came into Clotilde's eyes. She would have torn the necklace
from her neck if it had not been for Pascal. She talked about giving
it back at once, she was distracted and stammered:

"It is true, Martine is right .. Uncle is mad and it is wrong of
me to keep it for another minute. It will scorch me. I beg of you,
let me take it back."

But he proved adamant. He went so far as to sympathize with
them, agreed with their point of view, cried that he was incorrigible
and that they should have taken all the money away from him. He
ran to his desk, pulled out the remaining hundred francs and
insisted upon Martine taking charge of them:

"I tell you, I am not to be trusted, I will not keep a single sou!
I would only spend it .. Here! Martine! You are the only sensible
person in this house .. And you, dearest one, keep the necklace,
don't make me unhappy. Kiss me, go to your bedroom and dress
yourself."

Henceforth the subject of the catastrophe was tacitly avoided.
But Clotilde kept the necklace. She wore it underneath her blouse;
it gave her pleasure to feel it against her skin. It was her cherished

secret, a relatively harmless form of self-indulgence. Sometimes when they were alone together, she smiled at Pascal and pulled out the pearls, brandishing them in front of him without a word and tucked them away again, almost blushing because of the intensity of her delight in them and in him. They reminded her of the madly passionate element in their love for each other. They became a symbol. She always wore them, even at night.

Very gradually, the household began to feel the lack of money. At first, Pascal and Clotilde found it not unpleasant. Martine had made an inventory of their stocks of food and reported that potatoes were the only foodstuff of which they had a plentiful supply. As luck would have it, the jar of oil was nearly empty and the last barrel of wine was down to the dregs. The Souleiade was no longer productive; no more vineyards nor olive trees, only a few vegetables and a little fruit, pears which were not yet ripe and a few grapes from the vine arbour which would be their one luxury. Bread and meat had to be bought every day.

Hence from the first day, the servant rationed Pascal and Clotilde, never served them sweets or pastries and gave them smaller portions. She reverted to the position of authority which had been hers for so many years, treated them like children, no longer consulted their wishes or their tastes. It was she who decided what they were to eat, what was good for them; there was something maternal in the way she fussed over them. Besides, no one else could have managed so miraculously to keep up the appearance of plenty on such a beggarly pittance. Sometimes, not often, she admonished them, but it was for their own good as one admonishes a child who will not eat up his soup. It seemed as though this peculiar maternity, this final self-immolation gave her considerable satisfaction and aroused her from the state of apathetic despair into which she had lapsed. Now that she felt herself essential to their welfare she looked, once more, like a nun dedicated to celibacy with her placid white face and calm grey eyes, the colour of ashes. When, after the invariable potatoes and a minute cutlet lost among the vegetables, she managed, without compromising her budget, to serve them a dish of pancakes, she did so with an air of triumph and revelled in their delighted laughter.

Pascal and Clotilde found everything to their liking. This did not prevent them from laughing at her behind her back. They revived their old jokes about her avarice. They claimed that she counted the grains of pepper, so many for each dish! When the potatoes were too dry, cooked almost without oil, or the cutlets reduced to no more than a mouthful, they grinned at each other and, when she had gone, stifled their laughter in their napkins. Everything was a source of amusement to them, they even laughed at their poverty.

At the end of the first month, Pascal remembered Martine's wages. In the past, she had always taken her forty francs from the household money.

"My poor girl," he said to her one evening, " what are you going to do about your wages, as there is no more money?"

For a moment she seemed perplexed:

"Why to be sure! Monsieur, I shall have to wait."

But he could see that she had some idea at the back of her mind which she was reluctant to express and he nodded to her encouragingly.

"Well, if it will not offend monsieur, I would like him to sign a paper for me."

"What, a paper?"

"Yes, a paper on which monsieur could write, each month, that he owes me forty francs."

Pascal proceeded, immediately, to do what she wanted. She was very pleased with her bit of paper and put it away carefully in her purse just as though it had been real money.

Up till that time, it had been no effort for Pascal and Clotilde to retain their serenity in the face of their misfortune, which they did not even recognize. They were not living in the real world but in some distant, fabulously rich country of their fevered imaginations. At meals they paid no attention to what they were eating. They were dreaming of princely banquets, choice foods served on silver dishes. They were oblivious to everything that was happening around them, to the creeping threat of destitution, to the hungry servant who subsisted on the crumbs from their table; they walked about the empty house as if it were a palace, hung with silks and adorned with priceless works of art. It was during this period that they loved each other with greater intensity than ever before or afterwards. The bedroom was their whole world with its faded dawn-pink cotton print hangings, in which they kept finding new delight in each other, never growing tired of lying in each other's arms. They also spent days in the study, so full of happy memories, as if luxuriantly wrapped in the joy of having lived together for so long. Outside, at this time of year, royal summer had erected its blue tent, blazing with gold. Not knowing and not caring whether they were poor or rich, they strolled through the grounds of the Souleiade; in the morning, along the path through the fragrant trees; at midday, through the dense shade of the plane trees refreshed by the song of the spring; in the evening, on the cool terrace or in the yard which was still pleasantly warm and lit by the blue flush of the first stars. The earth was theirs with its treasures, with all its feast days and sovereign pomp!

Towards the end of August the situation was becoming so critical that even Pascal and Clotilde became disturbed. They began to realize that the idyllic existence which had been theirs, this life without ties or duties, even without work, could not last for ever. One evening, Martine announced that she was down to their last fifty francs which would only be enough to feed them for two more weeks and only on condition that they stopped drinking wine. The news about Pascal's money was equally bad; notary Grand-guillot was definitely insolvent, even the personal creditors would not get a penny. At first Pascal had counted on the house and two farms which still belonged to the notary; but now it appeared that this property had been transferred to his wife. As it was in her name, nothing could be done; and whilst the notary, according to reports, was admiring the beauty of the scenery in Switzerland, his wife was living in comfort in one of the farms, indifferent to the discom-fiture of his creditors. Plassans was seething with the scandalous story that his wife complacently tolerated his dissolute conduct and had not even protested at his taking two mistresses with him to Switzerland. And Pascal, careless as ever of his own material welfare, had not even bothered to visit the procurator of the republic to discuss his case. He claimed that the details of the nasty business were now common property, that nothing was to be gained by stirring up more mud, especially as there was obviously no hope of salvaging anything from the wreck.

Very soon they would be absolutely destitute. And Clotilde, who was by no means without common sense, was the first to be aware of the fact. She managed when Pascal was there to keep up an appearance of gaiety and to behave like her old carefree self. Alone, she became terror-stricken at the thought of his helplessness; her love for him made her more far-sighted and she kept asking herself what would become of him, how, at his age and without any income, could he possibly go on shouldering the heavy burden of the household? For some days she had been thinking out the details of a secret plan; she would work at her pastels and earn money by selling them. She had so often been told that she had great talent, exceptional and very individual talent. She took Martine into her confidence and sent her, one morning, to offer several of her most fantastic flower pastels to the art dealer in the Cours Sauvaire who, she had heard, was related to a painter in Paris. She gave Martine strict instructions to stipulate that her pictures should not be exhibited in Plassans, but should all be sent away. The result was disastrous. The dealer was disconcerted by the strange quality of her pictorial imagination and by the unusual boldness of colour and line and declared that there would be no sale for them. Her disappointment was so great that she wept bitter tears. Of what use was she? It was a scandal and a disgrace not to be able to earn her own living! The servant tried to console her by explaining that not all women were born to work, that some grow like flowers in a garden simply for the sake of their sweet perfume, whilst others are like the wheat which is crushed and eaten.

Martine, for her part, was ruminating another plan; to persuade the doctor to take up his practice again. She spoke about it to Clotilde, who pointed out the insuperable difficulties of such an undertaking. In fact, she had discussed it with Pascal himself the day before. He had been turning over the problem in his mind as he realized that it might be the only way to save the situation. His first thought had been to open up his consulting room again. But he had been a poor man's doctor for so long! How could he ask for fees after seeing patients for nothing for all these years? Besides, was it not too late to start a new career at his age? To say nothing of the absurd stories that were being told about him and the legend of half-cracked genius attached to his name. Not a patient would consult him, it would be cruel to force him to make an attempt so obviously foredoomed to failure. Clotilde was determined to prevent him from taking such a disastrous step and even Martine finally agreed that he would be exposing himself to certain disappointment. Besides, another idea had just occurred to her; she remembered discovering an old account book in a cupboard in which she had entered all medical visits to the doctor. Many of the patients had never paid. There were two pages filled with the names of patients who still owed their fees. Why, now that he was so desperately short of money, should these people not be made to pay what they owed? She could do it without saying anything to monsieur who had always refused to take legal action. And, this time, Clotilde agreed with her. They organized it between them; Clotilde picked out the amounts, made out the bills and the servant presented them in person. But she failed to collect a single penny. At every door she was met with the reply that they would look into the matter and see the doctor about it. They waited for ten days but none of these people put in an appearance. They were now down to their last six francs, enough to live on for two or three days.

The next day when Martine came back, empty-handed, from a visit to one of these old patients, she told Clotilde that she had seen and spoken to Madame Felicité at the corner of De la Banne Street. The old lady had, doubtless, been waiting for her. She still refused to set foot inside the Souleiade. Even her son's misfortune, the sudden loss of his income which was the talk of the town, had made no difference. In fact, she was quivering with impatience but maintained her attitude of the conventional mother who refused to condone immorality only because she was certain that Pascal would soon be at her mercy and that he was bound, sooner or later, to appeal to her for help. When he was penniless and knocked at her door she would dictate her own terms, would make him marry Clotilde or, better still, send her away. Time passed and still he did not come to see her. This was her reason for waylaying Martine, putting on a show of compassionate understanding, asking for news, protesting her surprise that Pascal had not asked her for money and making it clear that it would be beneath her dignity to take the first step.

"You should speak to monsieur," said the servant, "and urge him to appeal to his mother. What could be more natural?"

Clotilde was horrified:

"Oh! never! you must not count on me. The master would be furiously angry and he would be right. I am sure that he would rather die of starvation than eat grandmother's bread."

Two days later, as Martine served them the scanty remains of some boiled beef, she announced:

"I have no more money, monsieur, to-morrow there will only be potatoes without oil or butter .. You have been drinking water for three weeks. Now you will have to do without meat."

They laughed and made a joke of it:

"Have you any salt, my good Martine?"

"Oh! yes, monsieur, a little."

"Well, then! potatoes with salt taste very good when one is hungry."

She went back to her kitchen and, careful not to raise their voices, they repeated the old jokes about her avarice. It would never have occurred to her to lend them ten francs although she had her own treasure safely tucked away. They thought no less of her for it as they quite understood that such a gesture was as unthinkable as to expect her to unhook the stars and serve them up for dinner.

That night when they were in bed, Pascal realized that Clotilde was feverish. She was tossing about and could not go to sleep. When they were in each other's arms in the warm darkness, it was their time for speaking openly with each other; and she ventured to admit that she was worried about him, about herself, about the household. What was to become of them with no resources whatsoever? For a moment, she even considered talking to him about his mother. Then her courage failed her, but she did confess that she had tried, with Martine's assistance, to collect the money owed to him. At any other time this confession would have grieved and angered him, he would have been furious with them for taking such a step without consulting him. It was so contrary to the professional attitude he had adopted throughout his life. He said nothing at first, much moved by their pathetic attempts to help him. He expressed his gratitude to Clotilde by tightening his arms around her, almost convulsively. He freely admitted that she had done the right thing, that life was becoming impossible. They lay side by side, in silence, but Clotilde felt that he was not asleep and that his mind was active, as was hers, frantically trying to think of some means of finding the money necessary for their daily needs. This was their first night of unhappiness, both of them equally distressed, she, because of his tormented state of mind, and he, because it was agony to think of her deprived of the bare minimum of food for subsistence.

Next day at lunch there was nothing but fruit. The doctor had kept silent throughout the morning, visibly debating with himself about something. And it was only about three o'clock that he came to a decision:

"Come, we must bestir ourselves," he said to his companion. "I do not want you to go hungry again tonight .. Go and put on your hat, we are going out."

She looked at him, waiting for an explanation.

"Yes, we are owed money and as these people refused to give it to you, I want to see what will happen if I go and ask them for it in person."

His hands were trembling. To go and beg for his money after all these years was a dreadful ordeal; but he forced himself to smile and pretended that he was looking forward to it. And she who, from his tremulous voice, realized the extent of his sacrifice, was profoundly moved:

"No! No! master, don't go if it offends your pride too much .. Martine can try again."

But the servant was not of the same opinion. She highly approved of the doctor's proposal:

"Surely! why should monsieur not go? There is nothing shameful about asking these people for what they owe him .. Is that not so? To everyone his due .. I am proud that monsieur is showing himself a man, asserting himself at last."

Then, as in their palmy days, the old king David went out on Abishag's arm. Neither of them, as yet, were in rags. He still had his frockcoat, neatly buttoned up, and she wore her pretty linen dress with the red polka dots; but they were self-conscious about their poverty, made themselves as small as possible, careful to keep to the inside of the pavements and flattened themselves against the houses. The sun-drenched streets were almost empty. They shunned the few people they met and walked very slowly, reluctant and heavy-hearted.

Pascal wanted to begin with an ex-magistrate whom he had treated for some disease of the kidneys. He went in, leaving Clotilde on a bench in the Cours Sauvaire. He was actually relieved when the magistrate, aware of the object of the doctor's visit, explained to him that his income was due in the following October and that he would then settle the bill. His next visit was to an old lady, over seventy, and paralysed; she professed to have been insulted because he had sent his bill by a servant who had been rude to her; he hastened to beg her pardon and told her that he was in no hurry for payment. Next, he climbed three flights of stairs to see an employee in the tax collector's office. He found him still ailing and in extreme poverty. He could not think of asking him for money. Then, in succession, he visited the wife of a haberdasher, a solicitor's wife and an oil merchant. All these people were comfortably well off and either got rid of him on some pretext or other, or refused to see him; some of them even pretended to be surprised and indignant. This left the Marquise de Valqueyras, the only surviving member of a very old family, as wealthy as she was mean. She was a widow with a ten-year-old daughter. He had kept her to the last as she intimidated him. He finally nerved himself to ring the bell of the ancient mansion, at the end of the Cours Sauvaire, a monumental building dating back to Mazarin's time. He stayed inside for so long that Clotilde, who was walking up and down underneath the trees, began to worry.

When he reappeared after more than half an hour, she was so relieved that she said jokingly:

"Well, what have you been doing? Was she short of change?"

He had failed again. The marquise had not given him a penny on the pretext that her tenant-farmers had not paid her on time.

"You see," he continued to explain his long absence, "her little girl is ill. I am afraid that it may prove to be the onset of mucous fever .. So she insisted on my seeing the child and I examined the poor little mite .."

Clotilde could not help smiling:

"And you gave another free consultation?"

"Of course, what else could I do?"

As always, she was moved almost to tears by his good nature. She took his arm and pressed it against her heart. At first they could not make up their minds where to go. It was all over, there was nothing for it but to go home with empty hands. But he refused to give in, he was determined that she was going to have something else to eat beside potatoes and water. When they had walked to the other end of the Cours Sauvaire, they turned left into the new town. They were walking aimlessly as if some implacable wind of fate had blown them adrift.

"Listen," he said in the end, "I have an idea .. What about going to see Ramond, he would gladly lend us a thousand francs which we can repay when our affairs are settled."

She hesitated. Ramond, whom she had rejected, was now married with a fine house of his own in the new town, well on the way to becoming the most fashionable physician in the town and amassing a fortune! Fortunately, as she well knew, he was forthright, scrupulously honest, loyal and extremely good-natured. The fact that he had not been to see them was doubtless due to discretion. Whenever they ran across each other, he always saluted them as though he admired them and was delighted to see them so happy!

"Would it embarrass you?" asked Pascal, naively. She knew that he would have opened his house, his purse and his heart to the young physician.

"No, no! .. There was never anything between us except

202

affection and frankness. I believe that I made him very unhappy but he has forgiven me .. You are right, he is our only friend, we must appeal to Ramond."

Ill-luck dogged their footsteps. Ramond was away for a consultation at Marseilles, and was not expected back before the following evening; it was young Madame Ramond who received them, an old friend of Clotilde's, three years her junior. She seemed faintly embarrassed but welcomed them cordially. Naturally, the doctor did not disclose the real object of their visit and simply said that he had missed Ramond and was anxious to see him.

In the street outside Ramond's house, Pascal and Clotilde felt lonely and lost. Where were they to go now? What else could they do? They set off again, aimlessly.

"Master, I never told you," ventured Clotilde, "it appears that Martine met grandmother .. Yes, grandmother said that she was worried about us, asked her why we did not go to see her and whether we were in need of money .. And, look! there is her door, down there .."

They had reached De la Banne Street and could see the corner of the square of the Sous-Préfecture. Pascal caught the hint but refused to listen:

"Never! Please understand that once and for all .. You must never go there. You know that you mentioned her because you are distressed at seeing me in the gutter. My heart bleeds too, when I think of what you have to put up with. But it is better to go hungry and suffer want than to do something which we would regret bitterly for the rest of our lives .. I will not and cannot do it."

They came to the end of De la Banne Street and wandered into the old quarter.

"I would a thousand times rather appeal to a stranger .. Perhaps we still have some friends, but only among the poor."

And, resigned to beg for charity, David continued his walk on Abishag's arm, the old king begging from door to door, leaning on the shoulder of his loving subject whose youth remained his only support. It was nearly ten o'clock, the heat was no longer intense, the narrow streets were filling up with people; and, in this populous quarter, they were welcomed with smiles. There was an element of pity in the admiration which they aroused, everyone knew that they were ruined. Nevertheless, in spite of, or perhaps because of, their desperate straits, their beauty seemed to be intensified and etherealized. One felt them to be more united than ever, heads high, proud of their love for each other although stricken by misfortune; he, shaken, whilst she, valiant of heart, held him up and sustained him. Workmen, out for the night, passed them with well-lined pockets. No one dared to offer them the few sous they would gladly have given to a starving beggar. In Canquoin Street, they thought of paying Madame Guiraude a visit; she had died, in her turn, the week before. They were now reduced to the hope of finding ten francs somewhere, anywhere. They had been scouring the town for three hours.

It was the end of a limpid and ardent August day. They had walked from end to end of Plassans no less than three times, their footsteps lagging ever more slowly. The sun-baked town was deserted. All windows were shuttered. But beneath this lifeless exterior there seethed an active night life in clubs and gaming houses. Some ancient horse buses were standing in the cours; and, outside the cafés, in the dense shade of plane trees, the customers smilingly watched them pass. In the new town, with its servants standing at the doors of prosperous houses, they were looked upon with less favour than in the deserted streets of the Saint-Marc quarter, where the ancient houses gazed down at them in friendly silence. They returned to the old quarter and went as far as Saint-Saturnin, the cathedral. Here there was a delightfully peaceful corner; the chapter house garden which shaded the apse. From this haven they were driven by a beggar who came and demanded alms of them. They wandered towards the railway station, around which many new buildings were being erected; it was a whole new suburb. Then, for the last time, they returned to the square of the Sous-Préfecture in a sudden mood of optimism; they were convinced that they would end up by meeting someone they knew, that they would be given some money. But they were to be accompanied only by the admiring smiles of the town, pleased to see them so united and handsome. The pebbles of the Viorne and the pointed paving-stones bruised their feet. Finally, they had to go home to the Souleiade, empty-handed; old king David the beggar and his submissive subject, Abishag, in the flower of her youth bringing him back, stripped of his riches and tired of roaming the streets.

It was eight o'clock. Martine, who had been waiting for them, understood that she would not have to cook a meal for them. She claimed that she had eaten her own supper; and, as she seemed unwell, Pascal packed her off to bed at once.

"We can easily manage without you," repeated Clotilde. "As the potatoes are on the fire, we shall serve them up ourselves."

The servant, who was in a surly mood, went off muttering: "When there is nothing to eat, why sit down at the table?" Then, before shutting herself up in her room:

"Monsieur, there are no more oats for Bonhomme. I thought he looked poorly, perhaps monsieur would like to see for himself."

Pascal and Clotilde hastened to the stables to visit the old horse, now completely blind and crippled by rheumatism. Even Martine could not understand why the doctor did not have the poor beast put out of his misery. But they were sentimental about him and determined that he should be allowed to die a natural death in his own stable, like a faithful old servant. The doctor examined him carefully, lifted his legs, looked at his gums and listened to his heart beats:

"There is nothing wrong with him. It is simply old age .. The poor fellow is worn out."

Martine had brought out some grass and put in on the ground near Bonhomme's head. Clotilde picked up a handfull and they were both delighted when the old horse munched it and nuzzled her hand.

"I see," she said with a laugh, "that you still have an appetite. I am afraid that you were playing on our sympathy .. Goodnight and sleep well!"

They left, after they had each given him the ritual smacking kiss, one on each side of his muzzle.

Night was falling. Clotilde had a good idea; why stay downstairs in the empty house? They carried their dinner up to her bedroom, after locking the front door. She ran upstairs, carrying the dish of potatoes and a jug of ice-cold water; he came behind with a basket of grapes, the first fruits of the vine arbour underneath the terrace. They locked themselves in, laid the cloth on a small table, put the potatoes in the middle, between the salt-cellar and the jug, and the grapes on a chair. And it was a memorable feast, which reminded them of that delicious lunch the day after their wedding, when Martine had obstinately refused to answer them. They were just as childishly overjoyed at being alone together and at waiting on themselves. They sat close together and ate from the same plate.

This night of utter destitution, which they had done their utmost to avoid, was to give them the happiest hours of their lives. Now that they were back in that friendly room, as if a hundred leagues away from the indifferent town which they had been scouring, their depression and their fears left them. Even the memory of that distressing afternoon had been obliterated. Once more they were oblivious to anything outside their own feelings for each other. They forgot that they were destitute and would have to find a friend on the morrow to give them the wherewithal for their dinner. Why fear and grieve over their poverty, when just simply being together made them so deliriously happy?

But Pascal felt a twinge of fear:

"Clotilde, we were so worried about to-night. Is it reasonable to feel so happy? Who knows what to-morrow may have in store for us?"

But she put her little hand over his mouth:

"No, to-morrow we shall love each other as we love each other to-night . . Love me with all your might, as I love you."

They had never enjoyed a meal so much. She was ravenous and gobbled up her potatoes. With her mouth full of them, she laughed and pronounced them admirable, far more tasty than the most elaborate of dishes. He too had regained the hearty appetite of his youth. They praised the pure taste of the cold water. They were enchanted by the grapes, blood of the earth gilded by the sun. They gorged themselves. They were drunk with water and fruit and, above all, with their own spontaneous gaiety. They could not remember having eaten such a marvellous meal. Their first lunch, for all the cutlets and bread and wine, had not intoxicated them to the same extent. Their intense happiness, their joy in each other changed the coarse earthenware into golden platters and the meagre fare into a banquet cooked by some celestial cook.

Night had fallen upon the earth. In their haste to be in each other's arms, they had not even lit the lamp. But the windows were wide open to the vast summer sky. The evening breeze swept in, still burning hot, impregnated with the distant scent of lavender. Just over the horizon, the moon had risen. It loomed so large and full that the whole room was bathed in silvery light and they could see each other, infinitely bright as if in the light of a dream.

Then, her arms, her neck, her breasts naked and resplendent in the moonlight, she served him the last course of their banquet! Like a queen bestowing the highest of all honours, she gave him her body. The night before, they had shivered with instinctive terror at the approach of disaster. And now, the rest of the world seemed forgotten. Once more they were granted a night of supreme bliss and were sublimely unconscious of everything except their passion.

She had opened her arms, she delivered herself over to him, gave the whole of herself:

"Master, my master! I wanted to work for you and I found out that I was worthless, incapable of earning even a mouthful of bread for you. All I can do is to love you, give myself, pleasure you .. And, for me, it is enough to feel that I can thrill you with pleasure, master! If you knew how it delights me to know that you find me beautiful and that I can make you a present of my beauty. It is all I have and my only joy is to make you happy."

Enraptured, he pressed her to him and murmured:

"Oh! yes, beautiful! The most beautiful and desirable! .. All those poor jewels which I gave you, all that gold, all those precious stones are not worth the smallest fragment of the smooth satin of your skin. Each one of your nails, every hair on your head is incalculably precious to me. I worship you. I could kiss your eye-lashes, one by one, reverently."

"But listen, my master, listen to me; I am so thankful that you are older and that I am young, because the gift of my body means so much more to you. If you were as young as I am, the gift of my body would give you less pleasure and it would make me less happy .. It is only for your sake and because I can offer them to you that I am proud of my youth and beauty."

To feel that she had so completely surrendered herself to him made him quiver with ecstasy and his eyes were moist:

"You make me the richest and the most powerful of men, you overwhelm me with all the gifts men find most valuable. You pour out for me the most divine draught which could fill the heart of man."

She was seized with a fury of giving, she gave him her whole being, the very essence of it, even the blood in her veins:

"Take me, my master, let me disappear in you, annihilate myself in you .. Take my youth, drink it all down in a single kiss, drink it all until nothing is left except a faint taste of honey on your lips. You would make me so happy .. My master, take my lips because they are fresh, take my breath because it is pure, take my neck because it is soft to the mouth, take my whole body because it is a bud just opening, a delicate satin, a perfume which intoxicates you .. You hear, master, I am a living fragrance for you to inhale! I am a delicious young fruit for you to taste! I am an endless embrace for you to swoon in! .. I am your thing, the flower growing at your feet for your pleasure, running water to refresh you, hot sap to restore your youth! And I am nothing, my master, if I am not yours!"

She gave herself and he took her. At that moment, the moon's rays threw a flood of brightness over her sovereign nudity. She seemed the beauty of woman incarnate. He had never seen her so young, so shining white, so divine. And he thanked her for the gift of her body, as if she had given him all the treasures of the earth. She had given herself to him and would, perhaps, give him a child, their child! The thought was all they needed to complete their happiness.

CHAPTER ELEVEN

BUT, the following night, the tossing and the insomnia recurred. Neither Pascal nor Clotilde spoke about their anxiety to each other; and, in the darkness of the room, which now felt as gloomy as the grave, they lay side by side for hours, pretending to be asleep, both of them thinking about the rapidly deteriorating situation. They were both equally concerned about each other and indifferent to their own troubles. Martine was buying the bread, wine and a little meat on credit, feeling thoroughly ashamed and forced to tell ingenious lies, as it was common knowledge that her master was ruined. The doctor had not failed to consider mortgaging the Souleiade; but, it was his only asset, he possessed nothing else except this property, valued at about twenty thousand francs and which would barely fetch fifteen thousand, at a forced sale. Clotilde begged him to wait, not to take any irrevocable step, as long as there was a glimmer of hope.

Three or four more days passed. It was the beginning of September and, unfortunately, the weather changed; there were some terrible storms which ravaged the countryside, part of the garden wall of the Souleiade was blown over, which could not be patched up and left a jagged breach. The baker was beginning to be rude to Martine. Then, one morning when the old servant brought back a piece of stewing beef, she was in tears because the butcher had given her inferior meat. In a few days, no further buying on credit would be possible. It had become essential to find some way of raising enough money to cover the everyday household expenses.

One Monday, at the beginning of another week of mental torment for all of them, Clotilde was restless throughout the morning. She was finding it difficult to make up her mind, and it was only at lunch that she came to a definite decision, when she saw that Pascal refused his all too scanty portion of beef. After lunch she went out with Martine. She now looked calm and resolute and had given Martine a small parcel to put in her shopping basket, saying that it contained some old bits of clothing to give away.

She came back, two hours later, looking pale but with a gleam of triumph in her eye. She went up to the study, stood in front of the doctor and told him:

"I have just done something which you will disapprove of. I have disobeyed you."

He looked at her with an apprehensive and puzzled frown and asked:

"Now, what have you been doing?"

Without taking her eyes off his face, slowly and deliberately pulled out an envelope from her pocket. The flap was open and he could see that it was full of bank notes. Then, in a flash, he understood and cried:

"The jewels! All my presents!"

This sudden blow to his pride overwhelmed him and he lost his temper. Usually so gentle, he now toughly grasped her hands and was crushing her fingers, which were holding the notes:

"What a thing to do, you wretched girl! .. It is the best part of me, my heart, that you have taken away and sold! Those jewels were permeated with our love for each other, our deepest feelings. How could you give them back and take money for them? .. How can you expect me to spend money which represents the sacrifice of those jewels, my act of faith, my gift to you; mute witnesses of our most perfect moments together, your property, yours alone, which you should have kept, if only out of respect for my feelings? You must have known what unspeakable distress it would cause me!"

She answered, quietly:

"But, my master, did you expect me to let us all starve, with all those rings, necklaces and ear-rings sleeping at the bottom of a drawer. I found myself too revolting, I would have been horribly mean and selfish if I had kept them any longer .. Do you think I was not dreadfully upset at having to part with them? I was so sad that my courage almost failed me. I feel sure that I have done my duty and acted as you would have me act, as your obedient and adoring wife."

Then, as he was still crushing her hands, the tears came into her eyes and she added in the same quiet voice, with the ghost of a smile:

"Please, don't squeeze so hard, you are hurting me."

Then, he too burst into tears of contrition.

"I am a brute, it was unforgivable of me to lose my temper .. You were quite right, you were bound to act as you did. But forgive me, it was a bitter disappointment to see you stripped .. Give me your hands, those poor hands, let me heal them."

He put his own out and took her hands, with infinite gentleness; and he covered them with kisses. He found them even more lovely without a single ring. Now, relieved and happy, she told him the details; how she had taken Martine into her confidence and how they had both gone to the saleswoman from whom he had bought the French point lace shawl. Her original offer had been absurd and it had only been after endless bargaining that she had been induced to pay six thousand francs for the whole lot. He repressed a gesture of despair; six thousand francs! when the jewels had cost him more than three times that amount, at least twenty thousand francs.

"Listen," he said finally, "I will take the money, as you have brought it out of the goodness of your heart. But it must be clearly understood that it belongs to you. I swear that I shall be even more stingy with it than Martine. I will dole out to her the few sous indispensable for our bare keep, and you will always find the balance in my desk, even if I am never able to find enough money to make it good and give you back the whole amount."

He was sitting down with Clotilde on his knees, and was clasping her to him, still aquiver with emotion. Then, lowering his voice, he spoke into her ear:

"Did you sell them all, every one of them?"

Without speaking, she sat up a little, and, almost shyly, put her hand down and groped between her breasts. She was blushing with pleasure. Then she pulled out the thin chain from which the seven pearls dangled like milky stars; it was an exquisitely intimate gesture and the jewel seemed almost alive, as if her skin, on which it had lain hidden, had imbued it with her own particular radiance and made it redolent of her own delicate perfume. Then she quickly concealed it again.

His cheeks, too, were red and his eyes shone. He kissed her passionately:

"Oh! what an adorable child you are, and how I love you!"

But, from that evening onwards the memory of the sale of the jewels remained with him, like an ache in his chest; he could not look at the money in his desk without a pang of anguish. He became obsessed by the thought of poverty, gradually and inevitably closing in on them; even more infuriating was the fact of his age, his sixty years which had made him useless, incapable of earning a living for himself and the woman he loved. It shattered his deceptive dream of eternal love. No dream could mask the reality of poverty and old age; he was appalled, filled with remorse and futile rage against himself, as if he were being called upon to expiate some past crime.

Then he had a rude awakening. One morning, alone in the study, he received a letter. The postmark showed that it came from Plassans itself and he was surprised not to be able to recognize the writing. The letter was unsigned. After reading the first sentence, he made a gesture of annoyance and was about to tear it up; but it exerted a horrible fascination and he could not help reading it to the end. Besides, the phraseology was respectful, the style conventional but clear, and the sentences were long, measured and full of discretion, as if it had been written by a diplomat whose sole object was to convince him. The writer gave a number of excellent reasons for claiming that the scandal at the Souleiade had lasted too long. However carried away by his passions, a man of his age and in his position had no right to indulge in such immoral conduct towards his young relative; by so doing he was making himself universally despised. It was generally known that the young woman was entirely under his influence and that she was determined to sacrifice herself to him; but was it not up to him to understand that she could not possibly be in love with an old man and that her sentiments were merely those of pity and gratitude and it was about time that he ceased exerting his evil influence and freed her from the yoke of his senile passions, which would result in her being dishonoured and ostracized, neither wife nor mother? As he was no longer in a position to leave her a small fortune, it was to be hoped that he would come to his senses and have the decency to send her away, in order to salvage what might be left of her reputation and happiness. The letter ended with the comment that evil conduct was always punished in the end.

After the first few lines, Pascal realized that this anonymous letter came from his mother. Old Madame Rougon must have dictated it, he could even hear the inflections of her voice. After starting the letter in an access of rage he finished it in a mood of depression and dismay, which was to recur with increasing frequency. The letter was justified, it had aroused his conscience, intensified his remorse for being old, poor and keeping Clotilde near him. He rose to his feet, went over to the mirror and gazed at himself for a long time. He was horrified at his wrinkles and his white beard and shivered at the idea that a separation was becoming as necessary as it was inevitable. He pushed it away, he could not imagine himself becoming reconciled to it; but it was to besiege him henceforth; he would be continually torn by this conflict between love and reason, until, worn out with the useless struggle, he would become eventually resigned to it. At the moment he felt such a coward that he doubted whether he would ever be able to summon up enough courage. It was the beginning of the end. He had no choice, he must consider Clotilde's future; she was so young and his obvious duty was to save her from himself.

The next phase of his Calvary was his attempt to persuade himself haunted as he was by the words and phrases of the letter that she was not in love with him, and that all she felt for him was pity and gratitude .. It would have made the rupture much less painful if it were true, if he could convince himself that she was sacrificing herself and that in keeping her tied to him he was merely satisfying his own monstrous egoism. But the more he studied her, the more he put her to the test, the more affectionate he found her, the more passionate when in his arms. This made her doubly dear to him and the dreaded decision all the more difficult. He racked his brain to find legitimate reasons to justify the separation. The life they had been leading for months, without ties or duties, without even working, was thoroughly undesirable, it was bad for her. As far as he himself was concerned, he now believed that he was no longer good for anything, it would be better if he were sleeping under the sod; but it was a very different matter for her, would it not make her lazy, spoil her, sap her will-power? The scandal-mongers were probably right, he was perverting her by making her his idol. Then, all of a sudden, he was terror-stricken by a new train of thought; he saw her dead, left all alone, thrown into the street, penniless, reviled by everyone. Nobody would take her in, she would roam the streets and would never have a husband or children. No, it would be a crime—it would be unspeakably cruel of him to leave her such a heritage of shame and misery, just for the sake of his own selfish enjoyment.

One morning, Clotilde had gone out on an errand in the neighbourhood and came back, pale and trembling, in a state of frantic agitation. Upstairs she nearly fainted in Pascal's arms. She stammered incoherently:

"O, my God, O God, those women .."

Thoroughly alarmed, he bombarded her with questions:

"Come, answer me! What happened to you?"

Then, a flood of scarlet rose to her cheeks. She put her arms around him and clasped him tightly, hiding her face against his shoulder:

"Those women! .. I had crossed over into the shade, I was shutting my parasol and had the bad luck to collide with a child and knocked her over. .. And they all turned against me and shouted such vile things at me. Incredible things! That I should never have any children! That creatures of my sort were incapable of having children! .. And even worse things, dear God, things that I could not repeat—that I did not even understand!"

She was sobbing. He was livid and speechless, kissed her frantically, the tears pouring down his own face. He could easily reconstruct the scene, could see her hunted, sullied by foul words. Then, he stammered:

"It—it is my fault, it is because of me that you are unhappy .. Listen, we must go away, very far away, where we are not known, where you will be treated with respect and be happy again."

When she saw him weeping, she made a great effort, stood up and choked back her tears:

"What a coward I have been! I was determined not to tell you about it. Then when I came into the room, I was so upset that I lost control of myself .. But, it is all over now, you must not fret .. I love you .."

She was smiling and put her arms around him gently. Intent on consoling him, she, in her turn, covered his face with kisses:

"I love you so much that nothing matters! Nothing else in the world, I care about nothing but you! You are so good to me, you make me so happy!"

For a long time they both felt infinitely sad and kisses alternated with tears.

Pascal, when she had left him, felt conscience-stricken. He was acting like her worst enemy. It was his fault that this child whom he adored was exposed to such horrors. And, the evening of that same day, something happened which forced his hand. After dinner, Martine took him aside with an air of importance:

"Madame Felicité, whom I met in the street, told me to give you this letter, monsieur; and she told me to tell you that she would have brought it herself, but that it would be bad for her reputation to be seen here .. She asks you to send her back Monsieur Maxime's letter with mademoiselle's answer."

Felicité had been delighted to receive a letter from Maxime.

It was an excellent pretext for communicating with her son, whose visit she had been expecting with impatience; she had been sure that he would be driven to appeal to her by his lack of money. As neither Pascal nor Clotilde had been to see her, she had changed her plans, once again, and reverted to her old idea of separating them; and, this time, the opportunity seemed heaven-sent. Maxime's letter was most pressing; he sent the letter to his grandmother, urging her to plead with his sister. He had become definitely ataxic and he could only walk with great difficulty when supported by a servant. But, above all, he deplored the fact that he had been too weakminded to resist the charms of a ravishingly pretty brunette who had insinuated herself into his household and had allowed his passions to be aroused to such an extent that, in her arms he had squandered his little remaining nervous energy. Worst of all, he was now certain that this man-eater had been sent by his father, hoping that she would hasten the heritage he was counting on from his son. So, after throwing her out, Maxime had barricaded himself into his hotel and gone so far as to forbid his father the door, terrified that one morning he would see Saccard climbing in at the window. He was desperately lonely and implored his sister to come; he wanted her as a rampart against his father's abominable encroachments, he also needed someone gentle and loyal to look after him. The letter made it clear that she would be amply rewarded if she behaved well towards him; and it ended by reminding the young woman of her promise, made during his visit to Plassans to go to him if he ever really needed her.

Pascal was frozen with horror. He re-read the four pages. Here was the solution ready made! A refusal was unthinkable. It was a stroke of luck for Clotilde; but in spite of these unanswerable arguments he felt himself so undecided, so irresolute, that he collapsed into a chair, his legs trembling. But he was determined to make the heroic sacrifice, controlled himself and called his companion:

"Come here! Read this letter which grandmother sent along to me."

Clotilde read the letter attentively from beginning to end without word or gesture. Then firmly:

"Very well! Will you answer it? .. I refuse."

He had to exercise all his self-control not to give a shout of joy. But, as if an other self were speaking, he heard himself say, persuasively:

"You refuse? That is quite impossible .. You must think it over, let us wait until to-morrow before sending an answer."

But she was astounded and worked herself up into a state of excitement:

"Leave each other! Why? Would you really be willing? .. What madness! we love each other and yet we are to separate, and I am to go to that house in Paris, where nobody loves me! .. Come, how can you remotely consider it? It would be idiotic."

He avoided the issue and talked vaguely about her promise, her duty:

"Remember, my dearest, how upset you were when I first told you that Maxime was threatened with ataxia. To-day, the disease has progressed, as I anticipated. He is a cripple, helpless, alone and he needs you .. You cannot leave him in the lurch. It is your plain duty."

"Duty!" she cried. "What obligations have I to a brother who has never bothered his head about me? My duty is to you and to my own deepest feelings."

"But you gave your promise. I confirmed your promise and said that you were a reasonable person .. You must not make me appear a liar."

"Reasonable! It is you who are not reasonable. Is it reasonable to leave each other, when you know as well as I do that it would kill us both, that it would break our hearts?"

She made a sweeping motion to brush aside any further discussion:

"Besides, what is the use of arguing? .. It is quite simple. One word will be enough for me. Do you want to send me away?"

He uttered a cry of protest:

"Me, send you away!"

"Well, then! Unless you insist upon sending me away, I shall stay."

Her relief was so great that she broke into laughter. She ran to her desk and scribbled two words in red crayon across her brother's letter: "I refuse"; and she called Martine, insisted on her taking back the letter immediately. Pascal too was laughing, flooded with bliss. How could he listen to the voice of reason, when he was so overjoyed at the prospect of keeping her?

But that same night, when she was sleeping, he was overcome with remorse. Once again he had yielded to his need for happiness, the voluptuous delight of feeling her pressed close to him each night, so slender and soft in her long nightdress, inhaling her fresh, heady, scent. She was everything to him, all he had to live for, his last chance of loving. To be torn away from her, was to be torn away from love. His forehead was covered in cold sweat at the idea of being alone, without her, without the subtle enchantment of her presence, her breath, her courage, her forthrightness, all now as necessary to him as the light of day. But it was essential that she should leave him and he must if necessary find the strength to die from losing her. She was relaxed against his heart, breathing as lightly as a child. He was careful not to wake her and was filled with self-contempt, his brain was exceptionally clear and he was able to consider the situation objectively, with terrible lucidity. Up there, in Paris, she would be respected again and a fortune was hers for the asking; he could not allow himself to be dominated by senile egoism to the point of making her share his miserable poverty, exposed to the insults of washerwomen. He was almost swooning at the feel of her in his arms, so soft, so trusting, the subject who had given herself to the old king, but he swore a solemn oath that he would be firm and refuse to go on accepting the sacrifice of self from this child. He would give her back to happiness and life, in spite of herself.

The battle of abnegation was now joined. Some days passed, and he had succeeded in making her understand how unfeeling she had been in writing "I refuse" on Maxime's letter and she had written her grandmother a long letter, explaining the reasons for her refusal. But she was still unwilling to consider leaving the Souleiade. As he had become extremely stingy, in order to use as little of the money from the sale of the jewels as possible, she outdid him and chewed her dry bread cheerfully. One morning, he overheard her discussing even more draconian measures of economy with Martine. Ten times a day she scrutinized his face, threw her arms around his neck, covered him with kisses in an attempt to distract him from his horrible and fixed idea of separation which, as she could see from the look in his eye, was always with him. Then she was presented with a brand new argument. One evening, after dinner, he had an attack of palpitation. He nearly fainted. He was surprised, as he had never had anything wrong with his heart and he attributed the symptom to a recurrence of his nervous trouble. His transports of passion made him feel indefinably less well, as if something deep and fragile inside him had been broken. The attack had worried her and she was full of solicitude: Well now! That would put a stop to any talk about her going away! If those one loved were ill, one stayed near them and looked after them.

The conflict began to fill their lives, it loomed up every hour. It was one long assault, overflowing affection turned against itself, self-forgetfulness intent upon the happiness of the other. Her assiduous loving kindness made the necessity of her departure more atrocious for him, as he became daily more convinced that go she must. He was more firmly determined upon it than ever. He was at bay, hesitating only as to the best way of persuading her. He could not forget the scene of their mutual despair. What was he to do? What could he say? How could they nerve themselves to a final embrace and then never see each other again? And the days passed. No progress had been made. Every night, when she took him in her arms, happy and triumphant in her possession of him, he kept on reproaching himself with cowardice.

Often, she teased him with tender malice:

"Master, my master, you are too kind and good, say that you will keep me by your side."

But this angered him and he protested, frowning:

"No, no! Don't talk about my goodness! .. If I were really kind and good, you would have been in Paris long ago, respected and living in luxury, with the prospect of a quiet and happy life in front of you, instead of obstinately refusing to leave me and staying here, where you are insulted, miserably poor and with no hope, the unfortunate companion of an old fool like me! .. No! I am nothing but a coward and a dishonest man!"

She did her best to silence him, but his kindness and good nature were in fact his vulnerable points, that immense kindness and understanding derived from his love of life, which he lavished on everything and everybody. To want her to be happy, at the price of his own happiness, this was his duty to himself and to her and he felt that he would have the strength to fulfil it, to be decisive and heroic. But, like those unfortunate wretches who have decided to commit suicide, he was waiting for the opportunity, the moment and the means.

One morning, when he had been up since seven o'clock, she was surprised to find him in the study sitting at his table. For weeks he had not opened a book or touched a pen.

"Fancy! Working?"

"Yes. It is the Genealogical Tree, which I have not even kept up to date."

For some minutes she stood behind him watching him write. He was completing his entries on Tante Dide, Uncle Macquart and little Charles, writing in the deaths, with the dates. Then, as he remained bent over his work, seemingly oblivious of her presence, contrary to their usual habit of fondling each other and laughing together, she walked to the window and back disconcerted and forlorn.

"Well then, shall we both set to work?"

"Certainly. I should have entered up these deaths at least a month ago. I have neglected my work shamefully."

She looked at him, searchingly:

"Very well! let us get to work .. If there is anything you want me to look up or some notes to copy, let me have them."

From that day onwards, he made a great show of throwing himself into his work. Besides, it had always been a pet theory of his that idleness was undesirable and that absolute rest should never be prescribed, even to a man suffering from overwork. Man lives only by virtue of the external environment in which he is placed; and the sensations received from it are transformed into movement, thought and action; thus, at absolute rest, if he goes on receiving sensations without giving them back, in a digested and transformed condition, he becomes gorged with them, becomes ill and, inevitably, out of balance. His own experience had taught him that work was the best regulator of his own existence. Even when he felt unwell on waking, he set to work and soon felt the better for it. He was always at the top of his form if he managed to do his allotted task, method-ically planned in advance, so many pages each morning; and he compared this task to a pendulum which kept him in balance, amidst his daily worries, shortcomings and errors. He was also convinced that those weeks passed in idleness, were the sole cause of his palpitations, which had recurred at intervals. Hard work was the best remedy.

Pascal developed and explained these theories to Clotilde, for hours at a time, with feverish and exaggerated enthusiasm. His old love for science which, until he had become infatuated with Clotilde, had been the one passion of his life, seemed to be in the saddle once more. He explained to her that he could not leave his life's work unfinished, that he still had so much to do, before he could hope to erect a durable monument worthy of his name! His interest in the files was revived, he opened the big cupboard at least twenty times a day and kept on adding to them. His ideas on heredity were already changing, he would have liked to revise his whole treatise on the subject, alter everything, elaborate a vast synthesis on the basis of the natural and social history of his family, which was an epitome of the whole of humanity. This revived his interest in his injection treatment, he wanted to perfect it; he had a confused vision of a new system of treatment, a vague theory as to the favourable and dynamic influence of work, born of his conviction and his personal experience.

Every time he sat down at his table, he lamented:

"I have too few years ahead of me, life is too short!"

He appeared to believe that he could no longer afford to lose a single hour. And one morning, suddenly, he raised his head and said to his companion, who was copying a manuscript:

"Listen, Clotilde .. If I die .."

Disconcerted, she protested:

"What an idea!"

"If I should die, listen carefully .. I should want you to lock the doors, at once. Keep the files to yourself, strictly to yourself. And then, after collecting my other manuscripts, hand them over to Ramond .. Is that clear? These are my last wishes."

But she interrupted him, refused to listen:

"No, no! you are talking nonsense!"

"Clotilde, swear to me that you will keep the files and give all my other papers to Ramond."

In the end she gave him her word, with tears in her eyes. He had taken her in his arms, equally moved, kissed and caressed her, as if his love for her had suddenly been reborn. Then he calmed down and spoke of his fears. They had been revived ever since he had started work again. He was always keeping watch on the cupboard, he claimed that he had seen Martine lurking outside the door.

It would be only too easy to take advantage of the poor woman's blind devotion and to induce her to become a thief by persuading her that she would save her master by so doing. He had been forced to suspect the members of his own household for so long! The threat of approaching loneliness revived all his old fears, the mental torture of feeling himself persecuted by those nearest and dearest to him and the idea of a lifetime's patient scientific work jeopardized or even destroyed.

One evening, when he was back on this subject again, he had a slip of the tongue:

"You understand, when you are no longer here . ."

She went white in the face and seeing him hesitate, aquiver with emotion:

"What! Are you still thinking about that abomination? I can see it in your eyes, you are hiding something from me, your thoughts have strayed away from me .. But if I were to go away and you were to die, who would be here to defend your writings?"

He deluded himself that she was reconciling herself to the idea of going away, and managed to say, with forced gaiety:

"Do you think that I would allow myself to die without seeing you again? .. I will write to you, of course! You will be able to come back and close my eyes."

She fell into a chair, sobbing:

"My God! Is it possible? Do you really want us to part, we who never leave each other for a minute, who live in each others arms? Oh! if I had only had a child! .."

"You are condemning me out of your own mouth," he interrupted, violently, "if the child had come, I should never have let you go .. Can't you see that I am too old and that I despise myself? With me, you will always remain sterile, you will always regret not having known what it is to be a complete woman, a mother! Go away, then, as I am no good to you. I am not even half a man!"

She tried in vain to calm him.

"No! I am well aware of what your ideas are, we have agreed on them at least twenty times; if a child is not wanted, the act of love is useless and ignoble .. The other evening you threw away the novel you were reading because the heroes, dismayed at having a child, not even knowing that they were likely to have one, did not know how to get rid of it .. You know how I have longed for a child by you!"

That day, Pascal seemed to immerse himself in his work more than ever. He now had periods, lasting four or even five hours, whole afternoons, during which he never raised his head from his papers. His zeal was redoubled, he gave strict orders that he was not to be disturbed, that he was not even to be spoken to. Sometimes, when Clotilde tiptoed out of the room, to give an order downstairs or to run an errand, he looked around furtively to make sure that she was no longer there and let his head drop to the table, utterly dejected. It was a distressing reaction from the extraordinary strain of forcing himself to stay at his table and not taking her in his arms, keeping her pressed to him for hours, gently kissing her eyes and her hair ..

Work was an invaluable safety valve, his only hope of numbing the intolerable pain, of forgetting himself. But he was usually incapable of working. He had to pretend to be concentrating. His eyes were on the page but his thoughts were wandering. Was he to become intellectually as well as financially bankrupt, incapable of work, which he considered the sovereign remedy, the sole creator, the regulator of the world? Or was it all due to old age? Was it only senile incapacity for writing a single page, like his inability to fertilize and beget a child? Fear of impotence had always been his besetting anxiety. As he sat, collapsed, with his cheek against the table, overwhelmed by despair, he had a dream; he was a young man of thirty and, every night, in Clotilde's arms he drew from her the vitality necessary for his work the next day. Tears ran down into his white beard; and, when he heard her coming upstairs, he straightened up abruptly so that she would find him as she had left him, seemingly sunk in profound meditation.

It was the middle of September. After two more interminable weeks of anguish, with no solution in sight, Clotilde, one morning, was astonished to see her grandmother, Félicité, at the Souleiade. The day before, Pascal had met her in De la Banne Street. Impatient to consummate his sacrifice, but feeling that he was too weak to force the issue, he had with the greatest reluctance taken his mother into his confidence. He had asked her to come to the Souleiade the next day. She had just received another piteous letter from Maxime imploring Clotilde to come and look after him.

"Do not look so surprised, my dear," she said to Clotilde. "I did not want to come, but you may be sure that I would never have set foot inside this house, if it had not been for exceptional circumstances .. But you are really acting like a madwoman, I cannot let you ruin your life without making a last attempt to make you see reason."

She proceeded to read Maxime's letter aloud in a dramatic voice designed to play on Clotilde's feelings. It appeared that he was now confined to his armchair, that he was suffering from a rapidly progressive and extremely painful form of ataxia. He demanded an immediate answer from his sister, still hoping that she would come and dismayed at the idea of being reduced to looking for some other woman to nurse him. But he would be forced to do so, if his own family abandoned him to his fate. When she finished reading the letter, she pointed out the folly of allowing Maxime's fortune to fall into the hands of strangers; but, above all, she talked about duty, obligations towards a close relative, and also claimed that Clotilde had given her solemn promise.

"Come, my dear, you cannot have forgotten. You told him that if he ever needed you, you would go to him. I can hear you saying it .. Am I not right, my son?"

Ever since his mother's arrival, Pascal had kept silent. Pale and dejected he sat and listened to her. He answered by a barely perceptible nod.

Then Felicité proceeded to put forward all the arguments which Pascal himself had used; the scandal and the insults, the threat of destitution, which both of them would find increasingly hard to bear; this unnatural life, which would mean for him as he grew older, losing what was left of his health and, for her, still so young, the risk of ruining her life. What future could they look forward to, now that he had lost all his money? To be so obstinate was stupid and cruel.

Clotilde faced her, erect, with a stubborn look on her face and said nothing, she refused to argue. But when her grandmother pressed her insistently for an answer:

"For the last time, I am not under any obligation to my brother. My duty is to Pascal, here. Maxime can do what he likes with his money, I do not want it. When we are too poor to keep a servant, uncle will send Martine away and I will wait on him."

She cut short any further argument by a decisive gesture. All she wanted was to be able to devote herself to her lover, beg for him in the streets if necessary!

Old Madame Rougon raised her chin:

"You had far better think about being his wife than being his servant .. What an idea not to have married! It would have been so much simpler."

Felicité remembered her last visit, when she had come to beg them to marry, in order to stop any further scandalmongering; the young woman had seemed surprised, saying that neither she nor the doctor had thought about it, but that if it was necessary they would marry—later, as there was no hurry.

"Marry! I am quite willing!" cried Clotilde. "You are right, grandmother .."

And, turning to Pascal:

"You have assured me a hundred times that you would do what I wanted you to do .. Well then, marry me. As your wife, I can stay with you. A wife does not leave her husband."

But he answered only by a gesture, as if afraid that his voice would betray him. His gesture implied hesitation, refusal. When they were at their last gasp, what useful purpose could such a marriage serve?

"Very fine sentiments, no doubt," resumed Félicité. "Very nicely worked out in your little head. But marriage will not provide you both with an income; and, in the meanwhile, it costs money to keep you. You are a heavy burden to him."

This remark had an extraordinary effect on Clotilde, she turned towards Pascal, her cheeks a fiery red, her eyes streaming with tears:

"Master, is that true? Is grandmother right? Do you really grudge the money I cost you?"

His face grew paler still, but he made no move and sat hunched up, utterly depressed. In a voice which seemed to come from a distance, as if he were talking to himself, he murmured:

"I have so much work to do! I want to work on my files, my manuscripts, my notes and finish my life's work! . . If I were alone, perhaps I could manage it. I would sell the Souleiade, I would take a little room, just big enough for all my papers. I would work from morning to night and try not to be too unhappy."

But he avoided her eyes; this muttered explanation was far from adequate to calm her. On the contrary, it increased her anxiety, she was becoming frantic, because she felt that he was going to commit himself irrevocably to the dreaded decision.

"Look at me, master, look me in the face . . And, I beseech you, do not prevaricate, choose, once and for all, between your work and me, because you seem to have implied, just now, that you were sending me away so that you would be able to work better!"

Now was the time for his heroic lie. He raised his head, looked straight at her; and with the smile of a dying man who welcomes death, spoke in the tone of voice which she had heard so often in the past, infinitely gentle and kind:

"Why so excited? . . You should do your duty, quite simply, like everybody else. Is that beyond you? . . I have a great deal of work to do, I want to be alone; and you, my dear, should go to your brother."

There was a terrible silence of several seconds. She kept staring at him, hoping that he would weaken and change his mind. Had he told her the truth, or was he sacrificing himself for her sake?

For an instant, she felt intuitively that he was solely concerned with her happiness.

"And are you sending me away for good? Would you object to my coming back some time soon?"

He stood his ground. He smiled as if to imply that to go away was to stay away; her intuition failed her. She felt so bewildered and hurt that she really believed that he had made his choice, that he had chosen his work. After all as a man of science, his work was more important to him than a woman. She was as white as a sheet, she hesitated for a moment, in that deathly silence; then, slowly, gently and submissively:

"Very well, master, I will go as soon as you wish me to go, and I shall not come back unless you call me back."

Thus, the breach between them had become final, irrevocable. Félicité, surprised at not having to exert her powers of persuasion, was anxious to consolidate her easy victory by fixing the date of Clotilde's departure. It was Friday, it was arranged that Clotilde should leave on Sunday. They even sent a wire to Maxime.

There had been a mistral wind for three whole days. But, that evening, it blew with much greater violence; and Martine announced that according to the local weather prophets it would last for at least another three days. At the end of September, the wind swept across the valley of the Viorne with terrible force. Martine took the precaution of inspecting all the rooms upstairs to make sure that the shutters were fastened. When the mistral blew across the roofs of Plassans, it swept down sideways on the Souleiade, which stood on a little plateau. It was a raging, howling wind which hurled itself at the house, shaking it from cellar to attic for days and nights on end without any surcease. Tiles were blown off, window fastenings were torn off; and penetrating through the cracks, it whistled and whined through the rooms. Any door left open was slammed shut with a report like a cannon shot. To those inside the house, it felt like a siege, an incessant bombardment with nerve-racking noise.

Next day it was in a Souleiade as gloomy as the grave and swept by the furious wind, that Pascal asked Clotilde if she needed any help. Old Madame Rougon was to come back on Sunday at the last moment. When Martine had been told that Clotilde was definitely leaving, she had been dumbfounded. She had made no comment, but there had been a brief flicker of triumph in her eyes; and, as she had been sent away from the bedroom and been told that she was not needed for packing the trunks, she returned to the kitchen and set about her usual duties as if nothing out of the usual had happened. Whenever Pascal called her, however, she ran so promptly to do his bidding that she seemed rejuvenated. Pascal never left Clotilde's side. There were two large trunks open in the middle of the bedroom, which was in complete disorder and strewn with clothes and parcels. Both of them were equally distressed. He hovered over the trunks, making sure that everything was carefully packed without taking up too much room, using the hatbox for smaller things like scarves and slipping the boxes in between handkerchieves and blouses; whilst she took down her dresses, folded them on the bed before packing them at the top of the trunks. When the trunks were full and they were both tired, with nothing to distract them from their grief, they looked at each other and had the greatest difficulty in holding back their tears. Was it really true that they were no longer together? And, all the time, they could hear the wind howling mournfully, the terrible wind which was threatening to invade the house.

How many times, during the course of this last day together, did they go to the window, attracted by the storm, wishing that it would obliterate the whole world! In spite of the mistral, the sun was shining and the sky was blue, a livid, dust-stained blue; and the sun was pale, its pale rays tremulous, as if shrinking from the storm. In the distance, they could see immense clouds of dust whirling from the roads, the trees bent and cowering away from the wind, the whole countryside dried up, exhausted by the violence of the wind which never stopped blowing, sweeping along with the roar and rumble of distant thunder. Branches were broken off and whirled away, whole roofs lifted up and carried away so far that they could not be found. Why could they themselves not be picked up together by the mistral, whirled away and deposited in some distant land, where they could be happy? When the trunks had been locked, he tried to open a shutter which had been jammed by the wind; when he had succeeded in raising it a little, the inrush of air was so powerful that Clotilde had to help him and they needed all their combined strength to fasten the sash. As they were clearing up the room, they picked up the broken pieces of a hand mirror which had fallen from a chair. Was this a sign of death, as the old women of the town claimed?

That evening, after a gloomy meal in the cheerful dining-room, Pascal expressed his intention of going to bed early. Clotilde was taking the ten-fifteen train the next morning; he was afraid that she would be exhausted by such a long journey—twenty hours in the train. Then, at the door of her bedroom, he kissed her and went off to his own bedroom, determined to sleep alone. Besides, before the tiring journey of the morrow, it was essential for her to have a long sleep. If they slept together, neither of them would sleep. She looked at him with her large eyes full of mute supplication. She held out her arms; it required almost superhuman strength of will, but he managed to tear himself away and go back to her later, kiss her eyes, tuck her in like a child and wish her pleasant dreams. In any case, were they not already separated? If he had taken her again, now that they no longer belonged to each other it would have filled him with remorse and shame. But how he loathed his damp, neglected room! He felt abysmally depressed as he lay sleepless between the cold sheets of his bachelor bed. He felt as if old age were closing down on him, like the lid of a coffin. At first he thought that his sleeplessness was due to the wind, which filled the house with its many voices, some howling with rage, some imploring, some sobbing. On two occasions, he got up and listened at Clotilde's door. Nothing was to be heard. Then he went downstairs to shut a door which had been banging with intermittent regularity, as if some evil fate were hammering on the walls. The dark rooms were swept with an icy blast and he was shivering with cold when he crept back into bed and lay haunted by his melancholy thoughts. Then he realized that the loud voice which had filled his ears and prevented him from sleeping was not the voice of the mistral. It was the voice of Clotilde, mutely calling to him, the feeling that she was still in the house and that he had cut himself away from her. Then he was swept by a wave of frantic longing for her, abominable, desperate longing. My God! never to have her close to him again, when, with a word, he could stop her going and keep her for ever! In losing her he felt as if his own flesh was being torn away. She was young. A woman of thirty can always find happiness again, but he was at the end of his life. He would never find another woman anxious to pour the treasures of her youth at his feet! Not once, but ten times, he found himself throwing off the covers, about to rush to her room, to take her in his arms and keep her. He lay tormented with longing and despair, listening to the wind, until the morning.

At six o'clock, Martine, thinking that she had heard her master calling her by knocking on the floor, went up to his room, eager and excited. But she stopped short on the threshold, horrified by the sight of him lying across the bed, biting the pillow to stifle his sobs. He had made an effort to get up and dress, but had succumbed to one of his attacks of giddiness and palpitations.

He had been unconscious for a few moments and, on coming round, had stammered:

"I—I cannot go on like this, I cannot stand it .. I would rather die, die now .."

He recognized Martine and clutched at her, unburdened himself to her. He was at the end of his strength, overwhelmed with physical pain and mental anguish:

"My poor girl, I am in agony, my heart is breaking .. She is taking my heart and the rest of me, all that matters, away with her. I can't live without her .. I nearly died last night. I wish that I could die before she leaves and then I would not have to watch her going away from me .. Oh! my God! she is going, and I shall not have her with me any more, ever, she is leaving me alone, alone .."

The servant, who had run up the stairs so cheerfully, was now as pale as wax. She watched him tearing at the sheets, groaning, his lips glued to the blanket. Then she seemed to be making up her mind with a great effort:

"But, monsieur, there is no sense in your upsetting yourself like this. It is ridiculous .. If you feel like that and you cannot do without mademoiselle, I will go and tell her what a state you are in .."

He was staggering and had to hold on to the back of a chair, but he drew himself up and almost shouted:

"I forbid you to tell her, Martine!"

"Why should I listen to you, monsieur, when I find you half dead, crying your heart out? .. No, I will go and fetch mademoiselle, I will force her to stay with you!"

But he was digging his fingers into her arm and would not let her go, livid with rage:

"I order you to hold your tongue, do you hear? or I shall send you away, too .. Why did you come into my room? I was ill just because of the wind. That is nobody's business except my own."

Then, feeling that he had spoken too harshly to the old servant, he controlled himself, managed to smile and said in his usual kind voice:

"My poor girl, you made me lose my temper! Let me be the

judge of what is best for all of us. Do not say a word to Clotilde, it would distress me to no purpose."

Martine, in her turn, found it difficult to hold back her tears. Clotilde came in almost immediately; she had been up early, anxious to see Pascal and hoping, up to the last minute, that he would change his mind. She looked tired and drawn, as she had also spent a sleepless night. She searched his face and he looked so ill that she became anxious about him.

"There's nothing to worry about, I assure you. I should have had a good night, if it had not been for the mistral .. Isn't that right, Martine? I was telling you about it."

The servant nodded her head. And Clotilde allowed herself to be reassured. She said nothing about her own agony of mind, which had tortured her throughout the night, no less agonizing than his own torments in the room across the study. The two women were docility itself, ready to obey him and abet him in his self-forgetfulness.

"Wait," he continued, opening his desk, "I have something here for you .. Here you are! There are seven hundred francs in this envelope .."

In spite of her vehement protests, he insisted upon accounting for the original sum. Out of the proceeds of the sale of the jewels, six thousand francs, barely two hundred had been spent; he was keeping a hundred, which, with the strictest economy, would last till the end of the month. After that he would be able to manage as he intended to sell the Souleiade and concentrate on his work. He was determined to leave the balance of five thousand francs intact. He considered them her exclusive property and she would find them waiting for her in the drawer.

"Master, you are torturing me .."

He interrupted her:

"That is my wish, you would break my heart .. Come, it is half past seven, I will go and rope your trunks."

When Martine and Clotilde were left alone together, they gazed at each other in silence for a moment. Ever since she and Pascal had become lovers, there had been an atmosphere of latent antagonism between them, due to the triumph of the young mistress and the unconscious jealousy of the old servant, both of whom worshipped Pascal with equal fervour. To-day, it seemed that Martine was to be left triumphantly in possession of the field. But, at this last minute, they were both moved almost to tears and felt nearer to each other.

"Martine, you must not let him deprive himself of food. Promise me that he will have meat and wine every day!"

"Do not worry, mademoiselle."

"Those five thousand francs mouldering in the drawer really belong to him; I hope that you will not hesitate to use them. I want you to spoil him."

"Mademoiselle, that I will make it my business to look after him and you can be sure that he lacks nothing."

There was another short silence, as they scanned each other's faces, anxiously.

"You must watch him and see that he does not overwork. I am very worried about him, his health has been deteriorating lately. You will watch him, won't you?"

"Do not worry, mademoiselle, I will look after him."

"Well, I must leave him in your hands. He will have no one but you and the fact that you are so fond of him is the only thing that reassures me. Love him with all your might, for both of us."

They were both moved to tears, and Clotilde added:

"Will you kiss me, Martine?"

"Oh, mademoiselle, with all my heart!"

They were in each other's arms when Pascal came back into the room. He pretended not to notice, for fear of giving way to his own feelings. In an unnecessarily loud voice he talked about a few final details, as if he were concerned about missing the train. He had roped the trunks, Father Durieu had taken them away in his cart and they would find them at the station. However, it was barely eight o'clock and they had two full hours in front of them. They proved to be two hours of mortal anguish and painful boredom; they were both turning over in their minds, endlessly, all the implications of this appalling separation. Breakfast filled a bare quarter of an hour. They rose from the table and sat down again. Their eyes were on the clock. In this house of mourning the minutes seemed as eternal as death.

"Oh! what a wind!" said Clotilde, as an exceptionally violent blast shook the doors.

Pascal went to the window and looked at the tops of the trees, whipped by the mistral:

"It is blowing even harder this morning. Later on, I shall have to go and look at the roof. A lot of tiles have been blown away."

They felt as if they had already been separated. They were

oblivious of everything except the furious wind sweeping everything in front of it—including their own lives.

Finally, at half past eight, Pascal said quietly:

"It is time, Clotilde."

She rose from her chair. She had almost forgotten that she was going away. Suddenly, she was pierced by the horrible and final certainty of this dreadful separation. For the last time, she gazed at him, piteously. He made no move, no effort to keep her. It was all over. Her face sagged, it was deathly white. She was utterly crushed.

They exchanged a few stilted phrases, like strangers:

"Will you write to me?"

"Of course. You must send me all the news as often as possible."

"If you should fall ill, you will call me back at once?"

"I promise. But, you need have no fear, there is nothing wrong with my health."

Then, at the moment of leaving the beloved house, Clotilde looked around her with eyes blurred with tears. Then she collapsed, buried her face against his shoulder and threw her arms around him, stammering:

"I want to kiss you here, I want to thank you .. Master, you and you alone have made me what I am. As you have explained to me, so clearly and so often, you have corrected my hereditary tendencies. What would have become of me, in Paris, if I had been left in the environment in which Maxime grew up? .. If I am worth anything at all, I owe it to you, you who brought me to this house and surrounded me with an atmosphere of truth and kindness. You have helped me to grow worthy of your affection .. To-day, after having taken me and overwhelmed me with all the treasures of your mind and heart, you are sending me away. Thy will be done, you are my master and I needs must obey you. But I love you and will always love you."

He pressed her to his heart and answered:

"I am only concerned with your welfare, I must not spoil my own handiwork."

And, as they kissed for the last time, the last heart-rending kiss, she sighed and murmured:

"Oh! If only I had conceived a child!"

He was sobbing and she heard him mutter almost indistinguishably:

"Yes, the dream, the only true consummation. What I was unable to give you .. Forgive me, try and be happy."

Old Madame Rougon was at the station, very gay and lively in spite of her eighty years. It was a great day for her as she believed that Pascal would now be at her mercy. When she saw that they were both in a daze, she took charge, bought the ticket, registered the luggage and installed Clotilde in a compartment marked "Ladies Only". Then, she talked at length about Maxime, made some suggestions and asked Clotilde to be sure to keep her informed about the invalid's progress. But the train was not leaving for another five, atrocious, minutes, during which they faced each other without saying a word. Then the end came, the final embraces, a loud grinding of wheels, a waving of handkerchiefs.

Suddenly, Pascal realized that he was alone on the platform. The train had disappeared around a bend in the line. Shaking off his mother's hand, he ran out of the station, racing like a young man up the slope, up the stone steps to reach the terrace of the Souleiade in three minutes. The mistral was raging, a giant blast which bent the giant cypress trees as if they were straws. In the colourless sky, the sun seemed tired of this wind, which had blown violently across its face for six whole days. And Pascal stood firm, like the trunk of a tree, his clothes flapping like a flag, his beard and hair streaming in the wind. He could hardly breathe, his two hands pressed against his widly beating heart, he was watching the train recede into the distance across the barren plain, a tiny train which the mistral seemed to be sweeping away like a handful of autumn leaves.

CHAPTER TWELVE

THE next day, Pascal shut himself up, permanently, in the great empty house. He never went out, discontinued his medical visits and lived there in absolute solitude and silence with all doors and windows shut. Martine had strict orders not to admit anyone, on any pretext.

"But, monsieur, your mother, Madame Felicité?"

"Above all, not my mother. I have my reasons .. You can tell her that I am working, that I cannot think unless I am alone and that I must ask her to excuse me."

Old Madame Rougon paid three visits to the Souleiade, one after the other. She stormed at Martine. He heard her raising her voice, getting angry, trying to force her way in. Then the noise died away, he could only hear whispering. She was, doubtless, complaining and plotting against him as usual. But he stood his ground, never leaned over the banisters and called to her to come up.

One day, Martine ventured to say:

"It is a little hard all the same, monsieur, to bar the door to your own mother. Especially as Madame Felicité comes with the best of intentions, because she knows that monsieur is very hard pressed for money and keeps on coming only because she wants to help him."

He was exasperated and shouted:

"Money! I don't need any! .. I shall work. I can easily manage to earn a living!"

But the problem of money was becoming urgent. He was adamant about not taking a single sou of the five thousand francs in his drawer. Now that he was alone, he was completely indifferent to any material requirements. He would have been satisfied with bread and water; and, each time the servant asked him for money to buy wine, meat or anything else which was not absolutely essential to life, he shrugged his shoulders. What for? There was still a crust of bread from the day before, was that not enough? But she, who so loved him and pitied him, was distressed by this avarice, even more stringent than her own, this utter neglect of his own comfort and the welfare of the whole household. Compared with this miserable existence, the life of the poorest workman in the suburbs was relatively luxurious. Then, for a whole day, she wrestled with herself. Her love, the love of a docile dog, was fighting against her passion for money, accumulated sou by sou, hidden away, "making little ones", as she boasted. She would have preferred to sacrifice her flesh for him. So long as he had not been alone in his state of deprivation, the idea of having recourse to her private treasure would never have occurred to her. Thus, one morning, it was an act of extraordinary heroism when, driven to distraction by the fireless kitchen and the empty larder she disappeared for an hour and came back with a basketful of provisions and the change from a hundred franc note.

She met Pascal coming down the stairs. He was astonished and asked her where the money had come from. Thinking that she had appealed to his mother, he was about to fly into a violent rage.

"Indeed not! monsieur," she stammered, "you are quite wrong."

In the end she told him the lie which she had carefully thought out beforehand:

"You see, Monsieur Grandguillot's accounts have finally been made up and it looks as if there was something over .. This morning I thought of going along to see and they told me that you would surely get some of your money back and they gave me a hundred francs on account .. They even allowed me to sign a receipt. You can sign a proper one later on."

Pascal seemed not at all surprised. She prayed that he would not go out and verify the facts. But, she was relieved that he had not questioned her story and found it quite natural.

"All the better," he cried. "I have always said that it was wrong to give up hope. This will give me time to organize my affairs."

By affairs he meant the sale of the Souleiade, to which he had given but scanty thought. But how unutterably sad to have to leave this house, in which Clotilde had grown up, where he had lived with her for nearly eighteen years! He had allowed himself two or three weeks for reflection. Now that there seemed some hope of recovering something from the wreck, he dismissed the idea of selling from his mind. He forgot his surroundings again and let himself drift; he consumed everything which Martine put before him, not even noticing that the food was more abundant and varied. And Martine served him devotedly, heart-sick at having to draw on her precious savings, but delighted at being able to make him comfortable without his suspecting that he owed his life of relative luxury to her.

Besides, Pascal was not even grateful. He was sorry and said so, after he had been particularly violent and unfair towards her. But, in his present state of feverish despair, he kept losing his temper with her at the slightest excuse. One evening, after overhearing an interminable conversation between her and his mother in the kitchen, he burst into one of his violent rages:

"Listen to me, Martine, I will not have her in the Souleiade. This is the last time .. If you let her in and talk to her downstairs again, I shall dismiss you!"

"Monsieur, you would do that to me! Anyway, I wouldn't go away, I would lie down in the doorway."

He already felt ashamed of losing his temper and spoke more gently:

"I know perfectly well what is happening. She is plotting to get you on her side and turn you against me, isn't it true? .. She is plotting to get her hands on my papers, she would like to steal everything, destroy everything up there in my cupboard. I know her! When she has set her mind on something, she will stick at nothing .. Well, you can tell her that I am on my guard, that as long as I live I will not let her anywhere near the cupboard. And the key is here in my pocket."

All his old fears had been revived. Now that he was living alone, he felt in constant danger, of somebody lurking in ambush, in the dark. He was determined to repel all attempts at invasion with the utmost ruthlessness and to keep his mother at bay. He was under no illusion as to her real plans and he was afraid of not being firm enough with her. If he was to allow her to see and speak to him, she would overcome his resistance little by little and finally have him in her power. This was the beginning of another period of mental torture. He spent his days prowling the house, constantly on the watch. Every evening he locked the doors himself, at night he often got out of bed to make sure that the locks were not being forced. His great fear was that the servant, won over and convinced that it was the only way to ensure his eternal salvation, would open the door to his mother. He visualized his files blazing in the fireplace. He kept guard over them; he felt a passionate affection for them, a poignant tenderness towards these chilly papers, these cold pages of manuscript, to which he had sacrificed his one great love and to which he was determined to transfer his affections even to the extent of being able to forget Clotilde.

Ever since she had left him, Pascal had thrown himself into his work, trying to drown and lose himself in it. His only object was to annihilate himself by unceasing toil. That was why he had shut himself up and never even set foot in the garden. That was why he had been able to nerve himself to tell Martine that he would not see Doctor Ramond, one day when she had come up to his study to announce his visit. Poor Ramond, how happy he would have been to welcome him! He was well aware of his colleague's exquisite tact and that his visit could only have been animated by a desire to console his old teacher. But why lose an hour? From that day onwards, he never left his table, even for meals. He bent over it the whole morning, the whole afternoon and often continued by lamp-light late into the night. He was attempting to carry out his old cherished plan to revise his whole theory of heredity on a new basis, to use the files, all the family records, to establish laws according to which, in a group of human beings, life is distributed and leads mathematically from one man to another, taking the environment into consideration; a vast bible, the genesis of families, society, the whole of mankind. He hoped that the gigantic scope of such a plan, the effort necessary for carrying out such a colossal undertaking, would take complete possession of him, give him back his health, his faith, his pride, that he would find satisfaction in accomplishing such a herculean task. But for all his attempts to throw himself passionately and unreservedly into his work, he merely succeeded in exhausting himself. He could not concentrate. His heart was no longer in his work and his health suffered increasingly because he was desperately lonely and unhappy. Had he become definitely incapable of intellectual effort? Was he, whose existence had been devoured by incessant scientific labours, who considered work the mainspring of life, to be forced to come to the conclusion that to love and to be loved was more important than anything else in the world? He had moments of lucidity, during which his intellect functioned clearly and well. He was able to elaborate his new theory of the balance of forces, which consisted in establishing the fact that all sensation which impinges on man should be returned in the form of movement. How normal, full and happy life would be if it could be lived completely, functioning like a well-regulated machine, transforming into energy all its products of combustion, keeping itself vigorous and beautiful by means of the simultaneous and logical interplay of all its organs! He attributed equal importance to physical and intellectual labour, to sentiment and reason, to the reproductive and the cerebral functions. Excessive strain and overwork should be eliminated, because they lead to disturbance of the normal balance and thus to disease. One ought to start life again and learn how to live, dig the good earth, study the world, love women, attain human perfection, achieve the future city of universal happiness by using one's whole being wisely. What a fine legacy that would be for a medical philosopher to leave behind him! This dream, this theory glimpsed in the far future, filled him with bitterness, at the thought that he, henceforth, was nothing but a wasted and spent force.

Underlying his mounting depression, Pascal was dominated by the conviction that his life was finished. His longing for Clotilde, the unbearable pain of being without her, the certainty that he had lost her permanently, overwhelmed him. Work became impossible. Sometimes he let his head drop on the page he was trying to read and sobbed for hours, incapable of writing a line. He made a super-human effort to concentrate, but such days of voluntary annihilation resulted in terrible nights, nights of feverish insomnia, during which he bit the sheets to stop himself from calling aloud for Clotilde. She was everywhere in this mournful house, in which he was buried alive. He saw her in every room, sitting on all the chairs, standing behind all the doors. Downstairs in the dining-room, he could not sit down at table, without seeing her leaning forward in the chair opposite him. In the study, upstairs, where she had been closeted with him for so long, the atmosphere was impregnated with her personality; he had a vision of her ceaselessly moving around the room, or in front of her desk, bent over a pastel. He could not escape these haunting and torturing memories by leaving the house, as he was certain that she would be haunting the garden; he would visualize her dreaming on the terrace, strolling along the path through the pine trees, sitting in the cool shade of the plane trees listening to the everlasting murmur of the spring, or on her back in the yard, at twilight, gazing up at the sky and waiting for the stars. But there was one room in the house which terrified and fascinated him, which he never entered without trembling; it was Clotilde's sanctuary, her bedroom where she had given herself to him, where they had slept in each other's arms .. He kept the key on his person. Nothing in the room had been moved since the sad morning of her departure; an old discarded petticoat was still crumpled up on a chair. In there, he felt he was breathing the air she had breathed, impregnated with the faint heady scent of her young body, like a cloud of perfume. He opened his arms wide and closed them, clasped her ghostly presence, floating in the soft half-light of the shuttered room, in the faded pink of the cotton-print on the walls. He sobbed over her dressing-table, he kissed the bed. So powerful were the mixed emotions aroused in him by this room, that he did not dare visit the room every day and went to bed in his own chill bedroom, where, sometimes, he could sleep without being disturbed by the ever-present living image of Clotilde.

Clotilde's letters provided his only distraction from his work. He dreaded them almost as much as he delighted in them. She wrote regularly twice a week, never less than six pages, giving him a detailed account of her life. She did not seem to be very happy. Maxime was now never able to leave his invalid chair. Pascal could read between the lines and felt sure that Maxime was making her life a misery. He had always acted like a spoiled child and now that he was in constant pain he was bound to be continually pestering her with petulant demands for attention. He never allowed her out of his sight. He was even unwilling to let her look out of the window to watch the fashionable crowds promenading along the avenue. From a chance phrase here and there, he gathered that her brother was already becoming suspicious of her, beginning to distrust and hate her. This was the invariable sequel of events, due to his obsessional fear of being exploited and robbed. On two occasions she had seen his father, always jolly, full of himself and his innumerable political and financial commitments, converted to the republic and triumphantly successful. Saccard had taken her aside, made it clear that he considered poor Maxime completely insufferable and praised her courage in consenting to be his victim. The following day on the pretext that he knew that she had too much to do, he sent his barber's niece called Rose, eighteen years old, very blonde and very demure, to help her nurse the invalid. Clotilde never complained. She claimed that her life had its compensations and that she was resigned to it. Her letters were pathetically brave with never a word of anger at their cruel separation or of appeal to his feelings. But he felt that she loathed having anything to do with Maxime and, at one word from him, was ready to drop everything and hurry back immediately.

Still, Pascal steeled himself not to write that letter. She would settle down. Maxime would become accustomed to his sister. The sacrifice must be consummated. If, in a moment of weakness, he were to write a single line, his tremendous effort would have been in vain. When he sat down to answer Clotilde's letters Pascal needed all his courage and will-power. At night when he tossed feverishly in his bed her name was on his lips. It was all he could do to restrain himself from getting up to write to her or call her back by telegram. Then, in the daytime, after a long bout of weeping, he felt exhausted and resigned; and his answers were always very brief, almost cold. He scrutinized every sentence and rewrote it if he thought that there was any possibility of her misinterpreting it. But what torture to have to write such horrible letters, so short and frigid, so contrary to his real feelings, solely for the purpose of alienating her, of taking all the blame on his own shoulders and making her believe that she was justified in forgetting him! Afterwards, he found himself bathed in perspiration, drained, like a man recovering from an act of violent heroism.

It was nearly the end of October. Clotilde had been gone for a month, when Pascal, one morning had a sudden attack of agonizing pain. He had felt slight pain, almost more discomfort than pain, over his heart on several occasions in the past and had attributed it to overwork. But this time, there was no doubt about the diagnosis; excruciating pain over his heart, spreading across his chest and down the left arm, an appalling sensation of anxiety and cold sweats. It was a typical attack of angina pectoris. The acute attack passed off in a minute or two, leaving him, at first, more astonished than frightened. With the blindness characteristic of doctors when considering their own symptoms, he had never suspected that his heart might be affected.

As he was recovering, Martine came up to tell him that Doctor Ramond was downstairs and hoped that he could see monsieur for a few minutes. Pascal, feeling the need of reassurance and a confirmatory diagnosis, cried:

"Very well, let him come up. I shall be glad to see him."

The two men embraced and no allusion was made to Clotilde, other than an energetic and sympathetic handclasp.

"Can you guess the object of my visit?" asked Ramond at once. "I have news of your money .. My father-in-law, Monsieur Lévêque, the solicitor, spoke to me yesterday about your funds invested with Grandguillot. He advises you, most emphatically, to put in a claim, as he has been told that other people have been successful in recovering some of their money."

"But," said Pascal, "I know that something has been settled. Martine has already been given two hundred francs."

Ramond seemed very astonished:

"What! Martine? Without your own personal intervention? .. In any case, would you like my father-in-law to deal with the matter? If so, you must authorize him, officially. He will be able to clarify the situation, a job for which you have neither the time nor the inclination."

"Certainly I shall authorize Monsieur Lévêque. Please tell him that I am extremely grateful to him."

When this matter was out of the way the young man noticed that Pascal was looking pale and asked him about his health. Pascal answered with a smile:

"I must tell you, my friend, I have just had an acute attack of angina pectoris .. No, there's no doubt about it. I had all the classic symptoms .. And, as you are here, you might as well listen to my heart."

At first Ramond demurred and attempted to make fun of the whole idea. Could a raw conscript venture to express an opinion about his general? But he became concerned when he noted Pascal's drawn features, his look of anxiety and the characteristic expression of naked fear. He ended up by listening, very carefully, keeping his ear against the chest wall for a long time. Several minutes passed in profound silence.

"Well?" asked Pascal, when the young doctor had finished.

Ramond said nothing for a while. He felt Pascal's eyes boring into his own; and, in view of the tranquil assurance of Pascal's question, he answered simply:

"Well! in my opinion, there is definitely some degree of sclerosis."

"Good! I appreciate your not lying to me," said the doctor. "I was afraid, for a moment, that you were going to, and I would have been sadly disappointed in you."

Ramond bent over again and listened, murmuring:

"Yes, the impulse is heaving, the first sound is muffled, whereas the second, on the contrary, is increased and has a ringing sound .. I can feel the apex displaced downwards and outwards towards the axilla .. It is extremely probable that these signs are due to sclerosis."

Then, straightening up:

"I have known patients who have lived to a ripe old age with the disease. You should be good for at least another twenty years."

"You may be right, it can happen, but others die a fulminating death in the first or second attack."

The conversation then became impersonal and they discussed a strange case of cardiac sclerosis observed at the Plassans hospital. When the young doctor left, he promised to come back as soon as he had any news of the Grandguillot matter.

Alone in the study Pascal relapsed into despair. He felt that his case was hopeless. The symptoms of the last few weeks, the attacks of giddiness and pain, now fitted into the picture. The basic cause was undoubtedly organic. His poor heart muscle had been worn out by passion and overwork. This explained his sensations during the attack; utter exhaustion and a feeling of approaching death. But as yet he was not worried about dying. His first thought had been that he too, in his turn, was helpless in the grip of heredity, that sclerosis, which was a degenerative process, was his share of the family defect, the inevitable legacy of his abominable ancestry. In other members of the family, the neurosis, which was the original lesion, had manifested itself as vice or virtue, as genius, or crime, as drunkenness, or sanctity; others had died from tuberculosis, epilepsy or ataxia; he had lived on his passions and would die of heart disease. He was no longer afraid, nor did he resent this inevitable and, doubtless, necessary hereditary manifestation. Quite the contrary he was resigned to it, convinced that any rebellion against the laws of nature is undesirable. Why, therefore, had he boasted in the past that he did not belong to the family and had nothing in common with it? From a philosophical point of view nothing could be more misguided. Only monsters disobeyed the laws of heredity. To be part of the warp and woof of his family, why, he even began to think of it as an advantage, at least as desirable as belonging to any other family. Did not all families resemble each other? Was humanity not identical everywhere, with the same sum total of good and bad? The threat of severe pain and death had the effect of making him more modest and gentle, ready to accept anything which life might have in store for him.

Henceforth the thought never left Pascal that he might die from one hour to the next. It ennobled him and enabled him to achieve complete self-forgetfulness. He did not stop working and he now understood more clearly than ever that effort in itself was its own best reward and that all scientific work was transitory and could never be completed in a single lifetime. One evening, Martine informed him that Sarteur, the journeyman hatter and ex-inmate of the Tulettes asylum, had committed suicide by hanging himself. Throughout the evening he thought about this strange case; he had deluded himself that he had cured the man by his injection treatment. In fact he had been about to succumb to a new attack of homicidal mania and had been lucid enough to hang himself instead of strangling some helpless stranger. He remembered his last talk with the man, who had seemed so sensible when he had advised him to go back to his trade. What was the explanation of this destructive force, this urge to murder transformed into suicide, death claiming its victim in spite of everything? His last delusions of therapeutic grandeur accompanied this man into his grave; and, each morning, when he set to work, he felt like a schoolboy learning to spell, feebly groping towards the truth.

His new state of serenity was disturbed by the thought of what would happen to Bonhomme, his old horse, if he were to die first. Now, the poor beast, totally blind and legs paralysed, could not leave his litter. But, when his master visited him, he recognized his step and touch and turned his head. It was the joke of the neighbour-hood that the doctor refused to send the old animal to the slaughter-house. Was he to die first knowing that the knacker would be called in the very next day? But, one morning, when he entered the stable, Bonhomme did not hear him and did not raise his head. He was dead, stretched out peacefully, as if in relief. His master knelt down and kissed him for the last time. Two large tears rolled down his cheeks.

On that same day, Pascal's interest in his neighbour, M. Bellombre, was revived. He caught sight of him through the window, on the other side of the garden wall, taking his usual walk in the pale early November sun; and the sight of the old teacher, so perfectly con-tented with life, filled him with astonishment. Once again it seemed to him inconceivable that a man of seventy, without wife or child or even a dog should have found happiness in living so detached from life, so completely wrapped up in himself. He remembered how angry he had been with this man, how he had despised him, how he had mocked at the old man's fear of life and hoped that he would be chastized by some catastrophe. But no! M. Bellombre looked as hale as ever, he would almost certainly go on ageing for a long time, as hard, as miserly, as useless and happy as ever. But now he no longer hated the old man, he pitied him, realizing how ridiculous and miserable life must be for a man who had no one to love him. He, Pascal, was undergoing the tortures of the damned, just because he was alone! His heart felt like breaking because it was too full of other people's sorrows! How infinitely preferable he considered suffering and pain to this egoism, this death of all that was human and alive in man!

The following night, Pascal had another attack of angina pectoris. This time it lasted five minutes. He could not breathe and had no strength to call the servant. When he was able to breathe again, he did not call her, he preferred not to tell anyone about the increasing severity of his attacks; but he was more convinced than ever that he was doomed, that he would barely live the month out. His first thought was for Clotilde. Why not write to her and ask her to come back as soon as possible? He had, in fact, received a letter from her the day before and had intended to answer her that morning. Then the thought of his files flashed into his mind. If he were to die suddenly his mother would take possession of them and destroy them; and not only the files, but his manuscripts as well, all his papers, thirty years of the work of his brain. This would be the consummation of the crime which had haunted him, which he had dreaded to such an extent that he had risen from his bed, shivering as with fever, to make sure that they were not breaking open his cupboard. He broke out into a cold sweat at the idea of such an outrage; the ashes of a lifetime's work thrown to the four winds. All he had to do was to summon Clotilde; she would hurry back, watch over him, close his eyes and defend his memory. He sat down at his table, anxious to finish his letter so that it would catch the morning post.

But, when he took up his pen to write, all his scruples returned, he felt that he was acting like a coward. Was this solicitude for his files, this fine plan to set a guardian over them and save them, nothing but a sign of weakness, the promptings of his baser self as a pretext for seeing Clotilde? He was being selfish again. He was thinking of himself and not of her welfare. He visualized her coming back to this poverty-stricken house, condemned to nurse a sick old man; what a terrifying experience for her, if he died suddenly—before her very eyes—in one of his agonizingly painful attacks! No, she must be spared such an excruciating ordeal at all costs; it would be a crime on his part to harrow her feelings for a few days and then leave her to a life of poverty. His duty was to safeguard her peace of mind and future happiness. Nothing else mattered! He would die alone like a rat in a hole, happy not to have deprived her of happiness. As to his manuscripts, he hated parting with them, but he would make a great effort and hand them over to Ramond. Anyway, even if all his papers were to perish, he would not mind leaving nothing of himself behind, not even a thought, provided that his beloved Clotilde's life was not disturbed!

Pascal therefore proceeded to pen one of his usual stilted notes. In her last letter, Clotilde allowed it to be understood that Maxime was becoming indifferent to her, as he was finding Rose, Saccard's barber's niece, the demure little blonde, far more amusing. Pascal detected Saccard's hand in this; one of his wily manoeuvres to make sure of his son's rapid demise, by catering to the vices and depraved appetites of the invalid which were aggravated by the approach of death. Pascal, nevertheless, gave Clotilde the benefit of his wise counsel, repeating that her duty was to remain devoted to Maxime to the end. As he signed, tears blurred his vision. He was signing his own death warrant, a solitary death, without a kiss or a friendly hand. Then, he began to doubt his own judgement; was he right to leave her in Paris, in that atmosphere of vice and degeneracy?

At the Souleiade the postman brought the letters and newspapers at about nine each morning; and Pascal, when he wrote to Clotilde, was in the habit of keeping a look out for him and handing him the letter, to make sure that it would not be intercepted. This particular morning the postman gave him another letter from Clotilde, which he was not expecting for another two or three days. He was surprised, but he handed the postman his own letter. Then he went upstairs, sat down at his table and tore open the envelope.

He read the first few lines and sat back almost stupefied by the news. Clotilde wrote that she was two months pregnant. She had wanted to be absolutely certain before reporting to him. Now, there could be no doubt about it, she must have conceived at the end of August, probably during that delirious night when she had served him the royal feast of her youth, after scouring Plassans for money. They had been so extraordinarily happy, had they not sensed that their transports had kindled the spark of a new life? At the end of a month she had not been sure, she had accounted for the delay by her state of physical exhaustion and depression. But, after another month and a few days, she was now certain of being pregnant, besides, she now had all the symptoms. The letter was a short one, simply stating the facts, but it reflected her joy and her longing to be with him again.

Pascal was distracted and read the letter over again, fearing that he might have made a mistake. A child! How he had despised himself for not being able to give her a child, that last day, amidst the desolate howling of the mistral; and it had been there all the time and she had taken it away with her in the train which he had watched receding into the distance! What bliss! A new life was the only thing really worth creating! He beamed with happiness and pride. His own ideas, his fears of the family heredity were forgotten. They were going to have a child! What did anything matter, in comparison with the triumphant certainty of continuity, of life handed on and perpetuated, of his other self? He was indescribably moved, his whole being was aquiver with infinite tenderness. He found himself laughing aloud. He covered the letter with passionate kisses.

He calmed down when he heard footsteps. He turned his head and saw Martine.

"Doctor Ramond is downstairs."

"Ah! send him up, send him up at once."

More good news! Ramond was in the doorway, crying gaily:

"Victory! I am bringing you your money, not all of it, but a nice tidy sum!"

Ramond told him the story; an unexpected and fortunate stroke of luck, thanks to his father-in-law, M. Lévêque's patient investigations. The receipts for the hundred and twenty thousand francs, which established Pascal's right to be considered one of Grand-guillot's personal creditors, were worthless because of the notary's insolvency. His salvation was due to the power of attorney authorizing the notary to invest the whole or part of his money in mortgages. As the name of the beneficiary had been left blank, the notary had used one of his clerks as his man of straw, a common practice; and eighty thousand francs had been discovered, invested in sound mortgages, thanks to information laid by the good clerk, who was in no way involved in his principal's affairs. If Pascal had taken active steps and called on the public prosecutor, the matter would have been cleared up a long time ago. In any case, an assured income of four thousand francs was back in his pocket.

He had grasped the young man's hands and was pressing them in a state of happy excitement:

"My dear friend, if you knew how overwhelmed with joy I feel! This letter from Clotilde has given me a wonderful surprise. Yes, I was going to send for her; but the thought of my poverty, the privations which she would have to share, almost spoilt the joyful prospect of her return to this house .. And now you bring me money, a fortune! Well, enough at any rate to keep my little household in comfort!"

All this good news had made him expansive and he handed the letter to Ramond, insisted on his reading it. Then, when the young man handed it back with a smile, he was so moved by his affectionate understanding that he threw his great arms around him. The two men kissed each other warmly on both cheeks.

"As my lucky star has guided you here, I am going to ask you to render me yet another service. You know that I suspect everyone here, even my old servant. I want you to take my telegram to the post office."

He sat down and wrote: "Expect you leave tonight."

"Let me see," he continued, "am I right in thinking that today is November 6th? .. It is nearly ten o'clock, she will have my telegram about twelve. That will give her plenty of time to pack her trunks and catch the eight o'clock express tonight, which will get her to Marseilles tomorrow in time for lunch. But, as there is no train to connect with it, she cannot be here tomorrow the 7th until five o'clock in the afternoon."

He folded the telegram and rose to his feet:

"Five o'clock tomorrow! .. What a time to wait! What shall I do until then?"

A sudden thought struck him and his expression clouded over;

"Ramond, my comrade, will you do me yet another favour and be absolutely frank with me?"

"What do you mean, sir?"

"Yes, I am sure you understand my meaning .. The other day, you made a thorough examination. Do you think that I have a chance of lasting another year?"

He looked straight at the young man to prevent him from turning his eyes away. Ramond made an attempt at evading the issue by joking; was it reasonable for a medical man to ask such a question?"

"Please, Ramond, be serious."

Then Ramond gave his considered and sincere opinion that Pascal had every chance of living another year. He enumerated his reasons; the relatively early stage of the sclerosis, the healthy state of his other organs. It was obviously impossible to dogmatize, there was always an element of the unknown and the unexpected. No serious physician could absolutely exclude sudden death at any time. They proceeded to discuss the case, as calmly as if they had

246

been called to a bedside consultation, balancing the pros against the cons and agreeing on the inevitable prognosis, according to the recognized indications.

Pascal was as self-possessed and oblivious of himself, as if they were talking about a third person:

"Yes," he murmured, "in the end, you are right, it is not unjustifiable to hope for a year of life .. Do you know, my friend, what I would like would be two years. A mad wish, no doubt, but it would represent eternity of joy .."

And, abandoning himself to his dreams of the future:

"The child will be born about the end of May .. It would be such bliss to see him grow just up to eighteen months, twenty months, not more. Just time enough to see him take his first steps .. That is all I ask, to watch him walking. After that .."

He completed the sentence with a gesture. Then, carried away:

"Even two years are not out of the question. I had a very curious case, a suburban wheelwright who lived for four years, contrary to all my preconceived notions .. Two years, I *will* live two years! I *must* live them!"

Ramond made no further comment. He felt faintly embarrassed at the idea of having expressed an opinion which had erred on the optimistic side; his old colleague's exuberance worried him. It indicated a lack of mental balance, which might be a dangerous omen.

"Did you want me to send this telegram at once?"

"Yes, yes! Hurry, my dear Ramond, and I shall expect you the day after tomorrow. She will be here then and I want you to be the first to welcome her back home."

It was a long day. And, about four o'clock in the morning, when Pascal had just managed to doze off, after lying awake, too excited to sleep, he was aroused by a frightful attack. He felt as if an enormous weight, the whole house, was pressing on his chest heavy enough to flatten it and crush his ribs against his backbone; it was impossible to breathe, the pain spread to his shoulders and neck and paralyzed his left arm. He remained fully conscious and felt as if his heart were stopping and that his life was being crushed out of him by the jaws of a vice tightly clamped about him. In the early stages of the attack he had been able to get out of bed and call Martine by knocking on the floor with his cane. Then he had collapsed on his bed, soaked in cold sweat, unable to move or speak.

Fortunately Martine had heard him. She dressed, threw a shawl around her shoulders and hurried upstairs, candle in hand. It was just before dawn and the night was black as pitch. When she saw her master lying motionless, with his eyes the only living thing about him, watching her, his jaws tightly clenched, his tongue paralyzed, his features twisted with pain, she was terrified, frantic, and could only run towards the bed, crying:

"Monsieur .. monsieur, what is the matter? .. Answer me, monsieur! you frighten me!"

For another minute, which seemed endless, Pascal gasped for air, unable to breathe. Then as the jaws of the vice loosened a little, he managed to half whisper, half murmur:

"The five thousand francs in the desk belong to Clotilde .. Tell her that some of the notary's money has been recovered, that she will have enough to live on .."

Then Martine, who had listened, horrified, conscience-stricken, confessed that she had lied to him.

"Monsieur, you must forgive me, I told a lie. But it would be wrong of me to lie any more .. When I saw you so lonely, so unhappy, I drew on my own savings .."

"My poor girl, you actually did that?"

"Oh, I was hoping that monsieur would be able to pay me back some day!"

The attack was passing off, he was able to turn his head and look at her. He was stupefied and touched. How strange were the workings of the human heart. What had come over this miserly old maid, who had painfully accumulated her treasure over thirty years and never taken a sou from it either for herself or anybody else? He could not understand, but he was anxious to express his gratitude:

"You are a good woman, Martine. It will all be paid back .. But, I am going to die .."

She interrupted him, shocked to the core, unable to reconcile herself to such a dreadful prospect. Her beloved master! She uttered a wild cry of protest:

"Die? You, monsieur! .. Die before me! I cannot bear it. I won't let you!"

She had dropped on her knees by the side of the bed, grasped his hands and was pulling at them frantically, as if to keep him from slipping away from her, hoping that death would not dare to tear him away from her:

"Tell me what is wrong, I will look after you, I will save you.

If it will help, to give you my life, I will give it to you, monsieur ..
I can be with you all day and all night. I am still strong, I shall be
stronger than your illness, you will see .. To die, to die. Oh! no, it is
not possible! God cannot want to be so unjust. I have prayed to
him so much in my life, that he will listen to me, he will grant my
prayer, monsieur, he will save you!"

Pascal stared at her and listened to her. Suddenly, understanding
came to him. This poor woman loved him, had always loved him!
He remembered her thirty years of blind devotion, her mute
adoration, when she served him on her knees, when she had been
young; then, later, her latent jealousy of Clotilde. What she must
have suffered, unconsciously, during that period! And, here she was,
on her knees again, at his death bed, her hair now grey, with her
ash-coloured eyes in her pale face, with the expression of a nun
stupefied by celibacy. And he felt that she was vastly ignorant.
She did not even know that she had been in love. She loved him
simply for the sake of loving, of being with him and serving him.

Tears coursed down Pascal's cheeks. Infinite compassion and
infinite tenderness overflowed from his poor labouring heart,
which would soon cease to beat:

"My poor girl, you are the best of women .. Come here! Kiss me
like you love me, with all your might!"

Now she too was sobbing. She let her grey head, her toil-worn
face, fall against her master's chest. She kissed him, distractedly,
putting her whole being into that kiss.

"There, now! we must not allow ourselves to get sentimental
because, you see, whatever we do, I am finished .. If you want me
to love you, you must obey me."

His first impulse was to get away from his bedroom. It seemed
to him icy cold, gloomy, empty and black. He wanted to die in
Clotilde's room, where they had loved each other, which he could
not enter without a sensation of almost religious awe. Thus, Martine
was called upon to perform a last act of abnegation, help him to get
up, hold him up and guide him, staggering, to the bed still warm
with memories. He had brought the key of the cupboard, which he
kept under his pillow at night; and he put it under the other pillow
to watch over it as long as he was alive. The sky was a faint, pale
grey. The servant had put the candle down on the table.

"Now that I am comfortable in bed, and I can breathe more
freely, I want you to hurry to Doctor Ramond's .. Wake him up
and bring him back with you."

As she was leaving, a disquieting thought struck him:

"And, above all, I forbid you to go and tell my mother."

Flushing with embarrassment, she turned back and implored him:

"Oh, monsieur, Madame Felicité made me promise her . ."

But he was inflexible. Throughout his life he had treated his mother with deference, and he considered that he had earned the right to protect himself from her, now that he was about to die. He refused to see her. He forced the servant to swear to keep silence. Then his face cleared and he smiled at her:

"Hurry . . Oh! I shall be here when you come back, I am not leaving you just yet."

It was dawn, a sad hesitant dawn, in a pale November sky. At Pascal's wish, Martine had opened the shutters; now that he was alone, he lay watching the light slowly become brighter and spread, the light of the last day of his life, he felt sure. It had rained the day before, clouds had hidden the sun, though it had not been cold. From the plane trees outside the dressing room window he could hear the birds twittering and chirping and, far away, across the still slumbering countryside, a locomotive hooted, a prolonged and plaintive sound. And he was alone, alone in the great mournful house; he could feel the chill of its emptiness, he could almost hear its glabrous silence. The light was spreading slowly, he could see the reflection grow larger on the window panes. Then, the candle flame seemed drowned in the full light of day and the room sprang to life. As he had hoped, he was able to divert his attention from himself to the contemplation of the dawn-coloured wall coverings, the familiar furniture and the vast bed in which he had loved and was now going to die. The whole room, from floor to high ceiling, seemed filled with an invisible cloud of perfume, the delicate faint heady scent of his beloved; he was comforted by it, and transported to his intimate dream world in which he and Clotilde were reunited.

Although the acute phase of the attack was over, Pascal was still in pain, excruciating pain. He felt as if a dagger had been left in his heart, his left arm was numbed and felt like a leaden weight suspended from his shoulder. Ramond seemed to be interminably long in coming and his wandering thoughts reverted to this abominable pain, like talons clutching and tearing at his heart. But he was becoming resigned to it, he felt no trace of the leaping indignation which used to fill him at the sight of a patient writhing in pain. It had exasperated him. Pain had seemed to him monstrously cruel and useless. After his loss of faith in his own power to heal, his one object had been to alleviate pain when he visited his patients. Was the fact that he, to-day, no longer even resented the pain which was racking his own body proof that his faith in life had become even greater, more unquestioning, that he had climbed to that serene summit of objectivity, from the heights of which life seemed totally good, in spite of all its inevitable suffering, which, for all we know, may be its mainspring? Yes! live life with every fibre of one's being, surrender oneself to it, with no thought of rebellion, without deluding oneself that one can improve it and render it painless; all this was revealed to the dying man, as the only courageous and wise attitude possible for a man of science. And to make the time of waiting seem shorter and distract his mind from his pain, he thought about his latest theories; he tried to devise a means of utilizing pain, transforming it into action or into work. As man becomes civilized, he becomes more sensitive to pain, but he also becomes more powerful, controls his environment better. His brain, the dominant organ involved, develops and expands, on condition that the balance between the sensations which impinge on him and the work he performs is not disturbed. Was it not legitimate to aspire to a new humanity, in which the sum of work would be so accurately balanced against the sum of his sensations that pain itself would be involved in the process and thus, for practical purposes, be abolished?

Now the sun was rising. Pascal, his pain now dulled, was meditating on these hopes for the distant future, when he felt a new attack grumbling inside his chest and preparing to pounce upon him. He had a moment of atrocious anxiety; was this the end, was he going to die, all alone? But there were rapid footsteps on the stairs, Ramond hurried into the room followed by Martine. And Pascal had time to say to him:

"Give me an injection at once, an injection of plain water! At least ten grammes, fill the syringe twice!"

Unfortunately it took Ramond some time to find the syringe and prepare the injection, during which time Pascal was in excruciating agony. Ramond watched his face and saw his lips go blue. Finally, after the two injections, he noticed that the pain was beginning to diminish in intensity. The catastrophe seemed averted once again.

As soon as he was able to breathe, Pascal glanced at the clock and murmured in feeble but even tones:

"My friend, it is seven o'clock .. In twelve hours, at seven o'clock this evening, I shall be dead."

The young man was about to protest and argue, but he said:

"No, don't lie. You have watched the attack and now you know .. From now on, we can both prophesy what will happen with mathematical accuracy; and, hour by hour, I could describe the progress of the disease .."

He paused, managed to take a deep breath and added:

"Besides, all is well, I am glad .. Clotilde will be here at five o'clock, all I ask for is to be able to see her and die in her arms."

Very soon, however, he began to feel much better. The effect of the injections had been really miraculous; he was actually able to sit up in bed, propped up against some pillows. His voice became stronger, his brain had never been more lucid. "You know," said Ramond, "that I shall not be leaving you. I have sent a message to my wife that we are spending the day together; and, in spite of what you say, I hope that it will not be the last .. Will you allow me to stay and keep you company?"

Pascal smiled. He discussed the lunch with Martine, he wanted her to cook something special for Ramond. She must go and see to it. They would call her if they needed her. And the two men settled down to a long talk in an atmosphere of friendly intimacy; the one, semi-recumbent, with his great white beard, discoursing like a wise man of the East, the other, sitting by the bedside, listening with respect, like a disciple.

"It is a fact," murmured Pascal, as if talking to himself, "those injections are extraordinarily effective .."

Then, raising his voice, almost gaily:

"Ramond, my friend, it is perhaps not a gift of great value, but I am going to leave you my manuscripts. Yes, Clotilde has orders to hand them over to you when I am dead .. Look through them, you may find some ideas which are not devoid of interest. If, some day, you can make use of any of them, well, all the better."

He then proceeded to outline his scientific beliefs, to summarize his long career. He was fully aware of having been nothing but a solitary pioneer, a precursor, elaborating preliminary theories, trying to apply them gropingly, failing because his method was still in a rudimentary state. He recalled his enthusiasm, when he had believed that he had found the universal panacea, his injections of nerve substance; then his discomfortures and disasters, Lafouasse's

252

fulminating death, Valentin succumbing to phthisis despite his treatment, Sarteur relapsing into madness. For all these reasons he was full of doubts at the end of his life. He had lost the faith so indispensable to the physician-healer, but he was so in love with life that he was left with unlimited faith in life alone, convinced that life was the only source of health and strength. But he did not deny that the future might be pregnant with boundless possibilities and he was happy to bequeath his hypothesis to the younger generation. Theories changed every twenty years, only the acquired truths remained unshakable, the foundation on which science continued to build. Even if his sole merit had been to elaborate a hypothesis which proved to be untenable, his work would not have been in vain, because, surely, progress was the resultant of our ceaseless striving for knowledge and constantly increasing brain power. Who knows? although he was dying, weary and troubled in mind, without having been able to perfect his method of injections, other workers would come after him, young, ardent, confident, who would take up the idea, clarify and develop it. And perhaps it might usher in a new century, a whole new world.

"Ah! my dear Ramond," he continued, "if one could only have one's life to live over again! .. Yes, I would begin again, I would work on my idea, because it is most striking that injections of pure water have proved, recently, almost as effective as my extract .. It appears that the composition of the liquid injected is of no importance. It must, therefore, be simply a question of some mechanical action .. I have written a lot about this subject during the last month. You will find my notes and some interesting observations .. To sum up, I pin my faith on work, I should define health as the harmonious and balanced function of all the organs, a sort of dynamic therapy, if I may coin the word."

He became more and more carried away by his subject and even forgot his approaching end, alive with his ardent curiosity about life. He gave a rough account of his latest theory. Man was bathed in an environment, nature, which sets up a perpetual irritation of his sensory nerve endings, by direct contact. This stimulated, not only the senses, but all the surfaces of the body, both internal and external. These sensations, carried to the brain, the spinal cord and the nerve centres, were transformed into muscular tone, movements and ideas; he was convinced that health consisted of a normal rhythm of this sequence of events; to receive sensations, to transform them into ideas and movements, to nourish the human machine by the regular play of its organs. Hence, work became the great law, the regulator of the living universe. And, if the balance was disturbed, if the stimulation from outside became inadequate, it was necessary for the doctor to create artificial therapeutic stimuli, in order to re-establish tonicity or a state of optimum tone, which is synonymous with perfect health. And he was in favour of altogether new methods of treatment; suggestion, the authority of the doctor's personality which exerted such a powerful influence on the senses; electricity, frictions, massage for the skin and the tendons; diets for the stomach; fresh air cures at an altitude for the lungs; finally, transfusions and injections of distilled water for the circulatory apparatus. It was the undeniable and purely mechanical action of these injections which had put him on the track. He was now extending his hypothesis because of his passion for generalizations. He felt that he was being vouchsafed a glimpse of the world saved by this perfect balance, work performed in direct proportion to the exciting stimulus, the rhythm of the world re-established thanks to the virtue of eternal labour.

Then he burst into laughter:

"Oh dear! here I am off on my hobby horse again! Here am I, who have become convinced that true therapeutic wisdom consists in not interfering, leaving everything to nature! What an incorrigible old fool of an enthusiast I am!"

But Ramond had seized his two hands, in a transport of affection and admiration:

"You must not say that! Your passionate enthusiasm, even what you call your folly, is the essence of genius! You may be sure that I have listened and will remember what you have told me. I shall try to be worthy of your heritage; and I believe, as you do, that you have hit upon something with an unlimited future."

In the calm and intimate atmosphere of the room, Pascal continued the conversation with the tranquil bravery of a dying philosopher giving his last lecture. He reverted to his personal observations, he explained that he had often restored himself to health by work, according to a regular and methodical plan, without overworking. Eleven o'clock was striking and Ramond was to have his lunch. Pascal went on talking in a louder voice, while Martine served it. The sun, at last, had pierced the grey morning mist, a gentle sun, still half-veiled, which filled the room with golden radiance. Then after drinking a little milk, he fell silent.

The young doctor was eating a pear:

"Is your pain coming back?"

"No, no. Finish your meal."

But it was a palpable lie. It was another attack, a terrible one. It struck him like a thunderbolt, made him collapse against the pillows, his face convulsed and blue. He was clutching the sheet, as if to use it as a fulcrum to lever up the appalling weight which was crushing his chest. His eyes were wide open, fixed on the clock, with an agonized expression of despair and terror. For ten interminable minutes he fought with death.

Ramond had given him the injections without delay. But the effect was not so rapid and did not relieve him to the same extent.

Great tears came into Pascal's eyes as the acute pain began to abate, but he was still speechless. Then, gazing at the clock through eyes half-blinded with tears:

"My friend, I shall die at four o'clock, I shall not see her."

When Ramond, to change the subject, declared, against all the evidence, that his condition was not really so desperate, Pascal insisted, in the interests of scientific accuracy, in giving his young colleague a last lesson based on direct observation. He had looked after several cases almost identical to his own. He remembered having dissected the heart of an old pauper suffering from sclerosis at the Plassans hospital:

"I can see my heart, as if I were dissecting it .. It is the colour of dead leaves, the fibres are brittle, it is flaccid and there is some wasting of the muscle, although the volume has increased. The inflammatory process has hardened it, it would be hard to cut with a scalpel .."

He continued in a lower voice. During the attack he had felt his heart weakening, the contractions had become slower and less powerful. Instead of the normal rush of blood, spouting from the aorta, only a feeble trickle was coming from it. The veins were engorged with blood, becoming more and more overfilled, as the heart, the pump which sucks in and pushes out again, the regulator of the bodily machine, slowed down and lost its full power of contraction. And he had studied the action of the injection on himself, in spite of the pain, noted the progressive improvement in the heart beat; it had acted as a strong stimulant, revived the heart, which proceeded to suck in the black venous blood and spurt out the life-giving scarlet arterial blood, to revitalize the whole body. But he knew that he was in for another attack, as soon as the mechanical effect of the injection had worn off. He could predict

255

its onset to within a few minutes. Thanks to the injections, he would have three more attacks. The third would kill him and he would die at four o'clock.

Then, in a voice which grew progressively weaker, he expatiated, with a last flicker of enthusiasm, on that noble organ, the human heart, that obstinate and tireless worker, never stopping its life-giving labours even during sleep, whilst the other organs are lazily recuperating.

"Ah! great heart! how heroically you wage your battle! .. How faithful and generous your tireless muscles! .. You have loved too much, struggled too much and too often, and that is why you are breaking, stout heart, so reluctant to die, fighting to the last gasp!"

The first of the predicted attacks was starting. At the end of it Pascal emerged panting, haggard, hardly able to utter a few words in a harsh whisper. He was groaning, in spite of his stoicism. God! would this torture never end? But, his failing strength was concentrated on one object, his burning desire to live long enough to be able to kiss Clotilde for the last time, no matter how much he suffered in the meanwhile. If he were only mistaken, as Ramond persisted in claiming, if he could only survive until five o'clock! His eyes remained fixed on the clock, each minute was as important to him as eternity. In the past, they had often joked about this empire clock, a milestone of gilded bronze, with Cupid smiling at a sleeping Father Time. The hands were pointing to three o'clock. Then they pointed to half past three. Only two hours of life, two more hours of life. The sun was tilting towards the horizon, a great calm fell from the pale winter sky; from time to time he heard the distant whistle of a locomotive across the barren plain. That was a train going to the Tulettes. The other train, the one coming from Marseilles, would it never arrive?

At twenty minutes to four, Pascal beckoned to Ramond. His voice was so weak that it could not carry that far:

"If my pulse were less weak I might live to six o'clock. I was hoping, but it is all over .."

And his lips slowly formed the word Clotilde. It was his farewell to her. A long sighing murmur, expressing his anguish and despair at not seeing her again.

Then he began to worry about his manuscripts:

"Do not leave me .. the key is under my pillow. Tell Clotilde to take it. I have told her what to do."

At ten minutes to four another injection gave him no relief.

And, as four was about to strike, the second attack gripped him. Suddenly, stifling, he threw himself out of bed, he made a super-human effort to get up and walk. He must have space, light, fresh air, he must manage, somehow, to reach his study; it was calling to him, the irresistible call of life. And he managed to stagger through the door, unable to breathe, his body bent over to the left, holding on to the furniture.

Ramond stepped forward, quickly, to intercept him:

"Please, my old friend! go back to bed, I beg of you!"

But Pascal was determined to die on his feet. His was now a blind passion for survival, the heroic idea of work, more work, they carried him along, hardly more than an inert mass. There was a rattling sound in his throat, he stammered faintly:

"No, no .. over there, over there .."

His friend had to hold him up as far as the other end of the study. He collapsed on to his chair, in front of his table, on which there was a sheet of manuscript, half covered with his writing, in the middle of a disordered pile of papers and books.

His breathing was painfully laboured, his eyelids closed. He opened them again and his hands groped among the papers. He managed to find the Genealogical Tree. With trembling hands he pulled it towards him. Two days ago he had corrected some dates. Now ..

"My dear old friend! you are killing yourself!" repeated Ramond, shuddering and overwhelmed with pity and admiration.

Pascal was not listening. He heard nothing. He had felt a pencil rolling under his fingers. Fumblingly he picked it up, bent over the Tree, very low, as if his nearly lifeless eyes could barely see. And, for the last time, he reviewed the members of his family. His pencil hovered over the name Maxime and he wrote: "Dies of ataxia, in 1873", certain that his nephew would not survive for a year. Then, a little further on, Clotilde's name arrested his attention and he completed her case history in the leaf by writing: "Has, in 1874, son by her uncle Pascal". Now he was searching for his own name, exhausting himself, his hand wandering over the paper. Finally, when he found it, his hand steadied and he wrote in bold letters: "Dies, of heart disease, November 7, 1873". This was his supreme effort, the rattle became louder, his breathing stopped. Then he caught sight of the blank space in the leaf above Clotilde. His fingers could barely hold the pencil. However, he managed to write, almost illegibly, a few words which expressed his tortured feelings: "the child unknown, to be born in 1874. Boy or girl?" Then he collapsed, and Martine and Ramond just managed to carry him back to his bed.

The third attack took place at four-fifteen. His features were distorted, the pain was unbearable. But he was to endure his martyrdom to the end without loss of consciousness. His glazing eyes seemed still to be looking for the clock. His lips moved and Ramond bent over him, putting his ear against Pascal's mouth. The murmured words were more like a faint sigh:

"Four o'clock .. the heart is stopping, no more red blood in the aorta .. The valve flap is weakening and stopping .."

He was shaken by a terrifying rattle, the sighing murmur became even fainter:

"I am sinking, too fast .. Don't leave me, the key is under the pillow .. Clotilde, Clotilde .."

At the foot of the bed, Martine had fallen to her knees, choked with sobs. She could see that monsieur was dying. She had not dared to run and fetch a priest, much as she longed to do so; and she had to be satisfied with reciting the prayers for the dead herself. She prayed fervently to God, begging him to forgive monsieur and to admit him straight into paradise.

Pascal was dying. His face was blue. After a few seconds of complete immobility, he tried to take a breath. He pushed out his lips, opened his poor mouth, like a bird trying to take a last gulp of air. And death came to Pascal, swiftly and simply.

CHAPTER THIRTEEN

It was only after lunch, about one o'clock, that Clotilde received Pascal's telegram. On that particular day her brother had been very trying. He was sulking and venting his petulant spite on Clotilde. On the whole, she had not been a success as his nurse; he found her too simple and serious, he wanted somebody more cheerful around him; and now, he spent more and more time closeted with young Rose, the demure, little blonde, who amused him. Ever since he had been immobilized and enfeebled by his disease, he had become less prudent and was losing his distrust of women whom he had always suspected of being man-eaters. When his sister wanted to tell him that her uncle had sent for her, she had to wait for some time before his door was opened, as Rose was massaging him. He agreed, at once. He asked her to come back as soon as she had attended to her affairs at Plassans, but made no great point of it.

Clotilde spent the afternoon packing her trunks. In her fever of impatience, in her confusion at this sudden decision, she had had no time for reflection, she was simply wild with joy at the idea of going back home and seeing Pascal. But after a hurried meal, after saying goodbye to her brother and the interminable drive in a cab from the Avenue du Bois de Boulogne to the Gare de Lyon, when she was alone in a compartment reserved for ladies, in the rainy and cold November night, she calmed down; she began to think about the implications of the telegram and gradually fell a prey to foreboding thoughts. Why this urgent and laconic telegram: "Expect you leave tonight"? Doubtless it was the answer to her letter, in which she informed him of her pregnancy. On the other hand she knew how anxious he was for her to stay in Paris, where he deluded himself that she was happy and she found it surprising that he should have sent for her so hurriedly. She had not been expecting a telegram but a letter instructing her to make the necessary arrangements and go back to Plassans in a few weeks time. Was there, then, some other reason? Illness perhaps? Throughout the remainder of her journey these fears rankled in her mind and ended up by becoming a presentiment, which obsessed her.

Throughout the night all the way across the plains of Burgundy a driving rain had whipped the pane beside her. The deluge stopped only when the train reached Mâcon. After Lyons it would be day-light and she would be able to read. She waited impatiently for the dawn in order to re-read and study Pascal's letters. His handwriting seemed to have altered. In fact, she felt a pang of heightened anxiety when she examined it more closely; this was not his usual, regular, flowing writing, the sentences were broken and there were gaps in the words. He was ill, very ill; she was certain of it, not because of any process of reasoning but thanks to a sort of subtle intuition. The rest of the journey was horribly long and her anxiety increased as she approached her destination. The worst of it was that, although the train arrived at Marseilles at half past twelve, there was no connection for Plassans until three-twenty. Three hours to wait! She lunched at the station restaurant, feverishly wolfing her meal, as if afraid of missing her train; then she tried to kill time in a dusty garden, sat on one bench after another, under the pale, tepid sun, surrounded by buses and cabs. Finally her train started, but it stopped at every small station. She leaned out of the window, she felt as if she had been away for twenty years and that the whole countryside would be altered. The train was leaving Sainte-Marthe, when, by leaning out still further, she managed to catch a glimpse of the Souleiade on the horizon far in the distance, with the two ancient cypresses on the terrace. She felt unbearably excited.

It was five o'clock, early twilight. The turn-plates clanked, the train jarred to a stop and Clotilde jumped down to the platform. She had been bitterly disappointed that Pascal was not waiting for her on the platform. She had been saying to herself over and over again ever since Lyons: "If I don't see him at once, as soon as I arrive, I shall know that he is seriously ill." But perhaps he was in the waiting room, or outside in the carriage. She ran through the station and found only old Durieu, the hack coachman whom Pascal usually hired. She bombarded him with questions. The old man, a taciturn Provençal, was in no hurry to answer them. He had brought his handcart and asked for her luggage receipt, he wanted to attend to the trunks first. In a trembling voice, she repeated her question:

"Is everybody at home well, Monsieur Durieu?"

"Yes, mademoiselle."

It was only by patient and persistent questioning that she managed to extract the information that it was Martine, at about six the evening before, who had given him the order to meet the train with his carriage. He had not seen the doctor, nobody had seen him for at least two months. Perhaps, as he was not there, he had had to take to his bed, there were rumours in the town that his health was failing.

"Wait until I fetch the luggage, mademoiselle. There will be plenty of room for you on the back seat."

"No, I cannot wait. I shall walk."

She hurried up the station stairs. Her fears were flooding through her so violently that she could hardly breathe. The sun had disappeared behind the slopes of Sainte-Marthe, a faint mist like a shower of ashes was falling from the grey sky, the first damp shudder of November; and, when she turned into the lane of the Fenouillières she caught her second glimpse of the Souleiade, which sent a cold shiver of apprehension down her spine; in the twilight the façade looked dreadfully gloomy, all the shutters were closed, the house seemed sad and abandoned, as if in mourning.

But this was nothing compared with the shock of seeing Ramond standing on the threshold.

Anxious to try and deaden the blow of the catastrophic news he had come downstairs to wait for her. She arrived out of breath. She had taken a short cut through the plane trees, near the spring; up to the last moment she had been hoping to see Pascal at the door and, when she saw the young man, she felt in her bones that some frightful, irreparable disaster had happened to Pascal. Ramond was very pale and agitated, in spite of all his good resolutions. He said nothing and was bracing himself to answer her questions. Her anguish was so dreadful that she remained speechless. They went in together. He led her towards the dining room and they stood facing each other there for some seconds in mutual mute agony of mind.

"He is ill, isn't he?" she managed to ask.

"Yes, he is ill."

"That is what I assumed, when I saw you. He would have to be very ill not to be here to meet me." Then she repeated her question:

"He is very ill, then?"

He felt unable to answer her, his face grew even paler. Then a sort of sixth sense told her that Pascal was dead. The feeling of death emanated from Ramond, from his hands, still trembling from attending to the dying man, from his woe-begone expression, from his eyes, which darted away from hers and which had witnessed the agony of death, from the mental devastation which overwhelms a doctor who has been fighting death, unavailingly, for more than twelve hours.

She gave a heart-rending cry:

"He is dead!"

She swayed, utterly crushed, and collapsed into his arms. Ramond clasped her to him in a fraternal embrace. Then they sobbed bitterly in unison.

After he had made her sit down, he managed to say:

"It was I, yesterday, who took the telegram to the post office at about half past ten. At that time he was very happy and full of hope! He was building castles in Spain, he had wonderful plans for you and the child, he was convinced that he was going to live for a year, even two years .. It was this morning at four o'clock that he had his first acute attack and sent for me. He knew by then that his case was hopeless. But he expected to be able to last out until six o'clock, long enough to see you again .. But his diseased heart failed too rapidly. Until he drew his last breath, he continued reporting his own progress, minute by minute, like a professor demonstrating in a lecture hall. He died with your name on his lips, calm and despairing, like a hero."

Clotilde felt like rushing upstairs and bursting into the room, but she was unable to get out of her chair, all strength had been drained out of her. As she listened to him great tears welled up into her eyes and rolled down her cheeks in an interminable flood. Every one of Ramond's words, as he told the story of that stoical death, struck her like a blow and was engraved on her memory. She was able to reconstitute that abominable day in her mind. She was to re-live it over and over again throughout her life.

But her cup of intolerable grief overflowed when Martine, who had been standing there for a minute or two, said in a hard voice:

"Mademoiselle has every reason to cry, because it is mademoiselle's fault that monsieur is dead."

The old servant was standing near the door of the kitchen, distracted with grief, unable to bear the thought that her master had been taken away from her and she made no attempt to welcome or console this child whom she had brought up. Without considering the effect on Clotilde, she felt impelled to tell her everything and revealed her master's secret:

"Yes, monsieur is dead because mademoiselle went away."

Clotilde managed to find the strength to protest:

"But it was he who was angry with me and forced me to leave!"

"Oh, no! Mademoiselle must have been blind not to see what the master was feeling .. The night before you left, I found monsieur half suffocated, he was so upset; and when I wanted to tell mademoiselle, he stopped me .. And then, I could see very well what was happening to him when mademoiselle was not there any more. It was the same story every night, the poor man was in despair and it was all he could do not to write to you and call you back .. Now he is dead and I am telling you the truth, God's own truth."

Martine had explained what had so puzzled Clotilde. It was all clear to her now. In one way she felt relieved; in another it added to her mental torture. So it was true then, what she had suspected at first! She had ended by believing him, because of his violent and obstinately repeated statements that he was not lying, that he had genuinely preferred to put his work first, that this attitude was that of a scientist who loves his work more than he can love his wife. But he had been lying all the time. His devotion to her, his utter forgetfulness of self had driven him to immolate himself for the sake of what he considered best for her welfare. And it was the eternal irony of life that his unselfish action had proved to be a mistake, that it had led to misfortune and unhappiness for all of them.

Once more Clotilde protested vehemently:

"But how could I have known? .. I obeyed him, I loved him too much not to obey his slightest wish."

"Ah!" cried Martine, "if it had been me I would have guessed!"

Ramond intervened and spoke gently and kindly. He was holding his friend's hands and was explaining that mental perturbation might have hastened Pascal's inevitable end, but that his old colleague had been a condemned man for some time. His heart disease was not of recent origin, it must have started a long time ago and was due to constant overwork and overstrain—a definite hereditary element—and finally to his passionate nature.

"Let us go upstairs," said Clotilde, "I want to see him."

Upstairs in the bedroom the shutters had been closed, even the melancholy twilight had been kept out. Two wax tapers were burning on a little table at the foot of the bed, and they threw a pale yellow light on Pascal; he was stretched out, his legs together, his hands half joined on his chest. His eyelids had been piously closed. He seemed to be sleeping, the face was still tinged a faint blue, but the expression was peaceful. He had been dead for barely an hour and a half. He had set out on his last journey to infinite serenity and everlasting rest.

To see him like this, to know that he could not hear her voice, that he could not see her, that he was alone for ever, that, after a last kiss, she would lose him for ever, Clotilde felt drowned in an enormous wave of grief and had thrown herself on the bed, only able to stammer, lovingly:

"Oh! master, master, my master .."

Her lips were pressed against Pascal's cold forehead; and, as his body was still warm, she was able to delude herself for an instant that he could feel this last caress. Were those motionless features smiling, was he not happy at last, could he not die satisfied, now that he could feel them both near him, herself and the child within her? Then she felt the full impact of reality and burst uncontrollably into loud shuddering sobs.

Martine came into the room with a lamp which she put down on the corner of the mantelpiece.

Ramond, seeing Clotide so beside herself with grief and knowing that she was pregnant became seriously alarmed:

"My dear, you must make a great effort to control yourself, if not I shall have to take you away with me. You have the child to consider. The doctor's mind was full of your child just before he died. It had made him so happy."

The servant overhead this conversation and was now able to piece together the chance remarks heard earlier on; she looked at Clotilde with amazement and stood rooted to the spot, listening.

Ramond had lowered his voice:

"The key of the cupboard is under the pillow, he was most insistent upon your being told .. You know what you have to do."

Clotilde had to make an effort to remember:

"What I have to do? The pape.s, you mean ..? Yes, yes! I remember, I am to keep the files and give you the other manuscripts .. Do not worry, I am not out of my mind, I shall be very sensible. But I cannot tear myself away from him yet, I want to stay with him for one more night. I shall be quite calm, I promise you."

She looked so unhappy and so determined that Doctor Ramond did not feel justified in opposing her:

"Very well! I shall have to be going, they must be expecting me at home. Besides, there are all sorts of formalities which I can attend to and spare you as much as possible. Dismiss them from your mind.

When I come back tomorrow morning everything will have been done."

He embraced her once more and left her. And it was only then that Martine moved. She went out behind Ramond, locked the front door behind her and hurried through the early darkness of the winter night.

Clotilde was now alone in the room; she felt the empty house around and below her. Clotilde was alone with her dead Pascal. She had drawn up a chair against the head of the bed and was sitting like a graven image of grief. All feeling had been crushed out of her, the idea of washing and changing her dress did not occur to her, besides she would not have had the strength to move from the chair. Her tired brain kept returning to one thing; her one aching regret, her shattering remorse for having obeyed him! Why had she allowed herself to be persuaded? If she had stayed, she was convinced that he would not have died. She would have kept him alive, made him well again with her love and her caresses. Every night she would have rocked him to sleep in her arms, wrapped him around and warmed him with the soft cloak of her youth, breathed new life into him with her kisses. If one did not want death to rob one of a lover, one had to stay near him, give one's blood for him and put death to flight. It was her fault that she had lost him and that she was now powerless to wake him from his eternal sleep. There was no excuse for her unutterable stupidity; she should have understood. She had been a coward and was being pitilessly punished for going away.

The silence was so all pervading, so absolute that Clotilde aroused herself from her rapt contemplation of Pascal's face and looked around the room. All she could see was vague shadowy shapes; in the slanting light of the lamp the big cheval glass looked like a sheet of dull silver; everything was dim, except for two tawny patches of wavering light on the ceiling above the two tapers. At that moment his letters, those short, impersonal letters, came back into her mind, and she realized what anguish it must have caused him to write them. He had been determined to step out of her life in order to save her from poverty and the spectacle of his old age; he had deluded himself that he would be ensuring her a life of luxury and happiness in the full enjoyment of her twenty-six years. Her predominant feeling was one of gratitude. Then, all of a sudden, she began seeing vivid mental pictures of her childhood and adolescence by his side, always so kind and gay. Then, later, the successive stages of her falling in love with him flitted before her mind's eye. The misunderstanding which had separated them for a short time had made her eventual surrender to him even more complete! And now his body was slowly growing cold in this room which night after night had been so warm and aquiver with their passion.

The clock on the mantelpiece struck seven and Clotilde started, the thin metallic notes sounded loud in that deep silence. Had somebody spoken? Then she remembered and looked at the clock which had sounded so many joyful hours for Pascal and herself. The antique clock had the quavering voice of an aged friend, which had amused them as they lay in each other's arms in the darkness. And now every object of furniture in the room recalled memories of that happy past. It had been in that cheval-glass, against its silvered and pale background that she had admired herself when he had decked her out in some jewel, which he had been hiding until the last minute, carried away by his mania for showering her with presents. It was at that table, on which the tapers now stood, that they had eaten that frugal and unforgettable meal. What vestiges of their love she would find in that marble-topped chest-of-drawers! How they had rocked with laughter on that couch, on its stiff legs, when he had been helping her to pull on her stockings and had teased her unmercifully! Even the hangings, the old faded red cotton-print, seemed to be whispering to her, reminding her of their trifling and tender love passages and even seemed to be still redolent of the faint fragrance of her own hair, a scent reminiscent of violets, which had always sent him into transports of delight. The last vibrations of the strokes of the clock recalled her to the present and she turned her eyes back to Pascal's face and resumed her rapt contemplation.

It was in a state of prostration that Clotilde, a few minutes later heard the sound of sobbing behind her. She recognized her grandmother Felicité, who had rushed into the room unannounced. But she was so benumbed by her grief that she neither moved nor spoke. Martine had hastened to old Madame Rougon to acquaint her with the terrible news; and Felicité was dumbfounded at first by this sudden catastrophe and then distracted by genuine grief. She sobbed over her son, she kissed Clotilde who returned her embrace as if in a dream. From that moment onwards, even though still immersed in her dolorous apathy she could not help hearing the constant, restless stirring and rustling sounds in the room and realized that her solitary vigil had been broken. It was Felicité, either sobbing or coming in or going out on tip-toe, putting things in order or prying, whispering or dropping into a chair and getting up again. At about nine o'clock her grandmother tried to persuade Clotilde to eat something. Twice she had upbraided her grand-daughter for allowing herself to be overwhelmed by her bereavement. For the third time she came back to her and whispered in her ear:

"Clotilde, my dear, you must listen to me! you are wrong .. You must keep up your strength, you will make yourself ill."

Clotilde shook her head.

"Come, you must have had lunch in the station at Marseilles, am I right? and you have had nothing at all since .. Is that reasonable? We do not want another invalid on our hands .. Martine has some broth. I have told her to make a nice light soup with it and then give us a chicken .. Go down and eat a morsel, just a morsel, while I stay here."

Clotilde shook her head again wearily and managed to stammer:

"Leave me alone, grandmother, I implore you .. I could not possibly eat, it would choke me."

She had relapsed into silence, but she was not asleep. Her eyes were wide open and obstinately fixed on Pascal's face. She sat there for hours, not moving, erect and rigid in her chair. She was disturbed by a noise at ten o'clock. It was Martine who had brought back the lamp. At about eleven o'clock, Felicité, who had been dozing in an armchair, stirred restlessly, got up, went out of the room and came back. From then onwards, there was a constant coming and going, impatient movements and whisperings all around the young woman, who was still wide awake, still staring at Pascal. Midnight struck. One idea, her one obsession, remained in her tired brain which stopped her from sleeping; why had she obeyed him? If she had stayed by his side she would have kept him alive with the heat of her young body! It was only just before one o'clock that even this idea became confused and faded out into a kind of nightmare. Exhausted by grief and fatigue she fell into a heavy sleep.

When Martine had told old Madame Rougon about her son's sudden death, the old lady, though astounded and dismayed, had reacted by a cry of rage. What! Even when he was dying, Pascal had not wanted to see her, had made his servant swear not to inform her! It made her blood boil, as if her conflict with Pascal, which had lasted throughout his life, was to continue beyond the grave. Then, after putting on some clothes in a great hurry, when she was on the way to the Souleiade she had suddenly thought of those terrible files, all those manuscripts which filled the cupboard, and became frantically agitated. Now that Uncle Macquart and Tante Dide were safely out of the way, she had no further fear of what she called the abomination of the Tulettes; and poor little Charles's death had removed one of the most humiliating blemishes on the family honour. Now, there were only these files, these abominable files, which were a serious threat to that triumphant Rougon legend, which was the sole preoccupation of her old age and she was dedicating the not inconsiderable remnants of her abilities and all her capacity for intrigue to ensuring its triumph. She had been lying in wait for them over a very long period of years; she was tireless and ruthless, never admitted herself beaten and unswervingly tenacious. Ah! if she could only gain possession of them at last and destroy them! The execrable past would be blotted out, the glory of her family would become freely acknowledged and the legend, mendacious as it might be, would become an authentic fragment of history. She could visualize herself passing through the three quarters of Plassans, respectfully saluted by everybody, like a triumphal royal visit. Thus, when Martine had told her that Clotilde had arrived, she walked even faster towards the Souleiade, urged on by the fear of arriving too late.

As soon as she was installed in the house, she calmed down. There was no hurry. She had the whole night in front of her. Her first anxiety was to make sure that Martine was on her side; she knew just how to play on the superstitions of this simple creature steeped in the beliefs of her narrow religion. On the pretext of discussing the roasting of the chicken she trotted into the kitchen and pretended to be disconsolate at the thought of her son not having made his peace with the Church before his death. She pressed Martine for details of the deathbed scene. Martine confessed, to her despair, that no priest had been present, that monsieur had not even made the sign of the cross. She herself had kneeled down and recited the prayers for the dying, which, as she well knew, was not sufficient to ensure the salvation of his soul. But, with what devout fervour she had prayed to God to ask him to admit monsieur into Paradise!

With her eyes on the chicken turning on a spit in front of a blazing fire, Felicité continued in a low voice:

"Ah! my poor girl, what will prevent him from going to Paradise more than anything are those abominable papers that your poor master has left behind him. I cannot understand why they have not been reduced to ashes long since by lightning sent from heaven. If we let them out of this house, it will be the plague, dishonour and certain hell fire for Pascal!"

As she listened to the old lady Martine blanched:

"Holy mother of God! You may be sure that I believe you! .. If we had those horrible papers I would throw them in this fire! you could do without wood, just the manuscripts upstairs would be enough to roast three chickens like this one."

The servant had picked up a long ladle to baste the bird. She too seemed to be thinking hard:

"Only we haven't got them .. I heard a conversation about them that I can repeat to madame .. It was when Mademoiselle Clotilde went up to the bedroom. Doctor Ramond asked her if she remembered monsieur's orders; and she said that she remembered that she was to keep the files and give Doctor Ramond the other papers."

Felicité shuddered. She could see the papers slipping from her grasp; and it was not only the files which she coveted, but every single page with writing on it, all these mysterious, suspicious and loathsome documents which would only give rise to scandal:

"We must act!" she cried, "To-night! To-morrow may be too late."

"I know where to find the key of the cupboard," said Martine in a low conspiratorial tone. "Doctor Ramond told mademoiselle."

Felicité pricked up her ears:

"Where is it then?"

"Under the pillow, under monsieur's head."

Despite the hot fire, which had been fed with vine-shoots, the two old women shivered and fell silent. The only sounds were the sizzling of the bird and the fat dropping into the dripping pan.

When Madame Rougon had dined alone, she went back upstairs with Martine. By tacit consent the two were now in agreement. They were firmly resolved to take the papers before dawn by fair means or foul. The simplest way would be to take the key from under the pillow. Clotilde was certain to drop off to sleep; she seemed already too exhausted to do more than sit slumped in her chair. It was merely a question of waiting. They kept close watch on her. They kept going from room to room, from the bedroom to the study, waiting for the moment when Clotilde's eyes would finally close. They took it in turns to go and see. These manoeuvres continued, every quarter of an hour up till nearly midnight. Clotilde's great eyes, full of shadows and immense despair, remained wide open. Just before midnight, Felicité installed herself once more in an armchair at the foot of the bed, determined not to move out of the room until her granddaughter was sound asleep. She was disappointed and annoyed when she found that Clotilde went on staring interminably and fixedly without even blinking. Then she found herself nodding, unbearably sleepy. She was exasperated and jumped up to join Martine in the study.

"It is no use, she will not go to sleep!" she said in a muffled and trembling voice. "We must think of something else." She had considered the possibility of forcing the cupboard. But the oak framework seemed unbreakable and the old iron bands extremely strong. What tool could she use to force the lock? Besides, it would make a terrible noise, so loud that Clotilde would be sure to hear it in the next room.

They both stood in front of the cupboard and were running their hands over the thick doors, trying to find a weak spot.

"If I had a tool . . "

Martine, who was less excited and impatient, protested:

"No, no, madame! They would catch us! Wait, perhaps mademoiselle is asleep now."

She tip-toed into the bedroom and came back at once:

"Yes, she is asleep! . . Her eyes are shut and she is not moving."

Then both of them went into the bedroom to make sure, holding their breath, avoiding even the slightest creaking of the floor boards. Clotilde, in fact, had just gone to sleep, so profoundly plunged in sleep that the two old women became bolder. But they were still afraid of waking her if they touched her, as she was sitting near the bed. Besides, slipping a hand under the dead man's pillow and robbing him was a terrible act of sacrilege! Were they not about to disturb the rest of the dead? Would he move? They shuddered with apprehension.

Felicité had already stepped forward, her arm outstretched. But she recoiled:

"I am too short," she stammered. "You try, Martine."

The servant, in her turn, stepped up to the bed. But her whole body began to shake with such violent tremors that she too had to step backwards for fear of falling:

"No, no, I can't! it seems to me that monsieur will open his eyes."

They stood shivering and frantic with superstitious fear in the room which was full of the great silence and majesty of death, in the presence of Pascal motionless for ever and Clotilde, his widow, unconscious and crushed by the weight of her sorrow. Perhaps they had caught a glimpse of the nobility of a selfless life of scientific labour in the mute rigidity of the head which was keeping guard over the children of his brain. The flames of the tapers gleamed with a ghostly pallor. The terror of the unknown, sacred and mighty, came into the room and they fled.

Felicité, usually so fearless, who recoiled at nothing, not even bloodshed, fled as if the hounds of hell were at her heels.

"Come, come away, Martine. We will find some other way, let us look for a tool."

Once in the study, they breathed more freely. The servant remembered that she had seen the key of his desk on the bedside table. They went back into the bedroom, found the key and Felicité had no scruples in opening the desk. But she found nothing but the five thousand francs. She searched in vain for the genealogical Tree, which she knew was usually kept in the desk. It would have been a good beginning for her work of destruction!

But it was the cupboard which fascinated her and she returned to it and stood gazing at it. In spite of her short stature and her great age, she was full of extraordinary destructive energy:

"Oh!" she repeated, "if only I had the right tool!"

She proceeded to examine the massive cupboard, looking for a weak point, some small crack into which she could put her fingers and burst it open. Her busy brain was revolving every possible plan of attack, she considered using force and then realized the advantages of guile.

Suddenly a gleam came into her eyes. She had thought of something:

"Tell me, Martine, is one of the doors fastened by a hook?"

"Yes, madame, it hooks into a screw-ring just above the middle shelf .. Look, it is about here, behind this moulding."

Felicité was exultant:

"Have you a gimlet, a large gimlet? .. Give me a gimlet!"

Martine hurried downstairs to the kitchen and brought back the tool.

"You see, this makes practically no noise," continued the old lady, setting to work.

With singular strength and precision, which one would not have expected from her tiny hands which were knotted and dried up by old age, she made a first hole at the level of the moulding to which the servant had pointed. But it proved to be too low and she felt the point of the tool burying itself in the shelf. She made a second hole which revealed the iron hook. This was too central, so she made a whole series of holes, to the left and right of the first two. Then, using the point of the gimlet itself, she was able to dislodge the hook from its ring. The lock-bolt was easy to push and both doors were open.

"At last!" cried Felicité, beside herself with joy.

Then, uneasy, she stood without moving, listening, afraid of having aroused Clotilde. But the whole house was asleep in the deep black silence. Nothing came from the bedroom except the august peace of death. All she could hear was the clear high note of the clock striking once. And the cupboard was wide open and gaping. Then Felicité hurled herself forward and, in the shadow of death, the work of destruction began.

"At last," she muttered to herself, "I have been wanting and waiting for this for thirty years! .. Hurry, hurry, Martine! Help me!"

She had already fetched the high stool from Clotilde's desk and clambered on to it with her usual agility, in order to start with the papers on the top shelf, as she had remembered that the files were kept there. But she was surprised to find, instead of the files covered in thick blue paper, all Pascal's completed manuscripts, still unpublished, of inestimable scientific value, recording all his experiments and discoveries, the monument to his future glory, which he had left to Ramond to use as he thought fit. No doubt, some days before his death, realizing that his files were in danger and that nobody would dare to destroy his other writings, he had moved them.

"Ah! never mind!" murmured Felicité, "there are so many papers that it does not matter what we take first .. As I am up here, let us start with this rubbish .. Here, catch, Martine!"

And she emptied the shelf by throwing the manuscripts, one by one, into the servant's arms. Martine put them on the table, making as little noise as possible. Soon the shelf was bare and she jumped down.

"Into the fire! Burn them! .. We shall find the files I am looking for in the end .. In the fire! start with these! All of them down to every little bit of paper no bigger than my finger nail, even illegible notes. Into the fire with them! Burn them! We must be sure that the contagion will not spread!"

She herself, fanatical and savage in her hatred of the truth, passionately determined to annihilate everything which bore witness to scientific truth, tore the first page of manuscript, held it over the lamp and threw the flaming fragment into the fireplace, in which no fire had been lit for twenty years; and she fed the flames by throwing the rest of the manuscript page by page on the blazing pile. The servant, no less resolute than the old lady, was helping and had started with a large notebook, the pages of which she was tearing out and throwing on the fire. From then onwards the hungry flames leapt up ceaselessly, died down for a moment, to blaze up again as fresh fuel was added. The fireplace became a red-hot brazier, slowly spreading sideways, from which rose a shower of fine ashes and thick fragments of blackened paper, smouldering and sparking. But it was an endless task; because, if too many pages were thrown on the fire at once, they only smouldered, had to be shaken, turned over with the tongs; they found that the best way was to crumple up each page and wait until this had been consumed before throwing on the next. They became adepts at the task and the work of destruction progressed with greater speed.

In her haste to fetch another handful of papers, Félicité stumbled against an armchair.

"Oh, madame, be careful," said Martine. "Someone might hear us!"

"Hear us? Who? Clotilde is sleeping too soundly, the poor girl .. Besides, if she comes in when we have finished, what does it matter? I have nothing to hide. I shall leave the cupboard bare and wide open, I am proud of having purified this house .. Once we have burnt every single line my wretched son wrote, why, nothing else matters!"

The flames leapt and roared for nearly two hours. They had gone back to the cupboard and had emptied the two other shelves. All that now remained was a heaped-up accumulation of odd notes at the bottom of the cupboard. They were intoxicated by the heat of this bonfire, out of breath and covered in perspiration. They squatted down in front of the fireplace and blackened their hands by pushing back smouldering pages with such violence that strands of their grey hair hung down over their disordered clothes. It was a witches' gallop, a fanning of the devilish funeral-pile, thought in writing burnt in public, a whole world of truth and hope destroyed. And the brightness of the leaping flames which at times made the light of the lamp seem pale, made the vast room glow with unearthly

GENEALOGICAL TREE OF THE ROUGON-MACQUARTS

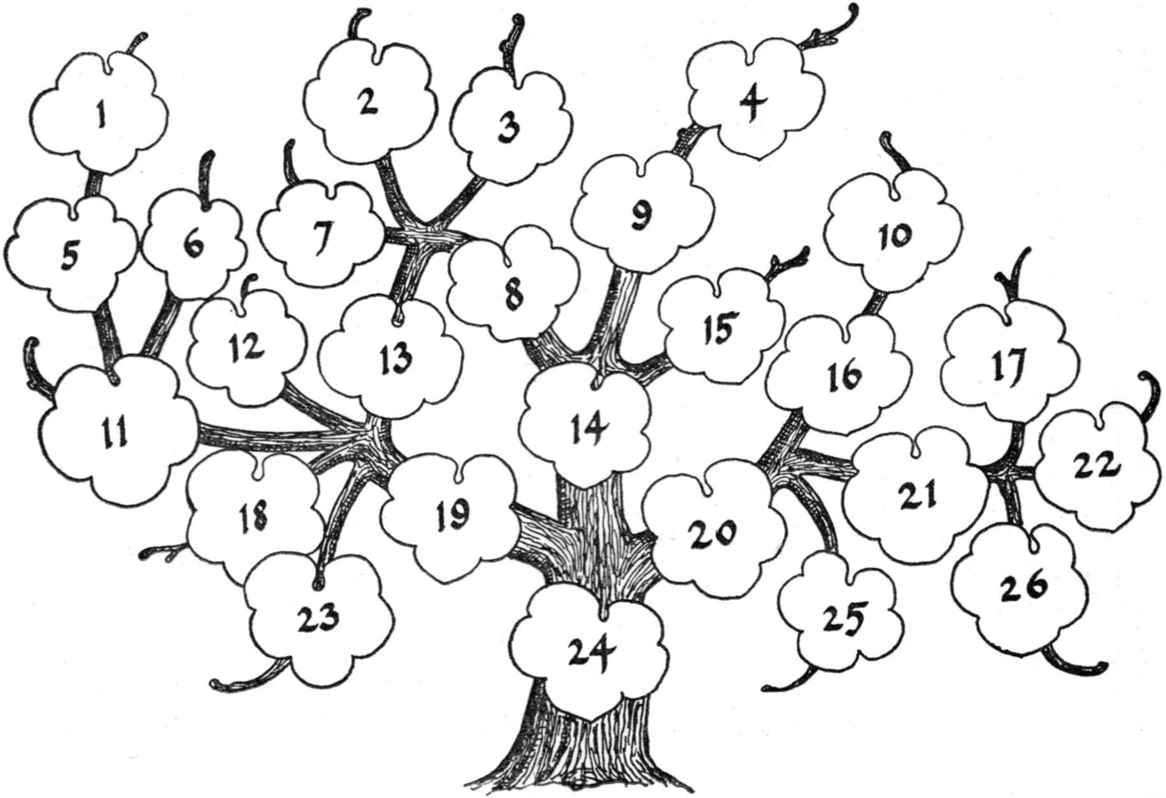

1. CHARLES ROUGON called SACCARD born 1857—latent heredity—skipping three generations—mental and physical resemblance to Adelaide Fouque—final expression of racial degeneration.

2. SERGE MOURET born 1841—"dissemination", mixture—mental and physical resemblance to mother more marked—father's mental state disturbed by mother's bad influence—heredity neurosis developing into religious mania—priest.

3. DÉSIRÉE MOURET born 1844—takes after mother—physical resemblance to mother—hereditary neurosis developing into insanity.

4. JEANNE GRANDJEAN born 1842—latent heredity, skipping two generations—physical resemblance to Adelaide Fouque.

5. MAXIME ROUGON called SACCARD born 1840—has a son by a servant whom he seduces—"dissemination" mixture—mental predominance of the father and physical resemblance to mother.

6. CLOTILDE ROUGON born 1847—takes after mother—physical resemblance to mother.

7. OCTAVE MOURET born 1840—takes after father—physical resemblance to father.

8. FRANÇOIS MOURET born 1817—marries his cousin Marthe Rougon in 1840—three children by her—takes after father—physical resemblance to mother—husband and wife resemble each other.

9. HÉLÈNE MOURET born 1824—marries Grandjean in 1841 by whom she has daughter who dies in 1850—takes after father—physical resemblance to father.

10. PAULINE QUENU born 1852—balanced mixture—physical and mental resemblance to both father and mother—worthy woman.

11. ARISTIDE ROUGON called SACCARD born 1815—marries Angèle Sicardot on 1836 by whom he has two children and who dies in 1854—remarried in 1855 to Renée Béraud Duchatel who dies childless in 1867—"linkage" mixture—mental preponderance of father and physical resemblance to mother—mother's ambitions frustrated by father's appetites.

12. SIDONIE ROUGON born 1818—takes after father—physical resemblance to mother.

13. MARTHE ROUGON born 1820—marries her cousin François Mouret in 1840 and dies in 1864—latent heredity, skipping one generation—mental and physical resemblance to Adelaide Fouque.

14. URSULE MACQUART born 1791—in 1810 married a hat maker, Mouret, by whom she has three children—dies from phthisis in 1840—"linkage" mixture—mental predominance of and physical resemblance to mother.

15. SILVÈRE MOURET born 1834—dies 1851—takes after mother—inborn physical resemblance.

16. LISA MACQUART born 1827—marries Quenu in 1852 and has a daughter by him the following year—takes after mother—physical resemblance to mother—pork-butcher.

17. CLAUDE LANTIER born 1842—"fusion" mixture—mental predominance of and physical resemblance to mother—hereditary neurosis developing into genius—painter.

18. PASCAL ROUGON born 1813—inborn factors only—no resemblance either physical or mental to his parents—entirely outside the family—physician.

19. PIERRE ROUGON born 1787—marries Félicité Puech in 1810 by whom he had five children—balanced mixture—mental resemblance shared, as well as physical resemblance to both mother and father.

20. ANTOINE MACQUART born 1789—soldier in 1809, returns in 1815, marries Joséphine Gavaud in 1826 by whom he has three children and who dies in 1851—"linkage" mental predominance of and physical resemblance to father—hereditary alcoholism handed down from father to son.

21. GERVAISE MACQUART born 1828—has two children by a lover, Lantier, with whom she runs away to Paris and who abandons her—in 1852 marries a workman, Copeau, by whom she has a daughter—dies in extreme poverty and sodden with drink in 1869—conceived in a drunken bout—lame—represents mother at moment of conception—laundress.

22. ETIENNE LANTIER born 1846—takes after mother—physical resemblance to father—hereditary alcoholism developing into homicidal mania—criminal.

23. EUGÈNE ROUGON born 1811—marries Véronique Beulin-d'Orchères in 1857—"fusion" mixture—inherits mental attributes and ambition of mother—physical resemblance to father—minister in government.

24. ADELAIDE FOUQUE born 1768—married to Rougon, who is a gardener, in 1786 and has son by him in 1787—loses her husband in 1783—takes lover, Macquart, has son by him in 1789 and daughter by him in 1791—goes mad and is shut up in lunatic asylum at the Tullettes in 1851—original neurosis.

25. JEAN MACQUART born 1831—takes after mother—physical resemblance to father—soldier.

26. ANNA COUPEAU—born 1852—"linkage" mixture—mental preponderance of father, physical resemblance to mother—hereditary alcoholism developing into hysteria—thoroughly vicious.

brilliance and threw their dancing shadows on the ceiling, vastly magnified.

Then, as she was emptying the last scraps of paper from the floor of the cupboard, having already burnt the bundles of notes, Felicité uttered a muffled cry of triumph:

"Ah! here they are! .. In the fire! burn them!"

She had at last discovered the files. Right at the back, behind the rampart of notes, the doctor had hidden the blue paper files. Then all the furies of devastation were let loose. Felicité was carried away by a mad passion of destruction. She filled her arms with the files, hurled them into the flames until the whole fireplace was one mass of blazing paper and dense clouds of smoke.

"They are burning, they are burning! .. At last, let them burn! .. Martine, another one! Yes, that one .. What a fire, what a wonderful fire!"

But the servant was becoming alarmed:

"Madame, be careful, you will set fire to the whole house .. Don't you hear that roaring noise?"

"What does it matter? For all I care, everything can burn! .. They are burning, burning, what a splendid sight! .. Only three left .. only two left .. Now! This is the last one .."

She was chuckling with glee, beside herself, a grotesque and frightening figure. At that moment lumps of burning soot fell into the fireplace. The roaring became much louder, the chimney had caught fire as it had never been swept. This seemed merely to add to her delirious excitement, whilst the servant, distracted, was shrieking and running around the room.

Clotilde was sleeping by the side of her dead Pascal in the sovereign calm of the bedroom. The only sound was the metallic vibration of the clock striking three. The tapers were burning with a long steady flame. But, from the depths of her heavy dreamless sleep, she began to hear noise, blurred and fantastic as in a nightmare. Then she opened her eyes. She was dazed and had no realization of the present or the immediate past. Where was she? Why this enormous weight which was crushing her heart? Reality came to her in a flash; she saw Pascal's face stilled in death; she heard Martine's cries in the next room. Terrified, she ran to the door to see what was happening.

From the threshold Clotilde grasped the significance of this scene of savage destruction; the cupboard open and completely empty, Martine distracted by her fear of a general conflagration, her grandmother Felicité radiant, pushing the last fragments of the files into the flames with her feet. Smoke and flying soot filled the study; the roar of the fire was like the rattling in a murderer's throat, like the noise she had heard in the depths of her sleep.

And the cry which rose to her lips was the cry which Pascal had uttered himself, that night of the storm, when he had surprised her in the act of stealing his papers:

"Thieves! Murderers!"

She had thrown herself forward and dropped to her knees in front of the blaze in the fireplace and, in spite of the terrible roaring and the incandescent lumps of soot which were falling, at the risk of burning her hair and hands, she was seizing handfuls of smouldering sheets of paper and was courageously trying to save them, pressing them against her dress. But these fragments were pitifully few. Not a single complete page was left of Pascal's unremitting labour, the patient and extensive work of a lifetime which the fire had destroyed in two hours. Clotilde's outraged fury expressed itself in an outburst of indignation:

"You are thieves, murderers! .. You have just committed the vilest of crimes! You have desecrated death, you have murdered thought, murdered genius itself!"

Old Madame Rougon held her ground. In fact, she stepped forward, remorseless, head held high, ready to defend the sentence of destruction pronounced and executed by herself:

"You are talking to me, your grandmother! .. I have done what needed to be done, what you were going to help us to do some time ago."

"Then! Then I was mad. You deliberately addled my brain. But, since then, I have lived. I have learnt to understand .. Besides, it was a sacred heritage, left to me, the last thought of a dying man, all that was left of a great brain and it was my sacred duty to make it known to all .. Yes, you are my grandmother! and you have just acted as if you had burnt your own son!"

"Burn Pascal, because I have burnt his papers!" cried Felicité. "I would burn the whole town to safeguard the glory of our family!"

She continued to advance towards Clotilde like a combatant flushed with victory; and Clotilde, who had put the charred fragments she had rescued down on the table, defended them with her body, fearing that the old lady might throw them back into the fire. But the old lady was now past caring about charred fragments, she was even oblivious of the burning chimney, which, fortunately, was extinguishing itself; whilst Martine, with the shovel, was crushing the incandescent lumps of soot and the last flames flickering from the burning ashes.

"You should know," continued the old lady, whose little figure seemed to swell and grow in stature, "that all my life I have had only one passion, the fortune and royalty of our family. I have fought for it, vigilantly watched over it and I believe that my life has been prolonged simply for the purpose of preventing any scandalous stories about us from being spread abroad and thus making sure that we should leave a glorious legend behind us .. Yes, I have never despaired, never disarmed, I have always been ready to take advantage of circumstances .. And I have been able to accomplish everything I set out to accomplish, simply because I have known how to bide my time."

She pointed towards the empty cupboard and the fireplace filled with smouldering embers:

"Now it is all over, our glory is saved. Those abominable papers can no longer accuse us and I shall leave no threat behind me .. The Rougons are triumphant."

Clotilde, exhausted and frantic, raised her arm as if to ward off the old tyrant. But she managed to control herself and went downstairs to the kitchen to wash her hands and do her hair. The servant was about to follow her but saw her young mistress's indignant gesture and stood still:

"Mademoiselle, I shall leave tomorrow, after monsieur has been laid to rest in the cemetery."

There was a silence.

"But I am not dismissing you, Martine, I know that you are not responsible for your actions .. You have been with us for thirty years. Stay, stay with me."

The old maid shook her grey head with its pale and faded features:

"No! I served monsieur, I shall serve nobody after monsieur."

"Not even me?"

Martine raised her eyes and gazed at the young woman, the beloved child whom she had seen grow up:

"You, no!"

Clotilde was embarrassed, she felt like appealing to her in the name of the child, the master's child, whom she might consent to serve. She was forestalled. Martine remembered the conversation she had overheard and looked at Clotilde's belly. She seemed to be reflecting. Then, decisively:

"The child, you mean? .. No!"

And she brought in her accounts, like a practical woman who knew the value of money:

"I am well provided for, I shall be able to live comfortably on my income .. I can leave you, mademoiselle, with a clear conscience because you are not poor. Monsieur Ramond will tell you to-morrow how they have saved an income of four thousand francs at the notary's. Here is the key of the desk, where you will find the five thousand francs that monsieur left there .. Oh! I know that we shall not quarrel about money. Monsieur did not pay my wages for three months, I have signed papers from him to prove it. Besides, in the last few weeks I have advanced about two hundred francs from my own pocket, without his knowing where it came from. All that is written down. I am sure that mademoiselle will pay me every sou of it .. The day after to-morrow, when monsieur has been taken away, I will leave."

She went down to the kitchen and Clotilde felt appallingly sad at being abandoned by her. As she was picking up the remains of the files, before going back to her room, she suddenly recognized the genealogical Tree, lying on the table and which had escaped the old women's attention. It was a holy relic, the only complete document saved from the wreck. She took it into her bedroom and locked it in her chest-of-drawers together with the charred fragments.

But she was overwhelmed with emotion when she found herself back in the august chamber. What sovereign calm, what immortal peace compared with the destructive savagery which had filled the next room with smoke and ashes! .. A sacred serenity stole from the shadows, the two wax tapers were burning with a pure motionless flame, without a flicker. And she saw that the pallor of Pascal's face had now become intensified. It was pure white like the hair and beard spread above and around it. He was sleeping in the light, aureolated, sovereignly beautiful. She bent down and kissed him once more. His lips and his face were as cold as marble. His eyelids were shut, he was dreaming his dream of eternity. She felt a poignant and piercing pang of remorse because she had not been able to save his scientific heritage which he had left in her care. She fell on her knees and sobbed. Genius had been violated. It seemed to her that the world was going to be destroyed, sucked down into the vortex of annihilation which had swallowed up the labours of a lifetime.

CHAPTER FOURTEEN

In the study, Clotilde was buttoning up her blouse after feeding the baby. It was after lunch, about three o'clock, on a blazing hot day at the end of August; the shutters were closed. The vast room was drowsing and relatively cool. The light was dim except for thin arrows of sunlight which came through the slits. The peace and contentment of an idle Sunday drifted in from outside; a distant peal of bells rang the last call to vespers. Inside, the empty house was hushed in a warm silence. The mother and baby were alone until dinner time, as the servant had been given permission to go and see a cousin on the outskirts of Plassans.

Clotilde's baby was now a strapping boy, three months old. She had given birth to him at the end of May. She had worn mourning for Pascal for nearly ten months, a simple, long black dress, which suited her to perfection; it enhanced the slender loveliness of her figure, the youthfulness of her pale, sad face, with its halo of gossamer fair hair. She was still incapable of smiling, but she felt soothed and almost satisfied when she looked at the beautiful baby, so fat and rosy and his mouth still wet with milk; his eyes were following one of the shafts of sunlight tremulous with dancing motes of dust. It seemed to fascinate him and he stared as if in mute adoration at this miracle of dazzling, golden light. Then he fell asleep. His little round head with its few pale hairs fell back on his mother's arm.

Then Clotilde got up very gently and put him in his cradle, which was near the table. She leaned over him for a moment, to make sure that he was sleeping and lowered the muslin curtain. She then busied herself about the room, noiselessly, walking so lightly that her feet hardly touched the floor. As she was alone in the house, she sank into a reverie, living over in her mind what had happened since Pascal's death.

First, there was Martine; after the appalling ordeal of the funeral, she had insisted on leaving immediately, without even working out her week. She had found someone to take her place, the young cousin of a neighbouring baker, a buxom, dark girl who had proved to be clean and devoted. Martine was living at Sainte-Marthe in an isolated cottage, in such a niggardly fashion that she was probably managing to save some of the income from her old savings. She had no surviving relatives, no heir. Who would profit by her miserliness? In ten months she had not once set foot in the Souleiade; monsieur was no longer there and she had not even wanted to see monsieur's son.

Then her thoughts turned to Felicité. The old lady visited her from time to time with the condescending manner of a distinguished relative who is broad-minded enough to forgive any fault as long as it has been cruelly expiated. She was in the habit of descending upon the Souleiade without notice, kissed the baby, gave Clotilde good advice and a lecture on some edifying subject; and the young mother invariably treated her with the same deference which Pascal had always manifested towards her. Besides, Felicité was now at the height of her triumphant career. At last she was about to realize an ambition, cherished and pondered over for a long time, which was to consecrate the glory of the family by an imperishable monument. Her idea was to devote her fortune, which was now very considerable, to the building and endowment of a home for old people, to be called the Rougon Asylum. She had already bought the land which was part of the old Jeu de Mail outside the town near the station; and that very Sunday, at about five o'clock, when the heat was less fierce, she was to lay the foundation stone, a ceremony which was to be honoured by the presence of the authorities, with Felicité hailed as its queen and applauded by an enormous crowd of the inhabitants of Plassans.

Clotilde, against her will, had been compelled to feel grateful to her grandmother who had shown herself completely disinterested when Pascal's will had been read. The doctor had made the young woman his residual legatee; and his mother, who was entitled to a quarter of his estate, after declaring that she wanted to respect her son's last wishes, had simply renounced her inheritance. Paradoxically enough she was about to disinherit her own relatives, leaving them nothing but glory, by lavishing the whole of her fortune on building this Asylum which would carry the respected and blessed name of Rougon on to future ages; after having been so intent upon amassing money for half a century, she now despised it and posed as a great and noble philanthropist. Clotilde, thanks to her generosity, was comfortably provided for; an income of four thousand francs would be ample for herself and the child. She would be able to give him a good education and make a man of him. She had even settled the five thousand francs in the desk on the child; she also owned the Souleiade which everybody advised her to sell. The upkeep, doubtless, was far from costly, but what a sad, lonely and solitary life in that big deserted house! Hitherto, however, she had not been able to bring herself to consider leaving it and she probably never would.

Ah! the Souleiade, that dear place, her love, her whole life, all her memories were connected with it! At times, it even seemed to her that Pascal was still living there, because the surroundings of their old life together had not been disturbed. The furniture had not been moved, the domestic ritual had not been changed. She had, it is true, locked his bedroom, to which no one had access except herself. And it was only when her burden of grief was too heavy to bear that she entered it, like a sanctuary, and relieved her aching heart with a flood of cleansing tears. In the room in which they had loved each other, in the bed where he had died, she slept each night, as she had always done as a child, a young girl and a woman; and the only addition was the cradle next to her own bed which she carried in at night time. It was still the same soft and welcoming room with its familiar old furniture. Downstairs in the cheerful dining room though she felt lonely and rather lost, she heard the echoes of their laughter and remembered the time when the two of them enjoyed their meals and drank their wine so gaily toasting each other and life, glorious life. And the garden too, the whole property was an indissoluble part of her life, intimately bound up with her earliest and dearest memories; she could not take a step without evoking the image of the two of them, so closely united; from the terrace, in the scanty shade of the two centuries-old cypresses, they had so often contemplated the valley of the Viorne, the rocky barriers of the Seille and the scorched slopes of Sainte-Marthe! Up the steps of dried stones, along the olive and almond trees, how they had vied with each to see who could reach the top first, just like children playing truant! And then there was the hot and fragrant shade of the pine trees, with the needles crackling under their feet and the immense yard, carpeted by soft grass, from which, flat on their backs at night when the stars came out, they had explored the vast expanse of the sky! And above all there were the giant plane trees, under which it had been their habit to sit in the summer, savouring the shade and the peace of them, listening to the silvery tinkle of the fountain. Even to the old stones of the house, to the very earth beneath it, there was not an atom of the Souleiade which had not taken part in their lives together.

But she preferred to spend her days in the study which revived her most cherished memories. And there also the only addition was the cradle. The doctor's table was in front of the window on the left as before. It was ready for him. He could come in and sit down at it. Even the chair had not been moved. On the long table in the middle of the room, amidst the untidy accumulation of books and pamphlets, the only new feature was a pile of white baby linen which she was mending. The same rows of books were in the bookcases. The massive oak cupboard seemed to be guarding the same treasure within its flanks and it was locked as before. Under the smoke-stained ceiling the atmosphere was still redolent of the faintly musty smell of their common labours. She felt particularly comforted by the sight of her old pastels, nailed to the walls, the faithful copies of his flowers as well as her own imaginative flights, the dream flowers.

As Clotilde finished her mending and was sorting out the baby linen, she raised her head and saw the pastel of the old king David, his hand resting on the bare shoulder of Abishag, the young Shunnamite. The memory of that day, when she had made the drawing, was poignant and still vivid. How tenderly moved he had been! How proud, how confident they both had been in their dream of an eternity together!

Clotilde sat down very quietly by the side of the cradle. The shafts of sunlight stole further into the room, the burning heat of the day became more oppressive in the somnolescent shade of the shutters; and the silence of the house seemed even deeper. She was languidly sewing the shoulder straps of a little garment, day-dreaming in the drowsy, peaceful warmth which enveloped and protected her from the blazing fury of the sun outside. Her thoughts strayed back to her pastels, her still lifes and her fantasies and the realization came to her that they were the perfect expression of her dual personality; the passion for truth which sometimes dominated her and made her spend hours accurately copying a single flower, then, at other times, because of her need for another world, she had been carried away by mad dreams of a paradise of unreal blossoms of inconceivable beauty. She had always been like that, essentially she was still the same, in spite of the flood of new impressions which were incessantly transforming her. Her thoughts came back to Pascal, how profoundly grateful to him she would always be for having made her as she was! A long time ago, when he had taken the little girl into his home out of an execrable environment, doubtless it had been out of sheer kindness of heart, but the motive must also have been partly a scientific one; to see how she would grow up in an environment of truth and affection. He had been constantly preoccupied with this problem. It had been one of his early theories, which he would have liked to test on a large scale; to use the environment as a sort of culture medium, to heal, to improve and save the individual, both physically and mentally. It was to him that she owed the best elements of her character, he was well aware of her mystical and violent tendencies and had given her passion and courage. Thanks to him she had unfolded like a flower in the fresh air and sunshine.

As she mused over the past, Clotilde understood for the first time the full extent of the profound, slow transformation which had taken place inside her. Pascal was correcting her heredity and she could now reconstruct the slow evolution, the conflict between the real and the chimerical. It had begun with her childish tantrums. Then came the religious period, accesses of devout prostration, her need for illusion and lies, immediate happiness, the strange illusion that inequality and injustice on earth should be compensated by eternal joy in some future paradise. It was during this period that she had fought Pascal tooth and nail, had tortured him and had even been determined to assassinate his genius. And then that night of the storm which had been the turning-point of her existence, when he had mastered her and swept her off her feet by that terrible lesson in real life. Since then, she had responded to the environment, she had evolved with great rapidity; she had ended up by becoming balanced and reasonable, ready to accept life and live it as it should be lived, in the hope that the sum total of human labours would one day liberate mankind from disease and pain. She had loved, she was a mother, she had achieved understanding.

Suddenly she remembered that other night in the yard. She could hear herself lamenting under the stars; atrocious nature, abominable humanity, the bankruptcy of science, and the necessity for losing oneself in God, in the mystery. No lasting happiness was possible in the absence of self-annihilation. Then she could hear him repeating his credo, the progress of reason by means of science, truths slowly and permanently accumulated were the only worthy objective, the belief that the sum total of these truths, ever increasing, would end in conferring on man incalculable power and serenity, if not happiness.

In this process of self-searching Clotilde realized that she no longer felt the anguished sense of apprehension which had so distressed her in the past when she had wondered what was to come after death. She was no longer tortured by her preoccupation with the beyond. In the old days she had felt like violently tearing the secret of destiny from the sky. She had felt infinitely sad at being alive without knowing the wherefore of life. What was one doing on earth? What was the sense of this execrable existence, without equality, without justice, which had appeared to her to resemble a nightmare in a night of delirium? She no longer shuddered with fear. She could think about these things, objectively and courageously. Perhaps it was because of the child, that continuation of herself, who blotted out the horror of the final ending. But it was also a question of balance; she was now living a sane, balanced life, understanding that the effort of living was its own justification and that the only possible peace on earth, was to appreciate the joy of accomplishing the appointed task. She remembered that Pascal had said to her, more than once, as he watched a peasant going home in the evening: "There is a man whose sleep will not be disturbed by thoughts of the after-life." He meant that such idle speculations merely trouble the disordered and feverish brains of those who "toil not, neither do they spin". If all men were to work at their allotted task, they would all sleep peacefully. She herself had found work the sovereign remedy when she had been in mental agony and in mourning. Ever since he had taught her to make proper use of every hour of the day, and especially since she had become a mother ceaselessly occupied with her child, she no longer felt the icy breath of the unknown. She had automatically stopped indulging in mystical reverie; and, if ever she still felt afraid, if ever she became unduly distressed by some trifling worry, she found comfort and invincible strength in the thought that her baby was one day older, that he would be yet another day older tomorrow, and that day by day, page by page, she was succeeding in writing the book of a new life. This consoled her for all her misfortunes. She had a function and an objective.

Nevertheless, even now, she realized that the mystical element in her was not altogether obliterated. A faint sound seemed to be quivering in the profound silence and she raised her head; who was the divine mediator passing through the room? Perhaps her dead beloved whom she mourned and whose presence she always felt around her. She would never be able to wholly eradicate the child in herself who believed, who was filled with awe and curiosity about the mystery. She had been able to assess the importance of this urge towards the unknown, even to clothe it in an adequate scientific explanation. However far science may extend human knowledge, there will always be a limit beyond which it can never aspire to penetrate; and this was exactly what Pascal meant when he claimed that the desire to know more, the ceaseless urge to extend the boundaries of knowledge was the main interest in life. She herself was convinced that the unknown forces which surround our world were an immense and obscure no-man's land, ten times larger than the ground which had already been covered and conquered, an unexplored infinity, a vast territory into which the men of the future would advance and go on exploring endlessly. This harmless form of day-dreaming slaked her imperious thirst for the beyond, the natural human need for escaping from the visible world and satisfied the illusion of absolute justice and future happiness. These last flights of fancy soothed the remnants of her old torments, seeing that suffering mankind cannot live without the consolation of lies. But everything was now satisfactorily fused in her. At this turning point in history, super-saturated with science, distressed at the havoc it had wrought apprehensive at the approach of the new century, terrified of advancing further and intent upon retreating into the past, she represented a happy mean, a passion for truth complemented by a concern for the unknown. Whilst the sectarian scientist, solely preoccupied with phenomena, barred the horizon, it was given to a good simple creature like herself to strike an even balance between what she did not know and what she would never know. And if Pascal's credo was the logical conclusion of his whole work, the eternal question of the beyond which she could not help continuing to put to the sky, reopened the door to the infinite to allow mankind to march through it.

Another faint rustling sound, like a great wing passing over her, the touch of a kiss on her hair, made her give a faint smile, for the first time. Pascal had surely come to visit her. A wave of immense tenderness swept through her and drowned her being. How kind and gay he was, and how his passion for life made him love his fellow men! He himself, perhaps, was only a dreamer, but he had dreamed the most beautiful of all dreams. He had believed in a better world in which science had given man incalculable power; he wanted to accept everything, use everything to ensure happiness, know everything and foresee everything, reduce nature to the status of a servant. In the meanwhile, work, freely undertaken and accomplished, would be enough to ensure well-being for all men. Perhaps even pain and suffering would be usefully harnessed one day. When she thought of the sum total of lives, good and bad, yet all of them admirable because of their courage and diligence, she thought of them as a fraternal body of mankind. She was filled with unlimited indulgence, infinite pity and burning charity. Love irradiates the earth like the sun, and kindness is the great river at which all hearts drink.

Clotilde had been sewing for nearly two hours. The shoulder straps had been sewn on the tiny garment. She had also marked some new napkins bought the day before. She got up to put the baby linen away. Outside, the sun was dipping towards the horizon, only a few attenuated golden shafts came slanting through the slits in the shutters. The light was now too dim and she opened one of the shutters; she gazed for a moment at the vast horizon. It was less hot, a slight breeze blew down from a cloudless blue sky. To the left, every branch of the pine trees stood out from the red and crumbling rocks of the Seille; whereas to the right, after the slopes of Sainte-Marthe, the valley of the Viorne extended into the infinite distance, powdered over with the dull gold of the setting sun. She looked for an instant at the tower of Saint-Saturnin, it too bathed in the same golden light, dominating the pink roofs of the town; she was about to turn away, when a spectacle arrested her attention and kept her leaning out of the window for a long time.

It was an enormous crowd packed into the old Jeu de Mail on the other side of the railway lines. Clotilde remembered the ceremony, in the course of which her grandmother Felicité was to lay the foundation stone of the Rougon Asylum. For a week beforehand there had been a great bustle of preparations, a solid silver hod and trowel had been especially made for the old lady's use when laying the stone. She had wanted everything to be as spectacular as possible for her great triumph at the age of eighty-two. She was particularly proud of the fact that to-day marked her conquest of Plassans for the third time; because the occasion forced the whole town to rally around her, to escort her and hail her as benefactress. There were to be a committee of lady patronesses chosen from the most aristocratic families of the Saint-Marc quarter, a delegation of trade guilds from the old quarter and finally the most prominent citizens of the new town, solicitors, notaries, doctors, without counting more humble folk, who were flocking to the ceremony as if to a festival. And the supreme triumph of all which fed her pride more than anything else, was the fact that she, one of the queens of the second empire, had vanquished the young republic in the person of the sub-prefect, by obliging it to hail and thank her. Originally, the organizers had only provided for one speech by the mayor; but now it was known that the sub-prefect proposed making a speech as well. It was too far away for Clotilde to distinguish more than a tumult of black frock-coats and light dresses under the dazzling sun. Then there was a deafening blare of music, the town band, whose brassy sonorities were wafted intermittently towards her by the breeze.

She left the window and went to the massive oak cupboard to put away the garments she had been mending. Clotilde was putting the vests and the napkins on one of the shelves, she caught sight of the large envelope which contained the charred fragments of the files saved from the fire. She remembered that Doctor Ramond had asked her to make a closer examination of the fragments; to find out whether one or other of the fragments might have more complete information on some subject of scientific importance. Immediately after Pascal's death Ramond had made an attempt to summarize their last conversation in writing, the dying man's all-embracing theories expounded with such heroic serenity; but he found that his summary contained too many gaps. He required more complete studies, the account of day by day observations, the results arrived at and the laws formulated in the light of these facts. It was an irreparable loss. The work would have to be started all over again and he complained that the indications were insufficient; he claimed that there would be a delay of at least twenty years before science could revive and utilize the ideas of this solitary pioneer, whose works had been destroyed by a savage and senseless catastrophe.

The genealogical Tree, the only document left intact, was attached to the envelope, and Clotilde brought them over to the table. She shook out the fragments and confirmed the fact that not a page of manuscript was left, not even a note complete which made sense; nothing but charred and blackened bits of paper! She again recalled the night of the storm and was able to complete sentences in her mind. She happened upon Maxime's name; and she felt able to reconstruct the existence of this brother who had remained a stranger to the last, whose death had left her almost indifferent. Next, an incomplete line contained her father's name; she shuddered with disapproval and disgust; she had heard that Saccard had pocketed Maxime's fortune as well as the proceeds of the sale of his hotel, thanks to the barber's niece, the innocent Rose rewarded by a generous percentage of the loot. Then she came across other names, her Uncle Eugène, the ex-vice-emperor now gone to rest, that of her cousin Serge, the curé of Saint-Eutrope, who, she had been told, was dying of phthisis. Every fragment came to life, the execrable and fraternal family arose reborn from these charred papers covered with incoherent syllables.

Then Clotilde had an impulse to unfold the genealogical Tree and spread it out on the table. These relics aroused her pity and recalled painful memories; and when she re-read the notes added in pencil by Pascal a few minutes before his death, tears came into her eyes. What gallantry to enter up the date of his own death! And how she felt his despair at being torn away from life, betrayed by the tremor of his hands as he wrote in the birth of the child! The great Tree pushed itself out of the ground, threw out its branches, unfolded its leaves. She sat for a long time lost in contemplation and realizing that this classification and description of their family contained the essence of Pascal's work. She remembered his words, as he commented each hereditary case history, but she had very naturally been especially interested in the children. The colleague to whom Pascal had written at Noumea for news of the child born to Etienne in the penal colony, had finally answered; but the information was confined to reporting that the child was a girl and in good health. Octave Mouret had nearly lost his little girl, whose frailty was a continual worry to him, but the little boy was flourishing. Besides, the real centre of health and fertility as far as the family was concerned, was at Valqueyras in Jean's house. His wife had given birth to two children in three years and she was already pregnant again. Her brood ran wild and grew tough and strong in the sunshine, like corn in well-fertilized ground, whilst the father ploughed and the mother cooked and attended to the children. Here in Jean and his family there was enough new sap, enough capacity and willingness to work, enough vitality to make a whole new world. Clotilde seemed to hear Pascal's voice asking: "What about our family, what is to become of it, what sort of human being will it end up by creating?" She herself began to speculate as to how these last twigs would grow and which would develop into the stout healthy branch of the future.

There was a faint cry from the cradle and the muslin cover moved, as if blown upon from below. It was the baby, awake and kicking. She picked him up at once and held him up above her head to bathe in the golden light of the setting sun. But he was indifferent to this golden seal at the end of a beautiful day; his eyes turned away from the vast sky and he opened his mouth, always agape with hunger like a nesting bird's beak. And he cried so loudly, so obviously famished that she gave him her breast. Besides it was time, it was three hours since his last feed.

Clotilde came back to the table and sat down with the baby on her knees. He was kicking and crying. She smiled at him as she unhooked her dress. She bared her small round breast. The baby attracted by the odour of the milk was greedily searching for the nipple. When she put it in his mouth he gave a little grunt of satisfaction and started sucking voraciously. At first he had grasped her breast in his hand, as if to establish his right of possession. Then, as the warm flood filled him with primitive sensual joy, his hand released the breast and he raised his arm straight up in the air like a flag. And the sight of him so vigorously drawing his nourishment from her brought an involuntary smile to Clotilde's face. For a few weeks after her confinement she had suffered much pain from cracked nipples; they were still sensitive, but this did not interfere with her satisfaction at being able to suckle him.

When she unhooked her bodice and bared her breast she had also revealed her zealously hidden secret; the fine gold chain with the seven pearls, the milky stars which Pascal had hung around her neck. Since then, not a single living soul except Pascal and the baby had seen it. As the baby sucked greedily, it gleamed softly above his head and brought back tender memories of a past which was like an idyllic dream.

A distant blare of music startled Clotilde. She turned her head and looked at the countryside, so bright and golden in the slanting sun. Ah! yes, the ceremony, the stone they were laying over there! Then she became engrossed again in the baby and watched him gorging himself. She pulled up a stool to raise one knee and leaned one shoulder against the table. Languid and content, she felt that her milk, pure essence of her maternal love, was binding this precious new being ever more closely to her. The child was come, the redeemer perhaps. The bells had pealed. The Wise Kings set forth on their journey, followed by the peoples, all nature rejoicing and smiling at the infant in his swaddling-clothes. She, the mother, as he sucked life from her breast, was dreaming about the future. If she devoted her whole life to him and made him big and strong, what would he become? A scholar who would pass on the eternal truths, a captain who would add to the glory of his country, or a pastor who would still the passions and usher in the reign of justice? Her son would be incomparably handsome, good and powerful. He would be the expected Messiah; it is fortunate for humanity that all mothers have this pathetic faith, without it mankind would not have the ever-renascent strength to go on living. What would he be like, this child? She looked at him closely, who did he resemble? He had his father's forehead and eyes, something of the elongated and massive shape of his head. He had her own rather small mouth and delicate chin. Then she realized, with a shiver of apprehension, that she was looking for traces of the others, those grisly antecedents, whose lives were summarized on the Tree beside her. Which, if any of them, would he take after? She soon felt reassured, thanks to her natural optimism. Besides, her master had inculcated her with his boundless faith in life. What matter the miseries, sufferings and abominations! Health and vitality depended upon work, the power which fertilizes and gives birth. Life was rounded off by the child, the object of love. When love culminated in a child, all hopes were justified, despite all the hidden sores, the black picture of human shame.

Clotilde had glanced involuntarily at the Tree of the ancestors, spread out by her side. Yes! the threat was there; so much mud amidst so many tears, so much virtue rewarded by suffering! What a strange mixture of the best and the worst in mankind, an epitome of humanity with all its defects and all its struggles! Might it not be a good thing if a stroke of lightning swept away this miserable and corrupt ant-hill once and for all? After so many terrible Rougons and abominable Macquarts, yet another was born. Life from its vantage point of eternity was not afraid to create one more life. It pursued its purpose, indifferent to all hypotheses, propagating itself according to its own laws, ever marching forward with infinite labour. Its mission was to create, go on creating, even at the risk of creating monsters, because, in spite of the maimed and the mad, there was always the hope that, in the end, it would create a new, healthier and wiser race. Life was like an enormous river, flowing endlessly towards its unknown objective! Life was never still, tossing us to and fro, with its currents and countercurrents, like an immense and boundless sea!

All Clotilde's perfervid maternal instinct was aroused by that voracious little mouth drinking insatiably. The nation had been conquered and brought low. Someone had to rebuild it, was it not possible that her boy was the one appointed for the purpose? He would carry out the great experiment, raise the walls again, lead man, still groping in the darkness, into the light of a new faith, build the city of justice in which work alone could ensure happiness. In these troubled times, men were waiting for a prophet. Or, perhaps, they were waiting for the Antichrist, the demon of devastation, the predicted beast who would cleanse the earth of the filth and corruption which defiled it. And life would continue in spite of everything. It might be necessary to wait patiently for thousands of years, until the other child, the enigma, the benefactor, appeared.

The baby had emptied the right breast; and as he was fuming with impatience Clotilde turned him around and gave him the left breast. As she felt his gluttonous gums close on her nipple, she could not help smiling once more. Surely a nursing mother was the emblem of hope, the image of salvation! As she bent over him, his eyes opened and he looked at her, limpid eyes enraptured by the light. She felt his heart beating against her breast. What was he trying to say as he tugged at her nipple? For what great cause would he shed his blood when he was a man, powerful and strong, thanks to all the milk he had drawn from her? Perhaps he was not trying to say anything, perhaps his lips were forming their first lie, but even this thought could not cloud her happiness, she felt so supremely confident in a glorious future for him!

She heard a flourish of trumpets in the distance. Doubtless the culminating point of the ceremony, the great moment, her grandmother Felicité with her silver trowel was laying the first stone of the monument erected to the glory of the Rougons. The great blue sky was rejoicing in such a festive Sunday. And, in the warm silence, in the peaceful solitude of the study, Clotilde smiled down at the baby who was still sucking—his little arm in the air, pointing upwards, a symbol of hope and life.